PRAISE FOR *SAINTS OF S...*

"Gabriella Buba writes the way the ocean moves: rhythmic and rolling, with dark currents and a powerful grace. *Saints of Storm and Sorrow* elegantly weaves the rich tapestry of Filipino folklore into a poignant, harrowing tale of magic and rebellion and sacrifice. Every page is drenched in the pain and hope that characterized our centuries-long struggle. This is fantasy at its finest, but it's also a story about us, and about how my love for you is one with our love for the motherland." THEA GUANZON, *NEW YORK TIMES*, *USA TODAY* AND *SUNDAY TIMES* BESTSELLING AUTHOR OF *THE HURRICANE WARS*

"Action, magic, romance... An unforgettable story filled with inspiration from myths across the Philippine islands. Crafted with exquisite detail that will resonate with fantasy fans—from those seeking new adventures to those like me, aching for the familiar." K.S. VILLOSO, AUTHOR OF *THE WOLF OF OREN-YARO*

"With prose as immersive and bracing as a sea storm, *Saints of Storm and Sorrow* is a stunning debut. Readers will be swept away by Lunurin's struggles as she is torn between the life she's building under the bonds of colonial rule and a vengeful goddess pounding at her mind's door. This aching, rage-soaked novel is a must-read." NICOLE JARVIS, AUTHOR OF *A PORTRAIT IN SHADOW* AND *THE LIGHTS OF PRAGUE*

"I am feral for this book. Buba has written a sublime, devastating tale that crackles with romance, dazzles with political intrigue, and snarls with the pent-up fury of those who suffer under colonization. And that fury must be released. *Saints of Storm and Sorrow* will hook you from its tumultuous beginning, draw you into a richly realized Filipino world, and crush you with emotion." MIA TSAI, AUTHOR OF *BITTER MEDICINE*

SAINTS OF STORM AND SORROW

GABRIELLA BUBA

TITAN BOOKS

Saints of Storm and Sorrow
Print edition ISBN: 9781803367804
E-book edition ISBN: 9781803367811

Published by Titan Books
A division of Titan Publishing Group Ltd
144 Southwark Street, London SE1 0UP
www.titanbooks.com

First edition: June 2024
10 9 8 7 6 5 4 3 2 1

Grateful acknowledgement is made to *Philippine Studies: Historical &
Ethnographic Viewpoints* for their permission to reprint an excerpt of
Bienvenido Lumbera's English translation of Tanaga poetry, from "Poetry
of the Early Tagalogs", Philippine Studies vol 16, no. 2 (1968): 221–45.

A CIP catalogue record for this title is available
from the British Library.

Printed and bound by CPI Group (UK) Ltd, Croydon, CR0 4YY.

To all the girls swallowing down their fury like broken glass.

PROLOGUE

LUNURIN CALILAN

◆—◆

The sea breezes keened of death in Lunurin's ears, a cacophony of voices urging her to act. The Stormfleet was under attack, the Inquisition's galleons on their way. Calilan was no longer safe.

Lunurin didn't fight her mother's grip as she was hauled down the beach toward a dual-sailed trading vessel from the island of Lusong. Her tiyas on the dock bargained with the captain, intent on sending Lunurin far away.

This was all her fault. She'd shattered everything her inay had worked toward. For years, the Codician Empire had overlooked the tiny island of Calilan, focusing instead on conquering rich harbor cities on Lusong and the other larger islands of the archipelago. The Stormfleet, its gods-blessed crews, and those training on Calilan had been safe from the Inquisition and its priests. Now, everyone would suffer for her failure.

For years, when they'd called her an ill-omen, better off returned to the sea, Lunurin had told herself things would be different when she joined the Stormfleet. She was fifteen, would soon have been assigned a berth and entrusted with guiding the ravaging typhoons of the Great South Sea around their islands.

Now that future tore from her grasp on winds stinking

of gunpowder. She was like a dugong wife from the stories, doomed to bring sorrow to all who loved her. Suddenly, wildly desperate, Lunurin reached for her mutya, where the mother-of-pearl comb and hairstick held her bun in place. She had to help. With the right winds, the Stormfleet vessels might still escape the Codicíans' larger, slower galleons. Lunurin's gift was too strong and the goddess of storms heard her voice too well, but even from this great distance—

Her inay seized her hand, her voice laced with fear. "Not again. Not ever. Don't forget who you are."

"You're a survivor," her tiya's tide-touched wife said, putting the dugong bone amulet she'd crafted around Lunurin's neck. Scavenged bone, never hunted; to kill a dugong or steal it away from the sea was grievous bad luck.

The deadening weight of the amulet stole the flavor and fervor from the wind, hiding Lunurin from the sight of the goddess of storms. Her gift dimmed to the barest thread, until the winds barely whispered at the farthest edge of her senses. At least they weren't trying to shave her head again.

"You're a stormcaller." Tiya Halili tucked her thick curling hair, grown back too fast, frighteningly fast, back into her bun, securing it with her mutya. "And we must never let our hair down unless we are prepared for the consequences, for what we are is vengeance."

But why shouldn't she have vengeance? If she were allowed to be useful...

The Inquisition's galleons would be so much shattered timber upon the waves.

Lunurin let the terrible voice of her goddess die behind her clenched teeth. This resentment was not hers. She'd caused this mess by listening to the angry goddess of storms, who longed for a typhoon that would destroy the Codicían colonizers' flotilla—along with the Stormfleet, and every lowland village and harbor city of the archipelago.

Lunurin wouldn't let her goddess use her for destruction. Not again.

She wished she could cast off this power entirely, cut her hair and give up her mutya—the gleaming mother-of-pearl comb and its matching hair prong, topped with the lightning-shaped pearl that marked her as one chosen by the Goddess of Storms and Sky, Anitun Tabu. She wished she could break them without breaking what little control she still had. More than that, better she'd never found a pearl at all. That she could be without any gift, with only a mother-of-pearl mutya from an empty shell to show for her naming dive. A daughter of Calilan, but one not doomed to bring destruction to her home, whose goddess did not whisper in her ear.

A true stormcaller would not struggle so, wouldn't need the dugong bone amulet achingly heavy on her chest. Perhaps her stepfather was right. Her Codicían blood made her baliw ka, crazy, and her inay was a fool for keeping the child of a shipwrecked Codicían priest.

Now not even her inay could protect her, though she was Datu and chief of the island, nor her Tiya Halili, to whom all the Stormfleet answered. A stormcaller must never be a liability to the fleet.

All the protections her mother and tiyas had left to give weighed upon her as they neared the ship. There was the dugong bone amulet—a precaution no captain would have her aboard without. There were the weights sewn into the tapiz skirt at her waist: a fortune in silver-grey pearls from the sacred oyster beds her Tiya Halili tended. From her inay, letters of entreaty to distant cousins in Lanao, begging them to teach Lunurin control. And—in case she was caught—a different set of letters in Codicían, declaring that she was the daughter of Father Mateo de Palma, and demanding she be taken to him before the Inquisition could mete out judgment. Letters to an aunt she'd never known in Aynila, an abbess at the Convent of Saint Augustine, letters of leverage and blackmail, in case having failed as her mother's daughter, she must try to live in her father's world.

Lunurin pressed the letters against her body, all her inay's hopes for her, every bit of politicking she knew and had tried to teach Lunurin. She clenched her hand around the bone amulet, a sign of how terribly she had failed her tiyas' training. She didn't dare beg their forgiveness. There was nothing more they could do. The thought of leaving Calilan and giving up on her place in the Stormfleet terrified her, but she knew she couldn't stay.

Her inay sealed the agreement with the captain, offering in thanks a purse full of the silvery black-lip pearls the gods-blessed of Calilan held sacred—though he turned them down. Along with a cargo of indigo dye and cloth, the captain and his tide-touched wife had brought warning—too late—of the Codicían flotilla that had been sighted chasing down a dozen Stormfleet vessels among the reef shoals west of the island.

As the sun sank low, her inay hugged Lunurin close, sniffing both her cheeks one last time. She tucked Lunurin into the prow alongside sacks of pounded rice, tart sheaves of lemongrass, and baskets of ginger, out of the way of the rowers and sails.

"They will take you south, to Lanao. The Codicíans have no established forts there. The rajs have repelled even the priests," her inay whispered as she pulled away.

Lunurin grasped after her skirts, desperate to prolong this parting, but was distracted when a scrawny ship's boy squeezed past. He scrambled into the narrow space beside her, pulling his legs in close. She wondered what he'd been told, if he was afraid her ill-luck was catching, like so many on Calilan.

"Sorry, my brother says I'm in way of the rowers." His gap-toothed grin flashed white in a deep brown face still round with baby fat. He couldn't be more than twelve, with black salt-stiff hair hanging down his back. Her longer limbs took up more space in the prow than was probably fair.

"I'm Alon," he added.

Lunurin answered in quick trader hand sign. "I'm Lunurin. Who's your brother?"

These Aynilans spoke a lowland dialect similar to Calilan's, but there was a lump in her throat she couldn't speak past. Hundreds of languages were spoken across the archipelago, many dozens across the Stormfleet. Everyone learned trader sign to smooth over difficulties, enabling all-important haggling.

Alon signed back his answer. "The captain, Jeian! Aizza is his wife. When she's aboard this is the fastest ship in the archipelago."

He pointed out the tall, sea-brown tide-touched woman who had approached the helm. In a low, melodic voice, she began a prayer for friendly currents that was familiar and yet subtly different from Calilan's. Her style of dress was distinct from the other Aynilan sailors. She was a bayok katalonan, raised a boy until she dove for her mutya and was called to serve the Sea Lady, Aman Sinaya, as one of her sacred priestesses.

The captain smiled at her. Several rowers tapped their mutya—bangles, amulets, and earrings, all of the gold-lip mother-of-pearl Aynila was famous for—dipping them into the sea or raising them to the breeze. Prayers for good luck to her and Aizza. No ship could be safer, with both a tide-touched and a stormcaller aboard.

They didn't know.

They were probably the only ones who didn't blame her for today's disaster. They had no idea what Lunurin had done. The thought filled her with relief.

Lunurin's chest tightened. She had no right to feel relieved. She bolted up, craning to see her mother and tiyas on the dock. Alon called out a warning and steadied her as the ship pulled away with a lurch. Lunurin couldn't take her eyes off the three figures dwindling in the distance. She would never be enough. Not as a stormcaller, not as a Datu's daughter. The sea went the color of blood in the sunset, the three women's features dark and indistinguishable. What if they were glad to see her go? Guilt gnawed at her insides, insidious and bitter.

Alon remained silent when she dropped into a crouch and buried her face into her knees, but he didn't pull away.

She might've grieved forever, as the full moon rose, and stars came wheeling out overhead. The ship skimmed over the water, until Calilan was not even a dark blot upon the horizon. The smooth rush of calm seas and the friendly push of the Sea Lady's power felt as familiar as breathing as the night slipped away.

Suddenly, she felt the tides change. A rogue wave crashed against the hull, dousing Lunurin in salt spray. It shunted the ship crosswise, spinning on Aizza's current. Lunurin and Alon were flung across the prow. Lunurin screamed and curled her arms around both their heads as sacks of grain crushed them against a wooden chest. How could a wave turn rogue against a ship with a tide-touched katalonan at the helm?

A wall of rain and wind caught them with a roar, as loud as when Calilan's caldera woke, howling ash and fury to the sky until the firetenders could soothe her back to sleep. A too-real roar, close to the ship.

Lunurin held tight to Alon, but he wriggled free. He scurried back with two tie-lines, and looped the end of one rope around Lunurin's waist, lashing it tight. The rowers fought with sails that cracked and strained in the wind.

Lunurin reached to loosen her hair. She could easily calm the gale. She grasped for the threads of her power, trying to decide where she should pull to bring the squall to heel, but though the wind roared past her ears, she couldn't parse the voices of the storm. Her power felt dim and far away.

Cursing, she pulled the dugong bone amulet over her head, tucking it into her waist pouch where it wouldn't touch her skin. It was a risk—her power was a liability on open water. But if they couldn't bring in the sails they would capsize and drown either way.

Then, through the driving wall of rain and ship-breaking swells, she saw it. A long, sinuous body, sea-dark, yet illuminated from within, as if each scale were outlined in glowing copper wire. Long fins trailed the water in its wake, each alight with different shades of bronze fire. At every flick and twist of the mesmerizing pattern of scales, the waves crashed higher and the storm's fury raged.

She could hear Aizza's voice above the wind, strong with all a katalonan's breath training, trying to wrestle control of the sea current away from the creature. But this was no ordinary sea beast. It was the laho, the bakunawa, a mooneater, and tonight was the full moon. The sea dragon was at the height of its power.

"Tabi, tabi po." Lunurin's whispered warding shredded in the wind.

It was a mistake, her voice too loud without her amulet to shield her. Hadn't she learned her lesson? Lunurin stared in horror as the laho reared up over the ship, higher and higher. Behind it rose a wave that blotted out the sky. Serpent and wave hung over the ship, its great horned face and frilled mane sluicing waterfalls of seawater across the deck, knocking men from their feet, tearing cargo free.

The huge pearl set in its brow glowed. Lunurin heard her goddess, Anitun Tabu, speak. *"Don't hide yourself, Daughter. Do not tear yourself from my arms! Come to Aynila. Together we could set things right. It has been too long since the eye of my storm has gazed on Aynila. Our people cry out for vengeance! How can you forswear your promise to me?"*

They were all still, trapped in the laho's burning gaze like the wave it held, ready to wipe them from the face of the sea.

Fury bloomed in Lunurin's chest. She lunged to her feet. "If I stay, I die; if I go to Aynila, I'll die! Is that what you want, Anitun Tabu? I'd rather just sink now, if that's your grand plan. They're killing us. One by one, they're killing us, all because of me, all because of what you made me do!"

The laho roared. Her goddess's fury half battered her to the deck.

Lunurin screamed back defiance, throat aching. "All you ever want is death. Even these people, your people, you would let them all die if it meant you got your way. No more! I am done. If this is what you want, I will not even think your name."

She pulled her mutya from her hair, freeing it to the wind and storm. She sang out above the rolling thunder, an old song, one every child on the archipelago knew. A song that could never be turned to devastation, no matter what Anitun Tabu desired. It was the song the katalonan sang when children were taken to dive for the sacred oysters to fashion their mutya from the mother-of-pearl-lined shells, and to discover if they might be named gods-blessed.

A song for an ambon, the sun shower.

An eye opened in the thunderheads above. The full moon stared down, and the laho became distracted. In one long, sinuous movement, the serpent launched upward as if it would swallow the moon whole. Its gleaming tail whipped the clouds to whirling cyclones before it vanished into the sky. The winds tore at the ship, sending debris shredding through the air.

Then the laho's wake crashed down. It caught Alon, with his half-fastened rope.

"ALON!" Lunurin screamed, and three goddesses leaned close to hear the name.

He caught the outrigger as he was swept overboard, but oars torn loose from their cradle crashed down over him and he was gone, his tie-line limp in the water, his body sinking into the midnight depths.

Lunurin took two running steps and dove.

The water pounded in her ears. Laho-riled currents tugged at her hair and salt stung her eyes, but she swam down and down. No one else would die because she couldn't control her power. She would not allow it.

And somehow in the crushing darkness of the water, just as she was sure she had no more breath left, her hand closed on wet cloth. She curled her arm around Alon's narrow waist and kicked for the surface. She chased the precious silvery stream of their breath up into the night air. They broke the surface not far behind the ship, the sea having gone eerily calm in the laho's absence.

A dozen hands hauled on Lunurin's tie-line, and helped pull them from the sea. Water and blood painted the deck black in the moonlight.

Aizza bent over Alon's body, palms dragging circular motions over his still chest. She drew the water from Alon's lungs till he heaved, sputtering saltwater and foam. Lunurin nearly wept with relief.

Then he opened his hand, offering her a huge, gnarled gold-lip oyster cradled in his bleeding palm. It seemed a miracle he'd been able to close his injured fingers around it at all. Bone shone white in the wash of blood streaming down his fingers.

Lunurin's heart beat a staccato rhythm of panic. Another disaster.

A cheer went up from the crew. The captain bent to kiss his brother's brow and sniff his cheeks. No matter the situation, a naming to the gods and a child's dive was a moment for celebration, one that was becoming rarer as the Codicians' Inquisition extended their reach and their disapproval of the old ways.

Lunurin seized Alon's still extended hand by the wrist and thrust it at Aizza. She couldn't be saddled with the responsibility of crafting someone's mutya. She'd contaminate Alon with her ill-luck, if she hadn't already.

Aizza ruffled Alon's hair. "Your mother will be beside herself she missed this. But who can argue with a naming like that?" Her hand traced the shape of the laho, rearing toward the moon. "Fit for the songs. I will write it myself."

Aizza shucked the oyster and plunged her fingers into the soft body, pulling a huge, round pearl from within. It gleamed bright as the full moon. "Alon Dakila, son of the Lakan, has been chosen by Aman Sinaya! A blessing for all Aynila!" she declared to a roar of approval from the crew.

Aizza leaned closer to Alon, and said in a conspiratorial whisper, "I knew you would be one for the Sea Lady like me. Your mother thought you'd take after your firetender cousins, but I knew."

Aizza tucked the pearl into Alon's uninjured hand and ate the oyster, completing the ritual. She then set to work stopping the bleeding of his injured hand.

Lunurin and Alon shared a dazed look. When he grinned at her, Lunurin couldn't help the answering smile that pulled her cheeks so taut they hurt. A bubble of incredulous laughter filled her throat.

A sailor pulled the captain aside, saying, "Even with Aizza we'll be lucky to make port in Aynila. With the damage to the ship and injured crew, there's no way we'll reach Lanao."

Lunurin's mirth died.

Anitun Tabu was never truly thwarted, only delayed. Old gods could afford to be patient.

I

MARÍA LUNURIN

TEN YEARS LATER

Lunurin drank in the scent of seagrass and salt, balancing on the dock above her oyster beds. She lowered the last seed-oyster platform into the water, arms burning.

She eyed the calm turquoise depths, rubbing together pruned fingertips gone fish-belly pale, stark against the browned backs of her hands. Worries swirled like a budding storm till the rope at her waist tugged. The brush of Catalina's hands checking the dive-line steadied her.

"Do you have to dive?" asked Cat, a fellow novice at the Convent of Saint Augustine.

Lunurin frowned down at the buckets of gold-lip oysters. "I don't have enough large oysters for the abbot's dinner. I can't take any more from the floating platforms." After four such dinners the platforms of young oysters were woefully bare. So now her decades-old pearl oysters would be dinner for Codicíans who lacked any reverence for the sacred creatures. What a waste.

"It's dangerous." Cat made the sign of the cross with ink-smudged hands. "The shipyard workers have seen witch ghosts in the water."

Tabi, tabi po. Lunurin touched her hidden mutya talisman to ward off anything Cat's words might've woken. She knew how far gods-blessed fury could twist the soul, even beyond death. And so many of Aynila's tide-touched healers had burned on the abbot's pyres when the Church labeled every woman with the old gods' magic a witch.

"You worry too much. It's just sailors'-tales," she lied.

Cat frowned, unconvinced.

"They're to scare people off from swimming where they shouldn't," Lunurin added.

Despite a life spent in the half-conquered city of Aynila, alongside the great Saliwain River whose delta split the city in three, Cat couldn't swim. She refused to learn on grounds of modesty and maintained a skepticism about the entire practice that the abbot would've approved of. Swimming was practically water witch perversity, in his mind.

Looking the way Cat did, Lunurin understood her hesitation. Catalina was mestiza too, but where Lunurin was all coarse curls, height, and muscle, and had never quite fit—not on Calilan and not in the convent—Cat was soft and small like her mother. With her lighter complexion and brown hair like chinannay red rice from the inland mountains of Lusong, she fit much more closely with the Codicían ideal. Even now she wore a broad-brim hat of woven palm over her veil to shield her from the sun. She was beautiful, and Lunurin was acutely aware of her.

Lunurin's usual helper, Cat's sister Inez, had slept in. Lunurin hadn't had the heart to wake her. Inez worked too hard. She was only thirteen, but already a postulant, and eager to take her novitiate's vows.

But Cat was right. She shouldn't dive this close to the coming wet season. Even with her dugong bone amulet, many things that should be sleeping became restive this time of year.

However, the abbot's ravenous dinner guests would not feed themselves. The abbot had demanded she serve pearl oyster paella. He intended to gift each of his guests one of Aynila's famous golden pearls. No doubt he hoped the captain of the *Santa Clarita*'s recounting of the lavish event would inspire more Codicíans to make the perilous crossing and enrich his congregation, much diminished after last year's harsh wet season fevers.

This dinner was just wasteful political theater.

Lunurin tightened her bun. Already, waving strands of her thick black hair were trying to win free. It didn't feel secure without the familiar weight of her pearl-topped gold hairstick and mother-of-pearl comb, both hidden in the band of her wrap skirt in preparation for diving. While her dugong bone pendant might be frowned upon as a quaint folk habit, if anyone but Catalina discovered she still wore her mutya, it would be enough to see her dragged before the abbot's Inquisition as a suspected witch.

Her tiya's admonishment, *A stormcaller must never let down their hair unless they mean it*, came back to her, as if they were not separated by years and a vast gulf of salt. A painful pressure rose in her chest, the weight of memory threatening to crush an unwary swimmer diving too deep.

Lunurin took deep breaths, banishing the recollection. One couldn't pearl dive with quivering lungs.

She pressed her toes into the sun-bleached wood of the dock and focused. The smell of sharp pine-pitch and hot metal from Aynila's shipyards overpowered her oysters. Memories of her childhood cut short on Calilan evaporated like the pre-dawn coolness before the metallic tang of industry. The last thing she needed was to call the attention of the old gods above their once-sacred oyster beds. After all, before the Codicíans burned the healing school and built the Palisade over the ashes, this was where the katalonan, the old priestesses, had gathered to sing the stories of the people to the gods' ears.

She dove, graceful as a cormorant, past floating bamboo oyster platforms to the beds once tended by the long-dead tide-touched healers of Aynila. With a short knife, she freed large, gnarled oysters from outcroppings of black lava rock. With no one to sing the harvester's prayer, surely she would go unnoticed this once. As she tucked the fourth oyster into her bag, three rapid tugs came on the rope tied at her waist. Lunurin went cold, studying the light-edged shadows dancing over her limbs for any sign they might grow hands and try to keep her below the waves. But it was only shafts of early dawn light filtering through the turquoise water of the bay.

Then a different shadow fell over her, cutting her off from the surface. She was buffeted to her knees, into the ridges of the reef. Lunurin stared up at an old dugong matriarch, longer than Lunurin was tall, her grey hide scarred and barnacled. Lunurin hadn't seen a dugong since she'd fled Calilan a decade ago and entered the Aynilan convent. Not since the Codicían governor started hunting them for sport. He'd stuffed one for display in his mansion, prompting his hired Aynilan servants to quit and forcing him to use conscripted workers instead. It was one reason the abbot hosted so many dinners in the governor's stead.

As though reacting to its fellow, the dugong bone amulet began to burn. Fear made her lungs tight, and she cursed her luck. She must not be seen. She couldn't let this dugong matriarch, a katalonan in her own right, sing of Lunurin to the old gods.

More panicked tugs came on the line. Lunurin's lungs were beginning to prickle, but she had at least another minute of air. Lunurin cut herself free before Cat pulled her into the dugong's path and tangled them both in the line. Then, Lunurin saw that the dugong was already entangled, a wad of weighted netting cutting into her tail. She'd never escape the next hunting party so encumbered.

Lunurin shouldn't intervene.

The dugong matriarch whistled sharply, her tone as plain as any aging tita demanding action. Lunurin couldn't leave her like this.

She kicked off the bottom, gliding alongside the old survivor. She curled her fingers into the twisted abaca fibers, angling her knife with care. She'd just cut the main knot when the dugong writhed with one strong sweep of her tail, and swam free. The dugong flung Lunurin and the tangle of net into the oyster beds. She peered down at Lunurin with brown, all-too knowing eyes. The dugong sang a thankful prayer, and cold terror filled Lunurin like rainwater. She should never have dived so near to the wet season.

Thunder grumbled over the bay in answer.

Lunurin shivered as the whisper of her thwarted goddess slid down her spine. *"Who tends these sacred beds but makes no offerings at my feet? Have all my prayers been forgotten? Pearl diver, won't you sing out my name?"*

As a child Lunurin had wanted nothing more than to dedicate her life to the goddess of storms. She knew better now. Knew better than to name the goddess, or offer her own name in return. So long as she had her amulet to conceal her, she might yet escape without discovery or her power spiraling out of control.

Lungs burning, Lunurin kicked off the ocean floor. Her head broke the surface, and she gasped for breath before a wave forced her under. She struggled against the waves, the tangle of rope dragging her down. Desperate to get out of the water, Lunurin abandoned the netting, and struck out for the ladder at the edge of the pier.

Dear, proper Catalina on the dock with her cut safety-line was near tears. "Asus! You frightened me. I thought it would eat you."

Lunurin forced a shaky smile of reassurance. "Dugong eat seagrass, Cat, not people."

Cat clutched the barb-tipped rattan cane Lunurin used to pull in the floating cages as if she intended to use it as a spear. "Please, say you have enough now? I think there's a storm coming."

"I heard the thunder. I'm done."

"Dugong are bad luck. They sink ships! The sky was clear when we started."

Lunurin grabbed the ladder with both hands. Dugong didn't sink ships—but they could cry so loudly the heavens themselves took heed. "You believe that old superstition?"

Cat frowned, caught out entertaining what the abbot called "heathen delusions." She hated to be seen as anything less than perfectly faithful, even by Lunurin.

"Climb faster, María," Cat griped. She held out a plain white wrap skirt to shield Lunurin, in her breast band and waist wrap, from the rest of the shipyards.

"I hate when you call me that." Even after ten years, Lunurin hadn't grown accustomed to the Christian name she'd been baptized into upon joining the convent. If not for Catalina, Lunurin never would have stayed. But with Catalina, Lunurin fit, as she never had on Calilan and never would with her Codicían relations here in Aynila.

Lunurin ducked behind the cloth, yanking on her white

habit. In her hurry, she put her hand through the worn elbow and grimaced. This had been her last good habit.

"You shouldn't have kept your heathen name as a surname. We're supposed to let our old self die away and be reborn," Cat admonished. "But you like to pretend you're only really María on the Saint's Day of Our Lady of the Drowned."

Sometimes Lunurin believed Cat had really achieved this, that who she'd been before entering the Church had been stripped away. Lunurin wished her own past could be banished so easily.

Cat half turned toward the *Santa Clarita*, which now sat in the Palisade shipyards for repairs. Lunurin followed her gaze. Aynilan men in white waistcloths clambered over the dry-docked behemoth like ants trying to carry off a banana spider. They glistened with sweat in the humidity, brown hands stained black with stone dust from the volcanic bricks being loaded as ballast.

"I'm sorry for taking you from your morning ministry. I would've been fine diving alone. Looks like you're busier than usual," Lunurin said.

"It's because the governor supplemented the laborers on this month's rota with arrests after the riots." Cat's expression creased in disapproval.

Many of those laboring hands had grasped bolo knives and torches during rioting after the governor had raised the labor exemption tax to drum up extra workers for the *Santa Clarita*'s repair in addition to this year's effort to complete the new bridge across the Saliwain River, allowing the Palisade to control the lifeblood of Aynila's commerce. The governor was getting greedy. The shipyards' forge fires never went out lately. He hoped to send the reefed galleon laden back to Canazco, the westernmost port of New Codicía, before wet season storms made the passage impossible and the rising river put the bridge completion on hold another year.

Under the polo agreement, every able-bodied Aynilan man between the ages of sixteen and sixty who couldn't afford the falla tax to pay for exemption joined the Palisade's public work gangs for forty days of every year. It sickened Lunurin to see her people forced to work for a pittance. She was grateful for Cat's efforts to ensure the agreement was honored, and the risks she took to ensure abuses of the system were minimized.

"You shouldn't dive alone. Bring one of the kitchen girls if Inez can't come." Cat poked Lunurin in the shoulder. "Who are you to say I'm busy? Between the abbot's dinners, the oyster beds, and your share of teaching at the abbey school… but it's Inez and I who work too hard."

"I don't know how my aunt managed. I still have to organize the Saint's Day festival procession and Mass on top of it all." Lunurin emptied her waist bag of oysters into the nearest bucket. Her aunt, Abbess Magdalena, had left near the end of the wet season last year for Canazco, to see doctors there for her health.

"You're doing your best. Everyone would understand if you delegated." Cat lifted the second bucket, grunting with effort.

Lunurin winced in mock hurt. "Cat, you wound me. Don't let Sister Philippa hear you agreeing with her. Are my efforts so lacking?"

"Standing in as acting-abbess is running you ragged. You're just being stubborn. Even God rested on the seventh day. You just don't want to give Sister Philippa the satisfaction."

Lunurin ducked her head at this frank assessment. Some days, she still felt like everything would fall apart, shattering the life she'd painstakingly carved out for herself with Cat and Inez as easily as she'd destroyed her life on Calilan.

Lunurin leaned down to press her brow to Cat's, breathing in the sesame oil and faintly feathery scent of her hair. "What would I do without you? After I get these delivered, I'll rest till my afternoon classes. I promise."

Cat lifted a hand to graze Lunurin's cheek—then snatched it back as Rosa, one of the kitchen girls, appeared at the end of the dock.

"Sister María! Biti didn't come to breakfast, and she's not in the girls' dormitory. No one can find her."

Lunurin jerked herself upright. Ha. What had she been thinking? She could rest when she was dead. Lunurin hooked the oyster buckets over both ends of the barb-tipped cane, lifting them onto her shoulders. Of course it would be Biti.

"I'm sure it's fine," Cat said soothingly. "I'll help you look so Sister Philippa doesn't panic."

Lunurin wished she were half so confident. But this wasn't the place to share her fears about the newest addition to the abbey school.

They hurried down the pier toward Rosa, who produced a stack of letters. "Sister Catalina, these came with the morning food delivery for you, one all the way from New Codicía with the *Santa Clarita*."

Cat accepted the letters, slowing as she riffled through them, eager for news. Thunder rumbled over the water as Lunurin strode ahead.

From this side of the Palisade Lunurin couldn't see the city of Aynila, only the wide blue stretch of the bay and Mount Hilaga, dominating the horizon to the north. The volcano's verdant green slopes were striped on the seaward side with narrow black lava flows, streaming from the peak into the sea. A bad sign. Hilaga, like all the archipelago's volcanoes, was a sacred place. Ever since the Codicíans had started mining volcanic ballast for the *Santa Clarita*, the peak had belched steam. Lunurin couldn't imagine the completion of the new bridge, the Puente de Hilaga, would improve things. The old gods were discontent.

Lunurin turned away from the brewing disaster across the water, toward the church belltower and the manmade rhythms of the Palisade. Only suffering came from listening to angry gods. They were old elemental beings of storm, sea, and land, with no grasp of the human consequences that came of wielding their powers. It was safest to avoid even thinking their names, lest she draw unwelcome attention. Like all the women in her family she had too much katalonan blood in her, like the dugong. Her voice was too loud.

It was better that she concerned herself only with the doings inside the walls of the convent. She'd built a good life for herself. She would not allow it to be undone, even by divine portents.

~

Lunurin rechecked the headcount at breakfast. Inez wasn't down yet. Lunurin asked Rosa to save Inez a snack so she wouldn't be late for classes when she woke. Then she joined the search for Biti.

She wound carefully through the packed kitchen storerooms with a coconut oil lamp in hand. She didn't call out. Servants had already been through the usual places students secreted themselves. Biti didn't want to be found.

Lunurin watched the little flame dancing before her. As she edged around large jars of coconut oil, the wavering flame stilled. It began to dim and flare, like the sleeping breaths of a child. Lunurin crouched. In the bare space between stacked crates of wine, bedded on a fallen rice sack lay Bituin Prinsa, fast asleep. The relieved sigh that puffed past Lunurin's lips didn't disturb the lamp's rhythm.

Biti was a recent addition to the church school. She wasn't adjusting well, and Lunurin couldn't blame her. Lunurin had lived in Aynila for ten years, and she'd never met anyone under twenty who still had their mutya. The Church had seen to that after the Codicíans burned the tide-touched healing school and built the Palisade. Few dared to wear their mother-of-pearl coming-of-age talismans openly, lest they be taken for one of the "wicked water witches of the tropics" the abbot eagerly hunted. Lunurin hadn't seen Biti's mutya, but judging by the breathing flame in Lunurin's hand, she must've been taken to dive for a sacred oyster, and found a tear-shaped pearl. Lunurin fingered the lightning-shaped pearl that topped the hairstick hidden at her waist, tracing the paired mother-of-pearl comb.

A young firetender hiding in the heart of a Codicían convent; she wouldn't remain hidden for long. Biti didn't have the benefit of a dugong amulet to suppress her growing abilities and hide her from her goddess. If Hilaga and the volcano's divine mistress truly woke, Biti would burn the convent down around their ears. Lunurin suppressed a shudder.

Lunurin had to get Biti out before the Codicíans discovered her or Biti lost control. It would happen. She was young. There was no other firetender to help her bank the flame or teach her not to pull on the fiery heart of the island. Lunurin couldn't help her. An untrained firetender and a stormcaller in hiding would be an explosive mix.

Lunurin laid a hand on Biti's head. She radiated heat. It was a wonder no one had quarantined her for fever. Lunurin brushed Biti's sleek, black hair from her burning brow, humming softly as the girl woke, eyes riveted by the flame in Lunurin's hand.

Biti's big dark eyes seemed to drink the firelight. Salt-rimed tear tracks glistened on her round, brown cheeks. "I know that song. My mother sings it."

The soothing rhythm died in Lunurin's throat and Biti picked up the song in her high child's soprano.

"Before our islands graced these seas, two lovers, Sea and Sky.
Between them flew a Kite, so free. O Aman Sinaya.
Anitun Tabu. Amihan. Goddesses three we sing
To please. Of Sea, of Sky, of Flame, three gods we know by name.

Alone flew wingéd Amihan. No land in sight to rest.
In pique, she stirred the saltwaters. Up rose the angry Sea.
Dodge quickly, wingéd Amihan. The Sea did strike the clouds.
Her lover's unrest wearied her, the Sky rained down great stones.

Aman Sinaya's churning breast was made a welcome home.
Our islands dot her vast blue breast, her tides now chase the moon.
The Sky ordered the Kite to cease and on the peak to rest.
Of Apo, the volcano great and there to make her nest."

Lunurin blinked back the rush of tears and memory and put a finger to Biti's lips. "My tiyas taught me that song, but this isn't the place to sing it."

The rest of the verses spooled out in Lunurin's soul, as if Biti's words had seized hold of a loose thread, the armored resolve of a decade unraveling before her eyes.

A nest she built, an egg she laid, yet no bird did she hatch,
Instead there was a hungry flame, to put her strength to test.
Fed first on dry abaca leaf, ate fast and sputtered low.
Poor Amihan had no relief. She flew where bamboo grows.

She split one sheath, and two halves fell. From each half they did rise,
A woman and a man they were, they went away to live.
Until the day Amihan came, their youngest child she chose.
A Firetender you shall be, to guard my living blaze.

Aman Sinaya, Merciful, she chose the middle son.
Tide-touched you are, salt seas and swells to brave, my blessed one.
Anitun Tabu, last to choose. The eldest she did take.
A Stormcaller they will call you and Typhoons you will face.

Fear made Lunurin's breath quiver, sweat beading on her upper lip. She'd never be able to carry a song to the goddess's ear if she couldn't control her breathing, her tiya's voice chided. But Lunurin thought, *Good, let my voice falter. May my song be unheard and unnoticed.*

Lunurin struggled to collect herself as Biti nodded solemnly. "What is your name again, Sister?"

"I am Sister María, but you may call me Lunurin."

"Lunurin is a better name."

"Why did you go wandering?"

"It's Hilaga. She's waking. Will you take me to my mother? She needs to know."

The lamp in Lunurin's hand trembled, and Biti reached out, rescuing the flame before sloshing oil could set dry sacking alight. The little flame crawled happily into her bare palms, flaring brightly in the grip of her power.

Lunurin choked. "Biti! You must never let anyone see that."

Biti licked her fingers and crushed the fire out with a frown. "But you feel like... a breeze over coals. You aren't like the others here."

Lunurin was saved from having to answer this startling

declaration by the door to the storeroom opening and Catalina calling out, "Bituin?"

"I found her. We're here," Lunurin called back.

She put a hand to Biti's brow and found her warm, but no longer burning. Had she fed the heat to the flame?

Cat wound into the maze of foodstuff and pulled Biti into her lap, rubbing the tear tracks from her cheeks. "Good morning, Bituin, what's wrong?"

Biti's expression crumpled, her words catching on a sob. "Why won't you take me to my mother?"

"Ahh, my dear, it's not so bad as that," Cat crooned.

But this couldn't appease poor Biti, now that whatever strange communion they'd shared had broken. Biti lapsed into disconsolate weeping.

Cat soothed the girl, rocking and patting her back, until she'd wrung herself dry and sunk into a fitful slumber. Cat sagged into Lunurin's side with a deep sigh of relief. Lunurin wrapped an arm around her, squeezing gently.

Cat turned toward her, whispering, "Sorry, I didn't mean to set her off again."

"She wasn't awake enough to be upset earlier," Lunurin assured Cat. "Has the situation with her mother improved at all?"

Biti's mother, Hiraya Prinsa, had recently been impressed upon to make new cannons for the Palisade.

Cat made a face, tucking her cheek in against Lunurin's neck. "I did try to bring up your concerns with DeSoto, but he says the governor won't hear of anything that takes a skilled metalworker from his shipyards."

The brush of Cat's lips at Lunurin's throat almost derailed her concentration entirely. They'd been unable to find the privacy or energy for anything more than a stolen kiss in months.

Lunurin dragged her attention back. "So she's still being held in the shipyards as a common laborer? Doesn't that completely go against the polo contracts?"

Hiraya Prinsa was the Lakan's sister-in-law and the head of the metalworkers' conclave on Hilaga. As the native ruler of Aynila, the Lakan held one of the few remaining positions of power that stood against the Codicíans' complete dominion of the island of Lusong. Tigas Dakila had assumed the role after his wife, Dalisay, ran afoul of the Codicíans. It didn't bode well that they were targeting another powerful matriarch of the family.

"She signed a labor contract agreeing to those terms," Cat hedged.

"But the Palisade shouldn't have been able to compel her to do anything..." Lunurin squeezed Cat closer.

"Maybe she thought it would look better, not using political connections or wealth in her favor, working the same as a common laborer," Cat suggested.

"She can't want her metalworkers to accept similar contracts."

"It's not ideal, but think of the benefits. It's meaningful to have a major Aynilan figure supporting Father DeSoto's efforts. He overhauled the design of the new bridge with her input, making it more resistant to flashfloods and sabotage."

Father DeSoto was the architect responsible for most of the major public buildings in the Palisade.

Lunurin frowned in thought. "So Biti's a hostage." It was the only thing that made sense of the timing of her enrollment, and the travesty of her mother's contract.

Catalina winced and laid a protective hand on Biti's head.

"We need to get Biti out," Lunurin hissed.

Cat lifted her head, staring at Lunurin. "Vanishing a student? Impossible."

Lunurin tried to pull Cat back to her, not wanting to give up this stolen moment of intimacy. "How is it any different from the workers and servants you've helped me vanish?"

"The governor cares about the students. They're high profile. A conscripted worker disappears, that's unremarkable, but a daughter of the principalia?"

"We could do it, if we were careful."

"It's not that I don't agree. Her mother won't find any fulfillment in her work while her daughter is being held here, but why Biti? Half the students are here as assurance of their parents' good behavior. The risks to us, to Biti—it's not worth it."

"Half the students won't burn the convent down in the midst of a temper tantrum," Lunurin murmured.

Cat stiffened, pulling away from Lunurin entirely. "What?"

Lunurin pointed out the singed and blackened sections of rice sacking everywhere Biti's skin had rested while she'd slept.

For an instant Cat seemed ready to thrust the sleeping child out of her lap, but then her expression firmed. "Maybe it's better she stays. Her fits might pass as she ages, the way yours did. She's younger than you were. It'll be easier for her."

Lunurin had failed on several occasions to correct Cat's misapprehensions about her "fits," but Cat needed to understand that Biti was dangerous to the life they'd built. The Codicians hadn't understood that the old gods' magic came in flavors other than the Inquisition's preferred prey. "Water witch: pulls saltwater and sinks galleons. To be exterminated with prejudice."

They must never discover girls like Biti—or Lunurin—existed.

"She's not like me. I can't help something like this. She needs family. The fires will be the least of it. Hilaga can pull on her, and she on the mountain. Eruptions, earthquakes…"

As if to corroborate her words, the ground shuddered under their feet. Lunurin threw herself over Cat and Biti to shield them as a stack of wine crates came hurtling down, thwacking her shoulders and back. Dust choked her throat. She squeezed Cat tight, half crushing Biti between them.

Biti shrieked.

Cat prayed fervently as the earth settled and dust sifted down from the bamboo flooring above. "Comfort them, O God—Be their rock when the earth refuses to stand still—"

When everything stopped moving, Lunurin pulled Cat, her eyes still clenched shut as she prayed, from the ground. Lunurin's battered back protested, but she heaved Biti into her arms and hurried them both out into the courtyard in case of aftershocks. Cat burst outside, crossing herself in thanksgiving, before calling out for her sister Inez. Everyone in the church compound poured out of buildings, dusty, frightened, and bleeding from falls and scrapes.

Lunurin pointed Inez out, following as Cat dashed to check her sister for injury. The four huddled close, Cat giving Lunurin's hand a convulsive squeeze with every aftershock. Black smoke rose from the peak of Hilaga, ringed in ashen storm clouds. She couldn't ignore such a threat. This was more serious than mining for volcanic ballast or even the near-finished Puente de Hilaga that would bring the metalworkers' conclave on Hilaga into the Palisade's sphere of influence. They had an untrained firetender held hostage. The old gods could use children to do things their parents knew better than to attempt.

Thunder rumbled in Lunurin's ears, reminding her that she wouldn't be safe from old promises forever, no matter how many fires she put out.

2

MARÍA LUNURIN

Morning classes were canceled while Father DeSoto inspected the foundations for structural damage.

This left Lunurin scrambling to occupy fifty-odd students with no classrooms and a dinner to plan. Sister Philippa, the female students' dorm mother and Lunurin's prime critic, was horrified by the suggestion to allow all the students, boys and girls, free time in the church courtyard.

Lunurin's head pounded at Philippa's shrill voice, her responsibilities pulling her a dozen ways.

"Lunurin's bleeding," Cat declared. "She'll come deal with everything once she's cleaned up."

"I've full faith that your supervision will ensure all propriety in my absence, Sister Philippa," Lunurin said to the older nun as she was pulled away.

Lunurin touched the edge of her hairline, sticky with blood and stiff with salt from her morning swim. "The river's running salty till low tide. I can't bathe in the river."

The Saliwain River was technically an estuary. This late in

the dry season, at high tide it ran backward into the mountain lake that fed it.

Cat shook her head. "You can't lug water with your shoulder like that. A rag bath for the dust will be fine. It's not healthy how much you bathe."

Lunurin had heard similar diatribes against the dangers of full-body bathing from her Aunt Magdalena and the other sisters for years. But since she hauled her own water, they could hardly call the practice slothful.

"I don't like when salt dries in my hair," she complained.

"I'll help you rinse," Cat offered. "I only wash mine once a month. Daily brushing is quite enough to keep it tidy."

Lunurin wrinkled her nose. Cat's hair was fine and straight, with none of the tendency to curl and snarl that hers had, requiring all manner of oils and washes to detangle.

As their shared cell was in one of the buildings declared sound, they headed up for privacy. Lunurin made do with a bucket and tabo for rinsing. Removing her faded blue veil, she secured her hair with her mutya. The familiar weight returned her sense of equilibrium, easing her pounding headache.

Lunurin crossed the room and caught Cat's hands, squeezing. "Thank you. I was pushing myself too hard."

The teasing arch of Cat's brow fell away. She squeezed back. "I know you are. Should I call the physician? We can't have you working to collapse again. I'm here, not everything has to fall on you. Have faith."

Lunurin wished she did. She had to believe Cat's faith would be enough. Surely her slipup with the dugong would pass unnoticed. All she had to do was stay away from the oyster beds till after the wet season festival.

And get Biti out of the Palisade before Hilaga woke to bury

the Palisade in lava and ash. All while maintaining her image as the perfect acting-abbess. Easy.

Lunurin stepped back reluctantly, wishing she could hide in Cat's embrace from everything, forever. "Thank you, but it's nothing serious. Just a headache and some scrapes. Could you dig for the salve in my chest?"

Cat frowned with concern but did as she asked.

Lunurin struggled to strip her torn habit, her shoulder protesting. Finally, she grasped the neck of the garment, tearing it enough to shimmy free. Craning her head, she eyed the gouge down the back of her shoulder, and gave it a good scrub with soap and water.

Cat picked up the tattered habit. "Careful, we don't get new clothing stipends till next year."

"I'll manage, I always do."

"Are you planning to call in a favor from a certain young noble? The one who trails after you so often when you minister to the sick, you'd think he planned to take the cloth?" Cat held out the indigo salve with an arched brow.

It was another gift from "a certain young noble," Alon, the Lakan's son. Lunurin wasn't sure if Cat disapproved more of Alon, or Lunurin using folk remedies instead of the Palisade physician. It was sometimes hard to tell if Cat's insecurity was simple jealousy, or if Lunurin's unorthodoxy was her true fear. Lunurin knew she made it hard for Cat to love her.

"I don't take advantage of Alon like that," Lunurin protested.

Cat's brow arched higher. "The way he moons after you, especially after the last 'favor,' doesn't make it seem that way."

Lunurin shook her head. "It's nothing like that with him. I have you, don't I?"

"Yes, you do," Cat affirmed, the arch edge melting away as if it had never been.

Cat helped her apply the salve and tied on a clean cloth. She softened, pressing her lips to Lunurin's shoulder. "Be careful."

"I was protecting you. Don't I deserve a kiss on the lips?" Lunurin asked, wanting to see Cat smile.

But Cat wrinkled her nose. "I thought your head hurt. Besides, what if someone comes looking for you?"

"On the cheek then?"

Cat acquiesced, giving Lunurin a quick peck that made Lunurin want to shower her in kisses.

Then Cat sat on her bed with her stack of letters while Lunurin finished her rag bath.

Lunurin scrubbed down quickly and wrapped a clean cloth around her body. "If you'll help me rinse, I'll be done."

Cat tore her gaze from her letters, her lips tightly pursed. "Hmm?"

"My hair?" Lunurin uncoiled her bun, making sure to keep several ties in place, securing the hair partly.

Cat, momentarily distracted from her letters, exclaimed, "How is it so long already? I trimmed it a month ago."

Lunurin inspected the ends. She rarely let her hair down, even this much. "It always grows fast."

"We wear veils. You should let me cut it short."

Lunurin shuddered, the memory of her tiya shaving her head after she'd flooded the rice fields out of season making her scalp ache. Even a trim was like tearing out a nail. She pressed her knuckles to the dugong bone amulet.

"I can't cut my hair. I'm sorry. But it gets so tangled when I wash it alone."

Yes, tangled. It certainly didn't trigger storms and flash flooding.

Cat squinted and shook her head.

"Please, Cat? I can't host a dinner tonight crunchy with salt," Lunurin wheedled.

Finally, Cat rose. Lunurin flipped her hair upside down into the rinse bucket. Cat ladled freshwater over her head, while Lunurin scrubbed her scalp.

"You know vanity is a sin. It's probably worse than your obsession with bathing." Cat's endless teasing always included pointed barbs about faith and propriety.

Lunurin loved Cat's prickles. Cat was allowed to be sharp and fitful with her anger in ways Lunurin didn't dare, but today she felt battered. Couldn't Cat see she was trying her best?

"Who sees my hair but you? I'll hurry and help you brush yours. I have the sesame hair oil you like," Lunurin promised.

Rather than brightening at this peace offering, Cat gave a despairing sigh.

Lunurin hated how much of a burden she was on Cat, with her secrets and her power. But something was wrong beyond Cat tiring of her hair troubles and the earthquake scare. Lunurin wrung and twisted her hair up, securing it with her mutya.

She traced a damp hand over Cat's round, golden cheek.

"What's wrong?" Lunurin pressed her brow to Cat's.

Cat could've pulled away if she wanted, made a hasty sign of the cross to ward off sinful thoughts. But she leaned in, brown eyes brimming with tears. "The Archdiocese in Canazco rejected my application to take my eternal vows. Again. You were right to not reapply. Your aunt sent word. I was sure this year would be different! With your father about to be named Archbishop over the Codician holdings in the East..."

"Oh, Cat, you know he's never claimed me. If my Aunt Magdalena weren't so stubborn, I wouldn't be here at all."

"She promised she'd make a case for me," Cat wailed, pressing herself into Lunurin's arms.

Lunurin's heart panged. Dedicating her life to the Church meant something real and vital to Catalina. Lunurin had only ever been leveraging her family connections to avoid being swept up in the abbot's witch hunts. Sometimes she suspected Cat—who could be more fervent than Abbot Rodrigo in some ways—justified the "sin" of their relationship because by love and dint of effort, she believed she'd be the one to save Lunurin's soul. A compromise that sat uneasily between them.

"Isn't it enough to be novices? How would our lives change if we were nuns? They'd make us get our own cells. How would I sleep without the sound of your delicate little snores?"

A wet laugh bubbled from Cat. "I don't snore!"

"You do, ever since we caught fever last year. It's comforting, it lets me know you're near even when I can't hold you," Lunurin insisted, squeezing Cat tight. "God knows your heart's in the right place, even if the Church thinks mestiza girls can't be truly devout."

Hiding in the convent, Lunurin had gotten good at telling the right lies.

Cat let out a shaky breath. "I know you're right. It's what's in my heart that matters, and being here, with you and Inez. I want to protect us too." She met Lunurin's eyes. "We are a family."

Lunurin's heart swelled.

"I am yours and you are mine," Lunurin promised her.

"If the Church still won't allow me to become a wife to Christ, at least we can be wives to each other," Cat agreed.

Cat gave her a hard kiss, and Lunurin lost herself in Cat's embrace, in the heat of her passion and sharp teeth, in the fierce love that was theirs and theirs alone.

Noon rang out from the church belltower.

Cat released her, panting, cheeks red. "There's never enough time, these days."

Lunurin damned the bell and her responsibilities as Cat pulled away, going to her letter desk. She retrieved one of the Palisade passes Father DeSoto regularly wrote for her to visit construction sites when he was busy elsewhere.

"I don't want to know how you manage it, but Biti should be with family too."

Lunurin accepted the pass. "It's the right thing to do."

"Now go, you've got afternoon classes to see to, and a dinner to host. I need to review the polo labor contracts. Unless there are natural disaster contingencies, we are losing half our workforce at the start of the wet season. With all the Palisade repairs I'm sure DeSoto will have conveniently forgotten." Cat shook her head in exasperation, and Lunurin gave her one last parting kiss before they both had to return to their duties.

~

Lunurin reached the courtyard in time to join the students in saying grace over a cold lunch. They recited the Lord's Prayer followed by a special Ave María for the patron saint of Aynila, Our Lady María of the Drowned.

According to Abbot Rodrigo, María of the Drowned was a local Aynilan woman who'd converted to Codicían faith on their arrival to the city thirty years ago. She'd been so distraught at her husband's and sons' refusal to convert, that when their ship went down in an early wet season storm, damning their souls to hell, she wept until she drowned in her own tears. For this act of devotion, Mary, Mother of God, sanctified her body, turning it entirely to wood, eternally salt-brined with her tears, which stood today in the sanctuary over the altar.

Though Lunurin did not dare speak or even think the goddess's name for risk of drawing her eye, she knew the statue over the altar was no Codicían saint.

When storms raged and the goddess's thwarted gaze roamed over Aynila, Lunurin could hear her in the thunder. *"Daughter, how can you hide from my sight? How can you let them defile me so? Can't you see they are erasing me? Won't you call me by my true name?"*

Shaking off the old gods' hopeless vengeance and the dread of being branded a witch, Lunurin hurried toward the kitchen where servants and workers streamed in and out, shoring up a buckling wall.

Sister Philippa, who taught catechism, and Father DeSoto, who taught weekly math lessons, huddled in discussion at the doorway. Lunurin needed their input on the afternoon classes. The abbot would be displeased if he discovered the students indolent and playing in the yard when his guests began arriving for dinner.

"I can extend my catechism lesson if you'll be busy with inspections and repair work, Father DeSoto. I heard you've had more trouble at the Puente de Hilaga. How low will those animals sink? Using natural disasters for sabotage." Sister Philippa shook her head. Her thin slash of a mouth twisted stark lines across a pale face that burned easily under the tropical sun. She was already pinking up from being outside.

Father DeSoto was a tall, heavyset Codicían man in his mid-fifties, with a face caught in a permanent unripe starfruit pucker. He furrowed his brow, his dark eyes lost in a maze of pale wrinkles. "Let's not feed the rumors. There's no sign the damage isn't from the quake."

"This time."

DeSoto waved this off. "I told the governor continuing the work on the Puente de Hilaga this close to the wet season was a risk. I've done my best shoring up the new stonework with brass buttressing. We're learning to build for the quakes. Anyway. If I don't get the class in now, they'll fall too far behind. I already had to cancel last week's lesson, and as helpful as Inez is, she can't take over everything for me."

"Will you teach a mixed class then? A double math session this afternoon would make up for last week," Lunurin interjected.

"That's a lot of students…" DeSoto protested.

Sister Philippa's expression twisted further in disapproval. "You know how I feel about mixing the students."

"I can help Father DeSoto and Inez manage everyone," Lunurin countered. She needed to keep close to Biti. She might react badly to aftershocks, and if people were already talking about sabotage…

Father DeSoto agreed, and went to summon Inez to prepare for class. She'd started as a teaching assistant last year when they'd been short-staffed during the fevers, but Father DeSoto was so busy he now monopolized Inez's time.

Lunurin headed farther into the kitchens to inspect the damage. The bamboo upper portions had held up well. It was the vast volcanic brick oven built into the wall that had taken the most damage. Her cook had no idea how they were going to feed everyone, much less host a formal dinner.

By the time Lunurin had talked the cook down from quitting and convinced her of a cold dinner menu, DeSoto's math class was well underway. A diagram of a galleon's hull was tacked on the wall. DeSoto was trying to explain the mathematics behind buoyancy, but he'd been derailed by more talk of sabotage.

"Could the earthquake trigger a tsunami?"

"Was it a tsunami that damaged the *Santa Clarita*?"

"Father, if buoyancy keeps ships afloat, why did it stop working on the *San Pedro*?"

Lunurin flinched at that. The sinking of the *San Pedro*, over a decade ago, was all the clergy, servants, and students of the convent could talk about since the *Santa Clarita* had limped into port. Endless similarities had been drawn, speculation that the *Santa Clarita*'s reefing had been no natural disaster, but water witch sabotage or even the doing of the terrible sea serpents for which these islands were known.

Father DeSoto clapped his hands. "No, there will not be another tsunami. There are no more water witches in Aynila who could summon one. The *Santa Clarita* didn't pay attention to their reef maps. It's nothing like the *San Pedro*."

"What is the *San Pedro*? And why does everyone keep mentioning it?" Biti asked.

Distant thunder rumbled in Lunurin's ears. She tried to find the breath to intervene.

"The tragedy of the *San Pedro* happened before you were born," said DeSoto. "It was lost at sea during the height of the dry season to a freak typhoon. The sailors might have escaped to safety in its longboats, had the foundering ship not been happened upon by a passing water witch who summoned a rogue wave to drown every one of the three hundred souls aboard."

"Did they ever find who did it?"

Lunurin was grateful Father DeSoto didn't deign to answer. She wondered if he was embarrassed at the failure of their famed Inquisition. The Codicians had chased the one responsible for the destruction of the *San Pedro* for years, hunting any mention of a witch powerful enough to single-handedly sink a galleon, and found... nothing. They'd been so thorough in their eradication of any woman with so much as a whisper of the sea in her blood, and yet there were still girls like Biti, hidden right under their nose. Still saboteurs who risked everything to delay DeSoto's damn bridge.

"Didn't you just say galleons are designed to sail even through a typhoon?" another student asked.

"The *San Pedro* was built before Codicían builders and sailors were familiar with these waters. The modern galleon is immune to the worst storms the Great South Sea stirs, and can ride out the largest conjured rogue waves."

One such sinking, not the *San Pedro*'s, had stranded Lunurin's father on Calilan, where he'd met her mother. But a Datu married to a Codicían priest? It never would've been allowed, not by the people or the katalonan. Her father had been sent back to the Codicían trading post in Aynila on the first available ship. He hadn't been pleased when Lunurin had appeared fifteen years later, the albatross of all his past sins, come home to roost.

Lunurin dismissed these painful memories, helping Inez pass out slates and chalk. Then she settled down with Biti and the youngest girls to work out an appropriately simplified volume problem.

Inez smothered a yawn, rubbing dark circles under her eyes as she hurried about the room on DeSoto's bidding. She'd been excited to help teach six months ago, but now she seemed exhausted. Still, Father DeSoto relied so heavily on her help that Lunurin was reluctant to intervene.

Lunurin touched Inez's arm. Inez started, and Lunurin raised her hand apologetically. "Are you getting enough sleep?"

Inez ducked her head, one hand gripping the nearest desk for balance. "I'm sorry about this morning. I've been sleeping poorly with how restless the volcano's been…"

Did lack of sleep account for all of it? If it was sickness… Lunurin would need to find her better help than the Palisade physician. "Don't worry about helping me with the oysters. I'd rather you get enough sleep."

"But Ate—my sister," Inez corrected herself, eyes flashing toward DeSoto to see if the priest had caught her slip into Aynilan. "Sister Catalina worries about you swimming alone."

"I'll ask Rosa to help me in the mornings," Lunurin promised; it warmed her how much Cat and Inez worried for her.

Inez tugged her overlong sleeves, a flush of embarrassment coloring her round cheeks. "If you think that's best."

Lunurin frowned. Inez's habit was far too big, and she hadn't tied on a belt. They were all low on clothing stipends, and the smaller girls wore mainly hand-me-downs, but surely they could find Inez a pair of shoes that weren't two sizes too large?

"Just until you're feeling better," Lunurin assured her.

They made it through the first hour with only two crying fits and a screaming match on the part of their students. Father DeSoto was in and out as workers and servants entered, requesting permission for building repairs. He spent half the lesson distracted, writing Palisade passes and purchase requisitions. When Lunurin saw Biti's chalk crack from the heat of the frustration she exuded, Lunurin suggested DeSoto show the students an example of buoyancy on the water trough near the kitchens.

Lunurin pulled several dried banana leaf boats from the shelf, sacrifices to everyone's restlessness. With DeSoto leading and Inez at the rear, they herded everyone out. Except Biti, who Lunurin held back to tidy her slate and chalk and maybe do some deep breathing exercises so as not to set everyone on fire.

The heat Biti radiated increased when she breathed in, like a miniature set of bellows over coals. Maybe deep breathing wasn't the answer to calming a firetender.

Biti twisted her smock in her hands, leaving ashen prints. "I'm sorry, Sister Lunurin. I'm not usually this bad. The volcano... my sister must be so worried."

"I'm worried too." Lunurin took the girl's hands, shocked at the heat. "Would it help you cool down if I lit a lamp?"

Just then, a woman Lunurin didn't recognize poked her head into the classroom.

"Hello, Sister, I am come on behalf of Señora Prinsa to bring Bituin to her in the shipyards," the woman said in accented Codicían. She was dressed like one of the church servants. But her hair was uncovered, cut far shorter than any of the women wore here except as punishment.

She dipped her head and made a botched sign of the cross, touching two fingers to her shoulder, brow, then opposite shoulder.

The women locked eyes. Lunurin mimicked her sign. Depending who you asked, it was Mount Hilaga. Others said it was a tsunami like the one the late Lakan, Dalisay Inanialon, had summoned, trying to wipe the Codicían Palisade from the delta. If the priests asked, Aynilans were forgetful and didn't mean to profane the Church's holy symbol.

Even if Lunurin hadn't been holding Biti's hand, the bright sizzle of her excitement was undeniable. Lunurin let go, and Biti bounded over to wrap her arms around the woman's waist, burying her face in the new arrival's middle.

They had the same pin-straight, sleek black hair, matching button noses and dimples. The heat in the room spiked, then dimmed, cold ash heaped over coals. This must be Biti's sister.

"You have somewhere safe for her?" Lunurin asked.

"Yes."

"You will need permission to leave the church grounds with one of the students. I'll write you a pass." Lunurin went to the desk and filled the travel slip Cat had given her from DeSoto. Mimicking DeSoto's crabbed hand, Lunurin wrote in "girl, mid-grade student and kitchen servant." It wasn't strictly correct to write a single slip for two people, lacking their names, but with the way DeSoto had written passes today, it should go unnoticed.

Lunurin pressed the slip into the other woman's hand, whispering in Aynilan, "You will need to show this to the soldiers at the gate. They'll let you through if you have it. If they question you, tell them you are on an errand for Father DeSoto himself, and if you are delayed the church belltower may collapse. Now go."

The woman grasped Lunurin's wrist with a fever-warm hand. "My mother, where is she?"

"I'm sorry; she's being held in the shipyards under guard with the rest of the workers. You won't be able to take them both. You have to get Biti out before they realize what she is."

The woman's jaw clenched tight, but she nodded curtly. "Thank you."

She seized Biti's hand, and they vanished into the bustle of people among the sprawling church complex.

Lunurin might regret this, but the last thing their testy volcano needed was a frightened young firetender. Not after Lunurin had been sung of by the dugong while tending the oyster beds. No matter what difficulties it caused, her little family would be safer with Biti far away.

Did she dare hope no other irregularities would derail the abbot's dinner tonight?

One of the older girls ran in. "Sister María! Inez fainted. She's got the worst nosebleed!"

3

MARÍA LUNURIN

Lunurin had sent Rosa for the Palisade physician. By the time she returned at last, cool water and shade had already revived Inez.

"Forgive me, Sister, he has too many injured from the earthquake. He wouldn't come," Rosa reported, wringing her hands.

"How's the bleeding now?" Lunurin crouched beside Inez who sat on the ground, head tipped forward, nose pinched shut.

"Stopped," Inez mumbled nasally, wiping helplessly at the bloodstains all down the white of her habit.

"Let's get you up to your bed where you can rest. I'll help you clean up," Lunurin suggested, reaching to lift her up.

Inez balked, sweat standing out on her brow. She held out both hands to stay Lunurin. "No, don't! I'll be sick for sure. I can walk," she insisted.

Lunurin gave her a hand up and helped her to the girls' dormitory.

"You should go. You have dinner. I just need to wait for the queasiness to pass." Inez curled onto her cot, rejecting all Lunurin's attempts to help her clean up and change.

Lunurin frowned down at her. "Alright. We'll get you to one of the herb-healers in Aynila tomorrow to make sure it's nothing serious. I'll send Cat up with dinner once you've had a chance to rest."

Inez cracked her eyes open to peer up at Lunurin pleadingly. "Please don't bother Ate, she's busy tonight. I just need to lie down a bit, I'll be fine. One of the other girls will bring me something."

Lunurin would've argued, but Rosa ran in with word the cook was threatening to walk out on them again. Between tonight's dinner and the festival Mass of Our Lady María of the Drowned, the ruined ovens put her in an impossible position.

Several hours later, Lunurin was dragged away from the kitchens by Sister Philippa. Philippa had just completed a headcount of the girls' dormitory. Lunurin hoped Inez was able to rest despite the commotion.

Muttering prayers to Saint Anthony under her breath, Philippa hauled Lunurin into Father DeSoto's study, and scowled to see him and Catalina bent over rosters of polo laborers.

"Father, we have a problem."

"A moment," he murmured, lifting a hand.

"If you *please*, Father. If you are so caught up in the building work, then you need to train someone to take your place in the school, Father Ortiz or someone with more time on their hands. We have the students' safety to think of!" Philippa cried.

"Safety? Safety! Sister Philippa, the coffin dam around the Puente de Hilaga's final pylon is taking on water, and as Sister Catalina so helpfully reminds me, half my workforce is overdue to be released from their contracts. But the governor still plans on announcing the entire delta will be connected by my bridges before the end of the month, despite stealing laborers for the *Santa Clarita*," DeSoto shot back, still deeply engrossed in the rosters on his desk.

"A student is missing!" Philippa exclaimed.

"Who is missing?"

"The Prinsa girl! Bitten—however you say it," Sister Philippa snapped.

"Bituin was in the group I supervised in the first math section. Father DeSoto, did she make it to your second session after the demonstration? I know we all got a little distracted by Inez's fall, and I had to leave you to manage everyone on your own to get Inez settled," Lunurin lied easily.

Father DeSoto looked up at last, frowning. "She must have."

"Do you have the attendance sheet?" She knew full well Father DeSoto relied on Inez to handle administrative tasks.

"Well no, I don't," he admitted.

Sister Philippa huffed in frustration. "Father! It is your job to record attendance for your classes."

"Now, Sister…"

"I have one twelve-year-old girl who could've wandered off into the Palisade at any time in the last five hours. *When* she vanished matters. Do I need to alert the Palisade guard, or can I keep this embarrassment private?"

"Let's not panic. How far can one girl have gone?"

"Easy for you to say. You're the one who lost her!"

Cat spoke up. "All the children have had a difficult day. It's likely she's hidden away on the church grounds and fallen asleep. She did the same thing last week, and I can't tell you the number of times I spent the night in some quiet corner rather than come out when I was her age," she counseled in an offhand tone.

"That's true. Father DeSoto, will you do a headcount on the boys, just to be safe?" Lunurin asked with all the earnestness she could muster.

He nodded.

Catalina rose to her feet. "I suggest we let the matter rest tonight. We don't want to rouse a search with the abbot's guests arriving. Come breakfast I wouldn't be surprised if Biti has reappeared. But I'll leave you three to sort it. I should check on my sister, and I've got another few contracts to review."

As expected, none of the boys were missing. Father DeSoto and Catalina had soon returned to the labor shortage problem, but Sister Philippa remained unconvinced.

"I'll search the girls' dormitories again," she said. "Maybe the girls are concealing her."

Unable to obfuscate the search further, Lunurin returned to preparations for dinner. Agitation swirled under her breastbone, but she pushed it down, and went to face her panicking cook and all the abbot's illustrious dinner guests.

~

The abbot's dinner had attracted every important inhabitant of the Palisade and no few members of Aynila's principalia, including the Lakan, Tigas Dakila, though Lunurin couldn't see his son, Alon. There were a dozen who showed despite previously declining the invitation. She could thank everyone's earthquake anxieties for that. While her guests were occupied with golden mango, buttery papaya, small tart siniguelas, and cold kinilaw-style dishes "cooked" in fresh calamansi juice and palm vinegar, Lunurin hoped desperately that the abbot's paella was cooking properly in its sealed clay pot in the coal pit behind the kitchens, and they wouldn't all break their teeth on raw rice.

The well-to-do of the Palisade had all the same concerns as the school children. "My wife thinks we ought to evacuate to high ground. What if there are more aftershocks, or some witch saboteur tries to pull in another wave?"

"Aynila is quite free of water witches thanks to the Inquisition's efforts." The abbot was always pleased at the opportunity to speak on his favorite topic.

"What about the three witches executed after sabotaging the Puente de Hilaga last All Saint's Feast?" the governor drawled. "It would've been completed months ago if not for that incident. Think how much more work our shipyards could take on with direct access to the resources on Hilaga's delta and the metalworking conclave."

"They were the last of a dying breed. We stamped out the scourge of witchcraft during the Inquest after their last attempt to stand in the way of progress. They will be erased, lost to myth, like the sea serpents from our navigational maps as we bring the light of God and civilization to the farthest reaches of the Empire," the abbot insisted.

Lunurin remembered those sleepless nights. How the stinging smoke from the women's pyres had lingered in her lungs, their screams in her ears, as she and Cat had desperately tried to get ahead of the Inquisition's broad definition of a collaborator. Anyone who'd run afoul of the overseers or the church became a target. A quarter of the women servants were dragged before the abbot to be "tested" for witch blood.

"Aynila won't stand for their ilk either. Jungle rebels and troublemakers, the lot of them," the Lakan agreed.

Lunurin wondered if he was only publicly distancing himself from his late wife's ill-fated attempt to destroy the Palisade, or if he truly believed in the abbot's witch hunts.

"You may be sure that any collaborators or sympathizers

remaining among us were rooted out, by hook and crook, and repented of the sinfulness in their hearts," the abbot concluded.

Lunurin remembered how even many of those found innocent had died after the canings and other "interrogation" methods the abbot so enjoyed employing. Cold sweat trickled down her back. There was so much zeal in the abbot's gleaming green eyes.

How small a slipup would it take for her piety to be deemed lacking, or her loyalty suspect? For the abbot to turn that flaying witching cane upon her?

The cook entered, freeing Lunurin from the memory of pyre smoke darkening the sky. The dinner must go on. The paella pot was wide and shallow, nearly as big as a kalesa wheel. It took four servants to set it before the abbot and his guests of honor at the head of the table. Lunurin accepted a small hammer from the cook and cracked the dish, shattering the clay sealing the top from hot coals and dirt. The cook lifted off the lid with a flourish, savory steam rushing out. Anito and turmeric had replaced saffron to achieve the rich golden color. Nestled into the rice, among half a bay's worth of smaller oysters, shrimp, and crabs, were the four huge gold-lip oysters.

"A gift, from Aynila's famous oyster beds." She served the guests of honor each a portion topped with one of the huge oysters.

The captain held up a golden pearl the size of his thumb. "Naturally gold? It's not the dish coloring it? Marvelous."

The Lakan, who knew exactly where these pearls had been harvested from, eyed her sharply.

"These *new* beds of yours seem quite mature," the Lakan commented.

Lunurin suddenly remembered the Codicíans' blithe claims that the old tide-touched oyster beds had all been destroyed and that these beds were new, the sole property of the Church and certainly not the product of Lunurin spending months diving for scattered survivors among the ransacked beds.

The abbot grinned. "It's the pearl-culturing methods we've introduced. Nothing of this size would've been possible with the backward ways previously employed."

Under your late wife went unsaid.

But before the Lakan could take insult, Sister Philippa burst in, shouting, "Explain this!"

She had a student's thin brown arm clenched in her talon-like hand, dragging them behind her as she marched toward the head table. *Inez.*

A dozen possible scenarios raced across Lunurin's mind. Philippa's wrath was legendary within the convent. No small part of Lunurin's youth had been spent developing elaborate deceptions to ensure she and Catalina evaded the woman's appetite for punishment. But what could Inez have done?

Lunurin intercepted Philippa, attempting to de-escalate the situation. "Now, Sister, let me help you deal with whatever it is."

"This little hussy is pregnant!" Sister Philippa declared. "This is what comes of allowing mixing of the students."

She hauled Inez forward and flung her into Lunurin's middle. Lunurin clutched Inez, baffled at the outlandish allegation.

In her arms, Inez shook and wept, wrapped in nothing but a sheet. Everyone stared. This was bad, very bad. Her mind raced, coming up with only flat denial.

"That's not possible. She just turned thirteen. This isn't a matter that concerns everyone, Sister Philippa. Let's take this back to the girls' dormitory and sort it out in privacy."

Lunurin took Philippa's arm and tried to sweep both her

and Inez back out of the dining room. But Philippa dug her heels in and reached to yank Inez's sheet. Lunurin knocked Philippa's hand aside, tucking Inez behind her. Along the way, her hand encountered a firm bump under the sheet. Lunurin nearly bit through her own tongue, but kept her face blank of everything besides mild confusion. "Please, Sister, decorum. Inez deserves her modesty."

"She's a lying whore!"

"Philippa!" Lunurin's stomach clenched tight at all the leering eyes, the abbot's face reddening with fury, Philippa smiling cruelly, oh-so satisfied at having proven Lunurin was failing as acting-abbess.

"How dare you allow this—this impropriety!" the abbot sputtered, then lapsed into silence, unable to find words for his outrage.

Lunurin curtseyed low. Somehow, she had to repair this. "Forgive me, Abbot. We're merely tired and stressed after the earthquake. I'm sure this is another case of tapeworms. It's been going around among the servants when they buy street food. Crushed papaya seeds and coconut oil will clear the ailment in a week."

She didn't wait for the abbot's response.

"What? I..." Philippa sputtered.

Lunurin urged Inez into the hands of the cook, who hustled her out the servants' entrance.

"This has all been a misunderstanding," Lunurin announced firmly.

An elderly nun gesticulated with a spoon. "It's not fever, is it?"

"Just worms, not contagious," Lunurin assured her.

The old woman shuddered. "Oh, poor dear. I got those when I first arrived. Thought I'd die. Sister Philippa, do stop interrupting a fine meal for no reason. Worms! As if anyone wants those on the mind when they're eating."

Lunurin curtseyed again to the head of the table. "My apologies. We take our responsibility for the health and welfare of our students very seriously. I will see that all is settled."

Lunurin seized Philippa's arm, hustling her away from the abbot, red-faced and beside himself at this breach in decorum, and the governor, who'd started to guffaw, his booming laugh chasing them out.

Once in the courtyard, Lunurin reiterated, "It was the washing girls, Rosa and Isa, last week. The worms are in the water at this time of year, anyone who uses river water for cooking is at risk. We should be drinking more tea, even the servants. Boiled water, that's the way."

Philippa snarled at her. "Even you can't make this vanish overnight. You may be acting-abbess because I can't fathom the servants' gibberish tongues, but you can't hide *this* from the abbot."

Well *now* she couldn't. Fury skated down her spine. If Magdalena were here, Philippa wouldn't have dared cause such a spectacle, but Lunurin kept her expression calm. If she was going to protect Inez, she had to sell the lie.

"I've lived on these islands all my life, Sister. I know our parasites. Tapeworms aren't even the worst. You should see flatworm snail fever. At least this will only give Inez a sore stomach for a few days. Cat and I will take her off your hands for the night. A worm purge isn't a pretty sight. It would disturb the other girls."

Philippa hesitated, glaring at Lunurin.

"Unless you'd like to administer the laxatives?" Lunurin offered. "Though I warn you, the worms sometimes try to spread to a new host once the purging process begins. It would be best to keep her isolated from the other children a short while."

"You can't really expect me—"

"Would you prefer the Palisade physician handles it? You know how busy he is, especially after the quake. Worms are hardly life-threatening."

Philippa's thin lips peeled back from her teeth in disgust. "It's ungodly the kinds of illnesses these islands spawn. I pray all is well in the morning. Good night, Sister María."

It took everything in her to keep her pleasant smile plastered in place, rather than bare her teeth right back at the horrible woman. Philippa dealt with, Lunurin hurried toward the kitchens.

Rosa intercepted her. "Cook took her up to your cell." She handed Lunurin a bag of crushed papaya seeds and a jar of coconut oil. The girl fidgeted with the rosary at her wrist, thumbing through the wooden beads till she held a golden cowry shell etched with a peak. "Tell Inez I'll pray she feels better. I shouldn't have shared those kwek kwek skewers. I thought they were fine!"

They had been. Lunurin had enjoyed a few of the crisp fried quail eggs coated in annato and sweet potato starch herself, but she appreciated Rosa's dedication to the story. Her brother had been one of those forced into hard labor sentences during the falla tax riots. Lunurin hoped Rosa wasn't showing anything but sympathy. It was too dangerous.

Lunurin was starting to see those subtle hatch marks everywhere. Waves and mountains, etched into the banana leaf-wrapped deliveries to the church kitchens, marking the goods that weren't day-old or otherwise subtly spoiled, and gratified near public worksites. The old gods weren't the only ones who were restless.

It would only get worse if the Codicíans completed the Puente de Hilaga, tightening their control over all the delta's river traffic.

Lunurin hurried up to find Inez.

Catalina had abandoned her contracts. Inez huddled on her sister's pallet.

"Lunurin, could it be tapeworms?" Cat asked, desperate hope in her expression.

"No." Lunurin set aside the deworming treatment and threw open the trunk at the foot of her bed, digging for the porcelain bottles of herbal medicine from Alon. She had a root decoction of abutra, a leaf tincture of sagilala, and tubang-bakod seed oil... but they were for when someone first missed their period. She thumped a fist into her thigh, her frustration dangerously close to fear. She couldn't panic; she had to think.

Lunurin went to sit beside Inez. "May I?"

Inez nodded, and Lunurin palpitated the hard bump of her stomach. Lunurin was no healer, but Inez must be well into her fourth month. Alon had given her tinctures to help the servants take care of things before anyone got fired. But they weren't safe this far along.

"What happened? Was it a boy from school?" Catalina asked.

Inez went white. "I can't tell you."

Catalina continued, "Inez, we want to help, you have to tell us. If it's a boy from the school—"

"It's not, Ate!"

"Inez, it's okay... these things happen," Lunurin tried.

"They're not supposed to!" Catalina hissed.

Lunurin knew when Cat's sharpness was fear. She put a hand on Cat's, trying to soothe her.

"You have to get it out of me." Inez seized Lunurin's arm.

"Don't say such things." Catalina crossed herself, then pressed a hand hard over her mouth.

Lunurin lifted her hand from Inez's belly, cradling her face. She was so young, her face rounded with lingering baby fat, her dark eyes red from weeping. Lunurin remembered her own confusion and terror in the aftermath of the many mistakes of her youth. How little her mother and stepfather had cared for her panicked explanations. Lunurin's gut twisted. She had to do better for Inez than had been done for her. Inez had only made a small mistake, not risked the lives of hundreds. Lunurin wouldn't let this ruin Inez's life.

"Is that what you want?" she asked.

"Please. Please, you have to. I'll drink anything, papaya seeds, coconut oil. I want everything back the way it was before—before—"

"Before what, Inez?" Catalina asked.

"Father DeSoto," Inez whispered, her face crumpling into tears.

The world dropped out from under Lunurin.

She drew both sisters into her arms, holding them too tightly. Catalina was shaking and swearing. Inez's little body shuddered with sobs.

Lunurin's blood roared in her ears. Thunder throbbed in the distance, a low rumble that vibrated into her skull through her mutya. The promise of a storm brewed over the warm seawater of the bay. With it, she could *drown them all*. She need only reach out and cry the goddess's true name, and she would have all the vengeance she needed for the terrible things the Codicians were doing to her people, to her islands, and to Inez, the child she and Catalina had practically raised.

Catalina pinched the soft skin under Lunurin's upper arm, hard. She snapped back into her body with a disorienting wrench, and took a deep breath, trying to shake off the goddess's rage.

She shot Cat a grateful look. No matter what the old gods wanted her to believe, she wasn't responsible for everyone—just Inez, just Cat, just preserving her little sliver of peace inside the convent. The old gods wouldn't be there in the aftermath of her destruction. They would have their vengeance, like they had with the sinking of the *San Pedro*, like when Lakan Dalisay called in the tsunami. But when the Codicíans retaliated by killing every gods-blessed they could find... the gods would be silent, and leave them to human mercies.

"I'm sorry!" Inez wept. "Please, you can't tell anyone! You can't! He said... he said if I told anyone I'd be thrown out of the convent. They'd never let me see Ate again."

Catalina shook her head in denial, her expression twisting in anguish, too distraught for words.

Lunurin struggled to keep her voice even. "We won't do anything rash. Only..." Words failed. Lunurin's rage tangled in on itself. She had suggested Inez help with Father DeSoto's math classes when his usual assistant, Ortiz, got sick—

"They'll send me away!"

"No, no, I won't let that happen." Lunurin forced surety into her voice. She wiped Inez's tears and squeezed Cat's shaking hands. "We can fix this."

"How? How? I don't—there isn't anyone—" Cat pressed her lips together, trying to smother her rising panic. She laid her cheek to the top of her sister's head, blinking back the tears gathering in the corners of her eyes.

Cat had no family who could take Inez in. Inez couldn't be expelled from the convent. She had no one in the world except for her big sister and Lunurin.

Lunurin bit her cheek, tasting the blunt edges of pain and wrestling with the impulse to tear DeSoto from his place at the abbot's table and push him out a window headfirst. She needed a plan. "Inez, when... when did it start? Your monthlies would've stopped. You might've felt nauseous and your breasts sore."

Inez shivered all over. "I thought I was dying. It feels like it's killing me."

"You're not dying," Lunurin assured her. "I remember you hardly ate anything at the Feast of the Three Kings. Half the Palisade were recovering from fever, I assumed..."

"I couldn't keep anything down. I was sick every day then," Inez whispered.

Cat clutched Inez tighter. "How could this happen? Why? Lunurin, what will we do?"

Lunurin ran the math. Five months, maybe more, no less than four, *damn*. She needed a better answer for the desperation in Cat's gaze, but she was still reeling. What was she supposed to do except gouge out DeSoto's eyes with a spoon?

On Calilan, there was a saying: "Go to a stormcaller for vengeance, for they do not heal, and they do not save." But no one had ever told Catalina this. For her, Lunurin would have to solve this another way.

"Nothing I have can help this far along," Lunurin admitted.

Catalina's eyes went wide. "What do you mean? What do you have?"

Lunurin stared back, unrepentant. "Sometimes the servants need help. The abbot does worse than dismiss those who become pregnant. It's no different than when we help a shipyard worker."

Cat's expression twisted with anguish. "It is! We can't—I can't—Saints have mercy."

Lunurin grabbed her hand. "We've done worse to help those less dear to us than Inez."

Catalina went very pale at her words. But they didn't have time for Cat's ever-shifting scales of right and wrong to take a hard dip toward repentance now. Inez needed them.

"We have to do this." Lunurin laid a clean habit and belt on the bed. "Come, Inez, up, up. Can you dress for me?"

When neither moved, Lunurin gently guided Inez behind the bamboo privacy screen.

Catalina fisted her hands in Lunurin's collar, pulling her down to whisper, "We have to stop. We'll only make things worse. I never should've helped you this morning. We went too far, and now Inez—"

"This isn't divine punishment." Lunurin cut off Cat's spiral, less kindly than she intended. She kissed Cat's white knuckles and held her gaze. "Repentance won't save your sister. We have to do that ourselves. Come, we have to go."

"Where? How? The convent is shut for the night."

"To Alon, he'll help."

"The Palisade gates are closed. How can he help with this?"

"He will," Lunurin insisted.

"What? Put her up till the baby is born? That's asking a lot of the Lakan's son, even if he does love you." Her voice dripped with venom. Lunurin flinched; Cat's fear could make her cruel.

She squeezed Cat's shoulders. "Inez doesn't want this baby. It would ruin her life. They will never let an unmarried mother remain in the convent, not as a postulant or servant. You know that."

Cat bit her lip. "It's a sin."

Why couldn't Cat see that to the Church, their very existence was a sin? What was one more?

The clouds over the bay were not yet heavy with rain, only illuminated from within by flashes of lightning and a dry rumble of thunder throbbing in her bones.

"What DeSoto did was the sin. This is harm reduction. We have to protect Inez."

Catalina's brow furrowed, torn between her love for her sister and her faith. "There's got to be another way. Why do you always run to *him* when things get difficult?"

Lunurin wanted to shout. They'd been working with Alon for years. When sickness came for the students and servants of the convent and the Palisade physician couldn't trouble himself, Alon could be depended on. Where did Catalina think she'd sent all the workers they'd disappeared? And during the latest inquest... yet Catalina had begrudged every hint of his involvement then too.

But sometimes the only thing left to do was to beg the mercy of the Sea Lady and a tide-touched healer. Alon was the last she knew of in Aynila.

"If there is, I don't know it. I'm sorry, Cat. Right now, we have no safe options. Alon will tell us what the safe options are. I can't do this alone."

In the face of her honesty, Cat's sharpness ebbed. She latched onto Lunurin's plan like a woman drowning. "Okay, options. Yes. Options."

Inez came out dressed. Catalina released her white-knuckled grip on Lunurin's habit. Cat helped Inez roll her sleeves, securing all the extra material around her neatly with the belt.

Oh dear, that made the problem apparent. No matter. If they met anyone the way Lunurin was taking them, they'd have bigger problems than a pregnant postulant.

Grateful once again for the placement of their room, Lunurin slid open the capiz shell window to peer into the deserted street outside. They were on the bamboo second floor jutting over the street, some twelve feet off the cobblestone. Below the window hung a sturdy planter, in which Cat grew orchids. Underneath the orchid baskets, Lunurin kept a rope ladder, which she unfurled down to the street.

Lunurin took Cat's and Inez's shaking hands in hers, squeezing tight. "It's not dangerous. You can do this. Trust me, we can fix this together."

4

MARÍA LUNURIN

By the time they'd snuck through darkened streets to the southern Palisade wall, even Lunurin was sweating with exertion. Built of three-needle pine, which grew over a hundred feet tall in the mountains, the bark-stripped trunks were painted in black pine-pitch. Like her, the trees had been uprooted and remade into something foreign. The Palisade stood at a modest eighty-five feet, with a narrow parapet along the top edge. Wooden guard towers and wide platforms supported hulking cannons.

Near marshy sections, iron grating had been installed to allow drainage during storms or when the Saliwain overflowed its banks. The salt of the river's reverse flow would help. Lunurin counted grates, looking for the telltale peaked hatch mark carved into the wall. *There!* She waded in.

Goddess willing, her handiwork three months before had gone unnoticed… *damn*.

Lunurin pulled her crucifix over her head. Dipping her

hand into the cool salty water, she touched the silver cross to the iron bars.

Addressing the dream of a storm over the water, Lunurin called softly, "Lintik, come to me."

She didn't need a storm. She didn't want a storm, but a seed of lightning? That would do nicely. The dugong amulet grew warm, warding off any attention this tiny draw of power might cause.

It came to her like one of the volcano's spark-striker birds, now a rare sight flitting indigo and turquoise along the flanks of Hilaga. The seed of lightning perched on her outstretched fingers, gentle as a firefly. She guided it through the crucifix into the iron grate. Iron bars pitted and crumbled like they'd been soaking in seawater for generations, not months.

Wrapping both hands around the grate, she lifted it free. The metal gave a protesting shriek, sending ice down her spine, as some unseen section she hadn't corroded completely gave way. Lunurin stopped breathing.

Catalina crushed Inez flat against the Palisade wall as a circle of light high overhead paused, an oil lantern swinging in a soldier's hand.

Lunurin's arms cramped. Her hands slicked with sweat. Her legs burned, but she didn't dare move. Discovery would mean expulsion from the convent at best, arrest and execution for sabotage at worst.

Catalina made the sign of the cross, her lips moving soundlessly. Lunurin envied the ease with which Cat prayed. She missed how the prayer ballads of her youth had tasted on her lips, but she'd learned long ago that prayer was dangerous. Some gods answered.

Finally, the guard moved on. Lunurin lowered the grate.

They were lucky the rains were late. Usually all but a foot of this grate would be underwater.

Inez went through first. Lunurin kicked a few brittle fingers of metal so Catalina could follow. She went last, her habit catching on the ragged edges. She heaved the grate back into place. They waded some distance before they were able to climb onto the bank.

Now, the tricky part: crossing the bridge into Aynila without being stopped by soldiers. While Catalina and Inez readjusted their habits, Lunurin reached again for the thread of power that still bound her to the goddess that made her a stormcaller. Her dugong bone amulet had thinned the connection, but never severed it like cutting her hair.

Without the amulet, hiding in the convent would be impossible. She'd have been burned as a witch years ago.

Now though, Lunurin could control the thread of her power. She let down a lock of hair with a quiet plea. This time, she didn't reach for the bay, but the peak of Hilaga. She curled her fingers, beckoning the swirling clouds that graced Hilaga's slopes like a lady's piña cloth shawl. Her mutya nestled in the thick bun at the nape of her neck hummed. She spread the clouds over the water, a haze that limited visibility and muted sound.

It was difficult to move cloud and not stir it into storm when it so wanted to soak up water from the river. She gripped the mists like a pack of spectral hounds, bidding them hold.

Catalina exclaimed in surprise. "When did it get so foggy?"

"It's good for us. We can walk across the Puente de Aynila and not wade clinging to the side."

Catalina bit her lip. "You've done this before."

"Yes."

"Why didn't you tell me?"

Lunurin tapped her knuckles to the amulet on her breast. "I put you at enough risk using your 'lost' passes from DeSoto.

If I got caught, I didn't want you in trouble with me." This was a half-truth, if not all of it. Lunurin had given up being too honest with Cat about her abilities, much less Alon's. For all that she loved Lunurin, Catalina was fearful of the full force of these islands' native magic.

The Church must never discover the Lakan's only heir was a water witch. Lunurin would not be the reason Aynila burned.

"How did you climb out the window without my noticing?" Cat asked.

Lunurin smiled fondly, glad this was the issue Cat had raised. "You are a very heavy sleeper, my love."

They had become good at tiptoeing around her power's existence and the fact that no amount of prayer or piety made it truly wane.

Lunurin dropped a light kiss onto Catalina's brow and reached for Inez.

"Almost there, Inez, I swear."

The poor girl panted, shivering in the muggy night air. Lunurin lifted her onto the bridge with care.

The ten-span bridge floated over the water, stone pilings disappearing into white mist below. Nothing moved on the river, the grates were lowered so no one could smuggle goods to the Aynilan port without paying the Palisade's toll. There were ways around on the far side of the central delta, for now, but the new Puente de Hilaga would fully span the Saliwain, connecting Aynila to Hilaga, and the metalworkers' conclave.

Soon the black bulk of the Palisade receded and before them lay only a white murk. No sounds from the city across the water reached them, although with no Palisade curfew Lunurin expected late-night carousing and social calls, while the evening air was cool and pleasant.

Her weather tricks wrapped silence around them like a cloak. The soft *thump-thump-thump* of their footfalls rippled through the mist.

The city came alive the farther they walked from Puente de Aynila and the strange sound-dampening mist. Music and laughter poured from upper-story windows where families and friends gathered, enjoying the night air and good company. They trudged on upstream toward Alon's estate bordering the river, inherited after his mother's death.

The main building was in the same mixed stone and wood style as the convent, but it had none of its dour presence. Alon's home was the heart of the community, more so than the Lakan's palace. The ground floor served as a local shop for raw dyes, ink, and cloth in every shade of blue from the palest sweet potato flower to deepest indigo. Alon's doors were always open to those who needed the sea's mercy.

The upper story was still illuminated. Most of the city kept late hours, sleeping in, enjoying afternoon naps during the hottest part of the day, and relegating work and social activities to the evenings. A schedule Lunurin had been trying to convince the convent to follow for years, but the sisters were adamant that rising with the sun was a godly thing.

They approached the wooden door to the shop, and Lunurin lifted a bronze door knocker shaped like a cresting wave. She wondered if the Lakan knew how rebellious his heir was these days.

The sound echoed hollowly. Catalina and Inez tucked themselves against Lunurin's sides, seeking reassurance. They waited.

An older Aynilan man with grey hair in a braid down his back answered the door, leaning on a cane. "Forgive me, we're closed for the evening—ah, Sister Lunurin."

"Mano po, Tito Kawit, I'm here to call on Gat Alon." Lunurin greeted him affectionately, pressing his hand to her brow when it was offered.

"I will see if the lord is awake." Kawit cast a critical eye over the three of them. His face softened, and he waved them inside. While the women removed their shoes, he bade them not to touch the wares while he went to see if Lord Alon was taking visitors.

Kawit left the oil lamp in a nook beside the door and stepped deeper into the shop around a wall, the *creak-tap* of his cane on the stair echoing as he ascended. The warm light lifted Lunurin's spirits. She'd gotten them this far. Whatever happened next, at least she wouldn't face the problem alone.

Lunurin coaxed Inez and Catalina to sit on a bench beside the door. Poor Inez was exhausted.

"What if he won't see us?" Inez whispered.

"He will," Lunurin assured her.

"What if he can't do anything?"

"He is a healer. He will do his very best," Lunurin promised.

Inez sucked in her full cheeks. "Is that different from the Palisade physician? He almost never comes, and he put leeches on Abbess Magdalena before she left for Canazco. They made her worse."

Lunurin squeezed Inez's hands. "Yes, a healer is very different."

A loud thump came from the upper floor, and Lunurin bit her lip on a smile of relief as it was followed by the fast tread of someone taking the stairs two at a time. Catalina, made dour by fear and her disapproval of these clandestine doings, frowned.

Alon, when he appeared, was very composed, walking calmly into the shop area. The Lakan's second son was tall, of an eye with Lunurin—he'd finally caught up to her when he was around twenty. He wore his shoulder-length black hair caught back from his face. Lunurin was glad he'd abandoned his attempt to grow a mustache matching his father's. She preferred him clean-shaven.

He approached Lunurin with his long easy stride, his deep brown complexion almost amber in the lamplight. He was comfortably dressed in the Aynilan style. His mutya was disguised as a false rosary, mother-of-pearl beads carved to mimic sampaguita flowers. A cross set with a perfectly round pearl at its center gleamed subtly gold against the deep indigo of his barong, as if spots of sunlight were shining through saltwater. A bold risk, one none but the son of the Lakan would dare. On his right hand, he wore an ornate set of gold rings set with mother-of-pearl. The blessing of Aman Sinaya upon him was a subtle push-pull in Lunurin's blood. He was one of the last tide-touched in Aynila.

His brow was furrowed with concern, but his arms he held open as if he would embrace her.

Lunurin dropped into a curtsey. "Gat Alon," she greeted him, and was pulled to her feet.

He leaned in, less a kiss of greeting than a soft press of his cheek against hers, as between visiting nobility or dear friends. She leaned into him.

"If this is about Biti, I swear I can explain," he murmured.

She wished she could drop her face onto his shoulder and groan. As if she didn't have enough worries tonight.

She took a deep breath—and regretted it, as his scent of indigo ink and salt flooded her senses. "It's not, but how do you already know about Biti?"

Alon squeezed her shoulders and released her in precisely the amount of time appropriate for an unmarried man greeting a married woman, bride of Christ, or whatever a nun was. Alon always remembered himself, even when Lunurin didn't, but Catalina still radiated disapproval.

Last Christmas she'd caught them smuggling lagundi leaf past the convent quarantine so Lunurin would have cough syrup for the students as the fever spread. You'd think she'd walked in on them kissing. She'd stubbornly rejected the remedy, her cough lingering weeks.

Lunurin shook herself. Alon was just as much to blame for the standoff as Cat. He had no patience for the inconstant nature of Cat's piety. Lunurin needed to drag herself free of the magnetism of his presence.

Just as a firetender's warmth could burn, the alluring depths of a tide-touched spirit could easily drown. The attraction she felt toward him now was only a trick of her magic, not real like her love for Cat, no matter how real it felt. Still, his nearness soothed the phantom thunder rumbling in her mutya, and eased the exhaustion weighing her muscles like lead. Tonight, he felt like resting in a brewing typhoon over warm saltwater. She was grateful for his strength, even if Cat never understood why she turned toward it, time and time again.

"Sister Lunurin. As pleased as I always am to see you, you never come with good news this late," Alon said, his words loud enough for the room at large.

"I'm not one to break with tradition," she responded, gesturing to the sisters rising from the bench. "You know Sister Catalina, and Inez."

Alon executed a shallow bow, greeting Cat as she preferred in the Codicían fashion. His dark eyes raking over each of them for hurt or malady, before settling with their usual accuracy on

Inez. Inez shivered against Cat, trying to melt into her side. The circles under her eyes were dark as bruises. How had Lunurin not noticed something was terribly wrong sooner?

Alon's stern expression softened, a look he reserved for injured animals and small children. "Hello, Inez. You look tired. Let's get you to my treatment room. Tea should warm you right up."

He led the way upstairs. Alon invited Inez to sit on a low cot in his treatment room.

"Excuse me, Sisters. I will return shortly," he said, stepping out.

Lunurin released a long deep breath and dropped onto a stool near the door. The fog she'd spread over the river reached chilly fingers into Aynila, searching for her. *"What would you have of us? What can we be? May we rage? May we rain? Stormcaller, but twist us into shape and tell us our names and so we will be."*

Did the tides pull so on Alon? How did he stop himself from pulling them in, until everything but the peak of Hilaga lay underwater? For surely Aman Sinaya saw how the Church had wrapped her lover in rosaries and set her above their false altar. They'd stripped from her all her power and rage and majesty, and left her with grief. Surely even the gentle Sea Lady must whisper, *"Drown them! Drown them all!"* with every slap of her waves on the beaches of Lusong.

How could she not, with so many of her blessed children dead on Codicían pyres? So many struggling to keep the Palisade from closing its iron fist around the city?

Lunurin was exhausted. As if the tug and pull of politics and greed alone weren't enough to tear Aynila apart. The energy of the world was drawn tight around her, her mutya ached with it, a powder keg waiting to go off. If the volcano didn't erupt, raining ash and fire from above, would the next earthquake allow a desperate tide-touched to pull in a tsunami? Or would she lose control and summon the storm of the century her goddess craved?

5

ALON DAKILA

I n the darkened hallway, Alon pressed his hand to his hammering
heart. The cool metal of his brace offered no relief. Sister
María Lunurin was a typhoon wrapped in warm brown skin
and white cotton. Her two disparate worlds were trying to
grind her people into dust, yet she still believed she could hold
them safe with nothing but a steely gaze and two strong hands.
Some of the incipient tragedies she brought to his door, Alon
wasn't sure he could help, but he'd never deny her. Being within
sight of her made him feel like a twelve-foot surge was bearing
down on him under the wings of a storm. It was exhilarating,
terrifying; it made him feel like he could do anything.

Nothing he did quelled her effect on him, not since she had
called his name and awoken the tide in his blood, when he'd
been a boy of thirteen. A decade of exposure hadn't diminished
her effect.

Alon shook his head to clear it and crossed to the kitchen
where Kawit was preparing a tray of snacks and tea for his
guests. Something was very wrong with Inez, and he could

already tell the cistern water Kawit had drawn wouldn't suffice. Catalina would never have agreed to come to him for anything minor. Nor would Lunurin risk such a visit.

"Tito Kawit, could I have a bowl of sea salt?"

Kawit pulled open his extensive salt cabinet. "Is it sickness or an injury? I've a theory that the Bool coconut salt is less draining when working on fever patients."

"I'm not sure. No fever, I think."

Kawit was also tide-touched, but his gift was quite the reverse of any tide-touched Alon had ever met. When he touched saltwater, all the salt flowed to him, rather than his spirit becoming one with the salt. His affinity was decidedly not one for healing, but he'd perfected myriad other skills. It had made it much easier for him to hide from the Inquisition's purges over the years.

Kawit's gnarled fingers danced over a dozen jars and bags of salt. He settled on a small wooden box. "Try the mangrove leaf salt. Let me know what you think."

A white salt with irregularly sized square crystals was scooped in a dish alongside the refreshments for the guests. Kawit ignored Alon's best efforts to take his burden. He managed the tray and his severe limp with his usual stubborn pride. Kawit had been injured in the same laho-riled storm that shattered Alon's right hand, necessitating the brace of gold rings Alon wore.

Back in the treatment room, Kawit passed around cups of ginger tea and suman, sweet rice cakes wrapped in banana leaves. Alon mixed salt into the water pitcher and eyed Inez inhaling the food with concern. She sat hunched, one arm wrapped protectively around her middle.

Alon settled on a stool, trying to make himself smaller, not liking the way the whites showed around Inez's eyes when he stood over her.

Lunurin wasn't normally this opaque about whatever problems she brought to his door. Tonight, she had volunteered nothing. Even she must be nearing the end of her impressive strength. There was a brittleness about the eyes that made him want to wrap a shawl around her shoulders and tuck her into a guest room for the night.

But given the way Sister Catalina eyed him, thin-lipped, he doubted that was an option. She'd never done more than tolerate him, and since Christmas she'd been downright chilly. She had no grasp of why Lunurin trusted him over any of the Tianchaowen herb-healers in Aynila, and begrudged every familiarity he showed her. As if he hadn't known her first.

Alon was one wrong move away from Catalina grabbing her sister and sprinting for the exit. Were it not for Lunurin, he'd be happy to let her. He didn't understand how Lunurin could love a woman who had no idea what she was, nor what her power meant, even if she was beautiful. Perhaps Lunurin preferred it that way, to be seen as only human, as Sister María and nothing more.

In the ten years since Alon had met her, she'd certainly adhered to the desperate furious promise she'd screamed into a laho's teeth that night on his brother's ship, when Alon had been sure they were all about to drown.

Once the women had recovered from their harrowing trip and Inez stopped shivering, Alon asked, "Inez, can you tell me what's wrong?"

She turned doe-brown eyes first on Catalina, then toward Lunurin. Even tucked into the corner on a stool, she seemed to stand sentinel.

Lunurin pressed the knuckles of two fingers to her sternum, a nervous quirk of hers, whenever she was upset. "Inez is pregnant. She's too far along for me to attempt the usual remedies. We need your opinion."

"How far along?" Alon held out his palm to the girl. "May I have your hand?"

Inez sat upright. The overlarge habit drew tight against her abdomen, the size and shape of the problem suddenly very apparent. Alon felt for her pulse, reaching for the salt-warm push-pull of her blood. Pregnancy in a girl this young was dangerous all on its own.

"How long do you think?" Alon repeated, when no one volunteered the information.

Inez shook her head in bafflement, her thin wrist trembling in his grip. Alon felt like he was cradling a bleeding-heart dove in his palm. He gentled his hold.

"No more than six months?" Lunurin hazarded, and there was something in her voice, an unspoken weight. Catalina flinched.

"Why did you wait so long?" The words slipped out, with less professional calm than Alon usually managed.

He instantly regretted them when Inez began to tear up. Aman Sinaya have mercy but she was a child, a little girl, how had this happened?

"We didn't know," Catalina snapped, looking like she'd rather stick a knife in his belly and feed him to the crocodiles in the Saliwain than ask for his help.

Alon released Inez's wrist and lifted his hands up in surrender. "Forgive me, but with these things the longer you wait to come to a healer, the fewer options there are. I'd like to try something, but I need access to her bare stomach. Will you step behind the screen with her? There is a tapis skirt and a shawl if she has no breast band."

The sisters went behind the screen in the corner of the room and Alon retreated to Lunurin's side, his back turned to give them privacy.

"Six months?" he asked softly.

She swallowed hard and nodded.

"Lunurin, I can try, but without another healer to help me, I could do more harm than good. I'm glad you didn't dose her. She'd have bled out before you could've gotten her here."

Lunurin turned faintly green. "I was afraid you'd say that."

She pressed her knuckles to her pendant so hard her hand shook. Alon gently touched her wrist. She dropped her hand and Alon snatched his back, startled and half-ashamed of his own audacity, but she looked stricken.

"Who's the boy? I can help him pay the bride-price to Catalina's father if that's the issue," Alon said. "She's young but we can monitor her closely, get her eating right..."

Lunurin hated to ask money of him, more even than she hated how her coming endangered the secret of his healing, but he didn't begrudge her gold any more than he begrudged her Aman Sinaya's mercy. He had a duty, that was what being tide-touched meant.

Lunurin shook her head. What came out of her mouth might have been a sob in a woman less stringently in control of herself. "Alon, Father DeSoto did this. Sister Philippa knows, and if I can't solve the problem by morning, she'll tell the abbot and he'll expel Inez from the convent. Catalina is her only family."

Bile crawled up Alon's throat, while the terrible knowledge in Lunurin found a home in his chest, weighing his middle with edges sharp as a dozen batangas swords.

Aman Sinaya have mercy. The old priest must be at least fifty. Inez was a little girl, she hardly came up to Alon's ribs, a child! Was she even twelve?

Lunurin seized his shoulder as every drop of water in the room leaped to his hand. Alon stared at the tea from Lunurin's cup that now balanced on the tip of his index finger. He couldn't usually pull water fresh enough to drink. It was the reason he tried to use freshwater for healing when people didn't know what he was. It was harder to affect freshwater.

Very slowly, he tipped the tea back into the cup. Alon folded into a cross-legged position. He locked his hands together over his ankles and held his breath until the nearness of the saltwater flowing up the Saliwain River did not pulse just outside the window, begging him to make use of it. He couldn't usually feel the bay this far inland, and that was a blessing. He prayed the rains would come soon and wash the salt back out to the bay. It was hard enough to conceal what he was without constant temptation.

Alon cleared his throat. "Forgive me."

Lunurin let him go. He tried not to miss her nearness.

Rustlings and muttering came from behind the screen, along with a low exclamation of alarm. Lunurin bent, pressing her face into her knees. For a terrible moment, he thought she would weep. But when she looked up, her eyes were dry, burning with a rage that was not human, brewing with the storm that always lived in her bones. How could everyone else not see it, and love it, and fear it in equal measure?

"Please, tell me there's something you can do. I can't let this happen. If this happens, I won't be able to let him live—" Her teeth clicked together.

Alon took her hands from her knees and pressed them to his brow. "Anything in my power, it is yours."

She sat, statue-still, for several beats, before pulling her hands from his. "Thank you, but you shouldn't. You are the Lakan's son."

"You are a Datu's daughter; your duty is the same as mine."

"Was. Now I am a nun, no one's daughter. I have only Catalina and Inez."

82

Lunurin's eyes burned as if to say, *Please, you must see, this is my family. So many strangers' lives we have saved, but they are all I have in the world.*

"She's decent."

Alon stared. Inez's distended belly was layered with bruises, some old and fading to yellow and green, some violent indigo, fresh as his dye-pots.

Alon sucked in a breath. "Are you bleeding?"

"No." Inez didn't meet his gaze.

"Did someone do this to you?"

"I did it."

Alon went to dip his hands in the pitcher of saltwater.

Very gently, he laid damp hands on Inez's belly, then closed his eyes and felt, not for Inez's blood but the warm salt of the womb, for the other heartbeat. Everyone, even those who had never been named to the three goddesses, had a hint of the tide in their blood. He sank into it like salt into solution, following the flow.

In Inez's belly, the fetus was well-formed with a strong heartbeat, perhaps five and a half months along. The afterbirth was large, with huge throbbing blood vessels and an alarming lack of small ones. She'd bleed out fast if he tried to force an early labor. He couldn't do this alone.

Alon opened his eyes. He could not let this tragedy play out. Alon checked Inez's pulse at her throat. He evaluated the color of her eyes and how much flesh clung to her narrow ribs. Then he dried his hands. For a full examination he'd need more water, and there was no way Catalina wouldn't recognize what he was.

"Is the baby healthy?" Catalina asked.

"Yes, it is, though I'm sure Inez hasn't felt that way with how underfed she is."

"Thank God in Heaven." Catalina made the sign of the cross.

"I'm not dying?" Inez asked.

"No, just hungry and stressed. Now that we know, I'll be able to help. We'll find you somewhere safe to stay until the baby is born. Make sure you're fed and resting. But you need to tell me, Inez, is that the kind of help you want?"

At last Inez met his eyes. "I want it to go away. I want it to stop growing and hurting, and making me so tired I want to die."

"Inez!" Catalina gasped, scandalized.

Alon held Inez's gaze. "Yes, alright."

"Can you make it go away?" Inez asked.

"Not alone, but I can take you to someone who can help," Alon promised.

Catalina let out a shout of frustration. "No! You aren't taking my sister anywhere else in the dead of night unless you tell me where and why. Why should I trust you to know anything about midwifery? We shouldn't be wandering around the city at night at all!"

Alon didn't have any answers Catalina would like.

Lunurin cut in sharply, "Cat, please, he's trying to help."

"How is this any safer than the Palisade doctor?" Catalina demanded.

Lunurin unfolded from her stool. "Alon won't tell the abbot. Alon won't hurt Inez. I trust him, and you trust me. You wouldn't have followed me this far if you didn't."

Catalina's expression crumpled. Inez, biting her lower lip, said, "It's okay, Ate. I trust Lunurin too. We'll go together."

Alon's gut twisted in unease. "I can't bring you all. Just Inez."

Catalina's rejection was flat. "You aren't taking my sister anywhere without me." *You aren't taking Lunurin out of my sight either* went unstated.

Even Lunurin turned to him, a furrow between her dark brows. "Who are you taking Inez to? I thought after last year all the others… were gone."

Alon winced. "My mother—my teacher—isn't dead, like I told you. The Lakan found it politically expedient to declare her dead. She went into exile."

6

MARÍA LUNURIN

Alon's mother, Dalisay Inanialon, the true Lakan of Aynila, was alive.

When Hilaga had turned in her sleep four years after Lunurin came to Aynila, the earthquake leveled every stone building within the Palisade and toppled one of the church's belltowers. After the quake, Alon's mother had tried to pull in a tsunami.

She'd nearly accomplished the vengeance the old gods demanded. Was it not a just repayment for the Codicíans burning the vast complex of temples and training halls on Aynila's central delta? The Codicíans' cruelty that day had been beyond belief—so few gods-blessed had the strength to do more than guide small watercraft.

But Alon's mother had failed. The Codicíans rebuilt, more entrenched. They'd handed her in chains to her husband, who'd announced she'd bled to death days later. The very next Sunday, he was publicly baptized at Mass and exiled his eldest son, Jeian, who wouldn't repudiate his own tide-touched bayok wife.

Lunurin had feared Alon would lose himself to the grief. They'd grown much closer after he lost his mother and became his father's liaison to the Palisade. They'd both needed someone to lean on.

Lunurin half turned to him. The moonlight gleamed blue off the sleek blackness of his hair. On the water, he was at ease and utterly in command of their bangka, even as she drew down and then released a mist to conceal them as they slipped through the single gap remaining in the Puente de Hilaga.

Its completion would make living free from the Palisade's control impossible. Without a single additional soldier, the Codicíans would have the lifeblood of Aynila in a stranglehold. Lunurin's afterhours activities would become much more dangerous.

But for now, Alon's power kept their double outrigger canoe cradled by favorable currents. He didn't need sightlines to guide them. He was all sharp angles, from the square cut of his jaw to cheekbones so sharp that in the hazy moonlight, his cheeks seemed hollowed. When had the last of boyhood melted from his features? No, that wasn't right. It had been scraped away against the black teeth of the Palisade. They'd grown up hard, but Alon at least hadn't grown twisted as she had, like a sapling starved of light. He had, somehow, held on to his gentleness, even when it cost him. Lunurin had lost that somewhere along the way.

He caught her gaze and smiled, the years and severity melting away until he was once more a boy of thirteen in her memory. He'd been so unexpectedly gentle when she was in the process of losing everything she'd ever known. Leaving Calilan, she'd been half suffocating under the unfamiliar weight of her dugong bone amulet as just out of sight, Calilan's Stormfleet burned, perfuming the air with smoke like some terrible ritual sacrifice.

She sometimes wondered why he did not hate her for naming him to Aman Sinaya. Her role in his magic, injury, and the host of casualties on his brother's ship still plagued her. She'd never dared ask him if the trade was worth all the sorrow and heartache that followed.

It hadn't even saved her from ending up right where the goddess wanted her, in Aynila.

"This time of year isn't the same without a proper wet season festival to look forward to," she said. "The Festival of Our Lady María of the Drowned happens at the same time, but…"

"I've never seen a wet season festival sung in the old way." Alon's voice was wistful and low, not carrying to the prow of the boat where Inez and Catalina lay sleeping.

Lunurin pulled a thread of breeze into a cocoon that would keep their words between them, as they left the Saliwain delta and the shadow of the Palisade for the bay's open waters.

"Why?" Lunurin asked. "The healing school didn't burn until you were what, ten?"

"But the Codicíans had a trading presence, and no liking for anything that smelled of witchery. My inay decided it was best if my father and I remained separate from what she and my kuya did. If she hadn't, I probably would've ended up exiled like Jeian. I can't fault her decision. Especially after…" He trailed off, and Lunurin knew he could smell the smoke of tide-touched pyres the way she did the shattering of the Stormfleet.

"Do you ever see him?"

"When his trading brings him past Lusong, we find ways. Though not as often as I'd like." Alon shrugged. "Will you tell me about the festival on Calilan? What was your favorite part?"

Lunurin's heart ached for him. She'd had to bind her power after the incident, but at least her family had never held her away from being a part of the community.

"When the stormcallers sing in the ambon, a sun shower, so the goddess of storms can see her people. While the goddess watches, the katalonan of all three orders will anoint the Datu of the island in rainwater, seawater, and ash, renewing their blessing to rule for another year. It is an auspicious time for agreements and treaties to be sealed with the goddesses' approval. Then the children old enough to be named will dive for the oysters that become their mutya," she said.

"I'd like to see that one day."

Lunurin tapped her chin. "She made a political decision, keeping you away from her magic. My mother made one like it. When my father discovered she was pregnant, he offered to give up his God and marry her. My mother refused him. She couldn't risk putting a Codicían priest that close to chieftainship of the island."

Alon cocked his head. "Does he know you are his? He doesn't act like it."

A short bitter laugh leaped to her lips. "He won't acknowledge it, but he knows. Abbess Magdalena knows. She includes messages to my mother when I write home. I sometimes think she insists on my staying in the convent as a reminder to him of his past sins, no matter how high he climbs in the eyes of the Church. But I will never be Codicían enough for him to acknowledge."

Alon nodded, pensive. "Family can be complicated. What would you be doing now to prepare for the festival?"

Lunurin was relieved to leave the subject of her father behind. "Tending Calilan's oyster beds, removing all the biggest diving dangers, and keeping kids away, to prevent accidental namings."

"Like you?" Alon asked with a grin.

"Like me," Lunurin acknowledged. "Maybe I'd put money down in my tiyas' yearly betting pool on if more children would be chosen tide-touched, stormcaller, or firetender."

Alon laughed. "What kept them from rigging the odds? I've seen you create some very uniquely shaped pearls based on the seed you start them from."

"Finding a natural pearl marks one as gods-blessed. The pearls I make don't convey any blessings at all."

Alon leaned forward suddenly, pointing with his chin over her shoulder. "There, can you see the smoke?" His voice was warm in her ear as she looked, seeking out smoke in the moonlight against the dark bulk of Hilaga. "On the seaward side of the volcano, where the lava flows, just there."

She glanced at him, and his warm gaze caught her in the chest, nagging her with guilt. She relied on him so heavily. What did he get in return, except a share in her problems?

"I see it."

"There is a hidden village in the jungle. Small eruptions conceal the smoke of their cook fires, and it's impossible to approach from the seaward side unless you craft your own currents."

They slipped into the shadow of the volcano, guided effortlessly around outcrops of black lava rock that would have shredded the hull of any ship with a deeper draft than theirs and eaten oars like toothpicks. Alon instructed Lunurin to pull her oar from the water. They let the current carry them. Lunurin hadn't known it would be so close.

"What will happen when the Puente de Hilaga is completed?"

"We have smugglers' routes to the harbor."

"And the village?"

"There are plans. Hilaga has a dozen hidden valleys, only accessible via the old lava tube caves."

"The volcano has been so active, is that safe?"

"Safer than being caught. They can't leave. In a storm surge, it takes at least twelve trained tide-touched to protect the harbor. We have a duty to Aynila." Alon paused. "I'm relieved you know now. My mother will be glad to see you."

"Her safety is important. Thank you for trusting me now, and for helping with…"

"I've always trusted you, and you can always come to me."

Lunurin didn't know what to say to such wholehearted generosity, so she said nothing.

Alon guided them in past the jagged teeth of the volcano and finally to a black sand beach almost too narrow to pull the bangka onto.

Once Lunurin and Alon had dragged the craft onto the sand, Lunurin bent to Catalina and Inez, sound asleep in the prow. She urged them to their feet, and they followed Alon across the uneven black surface of the lava flow. The ground shivered under her feet. Lunurin hoped somewhere in the metalworkers' conclave there were trained firetenders soothing Hilaga back to sleep.

As they stepped into the jungle, which grew thick and green out of rich volcanic soil, a grey-haired woman armed with a wickedly barbed fishing spear appeared from the foliage, blocking their way.

Alon bowed. "Pasamba, I bring a patient in dire need of my mother's expertise."

A smile creased Pasamba's face. "Gat Alon. I recognized you tugging on the currents and the draft of your bangka. The Dayang will be pleased you came."

Then they were in the heart of a small fishing village. Lunurin blinked. She could have been in any of the fishing villages of Calilan. Her heart twisted, nostalgic for the place of her birth and terribly ashamed of the peril she'd placed her people in. It had seemed such a simple thing, letting down her hair.

Alon ascended the steps of the largest nipa hut at the center of the village and knocked.

The door opened. An older Aynilan woman with Alon's exact smile and sculpted cheekbones gave a wordless exclamation of joy, dragging him into her arms.

Dayang Dalisay Inanialon pressed her face to each side of her son's, sniffing his cheeks thoroughly, before she stepped back, greeting him in rapid hand sign. "My son, what brings you at this hour?"

Alon's mother had no tongue. When the Codicíans captured her, they'd cut it out, silencing her prayer and collapsing her tsunami. Her mutya, a beautiful mother-of-pearl necklace modeled after the full moon hung in two parts, shattered, the partly smashed pearl cradled in a gold cage to hold the brittle remainder safe.

Without her tongue, she could never again sing the prayers that could command great waves to Aman Sinaya's ear. Luckily, unlike calling the ocean, healing did not require voice.

"Inay, I have a complicated case. I can't help her alone," Alon replied.

Rapid explanations were made and Dayang Dalisay took Inez in hand.

Lunurin and Catalina settled to wait while the healers took Inez behind a screen.

Eventually, Alon called out. "Lunurin, could you come here? My mother would like to show you something."

Catalina shot her a nervous look. Lunurin patted Cat's hand, then went, not entirely sure why. Stormcallers did not heal.

Behind the screen, Inez floated in a large tub of saltwater. Alon's mother took Lunurin's hands, inspecting them.

"Do you understand trader sign?" Dalisay signed.

"Yes," Lunurin responded. "Though it's been some time."

The rapid motions of Dalisay's hands slowed. "Alon can translate if you need. Can you call lightning? I know some stormcallers can't, but even a small amount will do."

Lunurin nodded. "Yes, but why? Stormcallers on Calilan never helped with healing."

Dalisay signed, "Calilan is still rich in magic. None of your tide-touched healers must work alone. In Aynila, there hasn't been a stormcaller chosen for more than a generation. When I was a girl, Aynila's last stormcaller still worked in the healing school. She used lightning not to heal, but to affect the body. You will see. You will help us."

"Show me," Lunurin said. Could there be some way to use the power in her blood that wasn't storms, and regret?

Alon's mother guided Lunurin's hands to Inez's back. Lunurin gave Inez a reassuring smile and waited for further instructions.

Dalisay's hands flashed complicated signs Lunurin had never been taught, though she caught "storm," "grasping," and "holding."

She shook her head. "Forgive me, I don't—" She looked to Alon whose brow was also furrowed.

He and his mother had a rapid discussion in sign. It impressed Lunurin how at ease Alon was speaking to his mother this way. He signed left-hand dominant to account for his old injury.

Alon tried to explain. "My mother says you must find the lightning that runs down her spine. Where your hands are you must create a loop, so the storm of her mind cannot detect anything below your hands. You must take great care with this technique. You cannot let the lightning arc into her body and interfere with her heart."

Alon's mother held up a pin and lifted Inez's foot from the water. Lunurin hoped her skepticism wasn't evident. Alon shrugged helplessly.

Bracing herself, Lunurin focused on Inez. "Alright. This may sting."

Inez had been doused with a calming brew. She floated, eyes half-lidded, her face serene.

She patted Lunurin's cheek. "I don't care how much it hurts. Just promise you'll get it out." She bit her lip. "Don't tell Catalina... tell her it was already dead."

A hard aching lump formed in Lunurin's throat. She nodded.

Alon dropped his mouth to her ear. "There will be no pain. My mother is concentrating the sedative in the fetus's blood. Soon she'll stop the flow of blood between them. It will be stillborn. While you hold her, my mother will deliver it. I'm here to stop the bleeding when the afterbirth separates."

Numbly, Lunurin nodded. She focused, trying to find the storm Alon's mother claimed was in Inez. But there was nothing save the lapping of the cool saltwater on her arms and Inez's warm breath against her neck.

"Healing isn't reaching for the tide coming in, it's like becoming the wave on the shore," Alon said in a low voice.

Everything a stormcaller did was huge and external, winds and rain far outside of the body. Lunurin made her focus smaller, within the room, and smaller yet, within the circle of her arms. She gave herself to the storm in the girl.

And then Lunurin wasn't trying to call phantom body lightning to herself. She sank into Inez's flesh, and there it was, a river of lightning running down Inez's spine and branching through her body. Inez's heart was a thunderhead pulsing with lightning and the *lub-dub* of thunder rolling through her blood. Lunurin focused on the column of lightning that lay between her hands. She plucked at the threads until they didn't branch and lay instead like a rope in her palm. She folded the rope back on itself, a closed loop.

Lunurin opened her eyes, holding her concentration through gritted teeth. "T-try now."

Dalisay stuck Inez's toe with her pin. Inez didn't make a sound.

Alon leaned over Lunurin to peer at Inez. "Could you feel that?"

"Mmm, no. Lunurin's hands tingle."

"I can't ask for better than that," he said.

The healers went to work in earnest.

Lunurin tuned them out, convincing the column of lightning she held to lie still. She slipped up once. Threads of lightning spread. Lunurin wrenched them back into her hand. Inez cried out, as the rhythm of her heart stuttered. Alon pressed a hand over Inez's chest, calming the rushing tide of her blood.

Dalisay signed, "You must take great care. The body's storm is still lightning."

Soon Inez floated in a pool more blood than water. Worse, both Alon and Dalisay were quietly, professionally frantic.

Alon's mother pulled a small bloody form from between the girl's legs and lowered it into a basin at the end of the tub. Alon kept his hands on either side of Inez's belly, his breathing deep and slow as he tried to stem the bleeding.

Dalisay came and took Lunurin's right hand from Inez's back, pressing it to the top of her abdomen between Alon's large hands.

She signed, "Call lightning, a small seed…" and a long series of other instructions Lunurin couldn't follow.

Through gritted teeth, Alon interpreted. "Call true lightning, the smallest seed. Find the places where Inez is losing the most blood. Cauterize the wound. The afterbirth detached badly."

Lunurin shook her head and tried to pull away. "No, I can't. I'll burn the hut down. I could kill her," she protested. "Catalina would never forgive me."

"She's dying," Alon admitted. "Lunurin, I can't—" His voice broke. "I'm just barely keeping her from bleeding out. She's not clotting like she should. If I lift my hands, she dies."

Alon's mother knelt opposite Alon. She wrapped her hands around his wrists, joining his silent war with the tide of Inez's blood, holding it back. But even two tide-touched couldn't hold back the sea forever.

Lunurin called lightning, her usual command a fearful whisper.

But lightning came. Like a swarm of fireflies twirled up out of the air, they lit on the tips of her fingers. Lunurin lowered her hand onto Inez's belly.

She reached for where Alon and his mother's magic gathered most thickly, urging the little fireflies of lightning to land and flit back to her fingertips before they burned too deep. Maybe she could do this. Maybe everything would be okay.

Lunurin heard a hiss and froze. Had she lost her grip on Inez's spine? Done permanent damage? She dragged the real lightning into the air, away from Inez.

"Don't stop," Alon ground out. "It's working."

Lunurin stared at him, trying to understand what she'd done wrong.

Then, Catalina walked around the screen. She saw them all bent over her sister, Inez floating in a tub of blood, and the poor red mess in the bowl.

Before Lunurin could come up with something to say that would make this all look less awful, Catalina screamed, made the sign of the cross, and fainted.

7

ALON DAKILA

Catalina fell. Alon winced as her head hit the bamboo screen, toppling it with a crash.

His mother lifted a hand from his wrist and signed, "Can you hold?"

"Yes," he answered, mostly sure he wasn't lying.

"Don't let the stormcaller stop until the girl starts to clot."

Alon relayed this directive to Lunurin, who was staring, stricken, at Catalina's fallen form.

His mother went to check Catalina hadn't split her head open.

"Lunurin, we have to finish. You can do this," Alon reminded her while his mother tugged Catalina over onto her back. She dipped her hand into a pitcher of seawater and touched three fingers to Catalina's brow.

Lunurin tore her gaze from Catalina and resumed her whispered instructions to the lightning. The threads of lightning in Alon's own body reacted to her voice, eager to answer her call, but she didn't pull on them. She drew from the air. The sparks that had dissipated from her grip returned to her fingertips and the searing electric burn of the gold rings on his right hand began again. Alon kept his right hand arched so only his fingertips touched Inez, making sure she wouldn't be burned.

He hoped his mother could do something for his hand later. He didn't want to imagine trying to remove his brace once the burns started to blister and swell.

When Inez's womb was no longer a net through which her blood poured like saltwater, Lunurin lifted her hands from the tub. Bloody water soaked her white sleeves, painting her habit red. The lightning she'd wielded danced along the waves of her disheveled black curls, peeking from beneath her veil.

Alon did a final check on his patient, then lifted her from the tub. He deposited her onto the cot along the wall.

Inez blinked at him sluggishly. "Is it over?"

"Yes, it's all over. You can sleep now."

Lunurin followed with a cloth to dry Inez and strip her out of her blood and salt drenched wraps.

Alon turned to check if his mother needed help with Catalina, but Lunurin caught him by the wrist.

"Hala! Alon, your hand."

Unwillingly, Alon looked. As he'd feared, the gold rings of his brace had proved particularly attractive to the threads of lightning Lunurin had wielded with such care that Inez didn't have the slightest scalds visible on her now empty abdomen. His flesh, however, had bubbled up red and angry at every point where gold touched his scarred skin.

"Ah… yes, I will remove my brace next time."

"I hurt you! How could you let me hurt you? I didn't think of your brace."

Alon shrugged. "But you didn't hurt her. My mother can fix my hand."

Lunurin's expression furrowed. Alon had the most insane, exhaustion-induced desire to press his lips to her brow.

"Don't add me to your flock of worries. I'll be fine." He squeezed her hand and lifted it from his wrist.

Turning to his mother he signed, "Inay, does she have a concussion? Why are you holding her under?"

His mother shook her head, signing, "Physically, she's fine, hardly a bump. Mentally, her spirit is all tangled up inside… I decided it best to keep her quiet while you worked. Shall I wake her now?"

Alon didn't translate for Lunurin, hoping she wasn't looking.

"Is Inez dressed?" Alon asked, keeping his back to the cot.

"Yes."

"Do you have something Lunurin might borrow? She looks a bit…" The benefit of the dark blues he favored meant he looked merely wet, not blood-drenched.

A tired smile creased his mother's face. "She looks like a manananggal come to feed on the blood of the stillbirth."

Unsure whether to laugh or not, Alon pressed a knuckle to his brow, trying to banish that disturbing mental image.

His mother snorted at her joke and signed, "She may take clothes from the chest by the wall."

Alon relayed this offer.

While Lunurin rummaged, Alon dragged the treatment tub outside, pouring out the bloody water. Then he covered the fetal mass in the bowl with a cloth.

After all signs of the terrible bloody ordeal were cleared away, Alon offered Inez a cup of sweet and salty fish broth to help restore her blood. Finally his mother lifted her fingertips from Catalina's brow. She came awake gasping.

Lunurin gathered her lover into her arms with a soothing murmur.

"Lunurin? I thought—I saw—There was so much blood!"

"Easy, easy, Catalina, you took a tumble and hit your head. But it's alright now. Inez is well."

"Inez?"

Lunurin helped Catalina lurch to her feet, guiding her to Inez. Alon stepped back, giving them space.

Inez's face was pale, her hair still damp, but she smiled. "Yes, Ate, I'm fine."

"You aren't hurt?"

Inez touched her now soft and tender abdomen. "It aches a bit, but I'm okay."

The sisters hugged. Then Catalina pulled Lunurin to join their embrace. Lunurin leaned in to kiss Cat's temple tenderly.

Alon tore his eyes from the intimate family scene, touching his inay's shoulder with his good hand. He gestured to his burns. Her dark brows shot up and she hissed in censure. She pulled him to the pitcher of saltwater and plunged his hand in, breathing over the surface of the liquid. Alon sighed as it cooled, pulling the heat from his burns.

His mother coaxed down the swelling, drawing the fluid from his blisters. She delicately wriggled his brace from his hand. His last three fingers curled toward his palm, aching and tingling with their usual phantom nerve pain. Still hissing her displeasure, his mother threaded his brace safely onto his beaded mutya necklace. With burn ointment and bandaging, she wrapped each of his fingers to ensure they wouldn't fuse as they healed.

She berated him. "You should have said. I could've held her blood while you removed the rings."

Alon ducked his head. His mother frowned, but took his face in her hands and sniffed his cheeks fiercely. He folded her into a one-armed hug.

"Salamat po, Inay," he thanked her.

He squeezed her tight against the bulk of him, not liking how thin she'd become. The last time he'd mentioned it, she complained eating was a chore. She tired of broths and soups that flowed without the aid of a tongue in swallowing and didn't risk choking her.

"You think too much of others, not yourself," she signed.

Silently, Alon signed, "Why didn't you warn me a stormcaller could pull on my blood like the moon? And the storm of my mind like lightning in a cloud? I thought I was losing my mind."

His inay pressed her lips together. "Does she still feel that way to you, even when it isn't your blood she reaches for?"

"Yes, does she not to you?"

"No. She has a strong presence, stronger than when she was a girl, or perhaps her amulet grows weaker. But she does not call to my heart."

His inay's blunt answer settled like a weight on his chest.

"Ahh… tang ina," he cursed at the realization.

A wry smile pulled his mother's lips. "My son, you are young. I assumed you'd figure it out… but, when you spoke of your stormcaller all these years, you didn't tell me she loved women." She shook a finger under his nose. "Nothing but sorrow comes of falling for one such as that."

Alon winced. "She is a nun. It doesn't matter one way or the other."

His inay's face grew almost sorrowful. "She is a nun for now. Not even the strongest amulet can hide a katalonan with that much power forever. Now. Get these mestiza girls back where they're meant to be."

"Can we move Inez so soon?" Alon asked. "I'd prefer she recover here."

"We can't stay," Lunurin spoke up. "We must get back before dawn."

His inay thrust a series of palm bundles into Cat's hands and signed to Alon, who said, "You must boil the contents in a pot of water and have her drink it every day for a week. She needs to eat. Meat if you can get it. Fish broth and coconut water to build her blood. Take her to Alon—I mean, to me—if the bleeding becomes heavier than her monthlies or goes on for more than three weeks."

Lunurin lifted Inez into her arms, and they headed back into the night. On the beach, as he handed Lunurin her oar, she laid her hand over his, leaning close. Alon took a startled breath, smelling salt, the rusted tang of blood, and the fragrant nuttiness of her sesame hair oil. It was less like the brutal energy burst of a storm surge than the subtle lift of high tide as she tugged on his flagging energy.

Lunurin let out a gentle sigh. "Don't let me hurt you like that again."

Alon stood straighter and thanked her. He suspected the heat of her skin and the brush of her fingers sliding from his would plague him every time he smelled sesame oil.

8

MARÍA LUNURIN

An insistent knock sounded on the door of their cell as Lunurin threw a habit over her head and did a final check of the room. The window was closed, the ladder hidden. Inez was tucked into bed beside Cat. In a chamber pot in the corner, Lunurin had concocted a horrible hodgepodge of human waste, crushed papaya seeds, coconut oil, and small white cotton threads.

She opened the door.

There stood a disgustingly well-rested Sister Philippa. "Well?"

Lunurin bared her teeth in a smile. "An unpleasant night for everyone involved, but most certainly worms. You can inspect the results if you like, lots of baby tapeworms in evidence. A week of papaya-seed purges and Inez will be as good as new."

Philippa had never liked Lunurin, not as a student, especially not as acting-abbess, but even she would find nothing out of order this morning.

Philippa cast a jaundiced eye over her and brushed past into the room. Lunurin, stupefied by exhaustion, didn't manage to grab her until after she'd marched up to the bed, and started prodding Inez's stomach.

Inez woke with a cry. Lunurin hauled Sister Philippa off her, biting back a curse.

"Sister! Inez has had a hard night. If you're interested you can poke the worms too. It's clear Inez wasn't pregnant."

Catalina, cradling her sister and wiping her tears, glared at Philippa. "Inez just turned thirteen! She hasn't started her monthlies. It's not possible for her to be pregnant."

"Fine, she wasn't pregnant, but she is a little thief. I found stolen food stashed in her mattress," Philippa spat, only to flinch when Lunurin shoved the "worm stool" concoction under her nose. Lunurin used it to herd her out of the room.

"She had worms; it makes one feel as if they're starving. Food hoarding is to be expected. Now please, Sister Philippa, I've had a long night. Why don't you see if Biti turns up to breakfast and wake me if there are any issues." Lunurin closed the door in Sister Philippa's face and collapsed on her pallet.

"Does she believe us?" Inez whispered.

"Yes, of course. The old hag is just angry Abbess Magdalena left Lunurin as acting-abbess and not her," Catalina responded heatedly.

Lunurin wasn't so sure, but she said nothing, hoping desperately to rest.

~

Far, far too soon by Lunurin's estimation there came a heavy rapping on the door. Lunurin dragged herself from her pallet with a groan. She re-pinned her veil over her hair and opened the door.

Abbot Rodrigo's manservant, a Black freeman called Juan, stood outside. "Forgive me, Sister María. Abbot Rodrigo wishes to speak to you."

"Of course. Give me a moment, would you?"

"Yes, Sister María."

Half ducking back inside, Lunurin paused. "Has Biti Prinsa been found?"

"She has not."

"I see. Thank you, Juan."

Juan had been illegally purchased from Lusitan slave traders, but that had been when Abbess Magdalena was still in Aynila. Sister Magdalena didn't stand for the breaking of the Empire's Law in the House of God, so Juan had been freed and assigned a wage like the other church servants. Lunurin didn't think Magdalena had any abolitionist principles, so much as the abbess disapproved of all Lusitan doings as a matter of national honor. The Lusitans were "upstart rebels who should never have been granted independence from the Empire" and "the Treaty of Lissipo was a farce."

Lunurin wiped her face and straightened her veil in the polished brass-plate mirror, before pulling her silver crucifix where it could be seen, and tucking the dugong bone pendant out of sight. She flicked off a piece of rust still clinging from her trick with the grate. Wrung out, Catalina and Inez slept on, undisturbed. Lunurin paused, running her hand over Inez's head, and dropped a light kiss on Cat's cheek.

Cat stirred, turning her face toward Lunurin.

"I'll be back. Don't wake on my account," Lunurin whispered.

Cat opened her eyes. "Inez and I should be seen at morning prayers. We'll get up."

A second soft rap at the door—Juan reminding her when it came to the abbot, time was of the essence. Lunurin hurried downstairs and across the abbey proper to the priests' cloister with Juan.

Juan had been brought into the abbey after Abbot Rodrigo's last manservant had poisoned him. Lunurin didn't know if it had really been poison or bad shrimp. She also didn't know where Alon had sent the manservant for safety, and she would never ask. If the abbot discovered her role in the disappearances of servants who caught his ire... well, like her mutya, it was better he never found out. It was enough for Lunurin that the man's corpse wasn't bloating in a starvation cage hanging from the Palisade wall. Abbot Rodrigo was fond of the starvation cages. The little metal boxes hung on chains, for all to see who'd drawn the Church's wrath.

They were supposedly for thieves, liars, and blasphemers. But the abbot would cage servants for the smallest of infractions— arriving late, bringing hot food cold or cold food hot, being slovenly, or worse, vain. He'd ordered the kitchen maid Isa's hair chopped off and caged her for two days with no water after hearing a younger priest rhapsodizing about her long black mane.

Lunurin instituted hair wraps for the women servants after that.

Resolutely, she tore her gaze from the blessedly empty cages. Only a week ago, Alon had convinced the governor to release the ringleaders of the falla tax insurrection to labor sentences in the shipyards.

"What sort of mood is the abbot in this morning?" she asked.

"Not a good one, Sister María," Juan said softly. "Got worse after you left dinner. The captain of the *Santa Clarita* insists the damage to his ship was unnatural. He's pushing for the abbot to authorize and the governor to fund another inquest into water witch saboteurs. He wants Father DeSoto to pull laborers away from his bridge to focus on the *Santa Clarita*. The captain and Father DeSoto got into a fight about the relative importance to the Empire of one ship versus the economic benefits of controlling all of the Saliwain's traffic and the metalworkers' conclave on Hilaga. The governor thinks agitators simply cross the river to escape justice and is sure the Puente de Hilaga is the key to peace."

"Oh dear."

Dread unfolded in her breast. She was so tired. Why couldn't Sister Philippa have kept this debacle with Inez away from the abbot? Soon, they reached the abbot's study. Lunurin paused, letting Juan announce her.

The abbot leaned over a desk gleaming with beautiful golden mother-of-pearl inlay. The desk, like the pearl-studded altar panels in the sanctuary, was made with mutya stolen from the tide-touched who'd been burned when Governor López laid waste to the healing school. All were drenched in the blood of Aynila's healers. Lunurin's skin crawled at the sight.

Lunurin curtseyed deeply. "Abbot Rodrigo."

The abbot didn't respond, trapping her in obeisance. Juan retreated, leaving her to her fate. Not that she blamed him. He'd lasted longer than any of the abbot's previous servants. His instincts for avoiding trouble were finely tuned.

"Novice María," the abbot drawled at last, giving her leave to rise. "Do you care to explain to me what unseemly mayhem is going on among the holy sisters of my flock?"

The bright morning sun shone through the open window behind the abbot, laying his face in shadow.

"I admit, Abbot, it's been a long night, but aside from Biti Prinsa, whose situation you were apprised of after Mass, all is well in the convent," Lunurin said, squinting in the bright mid-morning light.

"The Prinsa girl is my primary concern. How does one of our students vanish? I'm told the Palisade guard reported signing off on passes for one of our girl students and a servant no one recognized yesterday afternoon."

Lunurin frowned thoughtfully. "I didn't know we'd already heard back from the guard. You don't think Bituin really left the Palisade? She was in my section yesterday. I have the attendance sheet. Father DeSoto unfortunately forgot attendance for the second afternoon class, so there's no telling if she wandered off after first section or sometime before dinner. Inez became ill during the first section and I had to look after her." The lies came easy as breathing.

"Hmmm," Abbot Rodrigo considered this briefly. "Speaking of Inez, Sister Philippa won't stop bleating about the damn girl. Apparently embarrassing the order in front of half the Palisade wasn't enough. She's been hounding me all morning. You're doing a poor job as acting-abbess if I have to hear about every malady and missing child."

Lunurin's temper flared, but she tamped it down. "I apologize for burdening your esteemed person, and for the scene. Inez has tapeworms, and the symptoms frightened Sister Philippa. I dosed Inez with deworming purgatives. She will be good as new in a few days."

Her vision adjusted to the stark light of the study. Abbot Rodrigo's eyes gleamed coldly as he rolled a thin bamboo cane back and forth across the surface of his desk. They were the bright cold green of a mandadalag pit viper's scales, and more dangerous. *Tap, tap, tap* went the switch, often used to beat any woman suspected of witchcraft while glass bottles of salted holy water were watched for any unnatural movement. Lunurin was briefly so angry, she had no words.

"Abbess Magdalena's illness has put us all in a difficult position, but I was assured you could handle the responsibility. Based on the events of the last two days…" The abbot's mouth twisted.

Lunurin's back broke out in cold sweat. She had to convince the abbot not to intervene. When the abbot intervened, people died. "Abbot, I assure you I have the situations with Biti and Inez well in hand."

"Quite demonstrably, you do not. I resent being forced to intervene to preserve the reputation of the Augustinian order from your inability to maintain a certain level of propriety. This is how the situation will be handled going forward."

"Abbot, respectfully, Abbess Magdalena—"

"Unlike Magdalena, I wouldn't care if your father were His Holiness the Pope himself, girl. You will *not* interrupt your betters when they are speaking!" the abbot thundered.

Lunurin's face flushed hot with rage, but she dropped into a curtsey. "Forgive me, Abbot Rodrigo."

He sniffed. "As I was saying. I expect you will expel the postulant, Inez, from the convent by evening. I've spoken to Sister Philippa and Father DeSoto—"

Lunurin bolted upright. "Abbot Rodrigo! What warrants such a reaction? The poor girl merely had the misfortune of being ill while Sister Philippa was overwrought."

He stared at her in frigid silence.

Lunurin bit her lip and dropped into an even lower curtsey, though it was like breaking her own neck to do it. "Forgive me, Abbot Rodrigo, I was awake all night ministering to the girl. I'm… out of sorts this morning."

"Clearly, Sister Philippa isn't the only one who is overwrought," he observed. "She and Father DeSoto agree the girl is presenting concerning tendencies."

The conversation was slipping from her control like sand through her fingers. She scrambled for something, anything, to turn the implacable abbot from his chosen path.

"What tendencies? Father DeSoto has complimented Inez's diligence as an assistant instructor in his classes."

"I'm told she concealed stolen food when Sister Philippa turned over the dorms searching for the Prinsa girl."

"Worms make one incredibly hungry, as if you'll never get full. Surely she can be forgiven her hunger this time." Her voice sounded strained to her ears.

"I'm showing great leniency in only expelling her. A thief ought to be caned and caged until they repent."

"Abbot, please, she's a little girl!"

"Father DeSoto reports she is a haphazard assistant. She hands out Palisade passes without any discernment. She is a bad influence on his classes, encouraging slothfulness among the younger students and inducing lustful thoughts among the older ones. The school will be better off with her gone. In the unfortunate event the Prinsa girl isn't found, her disappearance is clearly the result of Inez's bad influence. When the governor demands persons to hold responsible for the disappearance of one of our most valuable students, I will personally laud you for acting quickly to remove such an ungodly influence from the convent."

They were going to scapegoat Inez to protect DeSoto.

Rage rippled through her like a bolt of lightning. Lunurin pressed her knuckles hard over her dugong bone amulet, struggling to contain her fury.

Thunder rumbled in the distance, and a desperate prayer hovered behind her clenched teeth. *Anitun Tabu! Please, please! Not now.*

Something under her hand cracked. Rage boiled through

her blood, like lava through an underwater fissure. *Lintik ka!* The curse nearly caused lightning to leap to her hand. It took all her will not to finish the ill-wish. This wrath wasn't hers, the curse on her tongue, not hers.

No, she had called out to her goddess by her true name, damaged her dugong bone amulet, and all the attention of the heavens rested upon her like the beating of the sun at high noon. If she moved a muscle, the full force of her suppressed power might overwhelm her, and the abbot would realize exactly what she was.

When she dared open her mouth she said softly, "Inez has done *nothing* wrong. Father DeSoto is responsible for his own haphazard writing of Palisade passes. Inez but delivers them as he directs and she did not deliver any yesterday. She fainted and I sent her to rest. He's blaming her for his lack of organization and conscientiousness writing passes, when Inez wasn't even helping with his class when Biti vanished."

Abbot Rodrigo was silent.

The roaring in Lunurin's ears increased, only this time it wasn't the formless rumble of distant thunder. *"Daughter, do you call to me? That is an old name, one I had almost forgotten. But you have called, and I am come. Daughter, do you see? Look how they are rotted from the inside out. There will be no peace while a single one of them breathes."*

Lunurin closed her heart to the goddess. She could solve this fiasco with human methods. She had to. Nothing good came of calling on the gods.

"Please, Abbot Rodrigo. She's a devout, hardworking little girl. All she wants to do is take her novitiate vows when she turns fifteen." Lunurin hated to beg, but she'd do anything to save Inez, to protect Cat, whose heart would break if her sister was expelled.

"She should've thought of that before she decided to steal."

"Her only family is Sister Catalina. It would be cruel to separate them," Lunurin tried, desperately. The abbot's earlier threat to cage Inez, when she was weak and still bleeding, terrified Lunurin. Inez was still so fragile.

It was the wrong thing to say. Abbot Rodrigo's eyes flashed. "I do not approve of your clear favoritism of Sister Catalina."

"Please, Abbot. The girl is very ill. Let us not do anything rash for a few more days. We will widen the search for Biti beyond the Palisade. I'm sure she'll be found. She is one little girl. If... if she isn't, I will take full responsibility for her disappearance and speak to the governor. There is no need to drag Inez into this."

Abbot Rodrigo rested his chin on his folded hands, his eyes alight with an eagerness that frightened Lunurin. Had he goaded her into taking responsibility for Biti's disappearance to get DeSoto off the hook? DeSoto was one of the abbot's favorites, and a credit to the Church with all he contributed to the public works of the Palisade. Unlike Lunurin, who was an unsightly reminder that the priesthood was not as devout as they made themselves out to be.

"You have until the Saint's Day Festival of Our Lady María of the Drowned to get everything in order. Then I'm informing the governor the Prinsa girl is in the wind."

Of course, because he only needed her to keep up public appearances until after the festival. After that she was out of public sight and mind. With both her aunt and father abroad, who would interfere in whatever punishment the governor deemed fit?

Lunurin curtseyed, so low her head was below the top of his awful desk. "Thank you, Abbot Rodrigo. You are generous and fair. I will do my utmost to resolve the situation, and take responsibility for whatever comes of it."

9

MARÍA LUNURIN

The abbot's god must still smile upon him, because Lunurin escaped the interview without shoving him out the window. The whispers of the goddess in her ears were so loud. Surely he must hear them too?

She fled past Juan at the door and abruptly changed course to avoid Sister Philippa, who was heading toward the abbot's office. Lunurin hoped desperately she would not see Father DeSoto. She would tear his throat out with her teeth and leave him bleeding out atop the abbot's desk. Lunurin sought the sanctuary, where she knelt before the altar. Her eyes slid over the cross on its central platform, past the great pearl-inlayed altar panels that lined the walls, to the face of Anitun Tabu, Goddess of Storms and Sky, High Lady of the Heavens.

Salt rimes graced her features, as if the dark wooden statue wept. Lunurin lifted her folded hands to her dugong bone amulet. She was afraid to see how much she'd damaged it. She groped for words, for a prayer, anything.

The statue of Anitun Tabu had been still and blind since Lunurin had arrived in Aynila.

"Why now?" Her stomach churned with dread. She hoped wildly that the goddess would not answer her.

Anitun Tabu's weeping eyes opened. Brewing in their dark depths was a typhoon that would take whole islands under the sea. *"You brought my name and my purpose back to me. I have been yoked and chained by false names, by prayers that stripped my majesty and power and granted me nothing but grief. But you prayed to me truly. My time is come. The season is right, and I have everything needed for the perfect storm."*

Lunurin didn't cry out in surprise, or flinch from the gaze of the goddess. "Your time is past. Aynila's tide-touched have tried before to wash the Codicíans out to sea. They have failed. They've been maimed, exiled, and burned alive. I won't die in some mad attempt at vengeance and abandon my family to the mercy of the Codicíans."

"You will call down the storm of the century, and you will do it in my name, Daughter."

"Do you remember what happened the last time I called a storm for you?" Lunurin hissed. She'd been so afraid.

A joyous peal of laughter filled Lunurin's head. *"We shattered a galleon. Hundreds drowned!"*

Lunurin's belly clenched, cold with fear, the only thing she had to hold fast against the divine, and the fury fizzing through her blood. "I was a child! I was a child and you made me a killer. I killed near as many of my own as the Codicíans. I sank two dozen fishing boats and a Stormfleet ship. My village stole my mutya and salted my legs, hoping it would turn me back into a dugong! The only reason they didn't hurl me into the sea was because my mother shaved my head and my tiya bound my power to hide me from your sight. You abandoned me! I gave you everything. You had your vengeance, and forgot I existed!"

Lunurin was still haunted by the smell of the wreck and ruin her typhoon had wrought. The bodies bloated in the sun, human and marine washed up by the brutal storm surge. So many they couldn't all be buried before they began to rot. The shattered bamboo splinters of homes. She'd brought death to their enemies, yes, but death had come home to roost.

Her hair had grown back with frightful speed. Her mother had to shave her head three times a day for a month before the hysteria passed. How could she blame them for their fear? She'd brought destruction to Calilan and fled rather than face the consequences. All who had died in her storm and when the Inquisition came, those deaths were her fault. How many innocent tide-touched had been hunted down and killed because she sank the *San Pedro* and her family hid her away?

"My time is come. I am Anitun Tabu, and I will rain such fury they will not dare to covet that which is mine and claim it for themselves."

"I will not kill for you again. I'm not a child you can cow into obedience," Lunurin swore.

"We shall see, Daughter. You made me a promise."

The noon bells tolled, and Lunurin bolted to her feet. She had to get away from the statue, from the whispers. As she fled the sanctuary, she ran into Catalina, red-eyed from weeping.

"Is it true?" Catalina demanded. "Sister Philippa told everyone Abbot Rodrigo will expel Inez from the convent!"

"No, Catalina. I won't let that happen."

"Sister Philippa says they'll cage her for theft—"

"Please, come with me. Let's discuss this elsewhere." Lunurin pulled Catalina with her, away from the dozens of staring eyes as the bell called everyone to the dining hall for lunch.

Lunurin shut them into one of the stone storerooms under the children's dorm, leaning into the door so the wood groaned.

"How did they find out about Inez? Sister Philippa believed us!" Catalina demanded.

Lunurin took Catalina's hands, bending her brow to Cat's. She somehow had to push the intoxicating power of the coming storm out of her blood. Her family was falling apart; they needed her. They needed her here and now, not swept up in the gods' useless bloody vengeance.

"It's not that, it's nothing to do with that. The Palisade guard said it was DeSoto who signed off the Palisade passes Biti used. They're scapegoating Inez to protect him."

Cat's hands squeezed until Lunurin's joints ached. "This is my fault. How could I not have realized?"

"It's not. It is not your fault. We had to get Biti out. We didn't know about Inez and DeSoto. If I'd even suspected— Catalina, I will never let him harm Inez, not ever again. I'll take responsibility for Biti's disappearance."

Cat pulled free from Lunurin's hold, and covering her face, she shook and shook. "We never should've done anything about Biti. If we hadn't interfered maybe… maybe… Saints preserve us. How could they do this to Inez?"

Lunurin tried to put her arms around Cat, but she broke away.

"This is punishment, isn't it? This is my punishment. I lacked faith!"

"No, Cat, of course not. Sometimes bad things happen to good people. It's nothing to do with Biti or anyone else we've helped."

"It is! I should never have let you convince me to interfere. It's God's plan. I shouldn't have questioned it, I should never…"

"Cat, easy, you don't believe that. You know it's wrong, the way our people are forced to work dangerous jobs for a pittance—"

"I don't know that! You think that. Properly run, it's a fair system. Left to their own devices the poor are indolent, spending their time on nothing but gambling and sin. Polo labor gives them a chance to better themselves, learn a trade, and attend Mass regularly. The polo system is the best way to win the hearts and souls of the working poor. Their good works toward the Church's endeavors are a credit to their station."

Lunurin stared at Cat in disbelief. Surely she didn't believe the Codicían propaganda? How could she believe it and still work so hard to better people's lives, to alleviate suffering where she could?

"How can it ever be properly run with a child rapist leading its work?" Lunurin asked, her hand straying to press her amulet to her chest.

Cat's eyes followed her motion. She frowned. "One man's sin does not condemn an institution that is bringing souls into God's light! Father DeSoto might yet repent, or the governor could select a new head of public works to run the program justly. None of us is free from sin, and yet through those who do God's work his light shines, despite our base natures."

"Since when is God's work empire building and enslaving our people?"

"It's not about empire! It's about winning hearts and souls to eternal salvation."

"And building bridges and ships," Lunurin observed dryly.

Cat's expression crumpled in anguish. "Stop talking like this! It makes you sound like you agree with the saboteurs.

Is it Biti? Are your fits getting worse like hers? Why don't you tell me these things?"

Lunurin saw that Cat had gone pale with fear. She was pushing too hard. If Cat could be convinced, it wouldn't be like this.

"I'm sorry. I didn't mean to frighten you," Lunurin whispered. "I love you. You know that."

"What if…" Cat chewed her lower lip. "What if you gave them up on the altar?"

"Gave them up?" Lunurin repeated slowly, not sure she understood. Surely Cat couldn't mean her mutya?

"Yes, your comb, the pearl hair prong, even that horrible bone pendant you always reach for. I know you think you need them, but what if keeping them is what's preventing you from truly embracing God? If you cast them off, maybe the fits would finally stop." Cat cradled Lunurin's face. "Look what it's doing to you. It's nothing good. I've seen how you can be when they aren't bothering you, how… at peace and faithful. You frighten me when you're like this. You become someone I don't recognize, not the wife I love."

Lunurin shook her head, regretting that she'd never tried harder to make Cat understand her "fits." "I'm sorry, Cat. I can't do that."

"It's that fear in your heart holding you back. If you put your trust in God and forswore all false gods—"

"Yes," Lunurin admitted. "It is fear. I'm sorry, I don't have your faith. I don't believe God can protect me from this power. Nothing can, but my mutya and dugong bone amulet, they help me hold back the storm. I need them."

Cat went white, tearing her hands away. "How can you say that? How can you let your fear keep you from the eternal peace of God's love? From me. This is your crisis of faith, the eye of the needle that you must pass through, but you're too busy clinging to your crutches like a rich man to his gold."

"Maybe, but would you leave me lying on the ground, rather than give me something to limp forward with?"

Cat covered her mouth, turning away. "Don't say that! Don't say you won't try. This is a sign we must repent and cast ourselves upon God's mercy. Can't you see how much safer you'd be… how much safer Inez and I would be if you would stop clutching this venom—"

Cat's tearful plea cut Lunurin's heart to ribbons, more than all her sharp words. Maybe Cat was right. Maybe it wasn't safety her mutya gave her, but a slow poison.

Lunurin was never more torn between the two halves of herself than when she faced Catalina and was found wanting. What did she care if Calilan rejected her, that her mother thought her unfit as a Datu's daughter? That to her father, she was nothing but proof of a crisis of faith? But if she couldn't be enough for Cat, who could she satisfy? Cat alone knew what it was to be caught between worlds. Cat alone had seen her at her lowest, when she had first come to the convent and loved her anyway. Lunurin reached for Cat, desperate for her regard, for her warmth. She drew Cat's hands into her own.

"I'll try harder," Lunurin promised. "For you I'll try harder. I'll keep you and Inez safe. I swear. I won't let anything happen to either of you. I'll take care of DeSoto, and my fits, all of it. I promise. Say you trust me. Have I ever let you down?"

Cat sobbed, but didn't answer. Instead, she pushed past Lunurin and fled.

Was she prepared to give it up. All of it? Could she cast off her blessing entirely? For Cat and Inez? For their life together?

Maybe. After one last thing.

After all the lives she'd taken for her goddess, what was one more dead Codicían, one final use of the terrible power in her blood? To keep her family safe. Then she'd give it up, even if it was like cutting off her own right hand. She'd keep her family safe.

~

Instead of chasing Cat, Lunurin hunted down Father DeSoto in his study. Two days without Inez's daily efforts and the space was already cluttered with heaps of reports and requisitions that needed sorting.

He stopped digging through the disorganization and shot her a worried frown. "Sister María?"

"We're overdue for a talk." Lunurin crossed the room in three strides.

He tried to rise, but she pushed him back into the chair hard, leaning over Father DeSoto with one hand braced on his sternum.

"Sister?" he sputtered. "What is the meaning of this—"

"Your students had concerning things to tell me."

His indignation gave way to fear. "I'm—I'm quite sure I don't know what you're talking about."

"I'm sure you don't." Lunurin sank her power into his skin and seized the storm of his heart. It beat quick as a hovering sunbird. She coaxed it faster.

Father DeSoto gasped, clutching her wrist. He was a big man, but he'd grown weak with age. Lunurin pressed his heart till he groaned in agony.

"What sins have you committed against God? Against the students in your care?" Lunurin asked.

"I—I—"

"Speak up, Father DeSoto. God can't hear you. Did you think lustful thoughts? Did you act upon them? Did you hurt children and lie to conceal your sins?"

"No, no, I—"

Lunurin flexed her fingers, momentarily stopping his heart.

DeSoto's mouth fell open in a soundless gasp. His face went dead white.

"God sees the sin in your heart, Father. Will you confess and absolve your eternal soul?" She released his heart, the storm within restarting the lump of flesh with difficulty.

"God, forgive me." His breath was short, sweat running down his face.

"For what?"

"I—I thought sinful thoughts," he gasped.

"And?"

"I acted on them. I could not help myself. God have mercy. I couldn't help myself."

"He won't. Just as I won't, not unless you tell the abbot it's your fault Biti is missing. You made baseless accusations against Inez because you feared being held accountable, but your conscience wouldn't let you live with the deception. I expect you to tell him you cannot teach anymore. You aren't able to ensure the safety of the children in your care."

He nodded, tears tracing the deep lines of his pale puckered cheeks. "Yes, yes, I'll tell him."

"If you breathe near my students again, I will pray God Himself strikes you down. I will ask Him to awaken the weakness in your twisted heart." Lunurin called a single firefly of lightning and bid it alight on the right side of Father DeSoto's heart, upsetting its rhythm. Not enough to kill him, just enough, that if he ever did anything too... *strenuous*, his heart might not recover.

Lunurin left him gasping, his heart beating at half capacity. Would Catalina ever forgive her for all Inez had suffered?

There was no time to worry about that now. Tomorrow was the first day of the wet season. Lunurin had an important role to play in the Festival of Our Lady María of the Drowned. She was building a house of cards in a frying pan over a fire— eventually, no matter how carefully she built, the bottom layer was going to catch. She'd called the goddess's true name and awakened her statue. The bottom cards were already smoking.

10

❖

ALON DAKILA

Everyone in Alon's life had a habit of dropping impending political disasters into his lap. It was his job description, as far as the Lakan was concerned. Sina adding to the pile wasn't new. But if she planned to consult his opinion then utterly ignore it, he wished she'd show a little more chagrin showing up, hunted by a dozen squadrons of Codícian soldiers undertaking a search of Aynila. They'd even sent a bully squad of "conquistadors" from the *Santa Clarita* to the metalworkers' conclave on Hilaga searching for Biti. Angry smoke still billowed from the volcano.

Across the low table sat his cousin, Sinagtala Prinsa, unperturbed. She was a tall, solid woman, a few years his elder, with a smith's bearing like her mother. She ignored him utterly in favor of teasing his foster brother, Isko, for risking a fire as he clicked cowrie shells up and down a sungka board, re-checking his math on inventory and supplies for the latest dye orders.

Isko retorted, "The only bad luck is playing the game indoors. You should be well able to prevent any house fires."

"Sina, you must see the position you're putting me in?" Alon interjected.

Sina paused in serving her sister, Biti, a second helping of Halabos na Hipon, delicately plucking the largest shrimp from the platter onto her plate and shelling it before depositing the choice flesh into her sister's bowl of garlic rice.

Sina kept the heads to suck on herself. "What did you expect me to do, Alon? Wait until the abbot discovered a fire witch in their midst and invented new and terrible ways to kill our people?"

"I've been in talks with Governor López. He was going to—"

"String you along a few more months while my mother makes cannons that will be pointed at this city and used to conquer others like it?" Sina shot back. "While they finish their Puente de Hilaga, proofed against quakes and flashflood with our metal? You saw how Hilaga liked having conquistadors on her flanks. What do you think she'll do when they can walk over on a stone bridge?"

Alon dropped his face into his hands. "Couldn't you have waited until after the festival?"

"There, there, Alon, she might yet enliven the festival by blowing up the bridge. She has those friends, remember?" Isko said dryly, sketching a quick mountain in the air and ignoring his meal to sip on ginger tea.

Because that's what Aynila needed, more acts of sabotage. Whether it was Sina and her metalworkers, or his mother's more zealous tide-touched, if it disrupted the largest festival of the year, instead of reveling in the coming of the rains, Aynila would take up bloody arms to dash themselves to pieces on the jagged black teeth of the Palisade. At this rate it would be worse than the falla tax riots.

Alon groaned. "I can't believe you told my father that aloud. I'm surprised he agreed to house arrest and didn't fling you in prison himself. The Puente de Hilaga was the very first joint effort between the Lakan and the Palisade. It's not even between the Palisade and Hilaga directly, the active lava flows and depth of the channel on the north side prevent it. It connects Aynila to Hilaga. My father will mediate any additional Codicían interference."

"Thanks for that," Sina said, acid sweet. "Nothing I like more than being trapped in Aynila while the conclave has been deprived of my mother's leadership. After all, your father's done so well mediating while my mother and sister are held hostage. I wonder why I don't trust him to prevent the Codicíans from wholesale controlling the bridge as soon as it's completed—which may be a matter of weeks. If I didn't know better, I'd think you were helping your father seize more power for himself."

"I'm trying to keep you safe, and you aren't cooperating," Alon pointed out.

"I saw my chance and I took it."

"You had no plan whatsoever aside from appearing on my doorstep and hoping I could hide you both."

"You did, didn't you? I saw the wave on your door. I'm not the only one you're helping."

"Helping is different."

Isko snorted. "If you don't want people washing up on your doorstep, you must first stop letting them all in." Alon glared at his foster brother, who shrugged one shoulder. "You're pulled in too many directions. Wave or mountain, 'help' or sabotage, your father won't appreciate the difference. He exiled Jeian for less. You can't afford to entertain dangerous soft spots."

"No one deserves Codicían justice." Alon turned to Sina. "You wouldn't have gotten out of the Palisade if Lunurin hadn't written you a pass."

"Oh no, you met Lunurin?" Isko frowned. "I bet you got along. That's terrible news."

The cousins ignored him.

"I had a plan for the guards," Sina insisted.

"Did your plan involve arson?" Alon asked archly.

"Maybe."

Alon groaned. "If your mother wanted you to kill them, she would have burned half the Palisade already."

His tiya, Hiraya Prinsa, was many things; easily cowed was not one of them. If she wished it, the shipyards would be nothing but ash.

Sina did not flinch. "While my mother is held captive, I speak for the firetenders on Hilaga, and I must keep my people safe. That means ensuring the Codicíans never learn what we are. We don't owe your father and his plans our allegiance."

Alon sucked on his teeth in frustration. "Please don't remind him of that. Not if you don't want to be conveniently married off, or worse."

"I've seen multiple lists of candidates. You wouldn't like them," Isko added helpfully.

The heat in the room increased. Sina stole Isko's teapot. "You need to eat solid food, not just tea."

Isko might possibly have *grinned* at Sina, before picking up his plate and sungka board and retreating to his study, where he wouldn't be disturbed by friendly family infighting.

"Sina, please, I'm trying to help," Alon said.

"If you really want to help, make the Lakan withdraw his half of the funding and materials for the bridge this year. It would delay them another wet season without any more sabotage. The rains are late! The funds should be reserved in case of drought. Can't he understand this bridge will be the end of us? It will be just like the tide-touched school, or worse. My people need more time to soothe Hilaga, riled as she is. We wouldn't make it a week without firetenders on her flanks. Hilaga will erupt and bury all of Aynila beside her children."

Alon rubbed a hand over his eyes in exhaustion. "Maybe the healing school's isolation was their downfall. If the firetenders could integrate, maybe they'd never develop the fearsome reputation that doomed the tide-touched. My father wants to see all of Aynila safe."

"You're wrong. He's always hated how independent we've kept our conclave. He's happy the Codicíans are holding my mother hostage. He agreed to the bridge project knowing she objected. Your father was afraid my mother was going to call a vote for a proper Lakan, one with the support of the principalia. She's right to doubt his intentions."

Alon didn't like the amount of truth to that.

Biti, busy shoveling rice and shrimp into her mouth at an alarming rate, shot worried looks between them. She swallowed hard. "If I'm causing trouble, you can send me back."

"No one's sending you back, Biti," Alon assured her, trying to ignore the triumphant grin Sina hid with her hand.

"Eventually, my father will realize it was you. What do you expect me to tell him?"

"Tell the Lakan the only thing I've been doing is becoming unseemly close with Isko, and I haven't left your care in days. He wouldn't doubt that you've been doing your job, watching me for signs of incipient insurrection. Isn't Isko tired of following me about constantly?"

"If he is, I can assign you a guard," Alon suggested helpfully.

Sina wrinkled her nose at him and pivoted the conversation. "Who's the nun, anyway? She recognized the sign. I thought I'd just make a nun angry enough for me and Biti to dash away very chastised. I didn't think we had anyone in the church."

"Sister Lunurin is a... friend," Alon fumbled, and Sina latched on with glee.

"How did you befriend a nun? And why does she feel"—Sina waved a hand—"different? Biti can't stop talking about her."

Alon struggled for an answer that wouldn't open him to more of Sina's probing questions.

"She's not one of yours. She just doesn't think servants should face torture for making mistakes," Alon said. "I trust her."

He wasn't about to share Lunurin's secrets. Not when she guarded his so fiercely.

"Ohhh, that's big from you," Sina said with that familiar teasing gleam in her eyes. "No wonder Isko doesn't like her. Is she how you got involved, 'helping?'"

"Speaking of my foster brother." Alon swirled his cup, trying to turn this back on Sina. "You never showed half this much interest in the indigo business when my mother tried to show you the ropes."

Sina's cheeks colored. "Isko, when he isn't following me to the bathhouse, happens to be very knowledgeable and surprisingly sweet."

Alon raised a brow. There were many admirable words he had for his no-nonsense foster brother, whose mother had been his wet nurse after his mother's milk had failed to come in. Sweet wasn't one he'd use.

"I didn't think *surprisingly sweet* was your type."

Sina sniffed. "I can try new things."

There came a loud knocking on the front door. Alon's heart stopped. He rose, strapping his batangas sword onto his hip.

Sina grabbed Biti, lifting her into one of the tall clay pots in the corner that normally held rice. Once Biti crouched inside, Sina set a false wicker top with a layer of concealing rice, and cleared away her place setting at the table.

Alon cracked the capiz shell window, peering into the street.

"Who would be calling this late at night? Do we need to sneak Biti to the outbuildings?" Sina whispered.

"We need to get her to my mother; she'll be safer there than in the conclave or here," Alon countered.

But there was no glint of steel and guns, only two small figures, sketching the sign of a wave in greeting to Kawit. The tightness in Alon's chest eased.

"Another healing emergency. You two stay quiet. I'll see what's wrong," Alon said as he pulled the cloth hanging across the door of the dining area. With the river running to salt with want of rain, there were more and more issues with contamination of the shallow wells in the city. They needed the rains to come soon. There'd been a cloudburst over the Palisade, but not a drop had fallen in Aynila for weeks. A plague of dysentery would be as disastrous as riots.

II

◆━◆━◆

MARÍA LUNURIN

Father DeSoto took the fall for Biti's disappearance. Claiming ill-health, he delegated his classes to Father Ortiz, who would finish the year with supervision from two sisters of the convent.

Despite the constant rumble of thunder, Lunurin was almost optimistic when the first day of the wet season dawned. It was overcast and cloudy, perfect to venerate Our Lady María of the Drowned.

Cat was busy ensuring everything was in place for the procession, so Lunurin prepared alone for her part in the pageantry of the day. She caked her face and hands in rice powder, lightening her brown skin to render her unrecognizable. It represented the salt of Santa María's tears. Her hair she bound up, covering her mutya with a veil and a huge gilt diadem. She swathed herself in a silvery-white gown, a matched set to the regalia worn by the stolen goddess's statue in the sanctuary. She, along with the statue, would be processed through the Palisade and the city of Aynila to the foot of the Lakan's palace, where she would weep upon his feet and beg him to renew his commitment to the one true God.

It was a role she'd filled every year since the Lakan converted. The Codicíans and the Lakan had conspired to turn the wet season festival into a horrible parody of the blessing of the three goddesses upon the Lakan and the re-swearing of a treaty blessed by the gods. As storm clouds billowed overhead, her goddess's rage swelled beneath her breastbone.

Lunurin breathed deep and wished for more substantial armor. If she made it through today and neither she nor Inez was expelled, she would cut her hair and shatter her mutya on the altar.

Then she would be free, and she wouldn't have to worry if Aynila would survive a loss of her control.

The door to their cell swung open. Catalina entered, her face an unreadable mask.

"What's wrong, Cat?"

"You told me you took care of it," Cat said in a low, dangerous voice.

"Yes, just like I promised. Why? Has the abbot said something?"

"You put some water witch curse on Father DeSoto! How does that not put even more scrutiny on whatever it is within you when we least need it?"

"It wasn't a water witch curse," Lunurin said weakly.

Cat's face darkened dangerously, a white ring appearing around her lips at how tightly she pressed them.

"He needed to be held accountable—"

"Who are you to hold him accountable? Who are you to decide who to punish? You aren't God. Stop holding all this anger and—and—violence inside you! Penance would have come in God's time."

"I couldn't wait on God's judgment!" Lunurin cried out. "I had to make sure it stopped. And now it has. I swear after this, I'll give it all up on the altar," Lunurin promised, rubbing her dugong bone charm for reassurance.

Cat looked sick. "You'll never give it up. You're turning away from me! I see how it pulls you toward *him*. You're so wrapped up in its hateful power. Can't you see every time you use it, it only makes everything worse?"

"Please, Cat, I'm doing everything I can to fix this. Just listen to me—" Lunurin tried to draw Catalina close, but Catalina pushed her away, jabbing her chest with an accusing finger.

"No! I'm done listening to you! I listened about letting Inez teach at the school, and I listened when you said we should go to Alon. I stood by while you worked some black magic deal with a water witch. And now look! Look where *he* got us. God is punishing me for my lack of faith, for consorting with devils, for letting you corrupt me with these unnatural feelings. No more! You're too dangerous!" On the last accusing jab, Cat grabbed the dugong bone amulet. In one swift jerk, she tore it from Lunurin's neck, flung it down, and stomped on it with all the force her tiny frame could muster. Lunurin gasped as the cracked amulet, already damaged from her episode in the abbot's study, sundered in two.

Her power flooded back. She was swamped with it, besieged, no longer a trickle but a raging torrent. She had dampened her power for over a decade. The dam walls were shattered by one dainty foot.

Lunurin dropped to her hands and knees, guiding the power down into the stone foundations, praying she could weather the deluge, that she would not kill everyone. Thunder rumbled so loud her bones ached.

Catalina stood over her, panting. "You have to stop! You have to stop before you're lost to me, before you do something truly unforgivable!"

Cat burst into tears and fled the room, leaving Lunurin on her knees, reeling. How could she be bleeding out without a single injury?

The goddess herself answered Lunurin's wordless query. *"Daughter of mine, years you have been covered over from my sight. But bare your wounded heart to me and I will avenge each hurt tenfold."*

"No! No! You did this! You and this terrible power you granted me," Lunurin cried out. "All I want is to keep Cat safe. I don't want your bloody vengeance!"

"Daughter, how can you forswear me when it is my power that swells in your heart? How can you deny me when I have granted you use of my blessing, even when you hid from my sight, paying lip service to other gods, and refused to call me by my name?"

Her head ached from the weight of her hair and the heavy diadem. Lunurin reached for the shattered pendant. She lifted the broken pieces around her neck, re-clasping the gold chain. A whimper slipped between her lips when the two halves of her amulet crumbled into white powder on her skin. She had to get away from the voice of her goddess in the thunder and the searing weight of her sight. Where could she hide? How could she hide?

The door reopened and Rosa hurried in. "Come, Sister María. They're waiting for you to start the procession."

Before she could protest, she was ushered downstairs. They helped her into the bed of a cart covered in flowers and cloth banners. Several of the youngest girls from the school, scrubbed clean and wearing brightly colored dresses, would accompany her and the statue.

Abbot Rodrigo, in a white mitre and his gold pectoral cross studded with pearls and emeralds, descended the church steps in stately fashion, followed by two priests bearing the statue of the goddess. All the residents of the Palisade who had attended the festival Mass were gathered in the courtyard. Every soldier that could be spared was arrayed in their parade day best.

The abbot walked among them, sprinkling holy water. Eventually, he reached the cart. The statue was lifted to a place of honor beside Lunurin. Mechanically—her head buzzing with panic—Lunurin curtseyed low, allowing him to anoint her brow and eyelids, the holy water leaving tear tracks through the powdered white makeup. He prayed over her as he did every year, blessing her as Santa María, Our Lady of the Drowned.

Only something was different. As he made the sign of the cross over her bowed head, a net of lightning crawled across the sky like a great hand. The eyes of Anitun Tabu's statue lit, searing into Lunurin's own with a blue-white glow.

The goddess spoke, though only Lunurin understood. *"You have dressed a vessel in my mantle. You have anointed her, and she knows my true name. I accept."*

A resounding crack of thunder split the sky, so loud Lunurin thought she'd been struck. Her head was all electric white heat. Lunurin lost herself to the memory of a storm she'd buried so deep she'd hoped to never see it again. She never should've gone down to the oyster beds without her tiyas.

The church courtyard faded, the scent of seagrass and salt filled her lungs like she was drowning on dry land.

~

Before her spread a wide bay, fed by a stream that crept down the side of Calilan's volcano like quicksilver. Lunurin walked to where low tide exposed a path to the wooden statue at the center of the bay. It was an anito idol of Anitun Tabu, dark wood weathered and half-gowned in salt. It was traditional to leave the Goddess of Storms and Sky where her lover could visit at least once a day.

With a murmured "Tabi, tabi po," Lunurin crossed to the small island. She knelt. The goddess stared up with a dark pensive expression. Her hair curved down her back and coiled around her feet. Lunurin untwisted a section of her wrap skirt, sprinkling pounded young rice grains onto the statue's open palms in offering.

Anitun Tabu's eyes dropped from their contemplation of the sky to stare straight at Lunurin. **"Hello, Daughter of mine."**

Lunurin shrieked, scrambling back until the waves lapping at the rock outcrop drenched her skirt. The voice of the goddess was like the rumble of distant thunder. It crashed through Lunurin's head, bypassing her ears. In its echoes were the moan of the wind and the crackle of lightning.

"Do not be afraid. I heard you singing and making offerings in my name. I have a task for you, little stormcaller."

"What task?" Lunurin asked.

Her eyes darted toward the stream, hoping her tiyas would appear, but there was no sign of them, only the wind whistling through the rocky cove entrance.

"There is a Codicían galleon hunting dugong in the seagrass beds. The sky is so clear and bright, the shadows of their bodies stand out too well. Let down your hair, Daughter. Help me hide the dugong."

Lunurin lifted her hand to her bun, but hesitated. "I'm not allowed to let down my hair without my tiyas."

"The mother dugong cry out to me as their children writhe

on barbed harpoons. Lunurin, would you have me leave their grief unanswered?"

Lunurin chewed the inside of her cheek. "Last time I flooded the rice fields out of season. Mother threatened to shave my head."

"I am Anitun Tabu, and you, Daughter, are a stormcaller. If it is not mine to say when there shall be storms, who shall say it?" *The voice of the goddess thundered through Lunurin's bones. There was no denying her.*

Lunurin pulled her mutya from her hair. Her hair tumbled down her shoulders, past her waist. It dipped even into the waves.

Overhead, clouds gathered to Lunurin's call like a school of swirling silver jackfish. Lunurin stared into the eye of a massive typhoon in horror. That was no light rain, enough to hide the bodies of dugong. That was a ship killer.

Her ears popped with the pressure change. Power surged through her. The storm spread out over the island of Calilan and headed westward on powerful winds, toward the seagrass beds, toward the Codician galleon. The sunlight came purpled and bruised through clouds, and Lunurin knelt transfixed before Anitun Tabu's statue, her arms upraised in unconscious mimic, her mind caught up in the eye of the storm, in the heart of the goddess.

She saw the ship. They'd anchored just off the seagrass beds and sent out a dozen shoreboats filled with white men with harpoons, filled with killers. Lunurin saw them through the eye of the goddess and she hated as she had never hated anything or anyone in her life.

The goddess seethed. **"Look at these Codicians. They come crawling over my islands like golden apple snails. They are foreign invaders, stripping greenery and life and magic,** *replacing it with conquistadors and priests and their soulless, joyless god."*

The storm wind struck the ship like a cannonball. The great galleon, unprepared for a clash with Calilan's Stormfleet, was still fully rigged. The sails caught the gale, and the galleon was flung like a child's toy onto its side. The shoreboats swirled away like leaves in floodwaters, dashing themselves upon reef and rock. Lightning struck the mast, sparking fire. Smoke boiled up, thick and black, unimpeded by the rain that slashed down.

An explosion ripped through the hull, cracking the ship open like a crab dropped by gulls onto the rocks. Men flung themselves into the water like rats, struggling to pull themselves away from the sinking behemoth, from the wrathful waves and the killer wind.

Anitun Tabu laughed. **"Yes, Daughter! We will drown them! Drown them all!"**

Her joy filled Lunurin to the brim like she'd stolen her stepfather's lambanog, till her head spun with the sick-making delight of strong coconut spirits. The goddess dragged Lunurin's attention across the water farther south, to the island of Lusong in the distance. Somehow, though it should be far, far too distant, Lunurin saw black smoke rising over the great city of Aynila.

"Do you see, Daughter? They are burning Aynila, where so many of my lover's healers go to train. Walk with me across the waters. Our typhoon will avenge the lost tide-touched of Aynila. We will sink every galleon in the bay and quench the pyres on which Aman Sinaya's chosen burn."

"Yes. Yes. Yes." Lunurin swore to it without thinking, without questioning. Wrapped up in Anitun Tabu's heart, those were her people dying, their prayers rising to her ear on ash-choked winds. How could she do anything but bring forth a bloody answer for their deaths?

Then strong arms seized Lunurin. Her mind snapped back into her body with a jolt. Cold rain slashed horizontally with the ferocious wind, as Tiya Kalaba struggled to tie back Lunurin's hair.

Tiya Halili was shouting at the statue of the goddess. "They're going to come for her now. Is that what you want? They will bring the death on Aynila here and sink our Stormfleet. They will come, with their guns and steel and Inquisition, and it will be your fault!"

~

As the sick-making combination of power and memory released Lunurin, her tiya's angry words followed her into the light. *She's just a little girl, and you've made her a killer!*

While Lunurin had been unaware, the procession had crossed into Aynila. The streets were lined with locals, some converts, who'd given up their mutya to the Church, but also those Aynilans who stubbornly had not. Lunurin could feel the presence of the hidden mother-of-pearl talismans guiding prayers to the ears of the goddess, and intentionally botched signs of the cross, mountains and waves, defiance on every other face. All joined the procession, as they wound their way toward the Lakan's palace, like a mudslide gathering weight.

The goddess was buoyed on the attention of her worshipers, as Lunurin choked on dread. The Lakan's palace was a wide bahay na bato set into the slopes of the hills that arced along the southern edge of the river delta with Tianchao-styled glazed tiled roofs gleaming golden in the storm-green light shining through the clouds. The goddess had created the perfect conditions for cyclones.

GABRIELLA BUBA

Lunurin clawed for a finger-hold of control in her own body. She was filled to the brim with lightning. It was nothing like calling a spark to her fingers or manipulating the internal storm of the body. Anitun Tabu was a primordial being of light and power. The goddess lay along Lunurin's nerves like a summer storm and Lunurin could not wrest back control.

When fighting had no effect, Lunurin tried begging, *Please, Anitun Tabu, look at the soldiers. There are six regiments. Look at their guns! If we do this, they will fire on our people. Bullets will fall like rain. So many will die!*

"It is time. I will not be denied again. I will not be forgotten!"

The Lakan won't listen! Lunurin cried. *He must protect his people. He can't side with you with half the Codician garrison on his doorstep.*

"Then he will die with them for his abandonment of me."

Please, Anitun Tabu, they have murdered all but two tide-touched in the entirety of Aynila. They will burn me for a witch.

"They are the ones who will burn. For how they have wronged my people, for how they have pillaged, raped, and tortured. I will burn them all and wash the ashes into the sea."

They were before the black stone steps leading to the Lakan's palace. The clouds flashed and roiled with lightning and thunder rumbled without end. The Lakan and most of the Aynilan principalia were arrayed on the steps. The plaza was packed with bodies. Yet more people had filed into the streets between buildings. Even the Codicians weren't oblivious to the tension in the air. The six regiments arrayed around the band and the abbot's attendants pointed their weapons toward the seething crowd. The upbeat drumming and piping of the band was barely audible. The Lakan tried to address the crowd, but Lunurin couldn't make out his words over the roaring in her ears.

The abbot and the governor approached her. Each took one of her powdered hands, helping her from the cart. Three little girls spread her long train as she mounted the terraced steps. The abbot's grip was too tight. Lunurin tried to squeeze back until his old bones ground together, anything to stop this tragedy.

She stared about, desperate to find someone, anyone who could help. There was Catalina, among the nuns' choir. Cat would see something was terribly wrong. Surely she'd stop Lunurin. Catalina's eyes skimmed over her without any recognition. If she could, Lunurin would've wept.

Anitun Tabu directed their gaze upward to the Lakan, Tigas Dakila. He was dressed in Codicían fashion, all in black, but for his stiff piña cloth ruffed collar, and the pearls buttoning his dark doublet. He wore an older style of breeches, legs bare below the knee, his feet encrusted with finery. Tambourine toe rings in gold filigree set with pearls and rubies, bangles of gold thick as shackles. His long white mustache was particularly dignified.

Behind him stood Alon, also dressed in the Codicían style, except for the batangas sword at his hip.

How could she let him know?

The abbot and governor released her hands, greeting the Lakan. The men bowed to one another. Words Lunurin couldn't hear were spoken and they all shared a drink of strong lambanog from one huge pearl-studded goblet, symbolically renewing the treaty between Aynila and the Palisade. If this were a true treaty renewal, blood and wine shared in the presence of Anitun Tabu, the clouds would have parted in an ambon, a sun shower, to indicate both parties acted in good faith. Instead, the clouds thickened and bellowed their discontent like a laho's roar.

When had leeches ever cared about the health and wellbeing of the carabao they sucked dry?

The time for Lunurin's role in this farcical pageantry approached. Her belly churned with terrible, addictive joy. She'd forgotten the euphoria of surrendering to the goddess. She'd forgotten the sweetness of it on her lips, and the power in her blood. She'd forgotten. She'd wanted to forget. She never, ever again wanted to feel this false joy gone rancid in her belly as bodies washed ashore and the death toll rose, as her terrible unspeakable storm raged on with no one to walk it into the open sea, where human lives wouldn't pay the cost for every drop of rain.

As Anitun Tabu gathered herself for one huge display of power, Lunurin silently begged Alon to stop her. Someone had to, before these steps ran with blood, painting the square. The power the goddess funneled into the clouds overhead would not discriminate in who it killed.

12

ALON DAKILA

Between the susurrant press of the crowd and the eerily green clouds piling higher, the air was so thick with humidity it was hard to breathe. Yet not a drop of rain fell. His bad hand ached with the pressure drop, throbbing in time with his heart.

Why didn't Lunurin calm the storm? If the threads of lightning spread like cloth-of-gold over low-hanging clouds touched down in the city…

A fire was the last thing they needed.

But Lunurin wasn't herself. Her movements were strange, too smooth, with none of her usual muscular grace. Her expression held none of her public pious solemnity. Instead, a red slash of a smile split the unnatural white of her face like a wound.

She was so close now, her dark eyes wheeling like a frenzied horse, her hands twitching. She'd tucked them together. Not quite in choir recitation posture. Her right hand fisted atop her left palm, her thumb gesturing toward herself. What was she doing? Not a mountain or a wave, not like the crowd below.

It was "Help Me" in trader sign.

"HELP ME. HELP ME. HELP ME." Over and over again, the storm reflected in her gaze like nothing he'd ever seen. There was nothing human in it, only pure fury.

While his father shared a cup of wine with the Codicían dignitaries, Alon signed back, "What's wrong?"

Lunurin's message didn't change. "Help me. Help me. Help me."

The abbot shouted into the storm, a prayer for Aynila. But the thunder stripped the meaning from his words. The air was so thick, Alon was afraid to breathe. There should be wind under such a storm, not this stillness. Was that a funnel, forming above?

Aman Sinaya have mercy. Was Lunurin spinning a cyclone?

Lunurin turned to the crowd. She lifted her hands. All fell silent, even the lightning stilled. Silence rolled out over the city. She smiled. This was *not* a usual part of the festival.

"*My People.*" Her voice cracked like thunder. "*My People, do you know me?*"

"Santa María! Our Lady María of the Drowned! Our Lady of Sorrows." The answer was a moan, a lamentation.

"*Do you remember my name? My children, surely you remember I was not always a Lady of Sorrows.*" The voice of the goddess held all of the storm, a caress like the gentlest fall of rain, the brittle edge of hail, and the keening of high wind.

A chant rose from the crowds packed into the square, forcing the Codicían regiments onto the terraced steps.

"Anitun Tabu, Anitun Tabu, High Lady of the Heavens, Mistress of Storms. On your wind comes vengeance."

"*My people know my true name!*" Lunurin whirled, the tracks of lightning that backlit her mirroring her white powdered hand through the air. She pointed at the Lakan.

"How have you, their anointed leader, forgotten me? How dare you defile my name, and share the goblet of peace with those who sup on the lifeblood of our people? You have forgotten who I am! Yet you would claim my blessing for your reign? You are unworthy of it! You are weak!"

Alon moved as though through water, the air thick with the charge of her power. She drew it around her like a typhoon growing heavy with rain over the open ocean. Terrified soldiers on the steps aimed their guns at the crowd and at Lunurin.

If Alon had any doubts that Lunurin wasn't in control of herself, they vanished when he reached her and laid a hand on the back of her neck. With a firm push, he folded her to the ground.

Lunurin would've grabbed him by the wrist and thrown him headlong down the steps. But the power that possessed Lunurin bent, unused to holding a material body upright. Alon held her, face down, at his father's feet. Her skin burned fever hot. His hands tingled with static. He breathed out, as if to cool seawater for healing. He drove cool and calm into her blood, drowning whatever maddened fever possessed her.

No longer whipped by her fury, the storm overhead eased. The budding cyclone receded into the clouds. The pressure in the air lifted, the green light fading from the sky. Almost at once, it was merely overcast, as if the whole episode had been nothing but a strange dream.

With a flick of his hand, he called the spilled wine dripping down the steps, seeping it into the bodice of her gown until the smell of fermented coconut sap clawed at the back of his throat.

"Witch!" the abbot shrieked, recovering himself enough to react.

"No," Alon retorted. "She's drunk and raving, nothing more. Lakan, the lady begs your forgiveness for the unseemly display and her insult to your noble person."

"She is a witch and must burn!" the abbot demanded. His hand slashed through the air, pointing at Lunurin like she was less than a dog, like she had pointed at his father.

Sweat broke out across his palms, but Alon couldn't afford to panic. "How many dozens of times has she passed your tests in the convent? You couldn't overlook a witch in your own house so long. She is a Datu's daughter, a noblewoman, who has given insult to her Lakan, nothing more. She begs your forgiveness."

The governor drew a hand through his dark beard. "Does she? Or do you in her place?"

"Lakan," Alon pleaded, begging his father to look at him, to listen for once. "Look at this crowd. You raised her up as Santa María, on a holy day. If we harm her, they will riot. Governor, your men might cut a bloody swath through my people, but how many will be torn apart before you reach your walls? You lost half a dozen to the falla riots. You have women and children. You cannot protect them all."

Beads of sweat stood out on his father's face as the Lakan surveyed the crowd, pressed like the lapping of a restless sea against the steps, hands tracing the wave and the mountain. It hardly looked like the sign of the cross anymore. "He's right. Look at them. One wrong word from us and the plaza will run red."

"What do you propose?" the governor asked.

"She has insulted her Lakan. Let it be known that my honor will be satisfied by no less than five taels of gold," his father intoned. "If she cannot pay, let her be put to death."

Alon tugged free the chains hanging at Lunurin's neck. One was gold, where her bone pendant hung, though the amulet was missing when he lifted it from inside her gown. The other was a heavy silver rosary.

Alon lay them at the Lakan's feet. "Two taels of gold. Five in silver. Is the Lakan's honor satisfied?"

The abbot whispered urgently in the governor's ear.

The governor's lip curled. "She comes short a few taels."

Glaring, Alon twisted free the gold signet ring he wore on his pinky finger. It was his mother's. He added it to the pile beside his father's bejeweled feet.

"It is enough," the Lakan said calmly, "for her insult. So she may remember her dignity in my presence, shear her hair as a sign of her shame."

"And two days in the starvation cages," the governor added. He inclined his head to the abbot. "She has not only insulted the Lakan, but the Church, and the Church has the right to punish heretics."

Despite the clinging humidity, a chill alighted on Alon's skin, raising the hairs on his arms. He didn't like the look on the abbot's face, no more than the gleam in his father's eyes. His father knew what a stormcaller's hair meant. Just as he knew a tide-touched needed their tongue to pull waves, and a firetender their hands to calm a volcano or shape flame.

"Let it be so," the Lakan agreed.

The nearest Codicían soldiers surged toward where Alon knelt beside Lunurin, overeager hunting dogs. Alon drew his sword, briefly, fully intending to cut down any man who touched her.

"Gat Alon." His father's voice was hard and cold.

Alon heaved for breath. The air was so thick, he could not catch it. He remembered so vividly how his mother's blood painted the hands of the soldiers who'd cut out her tongue. They'd brought her bleeding and bound. Her blood had bubbled past her lips so thick and red, Alon had feared she'd drown in it. His father's lie about her death had almost been truth. Alon hadn't been able to hold the tide of her blood; they'd severed her tongue at the root. He'd taken hot iron to his mother's poor mangled mouth to cauterize the wound, and spent days filtering infection from her blood. He'd been seventeen. His chest ached for want of air.

"I will do it," he ground out. "Let the whole city see what it means to insult the Lakan and the Church on the holiest day of the year." The words slid like wet chalk over his tongue, bitter and thick.

Dread filled his bones like lead. Lunurin was so still under his hand. Had he pushed too hard? Knocked her unconscious?

He grabbed a fistful of her dress, lifting her to her knees. Her head lolled, eyes half-lidded, but Alon saw no blood. His heart squeezed in an invisible fist.

The governor lifted a brow. "She's intoxicated. Abbot, what kind of convent are you keeping? Isn't this one of your nuns?"

"A blasphemous sea witch is what she is," the abbot hissed.

Alon's skin crawled as he reached into her elaborately done hair, freeing the pins that held her veil. In a sleight of hand aided by the slip of the veil, he tucked the pearl-topped hair prong and comb into his sleeve. He might as well strip her naked. Bad enough to touch the hair of a woman to whom he was not married, but to handle her mutya... His face burned with shame. If she lived, she would never forgive him this. He lifted the gilt diadem from her head, dropping it on the steps with a clang.

The sound or Alon lifting his hand from her neck roused her, and Lunurin struggled to stand. She moved like she was once more in charge of her body. Though she was sluggish with his healing magic, Alon nearly failed to wrestle her back to her knees. He folded forward with a grunt when she landed two well-placed elbow strikes to his liver.

Mouth at her ear he tasted rice powder, spilled wine, and the sour scent of her fear. "Please, stop, Lunurin. They'll kill you."

The fight drained out of her. She let Alon lower her to her knees before the Lakan, the governor, and the abbot.

Her hair was heavy as wet silk in his hand, its gathered mass sleek with oil, black waves gleaming. Alon found where the bun was tied at the nape of her neck. He drew it tight from her scalp and angled the edge of his blade between.

Gods forgive him.

The bun fell, rolling like a severed head down the steps. Lunurin folded with a cry, her hands clawing the shorn hair at her nape. The clouds overhead broke apart, the sun beating down hard and hot.

Alon stumbled back, unable to fathom what he'd done, as she was seized by Codicían soldiers. Her wail modulated higher. She keened; tears poured down her white cheeks, leaving messy trails in the powder. Her scream went on and on. The edges of it cut Alon's heart to tatters. They bound her and flung her into the bed of the cart. Soldiers arrayed like a bristling black porcupine, they backed out of the plaza, toward the Palisade.

Alon had just torn the last stormcaller in Aynila from the arms of her goddess and severed the root of her power. Would she ever forgive him?

Would he ever see her alive again?

13

ALON DAKILA

Alon stared numbly at the governor of the Codícían holdings in Lusong, Hector López de Lena.

"What do you mean, you can't release her? You said two days."

The governor was a large man, even without full parade armor. An old conquistador with a grizzled face, burned by the tropical sun and lined with scars from standing too close to a misfired cannon.

It was a shame the shrapnel had missed his eyes, but that would have impacted his main hobby: hunting, thinly shrouded as an anthropological endeavor. If a creature could be shot or snared, the governor had them pinned to his walls. Behind his desk, below a stuffed dugong, he even had four pairs of spark-striker birds from Hilaga. Only he'd mismatched the sacred birds after killing them, displaying the dimorphic pairs as separate species. A pair of turquoise females tended a nest full of paper flames across from a pair of the indigo males pinned to the wall with their wings and tails spread to display the iridescent hue.

If found dead or dying by any Aynilan, the birds would have been offered to Hilaga, for fear Amihan herself would come in search of the tigmamanukan, her missing messengers. The crude display made Alon's stomach twist. No wonder Hilaga had been so restive.

The governor drummed meaty fingers on his desk. "Look. Lord Alon, I agree with you. She is the daughter of a man who is about to be named Archbishop over all of the Codicían holdings in the East. I think she should be released, told to say her Ave Marías and lay off the wine. Let that be the end of it. This festival fiasco has already impacted the shipyards and public works. The polo workers are calling it a day of fasting and repentance since Santa María didn't bless us with rain, but a labor strike is what it is."

"Then why won't Abbot Rodrigo release her to me?" Alon tried so hard to keep his voice even, the words rasped.

Isko, at the back of the room, clicked his tongue in warning.

The governor dug gunpowder-stained fingers into his beard. "The abbot is a man of God, not politics. You and I, we are practical men. We understand exceptions must be made to keep the wheels of governance turning."

"Governor López, she's been two days without water. In this weather, she won't last three. What do you intend to tell her father when he returns? If your shipyard workers are striking now, it won't only be Aynila that burns in the riots if she dies."

The governor sniffed. "I believe that's precisely what the abbot intends, and I intend to leave the problem squarely in his lap. I think you misunderstand. My schedule is merely delayed. There will be no rioting in the Palisade. I have better control of my city than you. Walls and curfews, resources and civilization, that is the gift of empire. We will outlast whatever little unrest Aynila suffers."

Alon's protest died behind his teeth. "By what right do you hold her?"

"The Church is holding her for acts of heresy."

"Can't you order them to release her? She's been playing the part of Our Lady María of the Drowned for half a decade. She's practically become the saint herself in the eyes of Aynila. If it gets out that the Church executed her as a heretic…"

The look the governor gave him could best be described as *that does not sound like my problem.* Then he sighed. "We may not always see eye to eye, Lord Alon, but in this, if I could, I would aid you. The abbot's fixation with his water witches was all well and good when they were sinking galleons and raising tsunamis, but now his hunts cause me more trouble than they are worth. Likewise, it does me no good if your city burns, and the shipyards grind to a halt. Unfortunately, Archbishop Mateo de Palma has never officially acknowledged his daughter. She is a ward of the Church before she is a citizen of the Palisade. The abbot has every right to administer whatever punishment he deems fit. I have no say."

"A ward of the Church?" Alon repeated. "She's a woman well past majority, how is she still classed as a ward of the Church like an orphan child?"

The governor shrugged. "She's a woman. A woman is a ward of her father, or in this case the Church, until she becomes a ward of her husband."

Alon hoped his disdain for the Codicíans and their baffling belief that women were children wasn't apparent in his expression. He'd thought they were so precious about their women because few made the crossing from New Codicía, but at every brush with their intensely gendered social hierarchy, he came away equal parts mystified and repulsed.

The governor rose, ran a hand along a curving saber of ivory. Alon stared. This was no trophy from the far southern archipelago's rare elephants. Threads of copper veined the ivory and serrated edges gleamed. It was a laho's fang.

"I'm sorry I cannot be of more help to you, Lord Alon, but if that's all you came to discuss, I have scheduled appointments you've delayed long enough," the governor said, still stroking his terrible prize.

Alon left the governor's study, his expression so thunderous the soldiers knocked into each other clearing the way. Litao, his guard, broke into a jog to catch him. Isko, who had too much dignity to hurry, brought up the rear, his brow creased in thought.

Alon strode from the government buildings overlooking the shipyards, past the church, to a guard tower. He bid Litao wait on the ground. No one stopped him from climbing the parapet. Soon he came to the three huge chain-wheels that held the starvation cages.

A soldier with a bright red cloth wrapped at his neck to cushion the hot metal of his breastplate leaned there.

He tugged nervously at the cloth. "I can't let you release her without orders from the abbot."

Alon flipped the man a silver coin. "Pull her halfway up. I'd like to speak to her." He pulled out a second coin. "Privately."

"As you say, your lordship." The soldier released the wheel-lock, turning the crank. "Close enough for you, sir? You probably don't want her closer. They start to smell real ripe. Plus, this one's a witch. She might curse you."

Alon peered down. Lunurin, swinging in her cage, was half crouched, her hands clutching the bars overhead. She stared up with glassy eyes.

"My thanks, soldier."

Alon sat, his legs hanging over the edge, and waited till the soldier wandered to loiter near the guard tower and light a cigarillo.

"Alon?" Lunurin's voice was thin from thirst or screaming.

Aman Sinaya have mercy, her hair. It fluttered raggedly at chin level. Her skin had reacted to exposure by darkening to a rich hue Alon was more accustomed to on his captain of an older brother. A spate of freckles, dark as ink, graced her nose.

The air was dead still and thick with humidity. He didn't have the words needed to beg her forgiveness. They stuck like a too-large bite of sticky rice, gluing his jaw shut.

"They aren't going to let me down, are they?"

"No, forgive me. The abbot declared you a ward of the Church, and has the right to hold you as long as he deems fit."

"Until I die, you mean."

"Y—es." The word scraped out. It fell a long time through the open air before it struck her. Her dark eyes grew shuttered and hard.

"I'm so sorry, I never imagined..." Alon had no more words.

How many had Lunurin whisked out of the Palisade before they could be tortured and killed just like this? How many had he seeded into his brother's crew to be deposited far from Aynila? How many sent upriver to mountain villages?

Lunurin shifted, the cage juddered precariously. "I'd have preferred to be burned to death. It would've been quicker."

"I'm going to figure something out. I won't let you die like this." It sounded so trite. "Just hang on until tomorrow."

The noise she made could've been laughter, but there was too much derision in it.

"I'm sorry. I couldn't watch them kill you like they've killed so many tide-touched, like they nearly did my mother. Perhaps… perhaps it will rain."

If it rained, he would have three more days to try to convince the abbot to release her.

"Oh, Alon, if I die here, it will not rain over Aynila till every river reed is dust in a hot dry wind and every living thing a shriveled husk of leather and bone."

Even without her mutya, without her hair, the words of her curse curled around his heart, squeezing with implacable promise.

"You would kill us all for my father's faithlessness, for mine?"

"She—we—are so angry, Alon. I don't know anymore if it's her anger or mine. She cries out, but I cannot make her hear me. If I had but a thread of a storm I would kill every man, woman, and child gathered for Mass in their church below, praying to their god. I would watch them drown. As the water rose and hail pelted down, as cyclones spun over the bay and shredded their ships, as the flames climbed the Palisade walls and I choked on the smoke, I would die laughing."

She painted a picture so hauntingly clear, Alon tasted the resinous smoke as the pine-pitch Palisade bubbled and charred.

"Please, Lunurin. Give me one more day to try."

She said nothing. In her eyes Alon saw only death. Her mutya tucked into his sleeve throbbed against his skin. No one named to the old gods should die without their mutya.

He pulled hers out, mother-of-pearl gleaming like silver in the beating sun for an instant before he hid them in his palm.

Lunurin's throat worked, she lifted a hand toward him. "You?"

"I was afraid…" Alon gave up on excuses.

With great care he dropped the pearl-topped hairstick to her.

She snatched it from the air and pressed it into her chest. "Oh, oh, Alon, I thought they'd been destroyed."

He waited for her to raise her hand for the comb, but she didn't, shaking her head as she hid the pearl away in her shift. "No, keep it safe for me. I don't want it inlaid in their damn altar panels." With part of her mutya returned to her, her expression softened. "You'll look after Catalina and Inez for me, won't you? Get them out of the Palisade, before…"

From far above, Alon sensed the salt flow of tears. "Yes, of course. I'll send them far from Aynila. They won't get caught up. Don't cry. You can't spare the water."

Lunurin swiped a hand across her cheeks, quickly bracing herself again. Her tears dripped from her fingers onto the hot bars searing her flesh. Alon reached, not knowing if it would work. She was so far away. He breathed out and thought of one cold clear morning in the inland mountains of Lusong. At dawn, there had been a rime of frost flanking the mountain slopes that had melted away in the pale winter sunlight.

Alon remembered that cold morning and bid the saltwater of her tears to do the same, leaching the heat from the metal, till droplets of water formed, condensation dripping from the top of the cage. Not more than a mouthful or two.

She drank the pittance with a desperation that frightened him.

"Just one more day," he pleaded.

Her voice was thin and brittle as glass. "I'll give you as long as I can."

14

MARÍA LUNURIN

The thing the servants never mentioned about the starvation cages was how damned unsteady they were. Lunurin had expected the skin-searing heat of the metal, the beat of the sun, and the cramped quarters—but not the inability to rest. Too short to stand in, with the floor grating spaced so there was no way to kneel or sit, remaining constantly braced had been more draining than the lack of water. Now she lay crumpled in the cage, the bars scraping deeper with each clatter against the Palisade wall. Her blood dripped down and down.

Here she was once again in the aftermath of her goddess's fervor, alone, abandoned, scorned, and forgotten. There would be no divine intervention to save her from human retribution. Just as the sinking of the *San Pedro* had brought the Inquisition to Calilan, and half the Stormfleet had been sunk while she slipped safely away. How many more would die for her folly this time?

The baking heat rose off the tile roofs below. Someone had scrubbed the tiles into a wave pattern. But Lunurin wasn't tide-touched. Though Hilaga belched smoke, and the earth twitched like the hide of a great carabao, she could summon no tsunami.

Visions danced in the heat. Smoke rose, as if the healing school burned anew.

No. It was the *San Pedro,* gutted and burning.

Lunurin flinched from the memory. A dark mass of clouds, heavy and rain-wet, drew near. She stretched out a hand. Her parched throat made a croaking attempt at command.

The clouds did not shield her from the golden hammer of the sun, and no rain graced her skin. The absence of her hair was like a tooth torn out at the root, the space raw and broken, a familiar, yet terrible absence. Lunurin clawed her fingers into the shorn hair at her nape with a shriek of frustration. Only... far more than bristling tufts met her fingers.

Alon hadn't come through with a miracle for her, but he had returned the pearl of her mutya, and her hair had grown.

"I told you this would happen," she rasped.

The church belltower chimed three, seeming to shudder and fall, crushing the white-robed nuns scurrying up the steps for Prayers to Divine Mercy.

"I told you no one would listen!"

The afternoon heat lay thick and silent.

"Is this what you wanted? For me to die like a dog, with Codicían prayers in my ears? You said I wouldn't be burned to death, but it is the sun in your sky killing me now!"

Did thunder rumble in answer? No. Nothing.

"Anitun Tabu! Goddess, mine! Now? After all these years—now, you abandon me? Not when I was a child begging for reprieve. Not when my people tried to drown me for doing your will, because I was half-blooded and dangerous. Not when the Inquisition killed and killed, but let me slip through their fingers? Why me, out of all your other daughters? Why someone sullied with Codicían blood, blood that won't even save me now. Is it because if I die in your service, then half the blood spilt is Codicían? ANSWER ME, ANITUN TABU!"

Lunurin poured every drop of the power she'd nursed since her mutya's pearl was returned to her into her cry. She pushed it out of her skin into the air. Even if there wasn't a single real cloud in the sky, something had to come to her.

From the clear blue sky came a ball of lightning, circling her cage like a fallen star.

It was Anitun Tabu herself, garbed in light, the dark moon of her face too beautiful to gaze upon, the black river of her hair a halo lashing in unseen winds. She was crowned in lightning, the spear of heaven's judgment in her right hand.

"*You called my name, Daughter?*"

Had the goddess come at any other time, Lunurin would've prostrated herself.

Instead, Lunurin screamed, "Why now?"

"*I came when you called.*"

The cold fire of Lunurin's rage could've leveled more than one city. It could've laid whole islands under the sea. "Now, when I am dying."

"*I came when you called me by my name. Your fury is a beacon. I know how desperately you crave their deaths. You look upon them in their sanctuary and you hate every one that dares draw breath.*"

The goddess's words reached into her chest, tearing out her hate and unfurling its bloody banner.

"*Now at last, you hate, as I have hated. You will not stay your hand. All the mercy in the sea has run out. Now is the hour of death. Let me walk in you, once more, Daughter. If you but welcome me in, I will grant all the vengeance you desire.*"

Days ago, Lunurin had torn the goddess's victory from her fingertips. She'd almost had the Lakan, the governor, and the abbot in one fell swoop. But Lunurin had feared for the hundreds in the square, for Catalina and Inez, and for Alon, who'd protect his father with his life. He was a loyal son.

"Say the word and all my power will be yours," Anitun Tabu promised. *"A stormcaller no more, you will be called Stormbringer, and you will command typhoons."*

Lunurin had promised Alon time. He loved this city and its people on both sides of the river. Even when the Codicians had maimed his mother, he'd stayed his hand—even in her grief, Aman Sinaya loved her people too much to drown them.

He should never have returned her mutya.

A day ago, Lunurin would've denied Anitun Tabu as she had for the last decade. She would've closed her ears to temptation and refused even to think her name.

But now her goddess showed her a future written in blood, centuries of subjugation, exploitation, and suffering. Her people forced to grow small in the gauntleted grip of the Empire. Their histories half forgotten, their songs silenced, their gods unnamed, or remade in the image of the Church.

"Open your heart to me and we shall rain death from the heavens. Carry my name on your tongue, and I will be a Saint of Sorrow no more. Give me your hand, and we will be the Storm."

Lunurin had lived too long on her knees. Even if she failed, at least she would die with her goddess in her heart and a storm at her back.

Lunurin extended her arms toward the being in the light. "My heart is yours, Anitun Tabu. I promise it all if you will grant me their blood."

The Mistress of Storms stepped into Lunurin's skin like sinking into a mother's embrace. There was no pain, only warmth.

Electric fire crackled through her body, but it could no more harm her than lightning hurt the clouds. Lunurin knew her goddess. Anitun Tabu's tears were an endless rain, her laughter spawned the winds, the clouds her cooling raiment.

All Lunurin knew was rage.

She released a gale, striking the Palisade like a hammer. Roof tiles tore free, slicing the air, deadly as bullets. The church bell swung, ringing forth a dirge. Screams rose over the city, and the sisters in the sanctuary poured out like a froth of sea foam.

Lunurin reached for lightning. She stretched hungry fingers across the sky, grasping for the bronze bell in the tower. As the lightning leaped from her hand Lunurin looked down and down into Catalina's upraised face, white with fear.

15

ALON DAKILA

"Alon, you can't mean to do this!" Isko shouted after him. "She'll only be a liability."

"If you'd suggested it sooner, we could've gotten her down hours ago!" Alon retorted, taking the stairs three at a time.

"You can't be the one to do it." Isko chased Alon into the street. "Give me a chance to think!"

"We're out of chances! It's too late to find anyone else. Isko—she's dying. We don't have time." Alon flung himself onto the bay gelding Litao led out. His bad hand throbbed. Half of Lunurin's stolen mutya burned against his arm.

Alon rode hard for the bridge. Thunderheads piled over the Palisade, black as boiling tar. He wouldn't make it in time. The Palisade gates were closed. Likely the only thing left to do was die with her. That seemed fitting. He had put her into their hands.

Damn Catalina's stubborn pride. He'd told her Lunurin's wishes, asked her to leave the Palisade for a few days. He'd offered to pay for lodgings until everything was settled. No one should have to watch their lover tortured to death.

At her refusal, he'd begged her to let him take Inez. But Catalina cursed him, said it was his fault an evil spirit had possessed Lunurin. If he'd not brought Inez to a water witch, Lunurin wouldn't have gone mad.

He hadn't tried hard enough. He'd feared Catalina's hatred of magic would endanger his and Kawit's secret. He'd been sure he'd figure something out long before things became this dire. But he couldn't ignore the primordial rage brewing over the Palisade, the same as when his mother had pulled in the tsunami.

~

They'd just entered the walls of the Palisade when a gust of wind half ripped Alon from his horse's back. Rain came in sheets. Alon abandoned his horse to continue on foot.

He ran for the church, which miraculously was still standing. A surge of lightning cut across the heavens, clawing across the black underside of the clouds, like a great hand reaching for the church tower. The spread fingers of lightning hung suspended in the air, casting a terrible blue-white light over the city. Alon's hair stood on end. He tasted metal, and the sweet-pungent spark of burning air.

Then the great hand of the goddess folded in on itself and struck the small body in the metal cage.

The ground shuddered with the force of the thunder that followed. It went on and on, swallowing Alon's anguished cry.

The body in the cage fell, the tempest overhead faltering. Then, with another searing flash of light, the storm raged on, the rain slashing out of the sky almost horizontally.

Alon ran for the guard tower. He found four soldiers huddled at the base. He seized the man with the red neck cloth. "Up, man, if we don't get those cages on the ground, lightning will strike the Palisade. Everything will burn."

Men moved at his command. His brother always said he'd mastered a captain's knack for barking orders in a storm.

Alon went with them, struggling through the wind along the narrow parapet, to reach the huge chain-wheels.

"Cut the others free!" Alon roared. He and the first soldier seized the crank for Lunurin's cage, lowering it as fast as they dared.

Thumb-sized hail pelted Alon's arms, leaving welts. A fist-sized ball of ice took the soldier beside him in the head. The soldier's metal helmet crumpled like it was made of paper.

Alon lunged. Miraculously, he hooked three fingers in the red neck cloth. The two of them hung perilously off the parapet, Alon's grip on the rough wooden handle of the crank all that prevented them plummeting eighty feet down.

Alon's weakened right hand throbbed, his hold failing. The ground was dizzyingly far away. He tried to pull more fabric into his grip, but the wind slammed down, rain blinding him. The rough-spun fibers in his fist tore free, red threads catching on his gold brace.

The soldier fell.

Litao's hands closed around Alon's wrist and dragged him onto the parapet. Together they seized the crank, lowering Lunurin the last twenty feet.

Alon descended the guard tower stairs, terrified of what he would find below. Rain still sheeted down, but this near the wall they were sheltered from the wind. A flock of white-habited nuns and priests gathered around the bodies on the ground, one still in its cage, the other shattered across the ground, blood spreading black as ink across the cobbles in the strange bruised light under the storm. Alon flexed his aching hand. That man hadn't had to die.

But he'd known the soldier's fate the moment his grip faltered. Alon didn't yet know Lunurin's. He forced his way past the onlookers and found Catalina kneeling beside the cage, Lunurin's face cradled in her hands as she wept bitterly.

Lunurin's eyes were closed. She lay motionless, her body curled and broken. He was too late. How could this be all that was left of a woman who'd harnessed such awesome and terrible power?

"Shoot her! Pull her out and shoot her. Now!" the abbot demanded, shaking the soldier tending to his fallen compatriot.

Alon's head spun. By all the salt in the sea, she wasn't dead?

"No," he protested, his voice at once too quiet and too loud in the ringing shock of his own head.

A soldier approached the cage. Alon seized him. "No," he repeated, louder. "The abbot has no right to order her execution."

The soldier's hands went slack. Alon snatched the keys and shoved the man into a pack of sisters, who shrieked as they fell.

Alon turned on the abbot. "You have no right to hold Lunurin."

"Right? Right?! God gives me the right! She is a witch and needs to be put down before she kills us all."

"You can't kill her," Alon persevered, swiping the rain from his eyes to better hold the abbot's gaze.

"You may be the Lakan's son, Lord Alon," the abbot sneered. "But in these walls that is a courtesy title and nothing more. That nun is no citizen of your Lakan. Her life is in the hands of the Church. My hands—"

"She is not a nun," Alon said.

The abbot sputtered to a heaving stop, his expression furrowed in confusion.

Alon pressed his advantage. "She is a novice, who hasn't taken her lifelong vows to the Church. And we are engaged to be wed. She is as much a citizen of the Lakan as I am."

"What?" the abbot thundered. "What kind of farce—"

Alon wished he'd dragged Isko with him. This was Isko's idea. A way for Lunurin not to be a ward of the Church. Of course, he'd not meant for Alon to do it.

"It's true!" Catalina came swaying to her feet beside the cage. "I was witness, Abbot Rodrigo. I will swear to it! Sister María is engaged to wed Lord Alon."

16

MARÍA LUNURIN

Against Lunurin's every expectation, she opened her eyes. She was floating in the wooden tub in the cell she shared with Catalina. But it wasn't Cat holding her hair. Cat was digging in Lunurin's clothing chest at the foot of her cot. Thank the Merciful goddess above. Lunurin hadn't killed her. Filled to the brim with Anitun Tabu's rage and the euphoria of the storm, Lunurin had almost forgotten the most important thing: her family's safety.

"Salt, I need the box of salt," a man's voice said.

Was that Alon holding her? Yes, his hands supported her back as he chilled the water, pulling the fevered heat of the goddess's power from her body. The cold bit sharply at the scalds and festering wounds littering her skin. For one heart-twisting moment all she could think was, *He came back for me. Just like he promised.*

"Lunurin. Lunurin, keep your eyes open," Alon commanded. "Look at me. Yes, just like that. I have no idea what that lightning did to you. Nod if you can hear me."

Lunurin did her best to nod despite the drums pounding in her head, every heartbeat another blow. Her head throbbed and the water was so pleasantly cool. She'd just rest her eyes…

"You promised you'd get Catalina and Inez out," Lunurin rasped, trying to force accusation into her voice, anything to divorce herself from the desperate gratitude welling in her throat.

Something shook Alon's broad frame. Was it laughter? Sobs? His hands briefly wrapped around her ribs as if to encircle her in his arms. She wanted him to hold on. She wanted to be squeezed back into her body and reminded where the edges of her ended and the storm outside began.

"Forgive me, forgive me. I swear I tried. She is stubborn, your Cat."

"She is," Lunurin agreed.

Alon lifted a cup to her cracked lips. "Drink. Slowly, slowly. You'll make yourself sick."

Coconut water, faintly sweet, eased the broken glass ache of her throat, but he pulled it away too soon. Her tongue was still sandpaper.

"Found it." Catalina dumped the contents of a rosewood box into the tub. Flakes and clumps of salt landed on her wet shift, disappearing as Alon yanked them into solution.

"Is there anything I can do to help?" came Inez's small voice from where she perched on Catalina's pallet.

"What are you doing?" Lunurin asked.

"Shhh, easy, you are burning with fever or heat stroke or, I don't know, lightning. I'm bringing your temperature down before it cooks your brain," Alon explained as the saltwater cooled and Lunurin's skin broke out in gooseflesh.

"Did I hurt anyone?" It was a stupid question. Lunurin asked anyway.

Alon was quiet a long time, only breathing deep and steady, his ribs a set of bellows, drawing heat away instead of stoking it, till Lunurin shivered.

"Alon?"

"Yes, you did." His words were soft, bloody things.

Lunurin's heart ached. Alon was far too kind for what the world asked of him.

"She's going to hurt more people when she finds out what you did," Catalina muttered acidly.

"What?" Lunurin craned her head back. Alon's face looked odd upside down, quite a lot of chin. His Adam's apple bobbed.

"I ahh... I told the abbot we were engaged," he admitted, staring off into a corner.

Lunurin tried to sit up, the water in the tub sloshing precariously. "We're *what*?"

Catalina crouched, smoothing the short fringe of Lunurin's hair back. "Congratulations. You're engaged to wed the Lakan's son."

Lunurin's heart rate picked up. Aray! It hurt. Her chest ached like she'd been kicked by one of the sturdy ponies that drew kalesa through the streets.

"Calm. We need to keep her calm," Alon muttered.

Catalina went on, caressing Lunurin's cheeks. "As Alon has all the brains God gave a concussed chicken, he waited till you were practically dead to let us all know."

Alon's chest rumbled under her ear with some defense of himself. Then he seized hold of her blood, slowing everything down. She was grateful. She hoped everything would make more sense when she next woke.

~

It was no longer storming, only an endless rain drumming on the roof, when Lunurin next woke. Alon's shoulder jostled her head as he heaved her from the tub with a grunt.

"Careful! Careful!" Catalina chanted.

"I've got her."

"You nearly bashed her head in on the cage."

If her chest wasn't aching, Lunurin would've laughed at their bickering. Lunurin couldn't even will her weighted lids to open as Alon deposited her on her pallet.

Litao knocked and called in, "Gat Alon, I'm told the governor is on his way to speak to you."

Alon rose, his voice no longer beside her ear. "Catalina, would you dry and dress her? If anything is still actively raw or bleeding, let me know, but I don't think she needs bandages."

"She's to be your wife, isn't she?" Catalina shot back.

Catalina was angry. Lunurin finally broke the salt-rime sticking her lashes together. Catalina was up on her toes, nearly spitting in Alon's face.

"Please, Catalina. Help me get her through today alive. I—that's all I want." Alon sounded so tired. Was that blood running down his temple?

"You're both pathological liars, you know that?"

Alon turned from Catalina, releasing an angry breath through bared teeth. His eyes landed on Lunurin. He composed his expression.

"Lunurin, you should…" He rubbed a hand over his face, smearing the blood. "I have no idea if lightning is like a concussion and if I should let you sleep or not, salt bless it."

"Alon, you're bleeding," Lunurin rasped.

He stared at the blood on his fingers in confusion.

"Do you think he's the only one?" Catalina cut in. "Inez has a welt the size of a quail egg. And there are people who won't ever bleed again after all that hail and wind. The roof was ripped off the children's dorms!"

Lunurin's heart ached in her chest, but not with remorse. "I'm sorry, Catalina. I didn't mean—"

"You see! Liars! You deserve each other."

Lunurin's chest gave an ugly pulse. She gasped in pain. But wasn't it true? Wrapped in the arms of her goddess, she'd intended to kill every living person in the Palisade. How had she forgotten Catalina and Inez?

Alon crouched beside the tub, washing the blood from his face. He took the cloth Inez handed him with quiet thanks, mopping his brow. "Please lower your voice. We need to keep Lunurin's heart rate down. I don't know how her heart's still beating after the lightning strike, but it's not happy about it."

"By what devilry do you know that?!"

Inez wrapped her arms around Catalina's waist. "He's a healer, Ate. He's trying to help."

"Like he helped you?" Catalina snapped.

"Yes, like he helped me, Ate. Please don't hate me for it. It was hurting me. They made it stop hurting."

All the fight drained out of Catalina. She hugged Inez. "I don't hate you, Inez. I could never hate you. I just get scared. Don't mind what I say when I'm scared."

Alon's expression was so drawn and solemn. He must be hiding his rage. Certainly, he must hate Lunurin. He was just too good a healer to scream it in her face. She wanted to apologize, for being weak enough to get caught up in the goddess's rage without thinking of the consequences.

The knock on the door repeated. "Gat Alon, the abbot and the governor have requested your presence."

"Tell them the lady is awake. Soon, they can speak to us both."

Lunurin threw her legs, heavy and numb, out of bed. Taut patches of newly healed skin prickled and ached. Alon helped her to sit, then he reached into his sleeve, and held out the other half of her mutya. The comb gleamed like a fragment of moonlight.

"I'm sorry. I had no right to take them from you."

Lunurin's hands itched to pair her mutya. Their separation was a wound, like her shorn hair. It sapped her strength, rendering her control haphazard at best. She pulled her hairpin from where she'd stabbed it into a fold of her shift. She could feel the fury of her goddess dragging at her power through the pearl. She didn't trust herself to resist. Not tonight.

She folded his hands around them both. "I cannot wear them. You shouldn't have returned even this to me. If I die with them in reach... please, just do not let the Church have them."

Catalina sucked in a sharp breath. Lunurin couldn't bear to look at her. Did Cat still think her faith could save them?

The muscular cords of Alon's neck stood out in stark relief. He cradled her mutya so reverently.

"I'm not going to let you die," he swore.

"You don't owe me this, Alon. Don't ruin your life to save mine. I've taken so much from you. Don't let me take your future too."

Alon went down on his knees, bending till he could meet her downturned gaze. "You have taken nothing from me."

But she had, and she would. Lunurin was always taking, more than she deserved, hurting even those she loved. Lunurin silently tapped the back of his right hand above his ornate brace. His skin was cool with a faint grit of salt, the sight of the still reddened burns on his hands twisting her stomach. She didn't deserve him.

He shook his head. "If you had not named me, my mother would have bled out in my arms. If you hadn't named me, what would I do in the face of my people's suffering? You saved my life. Let me save yours. At least let me try."

"I—" Lunurin's voice caught. It was unspeakably selfish, but she did not want to die. "Alright. You may try."

She pressed his hands back into his chest. The phantom brush of his fingers on her mutya shivered down her back, gentle as fingertips in her hair. They locked eyes. Lunurin's drifted lower to the fullness of his lips. Alon flushed to the tips of his ears. He'd practically crawled into her lap, so close they breathed the same air.

He stood quickly, clearing his throat. "Catalina, Inez, please. Will you help her? It's not proper..." Alon flushed a deeper shade of red. Grabbing the changing screen he partitioned Lunurin off from the door.

A raw laugh scraped from Lunurin's throat. The lightning really had done something to her head. "Alon, when did we get engaged?"

"Eight months ago, just after your father left for Canazco. It's why you didn't renew your application to take your eternal vows. Catalina was your witness, Isko and Litao were mine," Alon mumbled. "This was all some stupid stunt to get you kicked out of the convent, so we could finally wed."

Lunurin raised her arms as Cat dragged her wet shift off. Her skin ached. "That's actually quite clever."

"I'll tell Isko you thought so, if they believe us."

"Don't... Not in a habit. Give me the indigo skirt and blouse," Lunurin said quietly, knowing she was breaking Cat's heart. But they were long past the time when false piety could save her. She'd die on her own terms.

"You have to cover your hair," Catalina protested.

Lunurin raked her fingers through the damp strands, already fighting gravity to curl. It reached almost to her chin now. Yes, she needed to cover her hair.

Soon she was dressed. Her head pounded sickeningly as Cat and Inez pulled her to her feet. Before she could falter, Alon was at her side. She leaned into his presence, steady as the tide coming in. Her vertigo eased. Perhaps it was weakness, but she needed his strength to hold the goddess at bay a little longer.

"I can do this alone," he assured her.

"No. If I'm to be dragged before a firing squad, I'm going to walk to the wall, not be hauled out of bed."

Alon's hands tightened. "That won't happen." He put an arm around her, tucking his hands under her elbows, lifting the weight off her feet.

Juan waited in the hall beside Litao. He spared Lunurin a nod and led the way to the abbot's study. They followed slowly. The courtyard was littered with debris, ceiling tiles, shutters, and drifts of melting hail. Lunurin had even felled one of the huge coconut palms that grew in the grassy quadrant. Without her mutya, her power couldn't whip the storm to further frenzy, but nor could she calm the deluge of the storm drawn to her, calling for her, crying out her name. The rain fell thick and soft.

Alon, bless him, lifted her over the worst puddles and heaps of debris as if she were made of spun glass and not the primary cause of the destruction. He had never treated her like the ill-luck she was, even when the evidence was staring him in the face.

The rain fell harder, splashy drops pelting her skin and dripping down her face. Finally, they entered the abbey and ascended to the abbot's study.

She almost asked Juan what mood Rodrigo was in. She wondered how politely he could convey "apoplectic." Shame clawed at her. Juan would've been one of the people killed if the goddess had her way. Lunurin truly didn't want to kill every living thing in the Palisade; not the children, not the servants and shipyard workers, who carried on their quiet everyday defiance. They didn't deserve what her goddess had in store for the Codicíans.

As Juan opened the door to the abbot's study, Lunurin tried to step free of Alon's hold to stand under her own power.

"Stay close," he urged her.

She subsided and let him guide her to stand before Abbot Rodrigo and Governor López. The abbot heaved for breath, his face a splotchy red. The governor's craggy features were impossible to read where he leaned against the bookshelf.

Governor López was an old-fashioned conquistador. He had been on campaign after campaign to tame lands for the Empire, all to escape his willful wife. She'd chased him across the world, but drawn the line at the witch-infested tropics. He'd found peace, until Abbess Magdalena made the crossing from Canazco with six Augustinian nuns, once more injecting women who experienced independent thought into his life. Abbess Magdalena had been the bane of his existence, constantly bringing her grievances with the abbot direct to his ear. He'd been a bit too pleased when Magdalena's illness forced her to return to New Codicía, and would have shipped all the nuns in the convent with her if he could.

"Lord Alon. I'm so glad you could finally join us," Governor López drawled.

"The lady was unwell. She needed care. Her wellbeing is my responsibility."

The governor waved this away. "Why precisely is she here, anyway? This is no business to involve a woman in."

"I disagree. It is Lady Lunurin's future we are discussing. She has every right to be here," Alon responded.

The governor frowned, but turned to the matter at hand. "You claim you are engaged?"

"Eight months ago, I gave my word I would marry her as soon as her father returned from Canazco to give his blessing," Alon answered steadily.

"You have sullied the sanctity of a nun's vows to the Church!" the abbot erupted.

"I have taken no vows, beyond novice's vows," Lunurin said. "Every year, I have applied, and every year I have been denied the right to take my eternal vows. I grow tired of waiting for a future that will never be mine."

"You will be silent, woman. You've caused me enough headaches," the governor snapped.

Lunurin's heart pulsed with rage, familiar as a friend. Oh, the ache in her chest was her goddess, awakening once more after Lunurin had denied her a third time. Alon squeezed her arms and Lunurin leaned into him, breathing in his calming presence. The chilling effect of his healing was melting too quickly, lightning and power rekindling in her blood. Her mutya were still so close, only kept from her skin by the cloth of Alon's sleeve.

"I'd intended us to wait, until Archbishop de Palma returned to Aynila, and our fathers could meet and arrange the match properly. However, with the wet season delaying the archbishop's return until next year, I am afraid the lady became impatient with me. She believed if she embarrassed the Church during the festival, she would be expelled from the convent and free to marry," Alon said.

The strained silence that met Alon's explanation wasn't promising. If the abbot got any redder, he might have a stroke. Dread filled her lungs. This was it. After this, the farce would be over, and she would die.

A barking laugh burst from the governor.

Abbot Rodrigo turned on him. "The Church will not take this insult! The woman blasphemed before the entire city. The punishment for such a crime is death."

The governor's laughter sounded like gravel crunching underfoot. "God in Heaven, Rodrigo, this is hilarious. You really want to kill a woman, the daughter of your archbishop, because she was angry her betrothed took too long to talk to her father?"

"She—I—" the abbot sputtered.

The governor howled, slapping his leg. "I'll tell you what, Lord Alon. I remember my own long walk to the altar. The gallows seemed preferable to being shackled to such a willful woman. But if the Lakan will bless the union, I'll make the abbot marry you tomorrow, so long as you ensure I am never troubled by your wife's theatrics again."

"She's a witch," the abbot protested.

The governor shook his head. "I think not. My captains noticed nothing amiss with the tides, and no tsunami swept the bay. Every one of the water witches you've burned pulled saltwater and blood. This nun got drunk and ranted during foul weather."

"What about the storm? She called lightning. I saw it!"

"Called lightning," Alon scoffed. "She was in a metal cage sixty feet in the air. Those cages are going to start a fire someday."

Anitun Tabu's rage reached a fever peak, crackling over her skin with a kiss of static. Lunurin tried to smother the electric spark, but Anitun Tabu was so very angry, and she was so tired. Alon curled his hands around her arms, breathing out, pressing cool and calm into her blood.

"I've said it a dozen times," the governor agreed. "A good set of stocks would serve the same purpose. Besides, I presume our archbishop would have noticed if his own daughter were a witch. So, we are agreed, Lord Alon?"

"Governor, I want your promise that my betrothed will face no further punishments from the Church while I seek the Lakan's blessing."

"You have my word. Your betrothed will remain among the convent nuns until your return."

Lunurin studied the governor's face. It simply couldn't be this easy. Surely they wouldn't let her slip away from their twisted justice for this farce of a marriage.

"My man will remain behind, to see to her safety," Alon insisted.

The abbot kicked the side of his desk and stormed out. A flush of heat spread through Lunurin's blood. Sweat broke out across her palms. Her heart raced. In matched time, the rain fell harder, like a hundred running feet. The windows creaked ominously. Alon's grip tightened, her mutya pressed between them and her power swelled.

The governor shook his head. "That, I cannot allow. No armed man who isn't sworn to me is remaining in the Palisade overnight."

Alon's breath hissed out of him. "If anything happens to her, I will be sure to inform my future father-in-law of how it came to pass."

A cold smile spread across the governor's face. "You do that, Lord Alon. But until you have the Lakan's seal of approval, I will do nothing."

"We need the banns to be read at Mass tonight," Alon reminded him.

The silence stretched, broken only by the rain.

The governor rubbed a knuckle through his beard. "Hmm... I suppose that can be arranged."

The men eyed each other, utterly ignoring her. Lunurin imagined the governor's head on a spear.

"For your understanding, and good humor, Governor, you have my thanks. Love makes fools of us all." Alon executed a shallow bow and pulled Lunurin from the room. A smattering of hail struck the roof. All Lunurin knew was rage. It welled along her nerves like lightning. It carved paths through her flesh, and deep inside her Anitun Tabu railed.

"Daughter! Daughter, you promised me that we would wipe them from Lusong! You called my name! You made me a vow!"

Distantly, Lunurin realized Alon had tugged her into his arms. She seized the lightning crawling through her body, holding it inside her skin with everything she was worth. She would not hurt him again.

His breath tickled her ear. "Please, please, Lunurin. I can't convince them a second time."

Lunurin forced her eyes open, let him see the storm that raged there, a storm beyond her will to fight.

"Anitun Tabu, High Lady of the Heavens, I beg you. Your daughter will surely die if you vent your wrath here," Alon prayed.

Lunurin grasped the back of his neck, dragging his brow to hers, half convinced that if she could lose herself in the salt-slow tides of his blood, she'd find the strength to hold back the goddess's wrath. Alon went with her hold, something unbearably soft in his dark gaze.

"My vengeance cannot be put off forever, not even by you, Son of the Sea." She didn't know if she spoke the words or if she only pressed them from her electric blood into his.

Alon cradled her face. "Goddess, please. I love her. I cannot watch her die like this."

The words pressed into her like a trio of hailstones, melting on her tongue. There was an ache to them, in her teeth, sweet with rot. She'd never meant to hurt him like this. She'd never intended to make him love her. All these years she'd closed her eyes to the truth of it. She hadn't been strong enough to turn away. She needed someone to rely on when the lies and deceptions weren't enough and all she had left was to beg Aman Sinaya's mercy.

She wasn't worthy of his love, his gentleness. She would let him down, just like she always failed Catalina. She couldn't bear it if he looked upon her with disappointment—or worse, disgust.

Then, the cold he urged into her blood through his palms broke through the rage and the hot ache of tears. The fury of her goddess drained from Lunurin like water from a cracked vessel. Outside, the storm abated its fury and the depths of Alon's tide-touched spirit closed over her head, dragging her down. The last thing she saw was the soft, yet fierce desperation in Alon's dark gaze.

17

MARÍA LUNURIN

Lunurin was used to being leaned on, being begged for energy and time, and treated like she had limitless strength and patience and will. Tonight, she had nothing. Alon had snatched her back from ruin, but her future balanced on the head of a pin. All it would take to bring it all crashing down would be one unwary breath, and *whoosh*... everything would fall to disaster again.

It was oddly comforting to be treated like she was fragile. It might've been ridiculous, trivializing, but Alon's innate gentleness held no condescension.

She rose slowly from the grip of Alon's power, and woke to rain misting her face as he tried to carry her across the courtyard without dousing her.

"Forgive me," she croaked. "She is so angry, and I am so tired."

"Drink water. Rest. I'll come for you in the morning."

"Alon, your father will never give his blessing."

"He will."

She didn't have the heart to contradict him. She'd promised she'd let him try. Soon, he would run out of lies to tell and last-minute saves to make. Love would not save her, not even Alon's love. Eventually they would come for her, and then they would die.

"Please don't look like that," he said, wiping rainwater from her brow before it ran into her eyes.

"Like what?" She turned her face into his hand, savoring this tenderness while she could.

"Like you are curled around a keg of powder, with a lit reed burning down in your hands."

Lunurin laughed and laughed. Each spasm of mirth ached in her chest and burned in her throat.

Alon's eyes went wide with fear. Lunurin bit down on her fist, pressing her face into the damp silk of his barong until her hysterical laughter smothered and died, breathing until the pain eased. She let herself be cradled against his strength. How strange to feel protected, as if the only thing keeping her from flying apart at the seams was his gentle grip.

In her cell, Alon tried once more to return her mutya, but Lunurin refused. Tonight, just tonight, she needed them far away. Her vow from the cage was still too near. "You may put them in my hair on my wedding morning."

"Tomorrow morning," he swore, a vow he couldn't possibly keep, but she didn't hold it against him. Then he left, so grave with determination she wished she believed it would save her.

When the door closed behind Alon, Catalina rounded the changing screen that bisected the cell, her eyes red with weeping.

"Where's Inez?" Lunurin asked.

"She's helping move the little ones into a dormitory that wasn't storm-wrecked. She's staying with them tonight." Cat's tone was accusatory.

"Please, Cat. I never meant to hurt anyone, but without my amulet, I couldn't fight it. I couldn't fight Her! And then they took my mutya…"

Catalina stared at her, stricken. Lunurin had nothing to offer her, but she spread her hands anyway. "Catalina, I am just as likely to be wed in the morning as I am to die, so you should say it all now."

"You're going to go through with it? You're going to abandon your life with God? With me?" Catalina demanded angrily, her hurt turning all her sharp edges outward.

As she always had, Lunurin opened herself up to be cut to the quick.

"If you were so against it, why did you corroborate Alon's story?" Lunurin asked, half exasperated, half relieved that Catalina had forgiven her enough to be upset she was leaving.

Catalina flung herself into Lunurin's lap, weeping. "I didn't want you to die! Lunurin, I was angry and scared, but I never wanted you to die. Whatever is in you, it frightens me so much."

Lunurin gathered Catalina into her arms, shushing her tears. "I will never hurt you. Not in a hundred thousand years would I let what I am hurt you."

"Then how can you leave me?!" Catalina keened, squeezing Lunurin till her ribs ached.

It had always been the two of them together, two lost, fatherless mestiza girls, at the mercy of the convent sisters. They'd always had each other. How could Lunurin ever leave her behind?

"Come with me, please," Lunurin begged. "Bring Inez. We'll take her away from here. It's no place for a mestiza girl, being taught to hate half herself. Let's give Inez something better than we had."

Catalina dragged her sleeve across her eyes. "Aren't you always saying we shouldn't take advantage of Alon? Even the Lakan's son has a limit to his patience, and it's always begun and ended with me."

"Alon's not like that. It wouldn't have to be like that if you didn't... You don't have to fight him for your place in my heart. It doesn't have to be one or the other. What I have with you is nothing like what I feel for him."

Catalina scoffed, brittle anger hardening into place, an edge for Lunurin to slip and cut herself to ribbons upon. "That's because you trust him. I see how you are with him, how different you are with him."

"What do you mean?" Lunurin's mouth formed the words, though she didn't have the air to voice them, the weight of Catalina's accusation crushing her chest. "I love you."

"Yes. But you haven't trusted me in a long time, if you ever did. You gave him your comb. You'd never give them up for me, never! But him—"

Lunurin flinched from this truth. "Cat..."

Catalina spat, "You've always told me half-truths, flecked with deception, and expected my blind faith. Not even a saint could be everything you ask of those you love, Lunurin. I'm no saint, but neither is he."

The words were a punch to the gut. A part of her wanted to shout back, *Every time I've tried to tell you the truth, you've asked me to cut off that part of me and destroy it.*

But... Lunurin had never raised her voice to Cat, could never hurl words like knives at her. Lunurin never wanted Cat cut open and bleeding out, the way Lunurin was now.

Lunurin did ask too much. Perhaps she *was* too much. How soon would it be before it was Alon turning from her with

184

dark hooded eyes, saying, *Why is it you always need so much? Can't you see I am just a man?*

"I'm not asking you…" The words caught in her raw throat, her heart panged with incipient grief. "Cat, can't you see how bad this place is for us? For our people? Every year, you apply to take your eternal vows and every year, they reject you for no other reason than they believe our mothers' blood is some kind of stain."

Cat hesitated. Lunurin latched onto her uncertainty, desperate to make her see that the Codicíans would never reward her faith, that there was nothing in the Church for them but shame and guilt and suffering.

"Please, I've never wanted to deceive you. I've always just been so afraid. We could be free of that if we left this place. I will make a place for you by my side. You and Inez, our little family, that's all I want."

Cat bit her lip. "Are you sure you can't cast it off for good? How can you abandon your divine calling?"

It took everything in Lunurin not to laugh until she wept. What divine calling could there be when a primordial goddess of the heavens, with lightning for blood and storms at her beck and call, curled under Lunurin's breastbone, whispering, *"Daughter, won't you drown them for me?"*

"I tried, but it only put you and Inez in danger. Even if I could, it's too late now. The abbot wants me burned as a witch."

"Not if you apologized!"

Lunurin did laugh then. The ache of it was grounding. All of her hurt. Her time in the cage made it impossible to swallow her bitterness. "Yes, I'll apologize, like the last three servants he had caned and caged till their backs festered. What shall I apologize for—my blood? My mother who seduced a priest? Shall I beg his pardon for being a soulless water witch?"

"You aren't a witch!" Catalina cried. "You are nothing like that woman in the jungle. She did something, put a demon in you, as payment for helping Inez. If you just told the abbot it was all her fault, I know he'd—"

"No." Lunurin's voice was hard.

Catalina tore from Lunurin's arms with a frustrated cry. "Why are you always too proud to beg for forgiveness? Can't you see it's what God wants? None of this would be happening if you would just humble yourself—"

"No," Lunurin repeated. "Ten years I've humbled myself. I have cut myself down and swallowed every offending sliver. The time for that is past. I certainly won't throw the woman who saved your sister's life at the abbot's feet in the hope that by the time his bloodlust was sated, he'd forget about wanting me dead."

Catalina paced, angry tears coursing down her cheeks. "Why do you always make me like this?" she wailed.

"All I want is for you and Inez to be safe. The convent, the Palisade, it's not safe for Inez. When I'm gone, I don't know if it will be safe for you." Lunurin wanted to go to Cat, to wrap her in her arms, but she didn't trust her strength to carry her.

"But Alon can keep us safe?" Cat's voice had a mocking edge.

"If I die tomorrow, he swore to me he'd keep you and Inez safe. Please let him try. He will ensure you are looked after."

Cat froze, her expression anguished. "You aren't going to die!"

Lunurin held out her arms, not caring if Cat cut out her heart. "Whatever comes with the dawn, would you let me hold you tonight?"

Cat's lower lip wobbled, her hard edges softening. With a watery sigh, she crawled onto Lunurin's pallet, draping herself across Lunurin's chest. Cat's kisses were hot and salty, with teeth and a fierce hunger that always surprised Lunurin. Catalina was not a woman who allowed herself to be seen to hunger. But when she let herself love Lunurin, she was ravenous.

Lunurin had always wanted to tell her, *There's no need to rush, I'm not going anywhere. I will always be here to give you all the love you need, whatever you'll accept.*

She didn't say these things tonight. Cat loved like a binge eater, fiercely, until she was half-sick, then abstained until she was half-starved. Her love and faith entangled her, forcing her to extremes. Tonight, Lunurin found the soft warm curves Cat hid under the flowing white of her habit. She bit back every hiss and grunt of discomfort as Catalina tried to devour her, a memory, a sacrifice, one final time to lie together in sin. The freshly knit edges of Lunurin's skin, where metal bars had gouged her flesh, gave. She bled sluggishly onto the pallet, but at last, Cat lay over her, drenched with sweat, panting, and smiling as she only did when she'd finally sated her appetite.

Lunurin drew her fingers from between Cat's thighs, and cradled her face. She admired the bloody nail marks Catalina had clawed between her knuckles and kissed her smiling mouth.

Blinking languidly, Cat returned her kiss, and reached between Lunurin's legs. Lunurin lay back, closed her eyes, and let herself tip very gradually into bliss. Lunurin had to be careful with love. The first time Catalina had kissed her, when they were sixteen, a sudden gust of wind had torn the shutters from their window.

She'd learned better since then. But without her mutya she felt unbalanced, the storm dragging dimly at her. She wasn't in control. She didn't know if the goddess could use her bliss the way she harnessed her rage. Tonight wasn't the night to find out, and tomorrow was unknown.

When the edge had been taken off Lunurin's need, Cat tried to rise from the pallet, but Lunurin rolled, tucking Cat into the curve of her body, preventing her from pulling away to sleep alone.

"Stay with me tonight, just this once. Even if they discover us, what can anyone possibly say? What worse can they do?"

Cat subsided. Lunurin covered her face in kisses.

"If I survive tomorrow, will you think about it? For Inez, at least. Do you think she will ever be able to find peace here after what happened to her?"

Cat chewed her lip, her eyes avoiding Lunurin's. "I'll think about it."

From Cat, this might as well be a blessing. And for one brief moment, Lunurin didn't care if she died tomorrow. Cat hadn't given up on her, on them, and that was all that mattered.

18

ALON DAKILA

That evening, Alon, Isko, and Litao climbed the steps to the Lakan's palace. Rain drummed a steady beat, marking the time slipping away from him.

"This is a terrible idea," Isko reiterated, as they ascended, water sluicing over their feet and off palm rain capes. "It's not too late to find a different groom."

"Are you volunteering?"

"No. She's a walking disaster."

"She's a woman, not an omen. And this was your idea. Now all we need is the Lakan's blessing." Alon steadied his salakót hat against a gust of wind.

"I don't know how you can still say that so confidently," Isko groused. "I'm capable of many things, but this may be beyond me."

"I hope she's still alive in the morning, otherwise it won't matter," Litao added.

As a married man Litao was out of the running, but the frank assessment mirrored Alon's own fears. "That's not going to happen."

The speed with which they were shown to the Lakan told Alon his father's spies were well informed.

Alon's father presided over the feasting hall, entertaining dozens of his favored nobles and warriors.

He made an expansive gesture to his guests as he rose from the low throne. It was polished teak inlayed with dizzyingly complex patterns in mother-of-pearl. Alon's earliest memories were of sitting in his mother's lap, tracing those patterns with short fingers.

"You will forgive me. It appears I have family matters to attend to. Please, enjoy your meal," the Lakan said.

Alon bowed, lifting his father's hand to his brow in a traditional mano po. "Magandang gabi po."

"God bless you." His father made the sign of the cross over his head. Then, he gestured, palm down, curling his fingers toward himself. "My son, come."

Alon obediently followed his father across the second story, into the small chapel installed when the Lakan had officially converted.

"Must we be seen to ask God's forgiveness for my sins?" Alon asked.

"I'm not the one who decided to fuck a nun."

"I didn't—" Alon's teeth clicked as Isko's hand closed hard on his elbow in warning. If anyone else had said such a thing about Lunurin... Alon let his anger drain away. He couldn't let his father rile him. He needed to explain the situation in words his father would understand.

"How tongues wag, my son. When you fought for her on the steps, the story was out. Half of Aynila swears you're in love with her. But surely, I said, my own son is not so foolish."

"Father, I need your blessing to marry her."

"Why should I bless the height of folly? There is no joy in

marriage to a woman who cannot abandon the old ways and adapt to the new reality. Fools like her tear at the fabric of Aynila's peace, inciting divisions that leave us vulnerable to Codicían greed. Isko, you cannot tell me you counseled my son to pursue this."

Isko bowed. "Lakan, the situation may yet be turned to our advantage. She is half Codicían. Her father is being ordained Archbishop of Lusong as we speak. Surely such a connection is in our favor. She is living proof of the new reality."

The Lakan frowned and dismissed Isko. He pulled Alon to stand before the altar. A crucifix gleaming in gold gilt hung there. The anguish depicted on Christ's face was too real. It was anguish like the kind found in the abbot's starvation cages, in men and women who'd died under Alon's hands, helpless to fix all that was broken in them.

"She is a rebellion waiting to happen, like your mother. Have you learned nothing from the suffering of your elders?" His father idly thumbed the gold tambourine rosary he wore. "This will end in tragedy."

Alon eyed his father's hard expression and abandoned all the pretty lies and logical reasons he'd lined up to explain the advantages of the match.

"Yes it will," Alon agreed.

His father had already drawn breath to point out the follies of this marriage. Alon's agreement stymied him. Alon didn't allow him to regain momentum.

"If we do nothing, she will destroy the fragile peace you so painstakingly maintain in Aynila. She is dangerous, a stormcaller with more power than I have seen in the whole of the Stormfleet. If she dies on Aynilan soil, bitterly cursing the Codicíans with her dying breaths, her goddess will not bring rain to Lusong for a generation."

GABRIELLA BUBA

"And you would invite such a sorceress into your home? Into your bed?" The sneering condescension was gone from his father's tone.

"If it means the Codicíans will hand her over and think themselves lucky to be rid of her, then yes. I can control her. If nothing else, let me be useful to you in this way. I can ensure she never again turns her power against Aynila, or you. I'm not a lovesick fool like they say. She is a danger. One we cannot allow to remain in Codicían hands." It was getting easier to say the right words, and seem to mean them. Perhaps he did mean them. Wasn't that a frightening thought? They certainly didn't stick in his throat the way his words had on the palace steps.

The Lakan lifted his rosary, sketching the sign of the cross. "What makes you think you can control her?"

"I brought her to heel on the steps, with all the rage of her goddess coiled to strike. But it will never come to that. She trusts me, and considers me an ally. She will be made to see the reason behind our cooperation with the Palisade."

"I fear you overestimate anyone's ability to reason with women like her. But at least you are entering the endeavor with eyes wide open. That's more of an advantage than I had at your age."

The silence stretched. The candlelight danced over his father's stern features.

"Father, I need your blessing to marry."

His father sighed. "Must I sacrifice a second son to a fanatic?"

Alon didn't respond, unsure if his father referred to his mother or his sister-in-law. Luckily the question had been posed to the golden figure upon the cross, not Alon.

"You have my blessing to marry. I pray it will not bring you the heartache it brought me."

Relief broke over Alon like a cresting wave. He bowed and pressed his father's hand to his brow. "Salamat po, Ama."

From the steps of the Lakan's palace, Alon sent two messages to the Palisade, informing the governor and the abbot he had the Lakan's blessing, and he planned to wed Lunurin at noon.

19

MARÍA LUNURIN

On the morning of her wedding, Lunurin kissed her sleeping lover and carried her to her own pallet. Her body protested, stiff and aching, but Alon's healing had been at work while she slept.

It still rained, in melancholy fits and starts, as if the sky were making up for being late for the wet season by three days. Lunurin's hands flew to her hair. Strands that had hardly reached past her ears now brushed her shoulders. She secured her hair into two tufts, hoping the Saliwain wouldn't flood its banks. Her distant mutya nagged at her with a phantom ache. This did not feel like a reprieve. It felt dangerous, a strange and untenable limbo. Had she been wrong to refuse her mutya?

Lunurin brought the pitcher in off the window ledge, and cleaned her hands and face. She wanted a bath, but refused to be caught unready this morning.

There came a soft knock. Lunurin pinned a blue veil over her hair, before cracking the door. The governor's soldiers wouldn't have bothered knocking. They'd have simply dragged her out of bed.

It was Rosa. "Sister María, this came for you."

She handed Lunurin a package wrapped in banana leaf to shield it from the rain.

Lunurin thanked her.

"Is it true you are marrying the Lakan's son today? They read the banns at Mass, but you weren't there."

Lunurin traced a fingertip over the note etched into the intricately folded banana leaf wrapping. Alon had written in looping baybayin script, the letters bruised dark against the silvery-green underside of the leaves.

> *My father has given his blessing.*
> *We wed at noon, if*
> *You don't mind walking on*
> *In spite of the unceasing rain.*

He was writing her love poems, old Aynilan tanaga poetry. Did he think she would not know the second couplet?

So why be so concerned that your heart
Is exposed as it heads for home.

Or was it that he hoped she did?

It wasn't how she had imagined her proposal, her lips tender from her lover's desperate kisses, her bed still warm where their bodies had been entangled. Alon, with his heart on his sleeve, deserved better than a wife like her.

"It would appear I am."

"Good. Though we'll be sad to see you go, I'd rather you marry than…" Rosa fiddled with her rosary, turning the wave-etched cowrie over and over.

Lunurin hesitated. In leaving the convent, she left the staff exposed to Sister Philippa and the abbot's whims. "You're sure I can't find you other work?"

"My brother is conscripted to the governor's house for another year. Cook will look out for us."

"You can always write to me if that changes."

"I'll remember," Rosa promised.

Lunurin ducked back into her room. She refilled and lit the lamp. In the warm yellow glow, Lunurin opened the package on the bed. Broad green leaves unfolded to reveal cloth dyed indigo and turquoise, the color of spark-striker birds, Amihan's birds of omen, lucky colors.

It was a baro't saya, in a jusi cloth polished to a silk-like sheen. The blouse was sheer piña cloth with long bell-like sleeves. The tapis overskirt was turquoise silk with an embroidered pattern of billowing clouds that shimmered in the lamplight. The shawl was such a saturated indigo it looked black, shot through with gold embroidery like lightning.

Lunurin didn't want to touch the silk, afraid the sweat from her hands would sully it. This was a lavish present, the kind of courtship gift to bestow on a Datu's daughter as part of a long softening up that culminated in a hefty bride-price. As if Lunurin were something precious.

The church bells rang out seven o'clock. Catalina stirred with her usual protesting groans about there being too much light for this early in the morning—then bolted upright, panicked, until her gaze landed on Lunurin.

She saw the gift. "Oh."

"He got the Lakan's blessing."

"Oh."

"We marry at noon."

A shutter fell behind Cat's eyes.

"Would you help me with my hair?" Lunurin begged, afraid Cat might simply leave.

Cat's expression softened. "Well, you can't marry with it like that." She pointed between her knees. "Sit."

Obediently, Lunurin sat at her feet. Her eyes fluttered closed. She reveled in Catalina's fingers carding through her hair, lifting the short strands this way and that.

Catalina gathered all the hair ribbons in the room.

She stared at her selection. "Hmm... we need more."

When Catalina returned, she brought Rosa and several others, turning Lunurin's wedding morning into a communal event.

There were ribbons in every color, orchids from the windowsill, vials of perfume oil, pots of rouge, and rice powder to lighten her complexion. Catalina ran sesame oil through Lunurin's hair and, using ribbons as hair extensions, coaxed Lunurin's short strands into a braided crown. "There, now you can dress."

When Lunurin was halfway dressed, Inez knocked, needing help with the younger girls.

"Go, go. I'll manage the last," Lunurin assured Catalina and the others, wanting a moment to collect herself.

Catalina lingered. On tiptoe she adjusted the orchids in Lunurin's hair. Lunurin traced the wrinkle of concentration between Cat's brows with a fingertip. It deepened. Their goodbyes had all been said last night. What promises were there left to make?

Lunurin didn't know, but she had to try. She couldn't lose Cat like this, not after everything. "Please, Cat, I swear—"

Catching Lunurin by the jaw, Cat pulled her down for one hard kiss. There was so much tangled inside them both. Lunurin recognized so much of her own anger in the hot press of Cat's mouth, but before Lunurin could coax it away for a more tender parting, Cat pulled back.

Her fingers dug into Lunurin's jaw bruising tight. "No more lies. No promises you can't keep."

Lunurin caught Cat in her arms and for once, she did not give way when Cat tried to break free. "I will find a way for us to be together. I promise you, Cat. I swear it."

Cat's breath caught in a sob, her voice strangled by her own bitter grief. "Oh, Lunurin..."

"Don't give up on us. Not yet."

Cat gave Lunurin one last kiss, then pulling back, she whispered, "I have to go. Inez needs me."

Lunurin let Cat pull from her arms at last, watching her vanish out the door.

20

ALON DAKILA

Alon had no idea how Isko had done it. His brother was an administrative terror. Even the Codicíans weren't immune to his skills. As Alon crossed the church courtyard, the belltower rang out. He was getting married in an hour, if he could find the bride. He needed to return her mutya to her.

All morning, servants had herded him away with various iterations of: "She's not ready yet!"

He was wrestling with going to knock on her door anyway when Catalina caught him loitering.

Alon understood why Catalina disliked him so intensely. But he was tiring of being a sandbag for her wildly vacillating emotions. He was doing everything in his power to help. He deserved a bit of slack.

He shot one panicked look at Litao, who shrugged helplessly and walked out to smoke, as Catalina dragged Alon into one of the storage areas.

"Is something wrong?" Alon asked.

Judging by Catalina's withering expression, she'd like to skewer his liver and feed it to the tilapia ponds.

"Catalina, what do you want from me? If you have any better ideas, I'm listening."

"Lunurin says you'll take my sister and I out of the convent if we wish it."

Alon blinked, rather blindsided by this. "Of course. I told you this days ago, but you refused."

"You mean it? Still? You'd take us in?"

And damn it, Alon hesitated. Alon was willing to sacrifice many things for Aynila's safety and peace, but taking Catalina into his home would be like lifting a blade to his own throat.

A bitter laugh leaped to Catalina's lips. "I knew you couldn't be that much a fool."

"If you and your sister want out of the convent, I'll help. Inez is owed that much and more. I'll see that you have a place and employment, and needn't fear the Church's reprisal."

"So I should give up Inez's chance to be educated, free of the expectation to marry and bear a dozen children, to be a servant or worse in Aynila? I think not."

"I can secure you better than servants' work. Whatever it is you wish to do, whatever trade Inez would take up, I'll see she is properly apprenticed."

Cat snorted derisively. "You think you're so much better than me, but charity for orphaned girls won't absolve you of coveting someone else's wife."

Alon flinched.

Cat bared her teeth at him in triumph. "She will never love you. Not when she could have me."

The words reached into his chest and punched holes in his lungs.

Alon forced his expression blank, refusing to give her further satisfaction. "I know."

"So why? Why do you care what happens to me and my sister at all?"

"What kind of monster do you think I am?" Alon asked. He and Catalina had spent a decade orbiting Lunurin like she was the sun. Even if they didn't like each other, they knew each other. "I care, because she cares. You are her family. Even if Lunurin didn't love you, I would still help. I'm the Lakan's son. If a wrong is done, and I know of it, I cannot do nothing. What happened to your sister was wrong. She is owed restitution. Let me help you leave this place."

The fight visibly drained out of her. "Neither of you understand. I can't leave. This is where I'm meant to be."

Alon lifted his hands in surrender. "I respect that, but if Inez wants something else for herself..."

Cat shook her head and turned to go, leaving him alone with his misgivings and guilt.

A crash from above sifted dust through the ceiling, followed by a scream. Alon ran for the stairs.

21

MARÍA LUNURIN

Lunurin secured the sliding window so it wouldn't clatter. A heavy tread sounded on the interior stair. A chill crept down her spine. The knock was loud. Lunurin went to answer, glad Catalina and the others weren't here.

The Codicían soldier outside was unfamiliar. He was unremarkable in every way, ruddy, tanned skin, dark hair and muddy hazel eyes, his peaked helm tucked under his arm. "Sister María?"

"Yes?"

"Lord Alon sent me to fetch you."

Prickles of unease raised the hair on her arms. Why hadn't he sent Litao or Isko? Had Alon ever in his life called her Sister María? "Fetch me where?"

"There is a boat, leaving with the tide for Tianchao. He knows you've no wish for this match. He's paid me to see you safely aboard before the ceremony."

At the word paid, the man tapped a gold signet ring on his index finger. Lunurin knew that ring. It was Alon's mother's signet. He wore it on the little finger of his left hand. She hadn't thought he'd part with it for anything.

But perhaps, to see her safely away, to ensure she could wreak no more vengeance upon his city, he'd been willing to use what he had to hand. The man produced another letter with Aynila's seal in indigo ink.

It was written in Codicían.

> María Lunurin,
> I hope you take this offer freely given for you to escape the bind in which we find ourselves. My man, a spy for the Lakan, will see you safely aboard a ship bound for Tianchao. If you remain here, it will be nothing but misery for both of us, for if we marry in the Codicían Church, we won't even have the option of divorce.
> Lord Alon

"I—"

"We must hurry, Sister, the ship leaves with the tide in the hour."

Which was also wrong. It was high tide now. All but the largest galleons could freely come in and out of the harbor for hours, and there were no galleons save the *Santa Clarita*.

Lunurin shook her head. "No. I won't be going with you."

The man's brow furrowed. "You can't mean to stay? Lord Alon was sure you'd wish nothing more than to leave."

"No. I can't run away." Not alone, certainly. Aynila she might convince Cat of, given time. Tianchao? Never.

She took a step back, but he followed, wedging his foot in the door to prevent her closing him out.

"I knew this was going to get messy," he muttered.

Then he threw his shoulder into the door, bursting in. The door crashed into the wall.

Lunurin shrieked as he lunged for her. She ducked away, but he managed to keep himself between her and the door, kicking it closed.

"Shut up, shut up! Goddamn, one gold ring for a runaway bride they said. It's never that easy."

He had his arms out, readying to lunge. "There is a ship, Sister. I just have no idea where it's headed. With the Lusitan, it could be anywhere, but no one else was willing to do a runner from under the governor's nose."

Lunurin's heart was a cold, hard thing. She'd envisioned a hundred ways this morning would end in tragedy, but Alon arranging for her to be kidnapped by Lusitan slavers hadn't been one of them. Catalina was right. No man, not even the Lakan's son, was a saint.

But could she blame him? One day soon she would get truly angry, and nothing would hold back Anitun Tabu's rage.

She couldn't dodge the spy's next wild grab. They crashed into the wall beside the window, the ribbed bamboo panels grinding into her shoulder blades. Pain exploded through her tender ribs. Was it raining too hard for anyone to hear their struggle?

"Gag, bag, boat. This would've been much easier with another set of hands," he muttered as he pinned her flat, his grimy fingers pressing gamely at her mouth, trying to pry her teeth apart.

Lunurin clenched her jaw, bracing her back, trying to get the leverage to heave him off. Her muscles screamed, but she ignored the warning.

He'd wiggled two fingers between her teeth and was cramming a wad of rags into her mouth when the door swung open.

Alon stood in the doorway. Rage burned through Lunurin's self-restraint like dried banana leaf. She bit down hard on the foul appendages prodding her tongue.

Blood gushed, hot and red, running down her face. The spy screamed, just once, as Lunurin reversed their positions. Except there was no wall to the right of her head. There was the window and a two-story drop. Lunurin had helped countless people climb out of her window without awakening Catalina. It was appallingly simple to aid one more. Though the scream as he fell would've woken even Cat.

"Lunurin?! Are you alright?" Alon exclaimed.

Lunurin spat two fingers into the palm of her hand. Alon's gold signet gleamed around the base of one.

Alon strode to the window, peering after her assailant. She fleetingly debated shoving him out as well.

Alon leaned back inside. "He's gone. What happened?"

Lunurin looked from Alon's baffled, horrified expression to the severed fingers in her hand. She started to laugh, more blood spilling down her chin.

22

ALON DAKILA

Lunurin made a terrible rasping gasp, no words. Yet she smiled as blood bubbled past her lips.

Alon stared at the blood spilling down Lunurin's chin, heart in his throat. Had they cut out her tongue? She looked so like his mother had he couldn't breathe.

He reached for her, desperate to stop the bleeding, but Lunurin intercepted his hand. She torqued his wrist, driving him to his knees.

Lunurin shoved her bloody hand in his face. "In Isko's calculations, was 'runaway bride' less riot-inducing than 'martyred by the Codicians'?"

Alon struggled to focus through his panic. She could talk; maybe she'd only bitten her tongue? Were those severed fingers under his nose? Important questions, along with—would she break his wrist?

"Lunurin, you're bleeding. Please…"

"I trusted you." She wrenched his wrist further. Pain shot through his shoulder. She smiled pleasantly, her red-tinted teeth very sharp.

"Lunurin, what happened? What do you think I've done?"

She released him. Alon folded, cradling his arm. She dropped the fingers in front of him.

"Does this ring look familiar?" she asked. "One of your father's spies came to tell me you'd purchased safe passage for me to Tianchao. But we both know that no sane captain would make that crossing in this weather."

Slowly, not believing his eyes, Alon twisted his mother's ring off the severed finger. On the face of the seal, a tooth impression marred the soft gold. He absently wiped away blood, saliva, and—was that a fleck of bone? Aman Sinaya have mercy. Three days ago he'd given this ring to pay Lunurin's fine.

"I can explain. My father—"

"Thinks I'm a failed rebellion waiting to happen? He's right. Tell me why I shouldn't end it all right now." Her mutya were hot against his skin and thunder boomed, loud as the *Santa Clarita*'s long-guns, and the drizzle outside thickened so the building across the street was lost in a grey haze. She was so close, her power filling the room.

Fear licked cold as melting hail down his spine. "Lunurin, please. Don't do this. You don't want this. Think of Catalina and Inez. Think of how many more of our people you will kill."

"Our people..." The fury of a thousand typhoons shone in her dark eyes. "Alon, have you been selling *our people* to Lusitan slavers?"

Alon reeled. "What?"

His father's hand was all over this, once again trying to make his sons' foolish mistakes disappear, with or without their cooperation.

"The ones I slipped out of the Palisade and sent trustingly into your hands. The ones I promised a better life. Did you put them aboard Lusitan ships? Your spy said no one else would risk the governor's displeasure. Is Aynila safer from the Codicíans if there are no firetenders either? Where are Biti Prinsa and her sister?" Lunurin's voice was so cold.

"They're safe, with my mother and in my home. Lunurin, how could you... No, I would never. I would never lie to you like that; I would never do that to our people. Why would you think that?" Alon's hand ached. The air crawled with static charge.

It grew stronger as she reached for him, her burning palms cradling his face. Alon prayed his bent knees would be read as supplication. He squeezed his mother's ring so hard it cut into his palm.

Anitun Tabu spoke through Lunurin. "*Son of the Sea, shame, censure, even reason means nothing to those responsible for the crimes against my people. You cannot negotiate with those who wish only to feast on your corpse. There will be more men and women, children and land, taken between the black teeth of their Palisade until they have swallowed all of Aynila to feed their insatiable hunger and greed. Will you spend your great strength only to feed them more slowly?*"

Her words should have shredded a human throat. They were low as thunder, yet loud as a howling gale, with all the softness of rain falling on his upturned face. It was for this a katalonan trained her voice, all the ballads and prayers, it was for this.

Lunurin's skin crackled with a kiss of lightning, her goddess burning in her eyes, and Alon knew she would destroy them all. Caught up in the riotous storm of her, he almost hesitated too long.

Like grappling through mud, Alon closed his hands around her wrists, feeding cold and the crash of the sea into her blood until Anitun Tabu's grip slackened. Lunurin would have collapsed in a heap, but Alon pulled her into his arms, and she went boneless against the bulk of his chest. It was a gentler landing than the floor.

Her head lolled, as it had on the steps, when he'd torn her from the arms of her goddess. Alon cradled the back of her head with shaking hands. What had he done? It was never supposed to be like this. He never wanted to hurt her like this, not again.

He bent his head to hers, apologies tripping over themselves. "I'm sorry, Sea Lady have mercy, I'm sorry. Lunurin, can you hear me? Can you blink? Please say something."

She hardly seemed to breathe, eyes gazing glassily toward the ceiling. His heart strangled him.

A knock on the door interrupted Alon's panic, as Sina stuck her head into the room. "Isko's worrying about his missing bride and groom, and Litao refuses to come in and 'disturb' you, so please don't be indecent."

Alon dragged his attention from Lunurin to his cousin. "Sina, help."

Sina blinked, taking in the scene: the room in disarray, Alon on his knees, and his bloody bride. "Is she dead?"

"No, no, she… I… there was an assailant. She shoved him out the window. I tried to heal her and I think I overdid it. I think it's mostly not her blood. I panicked."

"Oh well, that's alright then. Maybe stop touching her. I don't think it's helping."

Sina vanished from the door, and reappeared with Isko in tow. She grabbed a pitcher and cloth from the washstand and knelt beside Alon, pulling Lunurin from his lap.

Alon was reluctant to let Lunurin go, but as soon as he stopped touching her, she stirred. Her breathing evened out, eyelids fluttering.

"Are those fingers?" Isko asked.

GABRIELLA BUBA

Alon grimaced at the appendages, which lay not far from his knee. Once Sina had Lunurin, he grabbed for a banana leaf wrapper and scooped up the severed fingers.

After an uncomfortable moment, he flung them out of the window after their owner. "They're not mine or Lunurin's."

"Well, isn't that a relief," Isko snapped. "She's got other people's severed fingers."

Sina damped a cloth, and blotted Lunurin's cheeks, wiping the blood running down her chin and throat. "Lunurin? Can you hear us?"

Isko eyed Alon. "You're not supposed to render your fiancée insensate right before your wedding."

Alon groaned. "I didn't mean to." But that was a lie. It was this or letting her goddess tear the Palisade apart around them. He needed to get her to his mother. It couldn't wait. "Can we postpone the ceremony?"

Sina sat Lunurin up. Despite not responding to their words or Sina's ministrations, Lunurin remained upright.

Sina wrinkled her nose. "I'd say yes, but if you've already had to fend off assassination attempts, the sooner you get her out of the Palisade, the better."

"My father was trying to have her kidnapped and sold to Lusitan slavers," Alon admitted, wincing at how horrible it sounded stated plainly.

"Won't we all have a lot to discuss at the wedding feast?" Sina sounded far too cheerful.

"If we make it that far," Isko added.

"I'm afraid something's wrong. This isn't a normal reaction. I need to get her to my mother."

Isko sucked his teeth. "You think it's that dire?"

Sina pulled Lunurin to her feet. She swayed gently but stayed standing. "It's certainly unnerving. Whatever you did,

210

you need to undo it. Soon. I'll bring your regrets to the Lakan and beg him to delay the wedding feast, due to your new wife's ill-health."

"That's all well and good, but how do you propose we get through the wedding?" Isko asked.

Alon shrugged helplessly.

Sina handed Alon the bloody rag. "Get her cleaned up. Isko, get Litao to stall. I'll find something to make her look less... strange."

Isko went obediently and Sina started digging through Lunurin's trunk at the foot of the bed.

Hesitantly, Alon wiped the blood from the creases of her knuckles and palms, scrubbing at the crimson staining the edges of her fingernails.

The rust and copper smell of blood gave way to rainwater, her sesame hair oil, and the sweet scent of bruised orchids. How had he failed her so spectacularly?

Alon tried to meet her vacant gaze. "Lunurin, if you can hear me, I swear I had no idea what my father intended. But I will marry you. Today. Before there are any more incidents. I will make sure you're never again desperate enough that calling a typhoon is the only option you have left."

Had the cadence of her breathing shifted? Had her eyes focused on his? He couldn't tell. He felt foolish suddenly, pouring his heart out to a woman he was about to marry against her will. Sina pointedly ignoring him wasn't helping.

Gently, he wiped away the smear of blood running down Lunurin's strong jaw, and the splatter Sina had missed across her cheek and nose, like fresh freckles. In the lamplight, her skin gleamed like polished copper. She had a few dark spots down the left side of her neck, and similar discoloration where the swell of her breasts peeked above her neckline.

It took him longer than it should have to realize the discolorations he was wiping were in fact small, round bruises sucked into the column of her neck and shoulder. Were those bite marks? Why were they bloody?

The tips of his ears were suddenly so hot his hair must be smoking. He stepped back. Catalina had wanted him to know beyond a shadow of a doubt. Alon looked full in the face of his folly.

"I'm so sorry." The terrible emptiness within her was so much worse than her rage crackling against his skin, condemning him.

Isko returned. "That's only going to buy us twenty minutes. The church is packed."

Alon dropped the cloth into the washbasin and snatched the dark indigo shawl from the bed. "Can we pin it to cover the bloodstains?"

"Better idea." Taking the shawl, Sina unfolded it, draping it over Lunurin's head as a long, dark veil that concealed her from head to waist.

"There, no one will know," she declared.

"She has to say her vows, doesn't she?" Isko pointed out.

Sina grimaced. "I don't know if I'm that good at throwing my voice. I could try pinching her."

"Don't hurt her!" Alon winced, and lowered his voice. "She's been through enough."

Sina raised her hands placatingly. "I won't, but we need more than standing and swaying out of her, hopefully within the next twenty minutes."

Alon cursed his own stupidity. He pulled out Lunurin's mutya. They sat in his hands, her beating heart that he'd stolen from the safety of her ribs. It was a risk, but she needed something to ground her.

"Lift her veil. I need to give them back."

Sina sucked in a sharp breath, staring at the lightning-shaped pearl in his hands. "You took her mutya *and* cut her hair?"

"I didn't want the Codicíans to destroy it!"

"If we get through this wedding and she decides to kill you, I may help her," Sina muttered. "No wonder Biti liked her so much."

Alon didn't like those odds. It wasn't like Lunurin needed help to kill him.

He looked to his brother for support, but Isko shook his head. "I think this is a terrible idea. I'm helping you do it anyway. If your new wife wants your head, that's between you."

Alon tuned out Isko's and Sina's grim predictions on the outcome of his marriage. Gently he pressed Lunurin's comb and hairstick into the elaborate, beribboned crown of her hair, trying not to crush the pink and maroon orchids.

Alon let his hands drop away from her hair. Lunurin released a long, slow breath, and stood straighter.

"Lunurin?" he asked gently. "Can you hear me?"

Had the lines of strain around her eyes eased?

"Blink twice if you can hear me?"

The dark fringe of her lashes fluttered closed, once, twice.

"Can you speak at all? Please, Lunurin, I need you to say your vows so I can get you to my mother and we'll fix this, I swear."

Silence. Slowly, Lunurin shook her head.

"No, you can't speak?" Or no, she wouldn't marry him?

Her response tangled up behind her teeth in a wordless murmur.

Sina clapped her hands. "That's progress!"

"If that's progress, we're doomed," Isko lamented.

Sina swatted him. "You have to be encouraging. Can't you see how hard she's trying?"

Isko shrugged Sina off, but his forbidding expression softened.

Another knock sounded, and Alon hastily pulled the veil over Lunurin's face. The vacancy of her expression was frightening.

Litao called in, "There are now objections to the wedding. Isko, you didn't say what to do about objections. If we don't start soon, I'm not sure the abbot will marry them."

Sina met his gaze. "Do we try?"

"What happens if we get to the altar and she doesn't say anything? What if she says no?" Alon asked.

"How likely is the latter?" Sina asked.

He hesitated.

"Not a good sign, hesitating," said Isko.

"I know that," Alon growled.

"No need to snap. If you get up there and she can't nod, then do whatever you did to make her faint. Hopefully, the governor lets you take her home to recover," Sina said, as if it was all that simple.

Alon grimaced. "This is going to go horribly."

Sina crossed to his side, straightening his cuffs so the slashes of blue through black on his sleeves hung straight. She tugged free the mangled folds of the scratchy piña fiber ruff buttoned at his throat.

"You can do this, Alon. We're helping. You can pull this off."

Sina freed his mutya where the rosary tangled on the gold filigree buttons studding his chest. Isko held out his batangas sword. Alon accepted the hooked bronze pommel and secured it at his waist so the wooden sheath's inlaid pattern of schooling fish in coral and rosewood was visible.

"You look like a proper bride and groom, at least," Isko said.

"Take her hand and see if she'll follow. I'll go make sure no one's in the hall. Remember, there's the stairs," Sina said.

Alon and Isko were trying to coax Lunurin down the stairs when Inez appeared. She skewered Alon, crouched in the stairwell tugging on Lunurin's ankle, with a look. There was no mistaking that she was related to Catalina.

"Is something wrong?" Inez asked in a prim voice they must train into nuns early.

Alon bolted upright and tried to smile reassuringly. "No... not at all. Um. Lunurin cut her leg in the cage. She's finding the stairs difficult, but doesn't want to be carried."

It might even be true, Alon hadn't been able to check on any of her other injuries. This morning had to count as unwise strenuous activity.

"That's silly, Lunurin, you always tell me I should let people help when I'm hurting," Inez pointed out.

Alon stared panicked at Isko, hoping he'd convince Lunurin to nod, when muffled through the veil Lunurin said, "Mmm... Yes."

Possibly. Or maybe it was only a hissing exhale.

The arm Isko wasn't bracing lifted, fingertips fluttering in Inez's direction, before falling to her side.

Inez bit her lip. "I wanted to talk to Lunurin, but"—she eyed Isko and Alon—"you're busy. It can wait till after the wedding."

Alon smiled at Inez. "Thank you. Lunurin isn't feeling well right now, but I'm going to take care of her."

He carefully lifted Lunurin into his arms, carrying her down the stairs. Isko went ahead to find Sina and make sure all was in order at the church.

Left to his own devices, Alon decided damn the witnesses. It was faster to carry her. Besides, they'd both be soaked through in the rain at the rate she was moving.

If anyone asked, she was still tired from her ordeal.

Her head fell against his shoulder, a muffled sound escaping her.

"Lunurin, are you coming out of it?"

"Don't let me," Lunurin rasped, her words hot against his neck. "She's... angry."

At the top of the church steps Alon set her on her feet. "Lunurin—"

"Please..." Her hands closed around his wrists with a painful shock. Threads of lightning danced along her veil, crisping blue threads to black.

"I'm hurting you! You stayed down so long..."

"Please."

The sky overhead darkened, lightning flashed, and thunder shook the stones under their feet.

Alon returned her grip, dragging her down into the salt flow of his magic. Her posture slumped like a sleepwalker, the proud angle of her head bowing under the press of his power. The brewing storm overhead settled with an uneasy grumble into steady, drenching rain. A shiver of disgust crawled over his skin. Whatever he was doing to her, it wasn't good. It couldn't be right. He should never have taken her mutya.

He pushed open the door to the church. Isko ushered them into a side alcove.

"Any other issues come up?" Alon asked.

"Yes, several. Be prepared for a whole parade of objections," Isko warned.

"What've they got?" Alon asked.

"The abbot's paid a woman to claim she's pregnant with your firstborn son."

Alon shrugged. "Sure, why not? Did you try offering her more money?"

"I did, but the abbot has either deeper pockets or stronger threats than I do. On that cheerful note, you need to get your bride up there." Isko pointed Alon to the altar.

Alon hoped, briefly, that the governor hadn't been serious about the abbot marrying them. But a glance toward the altar disabused him of the notion.

From the choir loft there came a swell of music.

"That's your cue," Isko said.

Just like that, Alon was making the long, slow journey to the altar. He'd never imagined it like this.

Alon kept his eyes stubbornly forward. Flickering votive candles stood on tiered rows before the mother-of-pearl-inlayed altar panels, illuminating the statue of Anitun Tabu in the alcove above with a warm glow. Lunurin's pace was slow, her limp noticeable. Alon couldn't bring himself to tug her forward at a faster pace, even when the processional ended and the flustered choirmaster urged them into a different piece. The guests whispered and stared.

At the back sat most of the convent's servants. Inez had found a seat with the other girls from the school. Half the Palisade was in attendance, including Governor López in his Mass best. Alon's Tiya Hiraya was present, Sina at her side. A watchful member of the Palisade guard sat directly behind the two. Alon hoped Sina wouldn't do or say anything rash. He was relieved not to see his father or Catalina.

Lunurin's halting pace slowed further.

The abbot's scowl deepened. Outside, the rain lashed staccato beats across the roof, the wind keening through the belltower.

The atmosphere in the church shifted, the congregation nervously eyeing the ceiling. Alon squeezed her hand, urging calm and stillness. He ignored the abbot's venomous green glare. Finally, they reached the altar. The abbot greeted the congregation. Alon tried not to notice how much of that congregation signed waves rather than crossing themselves, as the abbot made the sign of the cross over Lunurin and Alon. Then, all rose to sing the opening Gloria.

They rose and knelt and processed through the readings, songs, and homilies of the Mass under the direction of the glowering abbot, who grew yet more irate when an even greater portion of the laity "failed" in their imitation of his sign of the cross before the gospel reading.

"A full wedding Mass?" Alon murmured to Isko, who stood as best man.

"Oh yes. Let no one say you weren't properly wed," he responded, while the boys' choir filed down from the loft.

At long last, when even Alon was weary from feeding his power into Lunurin's hot blood, the congregation came once more to their feet.

"We have come together into the house of the Church and the eyes of God..."

Alon fixed his gaze on Lunurin's veiled profile, hoping desperately she was coherent enough to speak. Lightning cast multicolored glints through the stained glass, followed by a long, low rumble of thunder. Abbot Rodrigo began the celebration of the matrimony.

As Isko had promised, the objections went on so long it was almost laughable.

First there was the pregnant Aynilan woman. Then, a man who claimed Lunurin's father had given him his blessing to marry her. Then came an allegation that Lunurin's mother was a sister to Alon's, making them first cousins, who couldn't wed for reasons of blood.

Alon narrowed his eyes. "My mother, Lakan Dalisay

Inanialon, only had brothers. I have met my wife-to-be's mother, Datu Talim of Calilan, and can assure you she has no relation to my family. In fact, Lord Bagay, given the marrying practices of Aynila's principalia, I am more closely related to every one of your daughters through my father's great-uncle than I am the Lady Lunurin."

A scatter of nervous laughter broke out, and a crack of thunder split the sky.

Someone shrieked. The governor cleared his throat. "I begin to tire of these diversions."

The governor and the abbot shared a long, hard look. The ceremony continued. Alon's bad hand ached, and sweat glued his barong to his back. Everything could still go so horribly wrong.

"Have you come here freely and without reservation to give yourself to each other in marriage?" the abbot asked.

"Yes," Alon answered, shocked at how confident he sounded. Hopefully confident enough to cover whether or not his bride responded.

"Will you honor each other as man and wife for the rest of your lives?"

"Yes." Had Lunurin's veil stirred with her breath?

"Will you accept children lovingly from God and bring them up according to the law of Christ and his Church?"

Lunurin's lax fingers in his grip twitched.

"Yes."

Alon turned her to face him, silently, desperately urging her to find her voice.

"Do you, Alon Dakila, take María Lunurin to be your wife? Do you promise to be true to her in good times and in bad, in sickness and in health? Will you love and honor her all the days of your life?" Abbot Rodrigo intoned solemnly.

"I do," Alon said.

He gave her hands another squeeze. All eyes fell on Lunurin.

"Do you, María Lunurin, take Alon Dakila to be your husband? Do you promise to be true to him in good times and in bad, in sickness and in health? Will you love and honor him all the days of your life?" Abbot Rodrigo repeated.

The silence dragged on. Alon shifted nervously. Should he let go of her hands? Would that help?

"Lunurin?" he whispered.

"I do." Her voice was so small it was almost lost in the crash of thunder that followed, but the abbot was eager to move on.

"You may exchange rings."

Isko produced two plain gold bands. Alon took them, but the ring he placed on Lunurin's finger was his mother's signet. The eight-pointed sun of Aynila glinted, surrounded by a ring of waves. Alon ran his thumb over Lunurin's toothmark on the face.

Alon laid his ring into Lunurin's lax open palm, and then fit it onto his left hand.

It was done. Did a wedding where the bride wasn't fully conscious count? Alon turned them both to face the abbot.

The abbot, whose pale gaze simmered with venom, declared, "What God joins together, let no one put asunder."

Then, without a sound, Lunurin collapsed.

Alon barely caught her before she split her head open on the altar.

He would've carried Lunurin as directly to his mother as possible if Isko hadn't reminded him about the marriage documents. So here he was, half holding his new wife upright, with Isko and the governor as their witnesses.

He dipped the bamboo split nib and signed without bothering to read the contract. He was far more concerned with

Lunurin's signature. Would the abbot accept her new ring as a seal?

He held out the inking reed to Lunurin, whom he supported on one side and Isko the other. When she accepted it, Alon hoped his relief wasn't too obvious.

Lunurin said nothing, but bent forward and scratched through where the abbot had written María Dakila and signed her name as Lunurin Calilan de Dakila.

The abbot glowered at Alon. "You allow this?"

"My wife may do as she deems fit," Alon said, a phrase he was prepared to repeat at great frequency for the foreseeable future.

"Your wife cannot abandon the Christian name she was baptized into," the abbot sputtered.

"Our marriage represents a diplomatic tie to Calilan that we will not erase."

Finally the legal necessities were concluded, and Litao informed him the kalesa had arrived.

Alon bowed to the governor. "My thanks, Governor, for your forbearance today, but now I must take my wife home to rest. She is unwell. We'll be postponing our wedding feast until her strength is returned."

"Surely you'll wait out the rain?" The governor squinted into the downpour.

"It's the wet season, Governor. A man could go grey waiting out the rain." Alon bent and hefted Lunurin into his arms.

A drenched Litao stood by holding aside the woven rain cape of the kalesa.

Alon lifted her into the bright orange vehicle. He pillowed her head in his lap. Litao would see to the horses. Isko and Sina had promised to carry his regrets to the Lakan. At least the storm would mean that he would be able to slip away to his mother easily. He checked Lunurin's sluggish pulse and gave her hand a squeeze.

23

LUNURIN CALILAN
DE DAKILA

The world came through in murky flashes. She was a drowner, gasping greedily for lungfuls of air. Lightning and salt warred in her blood. Alon's plea tangled around the divine rage that throbbed in her like a bloody wound.

Lunurin, please.

Cat and Inez.

Think of our people!

She held desperately on to these human things, but her very blood was electric, her mutya returned to her and the goddess railed, *"We have been wronged! Betrayed! And we will not swallow down our suffering, not when we are the storm."*

We will. We will. We will, Lunurin promised herself. If she could endure the crushing cold and pressure of drowning a little longer, surely someone would help her regain control. She needed something to root herself in, to dampen her magic to a trickle and not a torrent carrying her away on the will of her wronged goddess.

When at last Alon hauled her up from the depths, she was almost unsurprised to find herself floating in a tub of saltwater in his mother's home.

Kawit and Dayang Dalisay bent over a workbench nearby.

"Lunurin?" Alon hovered, trying to capture her gaze but she didn't want to see the fear in his eyes.

She didn't know if it would be of her or for her. She would deserve it, she knew that, but no man would suffer to live in fear of his own wife. And… she was his wife. At least, she thought so. Even if Alon's mother could help hide her from her goddess's eye, Alon would never forget what she was, and he'd never forgive it. No man was a saint.

"I'm afraid to ask." Lunurin cleared her throat. "Did I hurt anyone?"

"Only my father's spy, no one else. No one you didn't mean to hurt," Alon amended.

The fury lapping at her soul ebbed and flowed with the slosh of saltwater against her skin. "I'm cold."

"You were sparking lightning. We had to get you into saltwater to dissipate it before you caused a strike."

Lunurin could hear her storm raging overhead.

"Inay, she's waking," Alon called out.

Dalisay spun around and signed, "Finally. I thought you'd killed her. It's a wonder you haven't drowned her already. A spirit of wind and sky isn't meant to be dragged into the salt when there is no physical wound to repair."

Alon winced. This must be a continuation of an ongoing browbeating.

"I brought her as soon as I could… it got complicated."

"Forgive us, Dayang, we didn't know what else to do. Without my dugong bone amulet, I can't control myself," Lunurin added.

Dalisay threw up her hands, turning to Kawit signing, "Complicated they tell me! As if that is an explanation. My son appears with a drowning stormcaller, and married! And says it's complicated."

Kawit smiled wryly. "It's the exuberance of youth, Dayang. Give them a few years, when escapades start to ache in one's bones."

"They won't make it that long at the rate they're going," Dalisay declared.

Kawit proffered a gleaming pink salt crystal the size of his thumb. "This might help."

Dalisay weighed it in her palm. "Yes, the Bool salt didn't feel right. This is much better."

Kneeling beside the tub, Dalisay slid the pendant around Lunurin's neck. She pressed her hand down over the salt crystal.

Lunurin was so cold it was difficult to recognize the rage still clawing for a foothold in her body, but the ache in her chest intensified, centering on the sharp crystal digging into her sternum. Alon laid his hand over his mother's. When Kawit added his weight, she gasped.

"Focus, Alon," Kawit instructed. "You must center your power in the liquid heart of the crystal, not her blood."

Alon's power gripping her limbs ebbed until it fully coalesced into the pendant. The relentless beat of the rain and the wind dragging greedy fingers over the roof died. Lunurin breathed out slowly, unable to fathom the stillness. She wasn't angry, not at all. There was no low rumbled whisper in her ear urging her to drown them! Drown them all!

The hands pressing Lunurin down lifted away. The large crystal tipped, sloshing slightly.

"How'd you get seawater into the center?" Lunurin asked.

"Very tricky." Kawit tapped the side of his nose. "It's oversaturated, so it won't damage the rest of the crystal. Then we sealed it in Aynila copal resin so it won't dissolve from the outside. Dugong bone would be more stable, but we cannot trust that any we might acquire now wouldn't have been hunted."

"Did it work?" Lunurin asked, half disbelieving the silence in her own head.

So quiet, and gods but she was thirsty.

"The storm you were brewing has swept out to sea," Dalisay signed.

Alon helped her sit up. Her sense of equilibrium briefly sloshed with the crystal as it dropped to the end of its cord. She leaned into him, waiting for it to pass and relishing how, even now, after everything he'd seen, he did not flinch from her.

"Can I have—" Lunurin was shocked by the rasp in her own voice.

Kawit handed her a cup of water. "It's Alon's power. Normally it draws upon the spiritual well in a healer's own body, as well as the saltwater for healing. But you have healing magic acting on your body without being in contact with a healer, so it draws on your own stores of saltwater. You have to be very careful. You could become dangerously dehydrated, like a healer working too many fever cases."

Lunurin drank greedily, desperate to soothe her thirst. It was as bad as when she'd been dying in the cage.

As soon as she stopped, the momentary relief vanished.

Lunurin closed her eyes and swallowed hard, feeling the stick and scrape of the motion. There would be costs. Weren't there always?

"Lunurin? Are you alright?" Alon asked.

"Yes, please help me up. I'm cold."

Alon lifted her out of the tub. This time, Lunurin noticed how his touch eased the dry ache in her throat. She hadn't left behind every vestige of her power. She was still wrapped in it, drowning in it. She yearned toward him.

Resentment stirred in her. Even now, she couldn't trust her own feelings. She stepped away from Alon. Her tongue stuck to the insides of her teeth.

"Can I drink enough to quench it, or would that be a bad idea?"

Dalisay pinched the skin on the back of her hand. "Keep drinking. Alon and Kawit will monitor so you don't make yourself sick."

"And this will work? Or can I overwhelm it like I did the dugong bone charm?"

"Who can say? Most of the gods-blessed aren't strong enough to withstand unmediated communion with the gods. We go mad. There is a reason we trained katalonan, and even they had rituals and herbs they imbibed to protect themselves. I think your dugong bone hid you from notice. It dimmed your presence, dampening your magic. This one will only help to keep your spirit your own, so that your goddess cannot pull so strongly on you. Salt is a purifier, and with Alon's power it should help you remain in control. But nothing of human-make can hold off the divine forever. Not after the promise you made. I can feel it burning within you, as my vows to safeguard my people as their Lakan burn in me," Dalisay signed.

Lunurin's heart throbbed, as if her words were stitched in lightning across the vital organ. *My heart is yours, Anitun Tabu, I promise it all if you will grant me their blood.*

Lunurin clutched at the amulet. It seemed now such a paltry thing. "What have I done?"

Dalisay's expression was sympathetic. "No more than I did when I called the tsunami. No worse than what many of my tide-touched have done to prevent the Codicíans building their bridge to Hilaga. Once it is complete, we will have to take some of the firetenders with us into Hilaga's hidden valleys. But you aren't doomed to this life of hiding, as we are. You have other choices, and I don't begrudge you for rejecting the terrible burden your goddess would put on your shoulders."

Overwhelmed with gratitude and relief, Lunurin bent, offering her mother-in-law a proper mano po. "Dayang, salamat po. I've been so afraid I would destroy everything and everyone I love."

Dalisay greeted Lunurin as family, drawing her close to sniff both her cheeks.

"I am glad. I hope this amulet grants you peace for many years. You are now my beloved daughter, and I wouldn't want to see you torn apart by magic and divine fury."

Lunurin turned at last to meet Alon's searching gaze. "So, we did get married? I didn't dream that part? Even the woman pregnant with your son?"

Alon flushed. "We did. A claim was made to that effect, yes." He hesitated. "If you didn't want to be married, it's not too late to fake your death. You could stay here with my mother, like Biti."

Lunurin froze. Here it was, the escape she craved. She wouldn't have to fend off Codicían suspicion or the Lakan's spies. She needn't decipher Alon's incomprehensible gentleness, and whether she could trust her attraction toward him.

But it would mean abandoning Cat and Inez. Catalina would never consent to live in the jungle among water witches. She'd never raise Inez in hiding.

Alon was still stumbling through an apology. "Even if it was only your goddess's anger, I know you wouldn't have agreed if I hadn't... if we weren't forced. So, we needn't be married."

Lunurin studied his earnest expression. Did he love her enough to overlook all the reasons he should force her to remain in hiding? He'd have to be a fool or the bravest man alive to accept her as his wife after what he'd seen.

Her heart beat fast. Could he sense it? It was hard to lie to Alon with all his good intentions and loyalty held banner high.

He looked as exhausted as she felt. His outstretched hands signed, "Forgive me, forgive me, forgive me," in even cadence with his halting words.

Lunurin clasped his hands. His spirit washed over her like surf inspecting an unfamiliar shore. See, nothing to fear. He would not drown her again. With this amulet on her breast, he didn't need to. His power was coiled around her soul.

"There is nothing to forgive. I agreed to marry you. I shouldn't have allowed my fear and anger to make me doubt your intentions. Of course we are married, and I will return to Aynila with you." Lunurin squeezed his hands and hoped desperately he wouldn't tell her no.

It would be so expedient for him to abandon her. Alon was a busy man. He couldn't be expected to mind his wife's city-leveling furies forever.

Silence stretched, slow and acrid as burnt coconut caramel. Lunurin's mouth was so dry. Was it fear, or her new affliction?

"I know I can't be as useful to you as I was in the convent. But I'll find other ways. It's hard on you to heal alone. I'll learn how to use my lightning to help people. I can still help you."

And didn't Lunurin *hate* how desperate she sounded.

Don't abandon me, please, she wanted to beg. *Do you know how many times I've been cast away in the aftermath of Anitun Tabu's rage, and the terrible things I have done in her thrall?*

Had they been alone, she might have said these things. But she was aware of Alon's mother's heavy stare and Kawit's sharp attention.

Soon, they would remind Alon what a liability she was. That she was too dangerous to keep at his side. Surely Alon was only planning how to let her down gently.

Finally, Alon found his voice. "You *want* to return to Aynila with me?"

He sounded so surprised, but also happy. His hands unfolded, fingers threading through hers. His touch tingled, warm on her skin. But it was only relief. It was only the loosening of the vice of fear clamped around her chest. Right?

"Yes, of course. I wouldn't have agreed to marry you if I didn't think we could make this work." This lie was easier.

He was listening. Despite it all, he must still love her. What else explained the tender way his thumb stroked over the back of hers?

Alon smiled. "Then we are married." He untied his belt pouch and held it out. "Your bride-price. A woman should never become desperate in her husband's home."

Lunurin accepted. She didn't dare turn her head to see what his mother thought of this, the heft of the pouch frightened her enough.

Before the gentleness of Alon's warm gaze could gouge out her lying heart, Kawit crossed the hut, throwing open the door to announce, "It's settled. Gat Alon has a wife! Fetch the lambanog. We're celebrating!"

Lunurin stared. Most of the village was clustered on the porch and there was Biti in the crowd.

Alon groaned. "Do you have to bellow the announcement?"

Kawit grinned. "Grant an old tito his fun."

The tension and anxiety drawing the air tight gave way to

celebration. Alon drew Lunurin onto the porch as Pasamba opened a bottle of lambanog. A cup was poured and passed hand to hand till everyone had taken a swallow or two and granted the new couple a blessing. Biti tucked a huge gumamela bloom, deep crimson edged in gold, behind Lunurin's ear, and Kawit draped a garland of yellow ylang-ylang around Alon's shoulders. Even Dalisay smiled, as Kawit dragged the whole village into his impromptu wedding celebration.

"How did you meet? When did you know it was love?" Well-meaning questions abounded from a dozen listeners eager for the story.

Lunurin's throat was filled with powdered glass.

Alon squeezed her hand and refilled her cup with freshwater. Then, he proceeded to spin a tale of adolescent crushes, daring bravery, and the laho of Calilan. "We met the spring I went sailing on my brother Jeian's ship."

Lunurin remembered it, the dual-sailed guilalo cargo vessel that had slipped into Calilan's port just before the Codicían Inquisition had encountered the Stormfleet. Captained by the son of Aynila's Lakan, and guided by his bayok katalonan wife, Aizza, who'd lived as a man until she'd discovered she was tide-touched, it'd seemed the best way to send her safely beyond the Codicíans' clutches.

"Lunurin was fifteen, two years my senior and taller than any girl I'd ever met. When they tucked her in amongst the chests of spices and Calilan's silver pearls, I knew she must be just as special."

And damn him, he really seemed to mean it, lifting her fingers to his lips with a soft and tender air. She hated how he could tug on her heart as much as her magic.

"Of course, I had no idea how special until Aizza had swept us into the jaws of the worst storm I've yet seen. We were lucky to limp into port at Aynila, after the state the laho left the ship in."

Breaths were indrawn at the mention of the mooneater, or bakunawa, the vast sea serpents who stirred dangerous open-water storms. Lunurin drank till her stomach felt tight. Thirst and guilt still nagged at her.

"The laho was all dark water and copper fire, long enough to have encircled Hilaga's peak. No amount of bailing was going to save us once the laho had us in its sights." Alon shook his head, turning his gaze from his riveted audience to Lunurin. "But she did."

Lunurin's breath caught. Did he have to look at her so, his eyes dark and soft with tenderness?

"She was tall as the laho's mouth was wide, screaming her fury in its face as if it didn't have rows and rows of teeth curved like batangas swords. I was certain she was going to be snapped up, half the boat with her, and that we were all going to drown."

For the sake of their listeners Alon kept out her desperate vow.

But Lunurin remembered screaming it into the wind of the storm. *I will not even think your name!*

Here Kawit put in, "Got my limp thanks to that storm. Nothing Aizza or I could conjure would calm the laho-riled waves."

Alon continued, "Luckily, Lunurin is cleverer than I am by half. She sang up the ambon and when the full moon stared down, the laho forgot us."

Ridden by its eternal urge to swallow the moon, the laho had torn free of even Anitun Tabu's will.

"She was the last thing I saw before the laho's wake crashed down. When Lunurin hauled me up from the waves there it was, a sacred oyster, in my hand."

Kawit leaned into Alon's other side. "You should have seen Aizza's face when Alon told her that as much as he loved her, he didn't think he wanted to be a woman and katalonan. I've never laughed so hard. Thought I'd break a rib."

Alon smiled sheepishly. "After the initial shock, I was a bit distraught! All the tide-touched I knew were katalonan. Of course, Aizza—holding back her giggles only slightly more successfully than Kawit—explained that no, not every tide-touched was a woman. If I didn't feel so called, that was fine."

Gales of laughter met this conclusion to their harrowing meeting. Kawit and Alon received the bulk of ribbing and comments from the village of exiled women, on what a rare breed they were.

The storytelling, his tenderness, was all an act of course, for his mother and Kawit who doted on him, and the rest of their listening audience. It had to be.

Then Alon flexed his hand in its ornate golden brace, tracing the curve of her cheek. His eyes focused on her and her alone. "You made me who I am today. Do you know that?"

What was she supposed to say to that? The metal of his brace was cool on her cheek. His hand had never healed right, despite Aizza's and his mother's best efforts. Injuries gained diving for one's mutya were often like that. He should hate her for naming him to Aman Sinaya.

She'd only meant to sing apart the clouds to distract the laho with the moon, but her prayer was one katalonan sang when children dove for their mutya. How dare he take a moment of tragedy, her power spiraling out of control, and spin her as a clever heroine. How could he love her despite the ruin she'd swept into his life? Had his love so blinded him to what she truly was? At least Cat understood the danger Lunurin presented enough to protect herself.

24

LUNURIN CALILAN
DE DAKILA

Expecting a day to recover from her ordeal would be asking too much of the Lakan's forbearance. So, mere hours after returning to Aynila, Lunurin found herself at the center of a far less welcome wedding celebration.

The Lakan's wedding feast was tense and lurid, with whispers flowing freely as the tapuy rice wine. The room was overloud, with a heaviness the oppressive humidity didn't explain. They weren't in the mixed company one expected at a wedding feast. None of Alon's many tiyas were present, nor any of the older matriarchs of the Aynilan principalia. There were several young wives, but not one woman over thirty. It wasn't unusual for the Lakan to shun the counsel of the noble matriarchs of Aynila, but tonight their absence spoke volumes.

Lunurin hoped it was a simple social slight for the scandal she'd caused. But the night was young, and the Lakan had moved from tapuy to stronger palm spirits. As the boom of the Lakan's voice reverberated in the too-empty hall, Lunurin remembered the fear in his eyes on the palace steps.

Lunurin and Alon were on display, seated on a small, raised platform at the end of a long table opposite the Lakan. The seats of honor, before the feast's centerpiece—a lechon, whole roast suckling pig stuffed to the brim with crabs, shrimp, ginger, and lemongrass.

Conversation now turned from well-wishes and less well-meaning jibes about Lunurin eating for two, to current events.

A group of distant cousins to Lunurin's left were debating if the Codicíans' joint bridge project with the Lakan would be completed this month, as the governor claimed, and what profits they expected to make once the Puente de Hilaga was completed.

"That bridge has been a money sink for years. I don't think any amount of profit would justify it now. We'd all do better to cut our losses." With a start Lunurin recognized the speaker as the woman who'd spirited Biti out of the Palisade.

"Sina Prinsa, my cousin," Alon supplied quietly.

Sina was seated beside Alon's foster brother, Isko. Lunurin wasn't the only person suddenly interested in what she had to say.

"If these saboteurs weren't so fixated on it, the Codicíans would've abandoned the project years ago. Now they can't without losing face. It's like they think there's a city of gold on Hilaga, not a smoking smithy clinging to a shaky caldera. They've been trying to build it for twice as long as the Puente de Aynila took to construct," one man pointed out.

Alon quickly put in, "The Saliwain's channel runs deeper and wider before the river splits; these factors were known when the initial project was conceived. I have great faith that the contract the Lakan agreed upon will ensure that this joint venture will see benefit for all parties involved, despite the delays and difficulties we've encountered."

"When have the Codicíans ever fully honored a long-term contract before?" Sina asked archly. "How do we know they won't simply use this access to coerce more metalworkers into labor contracts for their shipyards?"

There were murmurs of discontent.

"Remember when the polo laborers' payment rate would surely incentivize everyone to work? How many times has the falla tax been raised? I know skilled carpenters, metalworkers, and artisans who couldn't provide the coinage to pay, and for their skilled labor were paid no more than a common day laborer," Sina said.

"Labor is another matter, rates fluctuate based on season, the type of labor involved, and the amount of public works underway," one of the original proponents of the Puente de Hilaga spoke up.

"And soon, when they have their final span built, and can block all trade down the Saliwain when the fancy takes them, how will that benefit Aynila? The Codicíans would prefer it if our riverfolk couldn't pay their tolls. They'd like the only work there is to be in their shipyards. Till all we do is build their ships faster, and bigger than the *Santa Clarita*. How will labor be valued then?" Sina shot back.

There was a ripple of quiet. Not only their end of the table was listening to Sina now; half the hall had lent an ear. Some even nodded agreement. At the far end of the table, the Lakan's eyes fastened on Sina. His gaze wasn't kind.

As much as Lunurin wanted to hear what Sina had to say, she was relieved when Isko steered the conversation toward who had been most inconvenienced by the prolonged dry season and the reverse flow of the Saliwain. It meant the Lakan's attention was no longer so baleful.

Lunurin ducked her attention back to her meal. She flushed

when Alon offered her choice pieces of cheek meat from his own grilled long-jawed mackerel, carefully deboning each morsel before setting them into the bowl of fresh steamed rice in front of her.

Did he have to be so doting?

"You need to eat as well as drink to regain your strength," he said gently.

It was just because she'd been injured. Nothing more. It meant nothing. Lunurin neatly pinched together bites of rice and fish in her right hand, eating with relish, the oily fish seeming to coat her throat and soothe the dry ache for longer than water.

But concern didn't explain the way his eyes lingered as she leaned forward to rinse her hand and wipe the rich grease from her fingers. And nothing explained the way she was blushing and smiling at his attention, like a real bride. She was almost glad when the meal was finished and the party split, men going off onto the porch to smoke and drink, while the few women remained indoors to drink tea and "prepare the bride for her wedding night."

Alon squeezed Lunurin's hand. "I need to have a word with my father. I will leave Litao with you."

"Yes, of course." Lunurin hesitated, keenly aware of the evening's tension, and the weight of the Lakan's anger. "I apologize if I've put you in an uncomfortable position with him."

Alon lifted her hand to his lips. "After this, we can go home and rest."

"I'd like that." Lunurin twisted the ring off her hand. "Here, you might need this."

Gravely, Alon accepted the gold signet.

It didn't escape Lunurin's notice that as soon as the Lakan exited the dining area, every other woman found somewhere to stand very far away from the two who had drawn the Lakan's ire.

Sina crossed to Lunurin, settling beside her as if they were the best of friends.

"Hello, cousin! We weren't properly introduced the morning of your wedding, but I'm pleased to see you so improved." Sina's boisterous greeting resulted in the trio of ladies across the room increasing the volume of their conversation, turning their backs on Sina and Lunurin as much as possible.

Sina grinned and leaned in conspiratorially. "They're not so bad. It's just that their husbands have told them associating with us will get them exiled from the capital."

"Are their husbands wrong?" Lunurin asked.

Sina rubbed at the shiny burn scar that bisected her right brow. "Probably not. They don't have the political connections you and I do, nor the independent clout to flout the Lakan's invitation altogether. I could've gotten away with not attending. The Lakan would have preferred that, but I didn't want to leave you to face his wrath alone." Sina smiled at Litao, who stood just out of earshot. "My cousin does his best, but he can't think of everything."

Lunurin huffed a laugh. "Don't tell me you got the Lakan riled up on my account."

Sina squeezed Lunurin's hands in her hot grip. "But he was glowering so fiercely at you, and I owed you help in a family matter. It's only fair."

Lunurin squeezed back. "I was glad to be able to help. I'd been concerned with Hilaga's restlessness."

"It would be better if my mother or I could be there ourselves, but things are cooling. Now tell me how you know so many of my and my cousin's secrets, yet I know so little of you." Sina's eyes gleamed, the oil lamps along the walls flaring.

"But you do know about me," Lunurin protested. "There are so few of us left."

There was no way the firetender wasn't intentionally flaring her spirit, not after how contained and invisible she had managed to appear in the Palisade. She couldn't *not* know.

"Not until after the steps. Before that, Alon had only told me you were a friend"—here Sina traced a small wave into the palm of Lunurin's hand—"and that he trusts you. And so I find myself terribly curious why he stopped you?"

"I begged him to. I had to be stopped."

Sina's heat tested Lunurin's spirit. She didn't flinch from Sina's seeking gaze.

"Ahh… so you agree with my cousin, that our gifts should only be used to help people."

"No, but—I couldn't let our people be slaughtered in the crossfire. It wasn't the time or place."

Sina tilted her head consideringly. "And if I could give you a better time and place to help our people? So there need be no risk of repeating the tragedies of the past?"

"I'm not sure I—"

"Together, we could grind their bridge into so much stone dust and char." The oil lamps crackled, echoing Sina's fervent promise.

Lunurin took a sharp breath, eyes darting about the room in a panic. The trio of women at the far end of the table called for more wine, quite red-faced and seemingly oblivious to Sina's declaration.

Still, such things shouldn't be said so openly. "I can't… and Alon, he…"

It wasn't that Lunurin didn't want to. But she didn't know how using her powers would affect this new amulet. Could she use them without jeopardizing the lifespan of the salt crystal?

Her head was so blessedly quiet. Anything that tested that was a risk. Hadn't Alon promised her that marriage to him would mean she wouldn't need to call typhoons?

A servant approached to refill their tea. Sina's intensity melted away as if it had never been.

She smiled warmly at Lunurin, giving her hands a final squeeze. "Think on what I've said. I have friends who would like to meet you."

25

ALON DAKILA

Alon watched Lunurin drink, ostensibly because he was concerned about the amulet's dehydrating properties, but really just to watch her full soft lips press the rim of her cup.

When a droplet ran from the corner of her mouth, and down the long line of her neck, Alon tore his gaze away, before he did something insane like lean over and lick it from her soft brown skin.

He was saved from the deranged suggestions of his own mind by the signal the men should join the Lakan outside.

Once he'd managed to navigate past a dozen back-patting titos, Alon crossed the porch to mano po to the Lakan.

"Father."

"Son."

The Lakan thumbed his golden rosary beads and pointed with his lips. "Walk with me."

Soon the strains of music and voices from the banquet were a dull buzz. Alon once more followed his father into the small chapel. The Lakan murmured his way through the Lord's Prayer.

Alon held out his palm. His mother's tooth-marked signet ring lay gleaming.

"My wife had a harrowing morning."

The Lakan did not turn from the crucifix. "I was trying to stop you from ruining your life."

"If you'd discussed the plan with me, we might've convinced her to go, instead of having her sink every ship in the bay in a fit of fury with Lusitan slavers."

"They were paid handsomely to put her ashore in Simsiman."

From deep down, like the inexorable tide coming in, a slow, cold anger built in Alon's veins. "I doubt they'd have gotten far with an angry stormcaller aboard. I admit I went into the endeavor thinking I'd have her trust, but your meddling has squashed any budding wifely loyalty."

"You put me on a short timeline to prevent you marrying a witch. Besides, you are in no position to pontificate about trust and loyalty," the Lakan spat. "It would seem even in my own son's eyes, I am not the true Lakan."

Alon drew up short. "My loyalty is to you above all others. You are the Lakan of Aynila."

His father sneered. "Is that what you call it? Is it loyalty, taking your new wife to pay respects to your mother and her village of saboteurs before me? I hear how even the principalia whisper about a returning 'wave.' This whole city keeps clinging to your mother's damn tsunami, even my own son!"

Alon's anger was ash in his mouth. He was suddenly scrambling. How could his father doubt him? "I wasn't taking her to pay respects. I needed help to bind her power, so she can no longer be overcome by her vengeful goddess and destroy your good work ensuring peace in Aynila. Only you can bind us together enough to resist the Codicíans despite our factions. When have I ever done other than your will?"

"When she appeared. She clouds your judgment."

"No, never. I acted with your interests and safety foremost. I couldn't bring her to you when I wasn't sure her nature was contained."

His father's simmering anger eased. "So she is constrained, by some witch work or another?"

"Yes, she is no longer a danger to you or peace with the Codicíans."

"How sure are you?"

"I have brought her before you, have I not? I would never endanger you. There will be no repeat of the incident on the steps."

"The Codicíans will not tolerate any further slipups, and nor will I."

"I understand." The words were heavy as stones.

"That's not enough. You will swear to me on your mother's life. You will control your new wife or bring me her head. If you can't, I will tell the Codicíans about your mother's village of witches. It must be getting very small now. How many of her failed saboteurs died last year? Three? Or was it only one, and the other two were just innocents caught up in your mother's suicidal quest? Maybe then I'll have peace from these idiotic wave agitators."

Alon couldn't breathe, couldn't do anything but bend to the iron press of the Lakan's decree.

"I know I can rely on you, my son. It grieves me to do this, but I too was once a young fool in love, who thought misplaced kindness and gentle words could solve everything. Soon you will see, women like her think only of their gods and power, and nothing of mortal men. Then, you will understand."

"Yes, Father." It rasped from his throat like broken glass. He bowed, pressing his father's ringed hand to his brow. "You can rely on me. My wife will cause no more friction." With the Codicíans or between his father and the nobles of Aynila, who had never officially selected him as their Lakan.

"And if she does?" his father prompted coldly.

"I'll handle the problem personally." Alon fought the bile crawling up his throat. "I swear it on my mother's life."

"May the Lord have mercy on you," his father intoned graciously, making the sign of the cross over Alon's head.

26

LUNURIN CALILAN DE DAKILA

Lunurin was braced for the worst when Isko slipped back in, offering to escort Sina home.

"Shouldn't Lunurin come with us? She's not fully recovered," Sina argued.

Isko shook his head. "Alon is not in a position to reject his father's hospitality."

Sina frowned. "Then let him drink till dawn, what's that got to do with his exhausted wife?"

Isko winced. "Everything. I'm sorry, Sina, let's just get you out before this devolves any further."

Then they were gone, leaving Lunurin with a cold pit of fear in her belly that made it impossible to even sip her tea, despite her thirst.

Shortly after, the rest of the party returned.

Alon's face was like stone. Lunurin studied the hard set of his jaw and wondered what had become of the kind and gentle friend she'd come to rely on so heavily. She'd seen him in the Palisade in his professional capacity many times. That was nothing on him now. She couldn't even feel the flow of his spirit. It was as if his internal sea were no more than pillars of salt.

She missed Sina's steady warmth. She didn't want to be here anymore. She was half convinced she'd be dragged out back and summarily executed. But Alon only returned to her side and pulled her to her feet. Nerves and sitting for too long had made Lunurin clumsy and stiff. A sharp pain pulled at the back of her knee as an injury from the cage reopened. *Damn.* Lunurin had hoped her last bout with the healers would've fixed the injury, but it was in a difficult place.

Alon slipped his mother's ring back onto her hand.

"Alon, what's going on?" she questioned.

He didn't speak, only squeezed her fingers warning-tight as the Lakan retook his throne and the celebration returned to full swing.

"My son, come. I have not yet given my congratulations to the new couple!" the Lakan declared.

Alon drew her to stand before the Lakan, his hold more and more like a shackle.

When Alon remained silent, Lunurin bowed and bowed again. "Lakan, your hospitality and generosity are beyond measure. My heart is overflowing to be welcomed so effusively into your family. Will you grant us your blessing to spend our first night together as a married couple?"

Raucous laughter rose from those hearty guests who remained. Lunurin twisted free of Alon's grip and knelt at the Lakan's feet. Her leg throbbed.

She lifted his hand to her brow. "My greatest wish is to be a good and loyal daughter to you. I hope I will have the chance to prove myself."

The Lakan caught her chin between his thumb and forefinger. He lifted her face.

"I hope you will be a good wife to my son." The words were only slightly slurred with drink.

Lunurin's skin prickled with unease, as Alon knelt rigidly beside her.

The Lakan placed a hand on both their heads. "Nawa'y pagpalain kayo ng Diyos."

As he said the blessing, he curled his fingers into Lunurin's hair, his fingertips skimming the mother-of-pearl comb, her mutya. Lunurin flinched, sure it was an accident, but he did not pull away. He pressed the comb in till its teeth scraped her scalp. A soul-deep revulsion stirred in her belly as every hair on her body stood on end. A terrible scraped glass sensation dragged down her spine with every pass of his fingers on her mutya.

Lunurin couldn't breathe. The Lakan might as well have torn open her robe and groped her breast.

He had finished the couple's blessing but was still speaking. The cadence was familiar, a prayer. He transferred both hands to her head, grasping her pearl-topped hair prong, like her mutya were horns.

Lunurin gagged, her throat so dry, the sensation stabbed deep. She was back on Calilan, her stepfather snatching her mutya while the headman of the fishers' village poured salt over her legs, rubbing the rough crystals into her calves till they were raw and bloody. Then she was on the steps of the palace, Alon lifting her mutya from her hair, his naked blade at her nape. She was in the cage, powerless and dying, her mutya torn from her, her hair shorn.

She tried to struggle but the Lakan tightened his grip, keeping her head bowed as he prayed, "O merciful Lord God, who in the beginning did take Eve out of the side of Adam and did give her to him as a helpmate: grant my daughter the grace to live worthy of the honorable estate of matrimony to which the Lord has called her, that she may acknowledge her husband as her head, and truly revere and obey him in all things…"

Lunurin's heart was so quiet. Anitun Tabu had abandoned her. Lunurin was empty of anything but herself. She was alone, so alone, without divine fury or even a storm to soak up her terror and revulsion. She'd been here before. She had silenced her screams, and swallowed down her tears. There were very human consequences for drawing on the power of the old gods, and she had always faced them alone.

Alon was as silent as her goddess beside her. He only moved once. The Lakan twisted her pearl hair prong and Lunurin voiced the smallest sound of protest, terribly afraid he would snap the pearl off. Alon took her hand, squeezing so tightly it hurt. And Lunurin hated him too.

"Keep from her all worldliness, vanity, and pride. This I pray through Jesus Christ our Lord. Amen." The Lakan released her, his expression benevolent, as if he hadn't just threatened to break her mutya.

Lunurin studied the bitterness in the Lakan's dark eyes, so like Alon's but without any of the gentleness she'd thought she could expect. She did not flinch.

Finally, the Lakan bid them rise. "An old man forgets what it is to be young. I had a wedding suite readied for you. Go, go. You have my blessing."

More congratulations were shouted from the guests along with ribald jokes and suggestions. Lunurin locked her gaze on the servant he'd indicated. She kept her shoulders back, and her head high. Her head ached. Her heart beat so fast. Her tongue was a shriveled dead thing in her mouth. At her side, Alon was unreadable. He said *nothing*. He did *nothing*. No more than a weight shackled to her left hand. Had she ever left the abbot's cage behind?

They were led to a lavish bridal suite, lit by a dozen candles, strewn with sampaguita garlands. The servant woman showed them in with a bow.

For the first time since he'd gone with his father, Alon spoke. "I need water."

"Are you sure you wouldn't like another bottle of tapuy, Gat Alon?"

"No. We've already overindulged."

The woman nodded solemnly. "Sometimes, my lord, it is good for a woman to be very relaxed for these things. Particularly the first time…" She gave them both a very kind look. "Be gentle with each other. Marriages that begin with that can be precious things."

"The water, if you will?"

"As you like." The servant bowed and returned with a porcelain pitcher and cups.

Litao gave them both a nod and slid the bamboo door closed, taking a post outside.

Alon released her hand and in the unexpected absence of his anchoring touch, everything came crashing down. The amulet on her chest burned, Alon's magic fighting the fervor in her blood.

Lunurin pressed her hands over her mouth and folded forward. Lightning crashed into the mountainside, so close that the air tasted of metal. Thunder rolled through the night, or was it another tremor? Hilaga had been so very active lately. Lunurin screamed out her anguish and fury and helplessness. She was so thirsty she couldn't even cry, though her eyes burned hot, and her head swam. Hail ricocheted off the tile roof like a hundred clay jars shattering.

And beyond the salt caging her spirit, her goddess keened, *"My daughter, my heart, let us rend the eyes from everyone who has seen our suffering and shame and done nothing, let ruin rain from the heavens! Why do you bury your heart in salt and smother your spirit? If you would but remember your vow, no man or god could tear you from my arms again!"*

She crouched, running her hands over her hair, assuring herself her mutya were both still intact, still there. When she opened her eyes, Alon was on his knees beside her.

"Please, Lunurin, you have to calm down," he urged. "The amulet—"

His hands were half-extended as he debated how best to calm her, to control her. Lunurin was dying for want of water, her goddess railing in the wind, and he was too busy trying to immure her in salt to protect her from his own father. This was his idea of protection? He'd only made her more vulnerable!

"They're still there. He didn't take them. He didn't take them, Lunurin."

"Why?" she rasped.

"It's not you, it's nothing you did. He's angry with me for showing respect to my mother before him. When he looks at you, all he sees is how my mother left him and failed Aynila, and I failed to protect you."

Lunurin shuddered, digging her fingers into her hair. She wanted nothing more than to tear it loose and let the storm inside her rage. Not even the amulet and all Alon's power could stop her if she cast herself into her goddess's arms and gave in to her vow. "He knows! He knows what it is to me!"

Alon reached for her, but did not presume to touch her. His expression was so distant, so strange. "Yes."

"It hurts." Lunurin's head throbbed in time with her leg, her tongue sticking to the roof of her mouth.

"Where? Can I help?"

She met his hands halfway. They closed around hers and she squeezed back, bruising tight, and dragged strength from the distant push-pull of his blood. Her amulet needed a body to pull from, but its magic was tide-touched and it preferred him. If he was to be her cage, then she would use what support he could provide. The voice of her goddess went quiet at last. For tonight at least, Lunurin would choose salt not vengeance. Though her voice rasped like broken pottery shards in her throat, she coaxed the clouds until the rain didn't threaten to wash the Lakan's palace from the hillside in an endless tide of mud. One could use even cage bars to stand. Lunurin had learned that well in the convent. Only she didn't want to think of all she'd left behind in her old life. What wouldn't she have given for Cat's merely human comfort in this moment? She didn't want this amulet like a noose around her neck, tying her ever more securely into the tidal nature of Alon's magic.

Alon gasped when she released his hands, but instead of scrambling away from her, he lifted her to the edge of the bed. Lunurin leaned her hot dry face into his neck, loving and hating the relief his cool touch brought.

She tried to speak but what came out was a croak, though her head spun less. Lunurin braced herself on his shoulders to sit upright.

Alon poured her a cup of water. "Here, drink. Is it dehydrating you faster, when your power overflows?"

She took the cup and drained it, then drank two more cups, till the sides of her throat didn't stick to themselves when she swallowed. "Yes."

"Does drawing on me like that help?" he asked, face turned away as he refilled her cup, and set it down on the bedside.

Lunurin couldn't parse his tone, but he'd created this problem. He could damn well help fix it. "Yes." ·

Alon turned to face her. He held out his hands. "If it helps, let me help."

Slowly, not sure what he intended, Lunurin nodded. Alon cradled her face in his hands, the hungry draw of the amulet eased to a bare trickle. Lunurin leaned into his touch, the relief too strong to be denied.

Lunurin could've stayed like that forever, but then Alon leaned forward, his breath slightly sweet with wine, as he pressed a gentle kiss to her brow. He rested his cheek on the top of her head.

Silently, Lunurin prayed Cat would forgive her. Then, she lifted her head and pressed her mouth over his. Alon froze. Undeterred, Lunurin curled her hand around the back of his neck, gentler than she had the last time, remembering the way he'd held her outside the abbot's study. She might be a terrible farce of a bride, but if she did this one thing, maybe she wouldn't be a failure as a wife. Maybe the Lakan would not look at her so. Maybe Alon would soften to her again. And if he didn't, she could at least drink in the relief of his touch.

She threaded her fingers into the hair at the nape of Alon's neck and he melted into her with a sigh. Her thirst evaporated as if it had never been. His kiss was so gentle, she almost didn't know what to do with herself. His lips were soft and full, and so warm. His cool hands cradled her cheeks, the contrast dizzying. The pads of his thumbs skimmed her cheekbones. Lunurin gave him a push, following his lips down, draping herself over his chest. Alon's arms locked around her and then, slowly, he pulled away.

"Stop. Please, stop," he whispered hoarsely, his breath warm on her skin.

Lunurin disentangled her hands from his sleek dark hair, dropping them to his chest. "I'm sorry, did I pull too hard?" What did it cost him to grant her this relief?

"You're bleeding."

Uncomprehending, Lunurin touched her fingers to her mouth. He hadn't bitten her. Cat had split her lip once or twice with overexuberant kisses. She still had a little white scar bisecting her upper lip. Alon sat them both back upright, his face flushed.

Alon gestured lower and Lunurin was once more aware of the dull distant ache of the rest of her body. Not even the good kind of ache. She hoped that would come later, but that was okay. Alon was gentle. He wouldn't hurt her.

She reached into her robe unselfconsciously, pressing her hand to the weal above the bend in her knee. Earlier, that pull...

Crimson smeared her palm.

Lunurin twisted. Pulling down the sheets, she painted a thin red line down the center of the bed.

"What are you doing?" Alon asked.

"Making amends to your father. I won't bleed for you. I don't think I bled the first time."

"Lunurin, I'm not. We're not..." Alon's brow furrowed in confusion. "You're bleeding." He repeated the words like an article of faith, holding it between them like a shield.

"I can handle it," Lunurin said.

Revulsion flared across Alon's face. "I can't."

"You won't hurt me," Lunurin assured him.

Something twisted in the deep shadows the candlelight cast, making his cheekbones sharper, the hollows beneath his brows endlessly deep. And Lunurin was almost afraid, but mostly she was angry, so very angry, and desperately grasping for something she could control.

"That doesn't make it right. I didn't marry you to be handled, to be endured."

Lunurin frowned. Despite everything, deep down, he must still be the grave, gentle boy she'd relied on all these years. She'd seen how he'd looked at her before he'd gone to talk with his father. How he'd always looked at her, in the quiet moments between healing emergencies and political nightmares. He *did* want her. He couldn't have done all this and not expect something in return. If the Church had taught her anything it was that love was the most selfish emotion there was.

"Your touch helps me. Let me do this for you. Let me be a proper wife. Please, you've done so much—"

"I didn't do it so you'd pay me back with sex," Alon hissed, disgust twisting his expression. He'd never looked so much like his father.

Lunurin, despite herself, recoiled, and hated the Lakan for putting this fear in her. But most of all she hated herself for daring to believe Alon could really protect her. Alon was a loyal son. She'd always known it. Catalina was right. What son could choose his wife over his father's will? If she couldn't make herself useful, she was only a liability.

"Then *why* by all the gods did you marry me?" she spat.

Something cracked in Alon's expression. He cursed and scrubbed his hands over his face. His shoulders trembled, and for a moment Lunurin thought he might cry.

"It wasn't supposed to be like this."

Lunurin laughed, the sound harsh in her throat. "Please, enlighten me, Alon. What did you expect? Tell me, and I swear I'll play the part."

Alon frowned. "Stop. Please, stop that. I know you've been through unmitigated torture. I know I failed you. I never should've dragged you before my father tonight. He was angry with me for showing my mother preference, angrier when he realized how much I care for you."

He took Lunurin's hands. The cool metal of his brace similar, yet so different from his father's ring-encrusted hands. "I never should've put you at his mercy. I know you're hurting, and tired… and scared. But I'm not here to play some cruel power game with you. I know I don't deserve your trust, but please, trust me that far at least."

A pressure deep inside Lunurin released, as though he'd lanced an abscess, deep and festering. She gasped for air, and started to cry, the rain falling harder with her tears. It was such a relief to cry. Before losing herself in Alon's touch, her body hadn't been able to spare the tears. Alon released Lunurin's hands like he'd been burned.

He stared at her in terror, paralyzed by her tears. Lunurin wiped fruitlessly at her cheeks. She tried to turn from him, to hide her face, but her leg protested. Lunurin hissed. She was trapped here as surely as in the abbot's terrible cage.

"I'm so, so tired," Lunurin gasped.

"Can I help with your leg, at least?" Alon asked softly.

Lunurin helped him pull aside her skirts to assess her injury. The back of her calf was painted in blood.

"Why didn't you say something? Walking must've been agony." Alon's terror of her tears melted in the face of a healing problem to focus on. He slipped the blood-drenched slipper from her foot and dropped a pinch of salt from his belt pouch into a cup. Saltwater crawled eagerly into his hands.

"Why do you think?"

Alon winced. "I deserved that. I've seen you walk through worse." His thumb skimmed a sunken star-shaped scar from where he'd once dug a harpoon out of her leg. "How did you end up with a barbed harpoon in your calf, again?"

A damp gasp of a laugh escaped her. "Oh no, that one I'm taking to the grave."

An almost smile curved his lips as he cleaned the wound with saltwater. Lunurin bit back a hiss at the sting. Realizing the folly of this, she let out a wet, heaving sob.

"Sorry," she hiccupped.

Alon patted her knee, not unlike how he might stroke the neck of a panicked mare. "You're fine."

The last remnant of her restraint crumbled. It was deeply cathartic to let the heat behind her eyes rise and run out over her cheeks instead of swallowing the tears until she couldn't breathe. Alon worked on, swift and sure, much more at ease as a healer than a new husband.

"If that won't seal up on its own, you may need stitches. But for now, a bandage and not walking on it should be enough." Alon stole a pillowcase for use as bandaging.

When he was done, Lunurin was still weeping, the rain coming down harder and harder. She needed to stop. She couldn't possibly spare the water. But once she'd started it was like pulling the plug on some huge untapped reservoir. There was no stemming the flow.

Alon proffered the half of the pillowcase he hadn't used to wrap her leg. "Lunurin, the storm."

Lunurin mopped her face. "The rain, the rain, I know. I'm just... I'm so tired."

"Can I help like earlier? Can you draw on my strength?"

Lunurin struggled to focus on Alon through the tears. She curled her hand around his wrist, but it did no good. Lunurin forced her breathing deep and slow. The tears kept coming, squeezing out of her eyes no matter how tightly she held them closed. She was too exhausted for even the lift of his magic to help.

She dropped his wrist, shaking her head. "I can't. I'm sorry, I can't. Can you stop me?"

Alon went green under his amber coloring. "No, gods no, Lunurin. I can't... I am so ashamed. What I did to you on the steps. I told myself I did it to protect you, to save your life. But after what my father did, how he hurt you… you screamed the same way when I cut…" His voice wavered and broke.

Lunurin held his gaze. "If you don't stop me, what will your father do to make it stop? How much of that… was a test, to see if I'd snap?"

Alon looked ill. "I don't want to hurt you again."

The lie to absolve him was on her tongue, but Lunurin did not speak it. She was too tired tonight for deception, too tired for anything but tears.

"The damage is already done. Help me stop the rain tonight."

Alon still hesitated. "There's got to be another way. Something to make the amulet work better?"

She pulled her mutya from her cropped curls. The rain fell harder. She tucked them into her sleeve. "Did I tell you? My tiya married a tide-touched woman. She told me it's because Anitun Tabu and Aman Sinaya are lovers, and to keep Anitun Tabu from killing all life when she rages, a tide-touched can dampen a stormcaller's power. It doesn't have to be… violent. My tiya's wife would always help me wash my hair so I didn't flood the fields. I'm so tired. Would you gather up my hair?"

The rain beat down harder and harder.

Then, light as a butterfly landing, Alon lowered his fingertips into her hair. "How?"

Lunurin frowned. "I'm not sure."

The rain continued to fall.

"Can you feel the rain through me the way you do blood?" Lunurin asked.

Alon's face scrunched in concentration. As they listened, the rain eased and finally, stopped. The silence after the unending downpour was so loud, the individual drops of water dripping off the roof tiles echoed like shouts.

Lunurin breathed out long and slow, the weight of responsibility falling away. "Oh. Thank you."

Somehow, relief made her cry harder.

Alon looked ill. "You're telling me I could have stopped everything like this? Without drowning you? Without—"

Lunurin wrapped her hand around his wrist. "This isn't Anitun Tabu, just me. You couldn't have stopped Her like this."

Alon's jaw relaxed, his touch as tentative as if he thought her skull were eggshell thin, and might shatter. "Do you want to lie down? I can sit by the bedside, and you can sleep."

Alon began pulling away from her, but then he yawned. Lunurin curled a hand into his sleeve. "Just lie down, Alon. Maybe for once in my life I won't wake with my hair ties coming loose, pulling in the morning rains."

"No, I—"

Lunurin gave his sleeve a tug. "Let a woman dramatically cry herself to sleep on her wedding night without dying of dehydration or worrying her husband will wake with a crick in his neck. It's a big bed."

Alon shifted onto the bed hesitantly, taking up the barest sliver he could and still claim he was in it. His hand in her hair was cautious, as if he were cradling a newborn.

She poked his shoulder. Alon had to flail to avoid tumbling to the floor, but at no point did he grip or tug her hair. When he glared, she hooked her fingers under his arm and pulled him toward her, so he had enough room to lie on his back. She tucked herself under the sheets, turned her back to him, and pressed the wad of pillowcase to her face. She cried without worrying how high the river would rise, or if anyone's roof was leaking, or if she'd start a mudslide. She wept without fearing her unspooling power would draw her father-in-law's or the Codicians' wrath. Alon sat up, his hand lifting away while he extinguished the candles and tugged closed the sheer bed netting. At last, he stilled, his hand returning to her hair, the drizzle falling silent, until her gasping sobs were the only sound disturbing the darkness. His touch was cooling relief, lifting the plaguing thirst, as if by touch alone he connected the salt amulet to the vast reservoir of seawater that was a healer's soul.

Alon's hand on her hair shifted to the back of her neck, where he rubbed light, soothing circles. At last, wrung out and spent, Lunurin slept, curled around the knowledge that with such a father-in-law as the Lakan, no matter how pure Alon's intentions were, she would never be safe. If she wasn't sure of her own security, how could she ask Cat to take such a risk, with Inez to think of?

27

ALON DAKILA

Alon woke late. He scrunched his eyes against the light pouring through the lace netting with an intensity that indicated Isko would be irritated when he hauled himself out of his bed. Only Alon was not in *his* bed. Worse, he was most certainly not alone in it, having tucked his face into the curve of Lunurin's neck. Her skin was softer than he'd imagined, and so warm...

Aman Sinaya preserve him, she even smelled good. The floral sweetness of the sampaguita garlands mingled with the nuttiness of her hair oil. He decided the better part of honor was not breathing.

The night before came back to him with a lurch. A flush of shame crawled up his neck, hot and prickly as a tide of red ants. Somehow his father had been right. They were going to make each other miserable.

As if to drive the point home, he heard his father's voice, raised in anger and getting closer.

Alon reached to wake Lunurin and found her eyes wide

open, her pulse beating so hard it throbbed against the delicate skin of her throat.

"Easy," Alon murmured. *You're safe*, he wanted to say, but he wasn't sure that was the truth.

Lunurin didn't respond. She scrambled upright, patting desperately about the bedding for her lost hairpins. Alon untied the ribbon from his hair and offered it. She tied her hair back ruthlessly tight. She didn't return her mutya to their rightful place, keeping them secreted away.

Alon scooped his brace from the side table, wriggling it back onto his fingers. He flexed his right hand a few times, settling the rings in place. His three smallest fingers had finally stopped aching with the nearness of rain.

Alon heard Litao's voice, just outside as he attempted to delay the Lakan. Lunurin seemed to be evaluating an escape out of the window. Alon lifted her from the edge of the bed to sit at the low breakfast table. He didn't want her to re-open her injury. "I'll handle my father."

"I want to believe you."

His previous failures mocked him.

Lunurin swiftly put the table between her and the door, keeping a window at her back. Alon watched, horrified, as she made herself small. Head bowed, her broad shoulders rounded, she vanished inside of herself.

And Alon couldn't stop it, because then the door slid open and his father strode in, consuming all his attention and energy.

The Lakan engulfed him in his arms. "I'd like to leave you to newlywed bliss, but there is no one else I trust to handle these difficult situations. No one understands their importance as you do."

His father's hold was warm and familiar. "How can I help?"

His father needed his support now more than ever. He was under immense pressure from the Codicíans. The finicky loyalty of the principalia didn't help. He felt abandoned by Alon's mother and brother. He'd never have doubted Alon's loyalty, never have acted so desperately, if he weren't under such stress. If Alon could just reassure his father nothing had changed, that he had Alon's complete loyalty, he wouldn't view Lunurin as such a threat.

"Tell me what I can do," Alon reiterated, returning his father's hold. Someone had to stay and fix things. Even if today that only meant distracting his father from his wife.

"It's the quicklime shortages! My buyers can't fulfill the amounts I promised the Codicíans for the bridge. We need this last span built. There are serious contract penalties if construction goes beyond this month, ones we can't afford to incur. The labor situation is too volatile after the polo riots," his father said.

Alon frowned, trying to buy time. "This time of year, getting lime is always tricky."

"I can't breach my contract with the Palisade and delay the bridge, again. The metalworkers' conclave has been stockpiling lime for months."

Did his father expect him to seize the conclave's lime supplies? Did Alon dare contemplate what Sina could have added to the lime in the time she'd had it?

"I need you to handle it," the Lakan demanded.

Of course he did.

"Let me speak to my suppliers. I'll meet with DeSoto about the schedule and his needs."

The Lakan frowned. "We cannot be found in breach."

Alon took his father by the arm, leading him out. "I'll handle the details. Show me our final contractual obligations, would you? How many additional laborers are we talking?"

As he passed Litao he signed, "Get her home. Don't let her walk."

"What have you done that the poor nun can't walk?" Litao signed with a wicked grin.

Alon glared, signing, "Cage! Leg! Bleeding! Punong-puno na ako sa'yo!"

28

LUNURIN CALILAN DE DAKILA

Lunurin felt like contraband goods being smuggled across the city, something to be hidden, something shameful. Bitterness churned in her belly. She held it close to ward off weaker emotions. Alon had abandoned her without a backward glance.

At last, Litao helped her down from the vividly painted red and yellow kalesa in front of Alon's home. The poor man wavered in evident exhaustion and Lunurin felt terrible for being such a burden.

As she was handed off to Kawit, Lunurin said, "You shouldn't go back to Alon today. Send one of the other men. You need rest."

Let Alon run ragged, jumping at his father's every request. The rest of them needn't play along.

Litao, who was directing the kalesa driver to return him to the palace, blinked glassily. "Yes, Dayang. That's… a good idea."

Litao dropped from the foot rail and trudged toward the guardhouse.

Lunurin balanced on one foot, keeping most of her weight on the doorframe, afraid she'd topple Kawit. She kept her face turned away from the older tide-touched man, trying to rearrange it into something pleasant. It was difficult, with how angry she was with Alon.

Kawit patted her hand on his arm, and expertly angled her weight through the cane at his side. "Come, Dayang. Tito Kawit is sturdier than he looks. Let's get you something to drink. I'll help get you settled into your room."

He leaned in conspiratorially. "Gat Alon wanted to tuck you away into a guestroom, but they're far too small. I've put your belongings in the blue room. Casama, our head dye mistress, will be along soon. She has the best eye for color and fabrics."

Lunurin desperately wanted to beg off, but Kawit seemed so determined.

She was soon settled in her new room, Kawit pouring her a cup of ginger tea.

"Drink plenty, it's salted and sweetened to keep your blood up."

She squeezed his hand. "Thank you, Tito, you've been too kind."

"It's nothing. By the time you and Casama are done, I'll have figured out where Gat Alon is off gallivanting and returned him to your side." Kawit clicked his tongue in disapproval as he left. "Leaving a bride alone so soon after the wedding—"

Her own irritation with Alon flared. She bit her tongue on agreeing, or worse, telling Kawit that Alon ought to stay gone.

Lunurin reached into her clothing chest at the foot of a frankly extravagant kalabasa-style four-poster bed draped in a blue lace mosquito netting. Her plain chest looked out of place in this huge room furnished in intricately carved dark wood. The rich indigo wall hangings made the room seem underwater; the polished bamboo flooring underfoot was smooth and golden as sand. She was out of place too. Was it any wonder Alon didn't know what to do with her?

Lunurin unfolded a threadbare white habit, her fingertips seeking the comfort of routine. The cloth still smelled of her and Cat's shared cell. She buried her face in it and breathed deeply.

"Oh no, that's for Kawit's rag pile," a dignified old lola declared from the doorway.

Sina followed the dye mistress, who must be Casama, her arms burdened down with cloth samples and clothes.

Casama tapped a finger alongside her nose where a mother-of-pearl hoop gleamed, her eyes suddenly bright. "It's good to see this room in use again. My wife made these tapestries... but that was before the Codicíans came."

Lunurin recognized the cadence of Casama's loss.

She studied the salt flowers blooming on her walls and wondered what other priceless arts they had lost to the Codicíans' fervor. "They're beautiful."

Casama nodded and held out a hand for the habit. "So, no more of smocks and dreary piety."

Lunurin folded the habit safely back into the chest. "I don't have much else to wear."

Sina flung her burdens on the bed. She lifted a silk wrap skirt striped with indigo and yellow from the top of the heap. "We're fixing that."

Casama began swatching colored fabric against Lunurin's deep brown skin. "We can't have our new Dayang dressing in rags."

That nervous quiver was back in her lungs. "This is too much."

She hadn't the temerity to open the coin purse Alon had gifted her in the tide-touched village. She was going to have to

266

pay all this back, somehow, she knew she was. Her debt was already too great.

"It's really not. You should absolutely keep milking Alon's guilt over cutting your hair and allowing you to be tortured. If you won't, I intend to do so in your stead," Sina said, matter-of-factly.

And it was silly, but laid bare like that, the careful weight of all she'd endured teetered precariously. Her eyes grew hot, her chest aching. Lunurin pressed her hands over her face. Why cry, now that she was safe? She breathed, forcing the tears down. Why did it make her so angry how Alon bent himself over backward to appease his father, after what he'd done?

She jumped when Sina laid a warm hand on her arm, foolishly wishing Cat were here to comfort her. "Oh, I'm sorry. You've had a hard few days."

"We can do this later. I'll just leave a few things for you to try," Casama agreed, gathering up most of her samples and withdrawing before Lunurin could pull herself together enough to pretend all was well.

"Forgive me, I'm just—"

"You're angry," Sina said bluntly.

Lunurin sucked in a breath, the air harsh on her parched throat. The amulet on her chest throbbed, and—oh. Oh, it wasn't just her anger at all, was it? With salt to guard her spirit she could see where her anger ended and Anitun Tabu's began. A simple reminder that Lunurin could spin her fury into a storm that would make all those who had wronged her pay. The gentlest of nudges; she couldn't avoid her vow forever. She'd promised her goddess everything. Anitun Tabu would not forget such a promise. She was discovering the limits of her new amulet far too quickly.

"Not with you. My goddess is feeling particularly vengeful. It's been difficult."

"Have you thought about my bridge dilemma?" Sina asked.

And maybe it was the divine fury leaking past her defenses, but this time Lunurin didn't hesitate. She'd done too little for too long. Years she'd made herself small thinking hiding was the best way to protect herself and others. That anything else was too big a risk. But it hadn't changed the outcome, she only lost a little more, and hurt more deeply, and watched more of her people suffer. She couldn't keep hoping that if she made herself innocuous enough, she would be safe. Someone would always find her wanting. Like her mother, like her father, like Magdalena and all the sisters of the convent... like Cat. Alon meant well, but he didn't understand what she was, how dangerous she was. Or how much his father and the Codicíans hated her. He'd fail again, despite his best intentions. She couldn't keep hoping he would be able to protect her. It was time to act.

"If I help you, I want a place in the metalworkers' conclave. I refuse to be trotted out for the entertainment of the Lakan. I'm done playing the blushing bride."

A place of her own, that was all she needed. Let Alon tell whatever lies he must to explain why his wife had entered seclusion. She'd make a place for her and Cat to continue on as they always had. On Hilaga, perhaps Inez would be able to grow up free from fear.

Sina smiled at her brilliantly. "You are my dearest cousin. Everyone will understand when very soon you enter a long confinement. It is only natural you would seek seclusion with your nearest female relations. What you do far from the public eye is of course no one's business. One of our contacts apprenticed under a Tianchaowen firework compounder. With the aid of lightning..."

Lunurin chewed the inside of her lip. She didn't intend to end up like the saboteurs on All Saint's Day. "No, that would draw too much attention. That man at the feast was right. Years of sabotage have made the Codicíans more determined to finish the bridge and not lose face."

"What did you have in mind?" Sina asked.

"What if the bridge was condemned? Damage that was slow but steady and seemingly natural. Are you orchestrating the lime shortages? That's what Alon's investigating for the Lakan."

Sina smiled, all teeth. "It took them longer to notice than we thought it would."

"The Lakan was in favor of seizing the conclave's stockpiles, but Alon persuaded him to take a diplomatic solution, utilizing Aynila Indigo's suppliers and talking to DeSoto about the schedule."

Sina frowned. "That's Alon for you, always putting himself on the line if it'll mean a second more of peace. I was hoping they'd go straight to seizure. Alon means well, but he's so conflict averse. And the Lakan has personal agendas that Alon will never admit have nothing to do with peace in Aynila."

This assessment aligned almost perfectly with Lunurin's own misgivings.

"How have you adulterated it?" Lunurin asked. Her oyster beds produced more than just pearls. Oyster shells were a valuable source of quicklime.

Sina blinked innocently. "You probably don't want to know. Ultimately, it won't matter if they don't seize this year's lime. I have contacts on the worksites who've been mixing the mortar on and off for years. Parts of the bridge are more fragile than others. It's where we planned to plant the explosives."

"Tell me anyway. It would help if we could get out to see the state it's in now. Any stress cracks, bubbling, or fissures might be places where heavy rain could wash out the lime.

And if there is no cracking yet, we can create some. High heat or lightning, followed by the river cooling. Then we could stand back and let a big storm do the rest naturally. You've already set up a perfect excuse for why suppliers coming up short would sell adulterated lime. How far can you—"

Isko knocked and peered in, eyeing their conspiratorial huddle.

"Ladies, Kawit is laying a feast. He'll be upset if it grows cold."

On the off chance that the acid churning in her belly at the thought of rebellion was partly hunger, Lunurin let herself be shown to the dining area.

Sina served, spooning adobo over steaming bowls of rice.

Lunurin picked at the tender shreds of chicken and mushrooms swimming in tangy, garlicky sauce. Isko had been convinced for years that she was going to get his brother into trouble his clever schemes couldn't fix. Given their current predicament, Isko had been absolutely correct. She'd hate for him to discover additional reasons to disapprove of her.

Sina waited until he'd taken a bite. "Isko, how do you feel about collapsing a bridge?"

Both Isko and Lunurin choked. Lunurin coughed, trying to clear an inhaled peppercorn from her lungs, while Isko thumped on his chest, hacking into the crook of his elbow. Sina pounded helpfully on Lunurin's back.

Isko, red in the face from coughing, shot Sina a glare. "Warn a man! What's possessed you to rope the nun in to your plans to get executed for treason?"

"She's a stormcaller. We can trust her."

"Those two statements do not logically follow," Isko retorted, then tilted his head to Lunurin. "Meaning no offense, of course."

Lunurin barked a laugh. "Why have you always distrusted me? How many years have I kept Alon's secret?"

Isko frowned at her. "You do things that don't make any sense, things against your family and the convent's interest. You tangle Alon into your schemes, and I can't get him to stop and think about what you're gaining from whatever impossible task you've proposed. Alon's loyalty to others always gets him in trouble."

Part of Lunurin wanted to spit back, *My family isn't my father, my loyalty is not to the Church. It's always been to Catalina and Inez. For their safety, I would let the rest drown.* But that wasn't a good way to seem sane and reasonable.

"How would her father, Archbishop de Palma, feel if he ever discovered her terrorism?"

"Technically, sabotage," Sina said.

Lunurin snapped. "Ten years I have tried to be a proper Codicían daughter, and he never once claimed me. My 'father' would've watched them burn me as a witch without protest. Why should I care how he'd feel?"

If Isko was taken aback at her vehemence, it didn't prevent him railing back. "You nearly got yourself executed for insurrection days ago. By all the gods, why do you want in on Sina's death wish?!"

"If we do nothing, we all die anyway," Sina muttered. "At least Lunurin tried."

Lunurin tucked her chin with a wince. "Tried is a strong word... The amulet keeping my powers manageable broke." She lifted her salt amulet. "I won't lose my head again. Alon's mother and Kawit think this could hold for years."

"I think I'd prefer if you ruined lives on purpose." Isko looked askance at Sina. "Why, oh why, would you trust the woman who almost *accidentally* incited a riot?"

"Well, you won't help me," Sina accused.

Isko pinched the bridge of his nose. "I'm supposed to be preventing you from committing treason and shattering this fragile peace."

"Then why haven't you told Alon what I've been doing?" Sina asked archly.

"Because he might be moved by his overdeveloped sense of duty to warn his father, fully believing you'd be shown leniency. But the Lakan isn't feeling lenient. Not after her stunt on the steps shamed him before all of Aynila. You'd be executed for inciting rebellion, and I won't be responsible for that."

"Oh. I thought you just didn't care," Sina said.

"I think I care too much," Isko admitted reluctantly.

Suddenly trespassing on this private revelation, Lunurin ducked her attention to her bowl.

Sina shifted as if to go to Isko's side, but she subsided, spreading her hands. "Will you help then? With my mother a hostage in the Palisade, I have to protect our people on Hilaga. If the Codicians realize what we are, they will wipe us out. If there are no firetenders to care for Hilaga, she will not just turn in her sleep, she will wake and bury us all in ash and fire. Once my people are secure, I will go back to them, and Alon and his father can continue their losing war of attrition with the governor for as long as they like. Think how much less likely we are to get caught if you help."

"This is a bad idea," Isko said. He rubbed hard at the deep furrow between his brows. "I'll think about it."

29

LUNURIN CALILAN DE DAKILA

In the distance, the Palisade church bell rang out two in the afternoon, calling the faithful to prayer. It was a Wednesday, the week after the wedding, so weather permitting, Cat would've packed her writing desk and be out visiting the public worksites beyond the Palisade. The perfect excuse for Lunurin and Sina to gain entry to the bridge worksite—and to distract Lunurin from the fact that Alon was avoiding her.

The afternoon steamed as they descended from the kalesa near the tract of land the Lakan had cleared the riverfolk from for the bridge. The worksite was visible from Alon's home, but with her thirst giving her bouts of lightheadedness and her leg still tender, Lunurin decided against walking.

Lunurin had penned excerpts of scripture on paper stolen from Isko's office. Cat preferred personalized stationery for her letters. In addition, Sina had packed several dozen boiled eggs into a basket. The meals provided to polo laborers in the workers' barracks were always deficient.

The fenced worksite was guarded by Palisade soldiers. The graffiti here was less subtle than inside the Palisade, with only a few waves and mountains and a great many insults. The soldiers regarded Lunurin and Sina with suspicion.

"Is Sister Catalina doing her rounds today, or are we early? She'd asked me to bring paper for her letters; she's running low." Lunurin hefted the stack in explanation.

Sina lifted the cloth to let the soldiers inspect the eggs. "For the laborers, but if you'd like a few?"

The soldiers relaxed at the mention of Cat. "Oh yes, Sister Catalina, she just arrived. You can set a clock by her. She'll be in the overseer's hut. She usually sets up on the porch, while the Father walks the site."

Passage paid on the credit of Catalina's name, they were ushered into the worksite.

Suddenly Lunurin's throat was tight with more than thirst. Somewhere in the back of her mind, where she'd been trying to ignore the fact that she'd be lying to Cat again, Lunurin had hoped they'd be early, or that maybe she wouldn't come today. The less she had to deceive Cat, the better.

Lunurin scanned the riverbank. Fifteen spans had been built across the Saliwain. The final pylon was still surrounded by the cofferdam, and workers were constructing the final arch that would finally, after five years, connect the bridge to the far bank.

At several points along the bridge, wooden arches supported freshly mortared stonework. There must already be damage from the recent tremors. Lunurin wondered if it would be easier to burn out the falseworks... but no. That would be discovered for sabotage far too quickly, and closer inspection revealed several of the falseworks were brass, not wood at all.

They passed mortar pits where freshwater, quicklime, crushed shells, and sand were being mixed. They didn't appear to be using traditional wet season additives, such as honey, egg whites, or molasses, to improve waterproofing. Sina's contacts would've ensured they weren't. Instead, nipa palm roofing had been constructed over the bridge to protect the curing mortar. Lunurin needed a way to drench the fresh mortar. Even if Sina's contacts hadn't been able to add additional water and metal-salts to the mix, rain on fresh mortar would dissolve away the lime, leaving the remaining material brittle. They only needed to destabilize one or two spans to ruin the bridge.

A muffled exclamation escaped Sina. Lunurin followed her gaze and saw a broad-shouldered Aynilan woman walking with the overseer along the bridge.

"Your mother?" Lunurin asked.

"She's probably consulting on the metalwork reinforcing the spans where there was earthquake damage," Sina murmured, her eyes drinking in her mother's form with a desperation Lunurin recognized.

"We can't," Lunurin said.

"I know. They would ransack every home and forge in the conclave looking for her if I tried. I know our people have to take priority."

And then it was Lunurin's turn to be struck. There, in the shade of the overseer's hut, was Cat, her Cat.

Lunurin lifted a hand to call out, but her voice lodged in her dry throat.

"How well do you know Sister Catalina?" Sina asked.

How to answer such a question? *She is my world. She has my heart.* Lunurin had broken vows to multiple gods for her and would break a dozen more if it meant her safety.

But Lunurin couldn't answer.

As they climbed onto the porch Sina said, "Sister Catalina, we brought the paper and eggs you requested."

Cat looked up, her expression sliding from confusion into hope squashed before it could fully surface.

"Oh yes, Sister María, I mean… Lady Lunurin, I wasn't sure you would come. With your recent marriage, I didn't expect you'd find time to support these humble charitable works."

She didn't miss the cutting edge to Cat's greeting. Lunurin made the sign of the cross, kissing her thumb in devotion, but not to God. "I would never let my marriage come between me and God."

Cat's brittle expression softened. "Sit, you might help me with these messages, if you've the time. Your companion could distribute the food to those waiting in line?"

Lunurin sat, drinking in the sight of Cat's golden cheek framed by the blue of her veil, her delicate fingers ink-flecked from her work. Were her eyes unusually bright? Or was it only the sunlight catching in their depths?

"I've missed you." Lunurin pulled her chair nearer, tucking her legs close beside Cat's. She took written messages, folding them so only the addressed side was visible.

Cat dropped a hand under the desk, resting it on Lunurin's knee.

The tension leached out of Lunurin. She leaned heavily into the points of contact between her hip and Cat's thigh, her arm and Cat's shoulder. There was something so sweetly familiar and good about leaning into someone without the risk of drowning in unfamiliar depths, without any pull on her spirit.

Lunurin handed over the extra paper. She'd chosen a line of scripture from Song of Songs 7:1–2. "How beautiful your sandaled feet, O prince's daughter! Your graceful legs are like jewels, the work of an artist's hands. Your navel is a rounded goblet that never lacks blended wine. Your waist is a mound of wheat encircled by lilies."

Cat had gotten stuck there, her fingertip pressed just under "lilies."

"I hadn't seen you use this verse on your letters," Lunurin said earnestly.

"Yes, well." Cat cleared her throat. "I guess some of their wives will be happy."

"But not you?" Lunurin teased.

Cat blushed and motioned for the next man to come forward.

Between the workers approaching with their messages and extra pay to be sent on to family, their conversation flowed haltingly.

"Cat, how are you?" Lunurin asked.

"You were right. Things are different without you in the convent. Sister Philippa is acting-abbess in your stead," Cat murmured.

"Bad different?" Lunurin asked, her mouth painfully dry.

"I don't know yet. I fear the abbot suspects... I'm not sure what. And I'm concerned for Inez. Even with DeSoto so ill, he tried to keep her as his assistant. I'm helping instead. Now after these letters, I will walk the site with the overseer and write DeSoto a report on the progress. He thinks with overtime the bridge can be completed in three weeks."

It took every shred of Lunurin's self-control not to tear the message she was folding. "Say you'll come to me, please. You must see it isn't safe."

She couldn't quite look at Cat head-on, only holding her profile in her peripheral vision.

Cat shook her head, her lips thinning. "Are you safe?"

Lunurin bit her tongue, hesitating, and Cat saw it. She turned her face away, addressing the next letter. She set it atop Lunurin's stack with a sigh.

"Inez I could send. But your husband was very clear I am not welcome in his home, and I won't part from her."

"Damn my husband," Lunurin snapped. The salt crystal around her neck sloshed, its draw on her increasing, her rage fighting with the magic holding her in check. Alon hadn't come home before midnight in days, if he came home at all. If he intended to avoid her, leaving her in the dark, she'd show him the same courtesy and make her own plans.

Cat pressed too hard with her bamboo dip pen, snapping off the tip and splattering ink across the page.

Lunurin offered the blotting cloth, brushing her fingertips over Cat's wrist in silent entreaty. "I'll make a place for you and Inez, well apart from him. I have a plan. Sina, Alon's cousin, has promised her help. We'll say I'm retiring into seclusion. I'm a disgraced nun, an embarrassment to the Lakan's son. No one will question it, or what I do in the privacy of my own home."

Cat accepted the cloth, but bit her lip and looked away, scrubbing at her mistake with fevered energy.

"Please, Cat, for Inez's safety."

"What about the safety of her immortal soul?" Cat snapped.

Lunurin spread her hands. "I'm not trying to steal her from you. Please, just think about it."

Why couldn't Cat see that Lunurin wanted what was best for them? Why did Cat always doubt her so? It hurt. It hurt how everything with Cat was always give and take, a careful balancing act of faith and favors.

Cat left off rubbing at her mistake. "I have. But can't you see? You and I, we're not like them." She jerked her chin at the Aynilan laborers bent over the mortar pits, muddy to their hips and worn with exhaustion under the beating sun, some of them risking their lives so the Puente de Hilaga would be just a little weaker. "We aren't just here to toil, feed our families, and die.

We have a higher work, a divine calling, souls that will be saved by our labor. Giving that up to pursue temporal comforts... How is that not a greater sin than anything they might do to offend God in their ignorance?"

"Is that what you think I've done?" Lunurin asked quietly.

"That's different. The abbot... He's convinced you really are a water witch."

"We'd be able to be together." Lunurin knew this plea was beginning to sound desperate, but what else did she have? Didn't Cat want to keep their family together as much as Lunurin did?

"What kind of life will that be for me? No one will take me for an Aynilan lady. I'm not like you. My Aynilan is clumsy. I've no family... I'd hardly be accepted as your companion. Ha, maybe as your maid? You know how important my work is, and you'd ask me to abandon it?"

"Cat, it wouldn't be like—"

The overseer stepped onto the porch. Cat pulled away from her, turning to business, to her work and her faith. After a brief conference with the man, she stood and followed him onto the bridge without a backward glance.

Every point of contact Lunurin had shared with Cat felt raw and skinned. Worse than the sting of Cat's rejection was the creeping fear that Cat was right. Was Lunurin really thinking of Cat's and Inez's safety, or was she being selfish?

30

***

ALON DAKILA

For the first time in more nights than he cared to count, Alon managed to tear away from his father's lime troubles soon enough to return to his own bed. After speaking to half the lime suppliers in the city and failed negotiations with DeSoto and the governor, he wasn't looking forward to convincing Isko to donate Aynila Indigo's lime stores to fulfill the Lakan's obligations. Half-drunk with exhaustion, all he wanted was to collapse into his own bed and deal with his disastrous personal life tomorrow.

So of course, that couldn't be allowed.

The first hint was the note from Kawit on his pillow. "Your wife is in the blue room. She deserves an apology. This standoff has gone on long enough."

Alon narrowed his eyes. Unlike the guestrooms, the blue room shared a sliding panel wall with his bedroom.

Muttering deprecations about meddling titos, Alon pulled down his bedding, to discover his sheets were drenched with distilled water.

So that's how it was going to be. Alon stripped the dripping sheets only to find the mattress had been scattered with gravel.

"Buwisit!" he swore. There was no way he'd successfully remove all the rocks by the light of one oil lamp.

Alon pinched the bridge of his nose and took a deep breath. Clearly, putting his wife off until tomorrow was not an option, according to Kawit.

Alon went to the sliding partition and knocked softly. "Lunurin, are you awake?"

"Alon?" Her voice, husky with sleep, sent a shiver down his spine.

No. Bad thoughts. She was a nun. Alon respected whatever those vows meant to her, and any promises she'd made to Catalina. Besides, she was probably raspy with thirst. Was she drinking enough?

"I need to apologize."

He heard creaks and rustling. The panel slid open.

Lunurin leaned into the doorframe. The light from the oil lamp threatened to lend translucence to her shift.

Alon jerked his gaze to her eyes. They were dark and hard. Though the night was quiet, Lunurin's spirit crackled.

Alon winced. "You're right to be angry. I... my father can be volatile when he's feeling threatened. Sometimes it's better to appease him. I couldn't have you caught in the crossfire of another fight. But I hated seeing how small he made you."

Lunurin let out a long, slow breath. "You have duties to Aynila, to your father. I understand why you did it. I just don't think I can remain small around him so you can keep playing the perfect son. Even if I wanted to do it for you, this amulet won't survive more of his tests."

Her words stabbed at all Alon's good intentions. "I don't want you to have to. I never intended this marriage to confine you—"

"Don't make promises you can't keep. I know you're trying, but look how this week has gone. I just don't know if it's going to be enough."

It frightened Alon how desperately he wanted to be enough for her. But Alon had been caught in a thorny net of duty long before he'd made any vows to her. He couldn't shrug it off, not even for love.

He felt his heart crack. "I understand. I'll find a way to—"

"No!" Lunurin's voice was sharp as a crack of thunder. "That's what I'm trying to tell you. Are we married or not? I need you to stop making decisions alone and trying to handle everything yourself. I am your wife, not your ward. If this can be fixed, let's fix it together. Won't you try with me?"

Relief rushed over Alon in a wave. She hadn't wholly given up on him. "Yes, of course, you're right."

Lunurin blinked at him in surprise. "I am?"

"Did you want me to say you were wrong?"

Lunurin shook her head, her expression strange. "No, I'm just tired. I don't want to fight."

"I don't either… I might not survive Kawit's encouragements to mend my marriage."

"Ganon ba?"

"My sheets are dripping wet and my bed is covered in gravel."

"Hay nako, gravel? Why is there—"

Alon held up a pebble for inspection, dropping it into her palms. Lunurin rolled it between her fingers. Then she started laughing. Aman Sinaya, but she was beautiful. It was riveting, except that it triggered a coughing fit.

"I'm sorry—" Her laughter ended in painful dry spasms in her throat. "It's just…" She waved him into her room. "Come lie down before Kawit resorts to more drastic measures."

Alon shook his head, refusing to enter the blue room. "Let me get you water."

"I have three pitchers on my bedside. Kawit's been very attentive. Now you need rest, and I'd like my throat to stop aching, both of which can be accomplished if you come and lie down."

Against his better judgment, Alon went. It was impossible to deny her.

He hesitated in the doorway. "About my father—"

"Come to bed," Lunurin repeated. "You can tell me what your father needs from you in the morning. We'll work on it together. If I'm to be your wife, let me be a help to you, not a burden."

31

❖

LUNURIN CALILAN
DE DAKILA

Did Lunurin feel terrible for manipulating Alon like this? Yes, but waking up without her head throbbing and her tongue the texture of sandpaper made it seem worth it. With him so near, she didn't even hear the whispers of her goddess in the wind. Her spirit was her own. Her emotions, her own. There was something so novel about how he was willing to work with her and trust her, how not every interaction devolved into a fight. But that wasn't the point. She and Sina had to keep abreast of Alon's involvement in the bridge project. If she could steer him into helping them, all the better.

"Did he say if he'd force the conclave to make up the shortfall? Isko says Aynila Indigo can only cover a quarter of what's needed," Sina asked the next morning as they bathed.

One of the dyeing huts, built half over the river, had its first level converted into a bathhouse. Lilies and reeds clustered around the stilts, but the bottom was firm and sandy and bamboo screens provided ample privacy and access to the clear river water.

"No," Lunurin grumbled. "He's still wavering; he plans to meet with a few traders about sourcing it outside of Aynila. It's cost prohibitive but might keep the peace."

"His father isn't going to like that, and the Codicíans even less," Sina observed as she dug through the basket of bathing supplies.

"I know but, Alon is still grimly optimistic he can avoid conflict if he twists himself in enough knots." Lunurin released her sleeping bun. Her hair was getting long again so quickly. If she let it loose, it would be well past her shoulder blades.

"Find out which suppliers and traders he's meeting with. My people can ramp up complaints of subpar lime deliveries."

A door in the main house opened and footsteps crunched down the gravel walk to the river.

"Will you help me wash my hair?" Lunurin asked Sina. "I'll scrub your back."

Sina snorted and waved her off. "Of course, I'll help. You don't have to trade me."

It made her uncomfortable how free with their aid and time everyone in Alon's household was toward her. Her life before had been very… transactional.

Despite Sina's best efforts, within moments a steady rain had started.

Lunurin winced. "Sorry, was I rinsing too vigorously?"

Sina laughed. "A bit. You pulled your hair right out of my hands. How do stormcallers manage this?"

"With help," Lunurin said honestly. "Someone tide-touched could briefly neutralize my ability."

Sina stared at her. "Really?"

"Yes, why?"

Sina raised her brows. "Why? So we put your husband on

285

hair duty and stop messing with the weather. Alon, is that you over there?"

Lunurin grabbed her hair with one hand and lunged to slap her other over Sina's mouth.

Sina went boneless and slippery as a squid, wriggling out of Lunurin's grip. "Alon! Get over here. Your wife needs help!"

From the unofficial men's side of the bathing area that was open to the river and all its traffic, Alon called back, "Sina, what are you caterwauling about?"

"Get over here," Sina ordered.

"You're bathing."

"We're both in wraps, and your wife needs help."

"Please ignore your cousin!" Lunurin put in.

With a mischievous grin, Sina let go of the ends of Lunurin's hair. Within seconds they couldn't hear the rush of the river over the rain. With a yelp, Lunurin tried to stem the rain before she brought down hail.

"Alon! Help me with your wife's hair!" Sina called out.

Alon peered hesitantly around the bamboo partition.

Lunurin froze, unaccountably interested in how her husband looked, wet and shirtless, a drenched salawal waistcloth hanging from his hips. Her mouth went dry, but it was just the rain and her salt amulet playing tug-of-war. Right?

"Why are we calling a storm off the bay?" Alon asked. His eyes were everywhere but on Lunurin, who discovered that her wrap had drenched to unexpected translucence.

Lunurin ducked into the water up to her neck while Sina grinned, pleased as a little queen cat.

"This always happens when my hair is loose. Even when I had my dugong bone amulet. It's just what being a stormcaller is," Lunurin explained.

286

Some of Alon's tension eased.

"I'm fine. I can handle it," Lunurin added, groping to collect her hair snaking wildly around her in the water. Faint rumbles of thunder throbbed in the distance.

Alon looked pleadingly at Sina. "Sina, why are you helping Kawit?"

"I don't know what you're talking about. No, there isn't a running betting pool," Sina replied glibly.

"Lunurin?"

"I'm struggling. How is there already so much hair?"

"Can I help?" Alon asked.

He shut his eyes and edged around the partition. Sina winked at Lunurin and vanished the way Alon had come, diving into the river with a slash.

Giving up on her hair, Lunurin stood and caught Alon's hand. The cool relief of his touch was so alluring. The longer she thirsted, the harder it was to deny. She tugged him onto the floating dock that supported the screen.

"Careful, careful, now sit." She pulled the basket of bathing supplies close.

Alon nodded, his throat bobbing visibly. His wet hair dripped down his broad chest.

Lunurin slipped into the water, and found an even more distracting sight, the trail of fine dark hair that ran from Alon's navel down...

Lunurin cleared her throat. "I'm going to put your hand on top of my head. Just hold it there while I finish washing my hair, then we can tie it back."

Alon hesitated. "You're sure it doesn't hurt you?"

"Yes." She lifted his hand off his knee.

His touch was light as a landing dragonfly. They both froze, listening to the rain. Alon reached out with his magic.

The downpour tapered and died. Lunurin smiled. It was so different from the spiritual drowning of driving her goddess out of her skin. This was… gentle, like floating on the surface of a vast calm sea. When he was with her like this, she really did feel protected.

"Thank you, this feels… safe."

Alon stopped scrunching his eyes closed. He stared at her with an expression caught between naked longing and awe. A pleasant shiver chased down her spine as Lunurin tilted her head into his touch. Alon slapped his other hand across his eyes with a wet smack.

"Aray… Are you okay?" she asked, doing her damnedest not to laugh.

Alon's voice had the nasal edge of someone unexpectedly popped in the nose. "Fine. I'm fine."

Lunurin reached for the gugo vine decoction. "Sorry about Sina—"

"You don't need to apologize. You married into my disaster of a family. Be glad Sina's stopped setting fires when she's angry. When I was ten, she set my hair on fire."

"Nako! I'll stay on her good side. What did you do?"

"I don't know what you're talking about. It was never conclusively proven that the eels in her wash water were my fault."

Lunurin giggled. She pulled her mother-of-pearl comb from where she'd tucked her mutya, using it to comb the decoction through her hair, root to tip.

When she brushed Alon's hand with the comb they both jumped, muttering apologies. Alon sifted his fingertips till they rested in the baby hairs just forward of her left ear. Which was fine until Lunurin reached for her hair oil and pressed her damp cheek directly into Alon's cupped palm.

Someone whimpered. To preserve Alon's dignity, Lunurin would pretend it was her. She snatched the bottle she needed and leaned away so only Alon's fingertips touched her. Gods, but it was so hard to resist the pull of him. He shouldn't feel this good. It was more than relief of her thirst. He felt—the way he felt… Was it just their tangled magic gone rogue? Did that explain it away?

"Sorry, sorry," Alon whispered hoarsely. "I know it's not proper for me to touch your hair. It's—"

"Don't say shameful. It's not shameful," Lunurin said.

Alon said nothing, a flush painting his chest and creeping up his neck. Did he have to blush so prettily?

"I'm going to rinse." Lunurin sank under the water. In comparison to the thick, steaming air, the river was deliciously refreshing from its time in upland lakes.

She surfaced with a gasp; the air tasted of fresh rain and wet earth. Wiping her eyes, she then poured the sesame oil into her wet palms, spreading it through her hair.

"It's intimate," Alon said at last. He'd dropped his hand from his face, but kept his eyes closed. "You shouldn't feel like you've no choice but to be intimate with me."

Lunurin didn't know how to untangle the pain and shame still knotted up in Alon. She shouldn't try. She intended to help Sina and leave him. She couldn't bear his good intentions and the way her body relaxed into his. Every intimacy she shared with him was a betrayal of Cat. She massaged the remnants of oil into her scalp. Alon's fingers slipped deeper into her hair, stroking through the strands.

"I think—" Lunurin leaned in, unable to stop herself, pleasant shivers tickling over her scalp. Her hair was so often ruthlessly constrained. Being able to relax like this was a luxury she hadn't realized she craved. She cleared her throat. "I could grow to appreciate it not requiring a three-step containment system to wash my hair."

A faint smile creased Alon's face. "Glad I'm good for something."

Lunurin wrung her hair, coiling it at the nape of her neck. She secured the low bun and slid her mutya in place. Alon lifted his hand away the instant she was done. Despite herself, Lunurin wished he'd lingered.

"I'll leave you to bathe in peace," Alon said, already rising.

But Lunurin still needed information. Before he could escape, Lunurin hooked a hand behind his knee.

"Where do you think you're going? I have to help you with your hair."

"You really don't—"

"Of course I do," Lunurin shot back. "I've done this a long time. No one enjoys the hassle of my hair."

Alon shook his head, eyes still scrunched closed. "Helping you isn't a hassle."

Lunurin shook off a pang at his sincerity. How different it'd been in the convent... and with Cat.

Lunurin cleared her tight throat, turning the sound into a scoff. "You're just afraid of reciprocity."

Alon sputtered. Lunurin heaved herself from the water, and knelt behind him on the dock. "Just relax and let me return the favor."

His shoulders tensed and Lunurin resisted a childish urge to push Alon into the water. Instead, she gathered his damp hair, noticing how a shiver skated over his skin at the slight scrape of her nails. His shoulders relaxed, his head lolling forward. She filed this information away under "future use," reaching for the coconut milk.

"Will you be busy again today?" she asked.

"Yes, I'm sorry."

"Could I help? You don't have to do everything yourself. Who do you still need to meet with?"

A flurried knock sounded on the door of the bathhouse. Litao called in, "Gat Alon! The Lakan sent for you."

Alon pushed to his feet. "Forgive me. I shouldn't keep my father waiting." His tone and bearing were suddenly distant and cold.

"Let me come with you," Lunurin said.

"I won't put you back in range while he's still so worked up about this." Alon dried off briskly and dragged his barong over his head.

"Don't I get a choice?" Lunurin asked, unaccountably angry at how the mere mention of his father changed Alon so much.

"Not while you're still affecting the weather. I don't need him noticing."

"I'm a stormcaller!" Lunurin exclaimed in frustration. "Unless you keep my hair shaved, I will call storms with it!"

But Alon only shook his head, and fled the bathhouse.

~

Lunurin made her way to the main house, grumbling under her breath. She'd hoped to get more information before Alon rushed off on his father's bidding. Now what?

Raised voices drew Lunurin to Isko's first-floor study. A trio of angry men, two women, and four chickens in a cage had packed into the limited space.

"I can't help you. Lord Alon isn't available. I don't know when he will return," Isko repeated.

"I've come every morning for days," one woman complained. "I need to lodge a complaint against Lord Bagay, but the Lakan turned me away. I haven't seen my son in months!"

"The Tianchaowen-owned rice mill is price gouging while ships are stuck in port and we've nowhere else to sell our rice," said the other.

"I can't begin construction without the Gat's seal of approval. He's had the plans to review for months. At this rate, the site will be rained out," the leader of the trio of laborers pointed out.

What had Alon been working on in his study this morning if it hadn't been Aynilan petitions? Lunurin wondered. With the right excuse for access, she could find out.

"If you'll come one at a time, and explain the problem, I'll give you a solution to hold you over until Gat Alon is available. Please, wait outside for now," Lunurin said.

The petitioners gawped at her, but gathered their things, including the cage of chickens and a heaping basket of rice, and traipsed out into the main shop area to wait.

Isko stood from where he'd sheltered behind the bulk of his desk. "I really don't think…"

Lunurin waggled her left hand. "Is this not the Seal of Aynila?"

"It is," Isko allowed.

"Am I not Alon's wife? I recall promising a great many people I would be his helpmeet in all things."

"He wouldn't expect you to take on——"

Lunurin threw her hands up, frustration boiling over. "Isn't that the problem? Alon doesn't expect anything of me. But I'm part of what's keeping him from his duties, the least I can do is keep him from falling behind."

Isko frowned. "I don't see how you can help. Alon's been run ragged with the Codician situation since the falla tax riots even before the wet season festival mess. All the Aynilan petitions have been delayed for weeks."

"Show me his study. If you point me in the right direction, I'll manage." Lunurin held Isko's gaze, imbuing her expression with good intentions.

Isko considered her from under black, hawkish brows. Then with a sigh he showed her into Alon's study. The surface of the desk was buried in literal mountains of paperwork.

"I've told him he needs a secretary or five, but that wouldn't solve the problem. The problem is politics." Isko helped her sift for the relevant petitions and left her to it.

Lunurin started with the rice mill, a miscommunication on conversion rates and slighted honor, which she patched over with a series of strongly worded letters and a promise to visit soon.

She moved on to Lord Bagay. He'd been operating as a loan broker, introducing a bafflingly complex interest rate system on his abaca farmers. When they couldn't pay up, he absconded with able-bodied family members to work his own fields. It was hours before she'd seen to the original parties, which bloated as more people arrived to offer their side of the story. While she waited, she sorted Alon's paperwork, and soon found exactly what she'd hoped for. She enlisted Sina to the task of cross-referencing which lime suppliers Alon had met with, and who'd sold lime to Aynila Indigo and the bridge project.

And maybe she'd only started so that she'd have a good excuse if Alon found her elbow-deep in his paperwork, but once she'd seen the state of things… she couldn't leave him like this.

Administration was all the same when it came down to it. She'd had the running of the convent for anything that required interfacing with Aynilan suppliers for years. She'd been raised to the arbitration and administration of Calilan and the maintenance of the Stormfleet. Aynila was just bigger. Luckily, Alon wasn't receiving every petition, requisition, and botched tax form in the city, only the disputes the Lakan's teams of accountants and secretaries deemed complicated enough, or involving easily offended nobility, who might require the fear of the Lakan put into them over the matter of doctored tax records.

Sina passed over a tray heaped with wedding congratulations. Lunurin didn't think any were time-sensitive, until moving the pile, a sheet with familiar handwriting fluttered to the floor.

Lunurin, I'm sure you're very busy, being newly married, and Cat says I shouldn't bother you, but I need to talk to you. Even if I can't stay, could I visit?

Inez

Lunurin swallowed hard. Did Inez want to stay? Was the note restrained because she worried Alon would read it, or because someone in the convent might? Did Cat know what Inez was so worried about? Hadn't Inez wanted to talk to Lunurin the morning of the wedding? Lunurin wracked her spotty memory of the day as she showed the note to Sina.

She still didn't have a satisfactory plan for what to do about Inez when Isko brought her a message from Alon.

Isko, I've been asked to host a dinner tonight for the Lakan and several codician stakeholders in the bridge project. It might be best if Lunurin and Sina were to claim ill-health.

Alon

Lunurin poured herself more water, only to find the pitcher empty. "Might be best" was more a strongly worded hope than an order. And clearly there was no better place to lay the groundwork for their lime adulteration rumors...

Sina leaned to read the missive. "Oh, we won't be missing that."

"Do we have to risk the Lakan's wrath twice in as many weeks?" Isko asked.

"We'll be on our best behavior," Sina promised. "Imagine all the worse things we could be doing than attending a dinner."

Isko grimaced. "I don't like that either."

"Alon needs a hostess," Lunurin pointed out. "I need to talk to Kawit. How many people is 'several'? Has Alon never hosted a dinner before? I'd like to open the eastern side of the house and move the table, so the Puente de Hilaga can be seen."

Sina nodded. "Yes. You take care of the food. I have an idea."

Isko eyed them and heaved a put-upon sigh. "I won't convince you this is a terrible idea, will I?"

"How badly can one dinner go?" Sina asked sweetly.

"Ask Lunurin," Isko shot back.

"Then you'll just have to attend."

"Before you get yourselves killed?" Isko pinched the bridge of his nose. "Oh, I'm going to regret this. How are you making the quicklime situation worse and what loose ends do I need to cover up?"

Sina squinted at him. "I thought you didn't want to know any details?"

"I'm keeping Alon's wife from being executed for treason. I'm fairly sure getting the only stormcaller in Aynila killed will be just as disastrous as Hilaga's firetenders being driven into hiding, or worse. If anything, this is for him, and the less he knows about it the better. Please tell me you at least have a solid cover story."

Sina's smile warmed the whole room.

32

ALON DAKILA

Alon was upset Lunurin had ignored him. Really, he was. But given the mayhem he'd expected to arrive to, Lunurin assuring him she'd already settled the menu with Kawit and that everything was in order was such a relief it was hard to stay upset.

He let her tug him away to dress.

Lunurin held open a white barong, heavily embroidered in gold thread, for him to shrug into. "Don't look so shocked. You know how often I hosted for the abbot."

"I'm not doubting you. I thought you wouldn't want to be at the center of any more political dinners, and I left rather abruptly this morning."

Lunurin buttoned his collar, tying on a lace kerchief, her fingertips brushing his throat. "Is that an apology?"

Alon caught her hand, lifting it to his lips. "It's trying to be one. You look lovely."

The furrow of concentration between Lunurin's brows melted away. Her smile caught him in the chest.

She wore an indigo silk robe, embroidered in matching geometric gold patterns. Her hair glimmered like moonlight on dark water, an effect accomplished by the net of indigo lace and pearls pinned over her hair, though he noticed her mutya were hidden. He didn't begrudge her the precaution.

"You need a hostess," Lunurin told him briskly. "You need to work on accepting help."

Which, maybe he did. But it seemed selfish to demand Lunurin fill that role. Still, if dinner went well, it might prove to his father Lunurin had been a good choice for a wife. If he could make his father see Lunurin as an asset, this marriage had a chance at keeping Lunurin as safe as he'd promised.

Then he learned that Father DeSoto was indisposed and had sent Sister Catalina in his place.

Alon blinked hard, hoping he'd fallen asleep in the kalesa and was having a nightmare. But no. Lunurin was conducting Catalina to a seat between Isko and Governor López. The abbot had arrived with Catalina, completing their party. Lunurin was so very gentle with her Cat. There was an undeniable softness in her eyes, her hands lingering on Cat's slim shoulders. Their gazes mingled intensely as lovers' breaths as they spoke about the trip from the Palisade.

Cat's warm regard turned to daggers as Lunurin retook her seat at Alon's side, her attention returning to her hosting duties.

His father was still talking to the governor. Alon dragged his attention back. Was he really promising the lime sooner and in greater quantity than discussed?

"Lime is an abundant local resource," his father said. "I'm certain that Lord Alon will reach an agreement with our suppliers before the end of the week and we'll be able to provide not just for the completion of the Puente de Hilaga, but for many more joint building projects in the future."

"In the convent, when I tended the oyster beds, I sold offcast shells with low quality mother-of-pearl to the lime kilns," Lunurin added. "I had no idea it was such an integral part of stonework. You'll forgive a woman's priorities; I thought it all went to soap and candle-making."

His father and the governor laughed. Alon feared his face might crack from the strain of maintaining a good-natured expression.

"It's always soap and candles with women," the governor said. "Keep them in soap and candles, and they'll keep their peace. Now, Lord Alon, my biggest concern is steady supply, and steady costs. I don't want to repeat the issues we've seen with this bridge. We've had construction grind to a halt for months at a time on account of supply shortages and price hikes."

"I'm working with my suppliers. I'm sure that we can negotiate an agreeable average year-round price, that is neither so high as these shortage price surges, nor so low as to disadvantage our local industries."

"You aren't likely to get quality lime, price-fixing like that," Sina observed.

Alon narrowed his eyes at his cousin, wishing she hadn't raised the point so blatantly.

Isko added, "It's true. Lately, we've had to use two, even three times the quantity of lime in the extraction cauldrons to get half the dye strength you'd usually see."

The governor's expression sharpened. "When was this? Do you buy local lime? Was it only one or two bad batches or have you been having consistent problems?"

Isko shrugged. "It's hard to tell. When there's a shortage like this, some vendors are incentivized to adulterate their lime. Quality issues are a constant fight when the seasons are changing and many additives are in flux. You must have similar problems on your build site with salt contamination when we get reverse flow to the upriver sand pits."

The abbot was frowning deeply now. Even Catalina looked concerned.

"Father DeSoto does say quality lime is what makes or breaks mortar integrity," she murmured, barely lifting her head.

The governor shot her a sidelong look. "Abbot, what is it with your lot and nuns? You mean to tell me none of your young priests have the head for numbers required to pass Father DeSoto's standards?"

The abbot gestured dismissively. "Forgive DeSoto and his ideas. He's convinced girls are more organized and keep better records. And if you've seen the man's records when he has no help... I'd rather he keep whatever neat handwriting he prefers. I'll speak to him about training a successor. We'll not leave the Palisade without a lead architect. You military sorts are all very well for fortification and ships, but it takes a more spiritually tuned eye for churches and bridges."

Alon put a staying touch over Lunurin's hand on the table. Her grip slid to the crook of his arm, fingertips digging deeper with every damning word from the abbot's mouth. Catalina's cup trembled in her grip. The conversation needed steering into safer waters before Catalina decided to poison DeSoto outright.

"And I do find the design quite eye-catching," Alon blurted out. "Now that the final arch is nearing completion, the whole effect does put one in mind of entering a holy place."

This pivoted the party's attention out the open capiz shell windows where the Puente de Hilaga, bathed in an almost firelight glow, looked like nothing so much as an undulating laho about to froth the river into chaos. Orange and red streaked the twilight sky, only a few large white fluffy clouds hovering far out to sea.

"It is quite impressive," his father commented. "Rare to see such a clear sky this time of year. I pray it heralds a mild typhoon season."

This last statement was directed pointedly toward Lunurin, whose expression of modest, but contented newlywed bliss didn't flicker.

Sea Lady have mercy, if Lunurin didn't release her grip he might bleed.

"What do you think of our chances for a mild typhoon season, Lord Alon?" his father prompted. "It would benefit your trading endeavors with Aynila Indigo."

His father indicated his empty cup to Lunurin, pointing with his lips. Alon did his level best not to wince as Lunurin let go of his arm. She thankfully only filled the Lakan's cup, rather than throwing the boiling tea in his face.

"I've spoken to some of my more experienced captains. They are hopeful, but are planning to wait out the unpredictable early season weather to see what comes before they'll commit to major voyages."

Keeping her hands busy, Lunurin served him and then his father more steamed puto rice cakes. Were those bamboo splinters from the steamer in the one she was about to serve the Lakan?

Alon caught Lunurin's hand in his before she could put it on his father's plate, drawing her to his side with what he hoped looked like an indulgent smile.

Lunurin smiled back, all teeth.

Catalina wishing a thousand deaths upon him when his gaze so much as lingered on Lunurin for too long wasn't helping.

"Will you travel yourself this wet season? Once the bridge has been completed, now that your home is in order, and your wife has settled into her proper place," his father asked next.

The governor stroked a hand through his beard. "I'm sure he'll be quite eager to get away. Business trips, hunting trips, bordello trips—a man will need any number of those once he has a wife waiting for him at home."

Alon forced himself to laugh with the older men, as the few bites of food in his stomach congealed into a solid brick of shame.

Thankfully, at that point Kawit determined that all their guests had arrived and began laying out the meal. This took at least his father's and the abbot's attention off Lunurin, for grace.

Alon wished DeSoto had sent anyone but Catalina. There were only so many incipient disasters he could be expected to fend off during one dinner. The chief of which was that his wife was seated between himself and his father. It was the last place he ever wanted her to be again. His father was tormenting Lunurin with calculating ease, a test to see if she was truly under his control or only feigning.

Catalina sat directly across from him and alternated between pointed commentary on the dangers of coveting that which was not one's own, and engaging in some unknowable communion with Lunurin entirely composed of their own subtle language.

Last, but not least, to his left sat Sina.

"Doesn't three weeks seem ambitious? I remember the last span took almost two months, and that was with good dry season weather. With all the recent rains, don't you worry about cure time for the new mortar?" Sina's needling questions were clearly getting on both the governor's and his father's nerves. Alon knew they were contractually tied to put up more money and higher labor quotas should construction extend beyond July.

Knowing Sina's next barb might hit its mark, Alon interjected, "On the subject of the Puente de Hilaga's completion—which I don't doubt will proceed according to DeSoto's schedule—would you be open to amending my aunt's labor contract to allow her to return to her forge on Hilaga? Her commissioned work could easily be transported from Hilaga to the Palisade, without her needing to be in the Palisade shipyards directly."

The governor nodded. "Let me think on it. Call on me tomorrow and we might try to hammer out the details of an amendment. She has done excellent work on the *Santa Clarita*'s new cannonry, but there are times of the year when I would like to ensure there is a dedicated smith in the shipyards."

Alon shot a quelling look at Sina, who toasted him. This didn't comfort him in the slightest. Couldn't she see diplomacy was the best way to achieve her mother's freedom?

33

LUNURIN CALILAN
DE DAKILA

Lunurin was going to have a meltdown. She'd never had one not tied to devastating weather events and was almost curious what it would be like. She'd severely miscalculated the level of polite torture that could be inflicted on her in her own home.

She was trapped in an actual tug-of-war between her husband and her father-in-law. Alon had all but pulled her into his lap, which hadn't stopped the Lakan from making her skin crawl. He'd started with a hand at the small of her back when he moved around the table, which escalated to giving her cheek a pinch or pat any time he laughed and leaned to thump Alon good-naturedly on the back.

Lunurin had thought her seating chart, arranged to give their esteemed visitors the best view of the river, would keep her well clear of her father-in-law, but the Lakan had undone all her strategizing by ignoring it.

Her mouth seemed to be filled with chalk. Her throat was so dry it was difficult to swallow her food. In the distance, far out over the water, rain pattered over the surface of the sea and her goddess asked, *"How long will you make yourself small for men who deserve nothing but scorn? How long will you cut into your own flesh to win even slivers back from their hunger and greed?"*

The salt guarding her spirit tightened. Alon's power swelled and her goddess's voice faded. Her distress was all hers. Hers alone.

And now the governor was goading the abbot into a sermon on the virtue of women marrying and submitting to their husbands, with the clear indication that Lunurin's situation should be applied to as many women of the Church as possible. Cat bit her lip, holding back tears.

It's an act! It's all an act! Lunurin wanted to shout. But all her fury was bound within her skin, reduced to an impotent churn of internal discomfort. When she knew she could *be so much more*—no.

Instead, she pointed out how many essential roles the women of the Church filled for the Palisade at large.

At least this brought Cat back to the conversation. She even smiled at Lunurin. With Cat's warm regard restored, Lunurin almost didn't flinch when the Lakan patted the top of her head before laying a paternal hand on her shoulder.

The room swam. Lunurin reminded herself her mutya were safely tucked into her sleeve. She drank more tea, trying to stave off a swoon. It was amazing that mere human fury could fill her up to the brim and not reach out of her body to stir the world to storm. She wouldn't allow these greedy, sneering men to tighten their hold on one of Aynila's last precious secrets. That beautiful bridge below could not be allowed to span the river.

Alon brushed a hand down her arm, subtly dislodging his father's hold. He gathered her into him, murmuring, "Easy, easy…"

The low rumble of his voice steadied her, the draw of the amulet easing.

Lunurin leaned in, needing the relief his touch provided. But when she opened her eyes, she saw Cat's face caught in an agony of jealousy and sorrow. Cat ducked her head, and wouldn't look at Lunurin again.

Lunurin pulled away from Alon, the buoying relief of his touch slipping away like water through a cracked cup. Shame replaced it, mixing with her impotent fury and thirst.

At last, dinner reached its natural conclusion. The men adjourned to the porch to smoke and drink heavier spirits than wine. Sina stepped away to the kitchen.

Lunurin forced herself to her feet and extended her hands to Catalina, trying to ignore the faint trembling of her fingers. "Sister Catalina, can I offer you sweet wine or more tea?"

Cat waved her off, her expression distant and cold. "I think I've seen… had quite enough."

"You are a guest. You must let me offer you something. It might be sometime before the men are done with their talk." Lunurin crossed to her side, desperate to make Cat look at her, to touch her, to hold her. She needed to remind herself of what was real and good, not just salt illusions and rogue magic.

Cat rose. "I'll not wait for them. I'd like to return to the Palisade before it gets too late."

"I need to talk to you."

Cat wasn't listening.

"It's about Inez."

Cat hesitated.

"She wrote to me. Cat, I think she wants to leave the convent. I think she's afraid."

Cat's expression hardened. "That's low, even from you. Inez is where she needs to be. Maybe we all are."

Cat brushed past. Lunurin shot out a hand, desperate to delay her. "Please, Cat. Let me explain—this wasn't about you."

Cat turned, eyes sharp as shattered porcelain, her voice hard and low. "I see that. I don't begrudge you whatever your new station requires. But I'll not stay to be your amusement when you are finished with hanging on your husband's arm at public functions. And I'd appreciate it if you stopped threatening to steal my sister to convince me I should."

Lunurin's hand went slack.

Cat stepped around her. "I have the dawn prayer slot, so I'll take my leave."

Lunurin counted each of her steps as they echoed down the stairs.

Sina returned with a tray of after-dinner snacks from the kitchen. "Did we offend your friend?"

Lunurin cleared her aching throat. Her eyes burned. She almost wished for the relief of tears. "Sister Catalina is very dedicated to her duties. She simply thinks these dinners frivolous. It's nothing to do with us."

"Would she not wait till we could call a kalesa?"

"I think she prefers the walk," Lunurin forced out.

Sina's brow furrowed with concern, but she said nothing. Their part in tonight's political showmanship wasn't finished.

She set aside her tray and gave Lunurin's hands a squeeze, pressing heat into her trembling fingers. "Come then, let's lay out an after-dinner spread. I fear the rain will chase the men indoors soon enough."

Reminded of their purpose tonight, Lunurin firmed her jaw against a tremble. Her personal tragedy could wait. She searched Sina's burning gaze. She'd wondered if Alon's negotiations on Hiraya's behalf might pause Sina's plans. But there was no hint of hesitation in the burning heat of her presence.

"Are we ready?" Lunurin asked.

"Yes."

Lunurin released a few curls from the edge of her mantilla. At least the amulet had given her this. Precision that didn't dampen her power. Instead it prevented her goddess from reaching through, twisting a drizzle into a thunderstorm if Lunurin's attention slipped. Slowly, those white clouds over the bay crept inland, up the Saliwain. They were hardly a storm, bringing no wind or lightning, only steady, drenching rain, heavy as the tears she couldn't afford to shed.

~

After all the guests had left, Sina and Lunurin retreated to "bathe." There was heavy security on the Aynilan-facing side of the worksite, but its access by water wasn't nearly so well guarded. Perhaps the Codicians had grown complacent during the dry season, accustomed to being able to look out over the whole site from the guard tower built into the fencing. Through the rain, the faint glow of lantern light was visible at the top of the tower and within the windows of the overseer's hut. Luckily, she and Sina wouldn't need to go near either.

Instead, they rowed the small bangka under the third arch from the center. Someone had tied white flagging from the falseworks there in the vague shape of a peaked mountain. Lunurin saw several places so flagged.

"That's where we would've placed the black powder," Sina explained. "Will we be able to do enough with just us?"

"You're the one who said multiple firetenders working together might rouse Hilaga too close to waking."

Sina waggled a hand. "In large groups, some aren't good at using only the inner flame with our own breath to stoke it, just

307

as Amihan rides the wind. They tug on the fires of the earth instead, Amihan's primordial child, who we are charged to tend. These islands were born of fire, and wake to it easily."

"If we need more heat, I'll call down lightning," Lunurin promised.

Sina stood wobbling, before throwing her hands flat against the pylon. "Perfect. It's not hardened yet, more kinda… rubbery," she said, scraping the mortar with a nail.

"The surface could just be wet from water absorbed during the recent storms. But I'm hoping there's still plenty of moisture deeper in the stonework. Tie us to the falseworks. I want to be moored before I call the wind."

Lunurin pulled more pins from her hair, dragging down some less than friendly winds. The first energetic rush of high-altitude air swung their craft out horizontally, nearly pitching Sina into the river, before Lunurin harnessed the wind and sent it up off the water to carry away large sections of the nipa palm roofing.

Drifts of roofing swirled away downriver. Rain beat down on either side of the arch.

"Now we wait," said Lunurin. "The rain has to seep into the cracks in the stonework before our trick has a chance of working."

Sina nodded. "I'll try to heat the metal reinforcements enough to warp or damage the foundations. There's wood right alongside the metal, some moisture is sure to be trapped." She made an expanding gesture with her hands.

Lunurin eyed the dark water streaming past their craft. "I don't want to be here when the river starts boiling. I'll climb up on the bridge and blow off more roofing. When it's wet enough, you can heat the mortar. The water will flash, even if the mortar doesn't immediately crumble out. It's best if the damage takes a few weeks to show."

Lunurin jumped, grabbed the falseworks and climbed, throwing a leg over the top of the bridge, scrambling the rest of the way up.

A gout of steam boiled from below, threatening to scald her even at this distance. Lunurin lifted her mutya from her bun, letting more of her hair tumble down her back.

Winds swirled around her to nudge at her face and hands like eager hounds.

The salt amulet on her chest warmed, her goddess's power pressing on the barrier. *"They love you because you are my blessed daughter. Why do you settle for mere sabotage? With a firetender by your side, you could reduce the Palisade to ash floating on the surface of the sea. If you would but take my hand, I would grant you so much more than this."*

Lunurin ignored the goddess's alluring promises. She needed to focus. She needed to stop listening so intently to what was whispered outside the salt shelter around her spirit. But Lunurin knew that was an impossibility for as long as she continued to use her magic. She'd have to learn to live with the whispers. She could do that. So long as her emotions were her own. She wouldn't lose control.

Her winds charged down the length of the bridge, sending woven chunks of nipa palm spinning off into the night.

Lunurin heard a familiar scream as her winds found the nipa roof of the overseer's hut on the bank.

She wheeled about, and through the gloom of the rain, saw Catalina dash out onto the porch. Lunurin's rains must have driven her to seek shelter here on her way back to the Palisade. More debris whirled into the air, crashing through the window of the hut, before Lunurin called off her pack, scattering the winds like scolded children.

Lunurin knew she should scramble under the bridge with Sina, damn the heat. She couldn't be seen. But Cat looked so alone huddled under the still intact portions of the building, and Lunurin's feet were already carrying her off the bridge, up the muddy bank.

"Lunurin?! What are you doing here?" Cat called out.

"I came looking for you. The rain blew in so quickly after you left, and Kawit told me you didn't wait for him to call a kalesa. I assumed you'd stop along the way to wait out the rain."

"You came for me?" Catalina asked, her voice small and hopeful.

Lunurin leaped the few steps to the porch, sweeping Cat out of the way as the storm debris jammed through the window and clattered to the ground.

"I couldn't let you leave like that. I said things all wrong. I'm so sorry for hurting you. I never want you to think you're an amusement to me. You mean everything to me."

Cat threw her arms around Lunurin's neck. "It just hurts so much to see you with him, knowing we can never be together like that. Not in public. Not where anyone can know."

"I'm so sorry you had to see it. It's not real. What I feel for him, what I do with him, it's all political theater and lies. It's not real like the love we have," Lunurin swore, trying to make herself believe the words as much as Cat.

"It makes me feel dirty, like I'm some terrible secret! Loving you must be a sin. Surely if it were right, we wouldn't have to hide it." Cat wept, her tears hot on Lunurin's rain-cooled skin.

Lunurin cradled Cat close, lowering them to the stoop of the porch. "You are my beloved, you are so precious to me. The world does not deserve our love. How can it be wrong? Who do we hurt with it but ourselves?"

This drew a watery laugh from Cat.

Lunurin smiled down at her in relief. "Oh, Cat, I'm so sorry for hurting you. I never meant to make you feel second to him. I'm doing everything so we can have a place of our own, where no one will harass us, not the Lakan, not the Codicians. There will be no one to pretend for."

Lunurin had to believe that without those constant threats, maybe she and Cat could learn to be as gentle with each other as they deserved. Without Cat's faith constantly cutting her to ribbons, surely, surely it would be different. Cat would be different.

Cat pulled her down for a kiss. "I want to believe you. I do."

Their breath was hot in the space between them, a delicious contrast to the splattering rain covering the back of Lunurin's neck and arms in a fine mist. She dropped kisses on Cat's pert button nose, her sloping golden brow, and the delicate skin of her eyelids. She kissed Cat until her breath ached in her lungs for want of air.

"Believe in me, just a little longer. I'll make it right. I promise. You and Inez are my world. I won't give you up for anything." Holding Cat, Lunurin could almost ignore the dizzying joy of her winds, how lightheaded she was with thirst.

Just then, a low rumble crawled through the night. It went on and on.

Cat clutched Lunurin tight. Lunurin stared out over the darkness of the river. This rain carried no lightning. There should be no thunder. Had Hilaga finally woken to roar her fury? Then she saw, through the mist and rain, the pale expanse of the bridge was... crumbling, great chunks of the fifteen stone arches giving way and tumbling down into the water.

Sina wasn't under there, was she?!

"Another earthquake?" Cat asked in a quavering voice, covering her head with her hands.

Lunurin clutched her tight, ready to drag them both off the stoop and away from the hut, but the ground was still under her feet.

"Yes, it must be," Lunurin lied.

Cat sat up, following her gaze. "Saints have mercy, I hardly felt the porch shake. How could it do that to the bridge?"

"Bamboo," Lunurin said through numb lips. "It's more resilient to tremors."

Cat pulled out of Lunurin's arms, and strode into the rain.

Lunurin chased her. "Wait, there could be aftershocks!"

Cat stood on the bank, staring in shock at the steaming rubble pockmarking the river.

"Why is it so hot? There can't have been an eruption. We wouldn't feel the heat before we saw the lava, right?" Cat whirled, confusion furrowing her brow.

Lunurin shrugged helplessly. "Come away from there. It's dangerous."

But Cat was moving closer, inspecting the damage. "The stones are hot as a stove!"

"Lunurin!" Sina called her name from somewhere out on the water.

Lunurin spun toward the cry, fearful the firetender had gone into the water under the stones, but no, she'd pulled clear of the collapse and was now paddling down the bank.

Cat backed away from the rubble, up toward the guardhouse, crossing herself. "Lunurin, you did this! You and those water witch saboteurs in the jungle!"

Lunurin held her hands out. "I didn't. Cat, it's not what you think."

Cat shook her head. "I should've known you weren't here to see me. Why would you be? You never stop with your plots and schemes. This hateful thing inside you, it's twisted you into a stranger. This is treason!"

Then she turned and fled toward the lighted guardhouse.

"Cat!" The cry scraped raw and painful from Lunurin's throat, but Cat didn't turn.

Lunurin would've run after her, but Sina called out, "We need to go."

Lunurin's heart shattered. She turned from Cat and waded into the river.

34

ALON DAKILA

The Palisade was like a kicked anthill with the news of the bridge collapse overnight. Some said they'd felt an earthquake, others swore it was water witch sabotage. Alon sent Kawit to one of the safe houses he used when people had to be moved out of Aynila to find out if any of his mother's people had been involved, and make sure they got well clear of the city.

Alon heard other rumors as he was ushered in to meet the governor. He was surprised to see the Lakan in attendance. They were poring over a series of documents Alon recognized from Aynila Indigo. Had Isko already sent something about the faulty lime? That seemed… quick. The earlier lime shortage issue had been tabled for failure analysis. A frankly unhealthy-looking Father DeSoto arrived after walking the worksite. Father Ortiz assisted him, bearing samples of rubble and damaged mortar, to set on the governor's desk.

As discussion shifted to the samples, Alon picked up the Aynila Indigo documents. They were expenditure logs going back several months, showing the volume of purchased lime had nearly tripled. It was on familiar paper, the sort Isko used to maintain accounts, and bore Alon's seal, the Seal of Aynila. But Alon had no memory of them.

His seal on the monthly expenditures looked slightly off. It was a small thing, a thick blot of ink along the top of the sun seal, interrupting the smooth circle of the ring face. Of course, Alon had been busy these last months, but so busy neither Isko nor Casama had mentioned their lime purchases had tripled? Why had he only heard of the problem yesterday?

DeSoto sketched with a shaking hand the pattern of debris. "Planted explosives, as initial witnesses suggested, would've spread the rubble a great deal more. There would be evidence of fire, saltpeter and nitrate, of which I could find none. It does truly look like a natural collapse. It has to do with load, the completed spans rely on each other for strength. If one was damaged in the earthquake a few weeks ago, and finally gave way, it could have destabilized the entire bridge."

This was the first Alon had heard of witnesses.

"That doesn't rule out the influence of devilry. We've all seen the unnatural powers of these saboteurs," Ortiz pointed out. "The abbot's witness testified to unnatural happenings last night. I heard her myself."

"Had the damage been done by a rogue wave, wouldn't there be damage to structures on the banks and signs of how high the wave crested?" Alon said, desperate to turn talk away from another witch hunt. "There was no such evidence affecting my property."

The governor frowned. "I'm not sure how far I'm willing to trust the word of the abbot's witness. The guards say it was a beast of a storm, and the woman was speaking gibberish for hours."

DeSoto opened his mouth to say something, but he seemed winded, subsiding into silence.

Alon pressed his thumb over the face of his sealing ring. The uncomfortable nerve tingle of his bad hand was strong today. He went to finish the habitual fidget by twisting his mother's ring around his pinky, only to meet bare skin.

"Sister Catalina may be confused on some of the details, but she was quite clear it was the doing of water witches," Ortiz put in.

Alarm sent chills down Alon's spine.

"Where is your abbot this morning, Father Ortiz?" the governor asked. "It's not like him to send proxies for his opinions when he wants me to sign off on another witch hunt."

Alon's teeth clicked together, the talk around the table fading to a distant buzz, as the pieces fell into place. The lime documents did not bear his seal. They bore his mother's. The face of his mother's sealing ring, Lunurin's wedding ring, had a small imperfection on its face, a tooth mark. Sea Lady have mercy, what had Lunurin and Sina done? And what had Catalina told the abbot?!

"The abbot's already started another witch hunt, hasn't he? And this is all a distraction," Alon said slowly.

The study went silent.

Alon pinned Ortiz under his stare. "What is it then? Another pointless raid on Aynila Indigo? No matter how many times you terrify my dye workers, they won't turn into witches."

The priest scowled at him. "This time we have a witness."

Would Catalina betray Lunurin? Never. But Catalina hated him, and feared his magic. She would betray the tide-touched.

Alon whirled on his father. "I expect this kind of underhandedness from the Codicíans, but from you? How could you allow a raid on Aynila, on my home?"

The Lakan's eyes were hard. "If your people have nothing to hide…"

"My people don't deserve to be terrorized because the abbot wants to indulge in superstitious fearmongering. The evidence suggests the mortar never set properly. That paired with the earthquake two weeks ago could easily be the reason the bridge collapsed. But if you would all prefer to seek devilment in ill-luck, rather than listen to your resident architect, I have nothing to add to the discussion. I'm certainly not staying here while my people are harassed."

"You'll stay if you want your wife properly cleared of suspicion," his father snapped.

Alon froze. Logic said he had to stay, convince his father that he was loyal, that he wouldn't endanger their partnership with the Codicíans. That he'd give up every tie if it meant the Lakan's interests were served. Only… he wasn't sure whether his father was working to protect Aynila, or for his own profit. And if it wasn't for Aynila's safety—if it hadn't been for a long time—what was Alon doing helping him?

He wasn't even protecting his mother anymore, was he? Catalina had betrayed them. The Codicíans might already know about his mother's village.

"My wife has been through every test and trial you've asked of her. For what? The abbot's petty vengeance? No, I won't stand aside. Not this time." Alon turned his back on his father.

In the silence after Alon's outburst, DeSoto pressed a shaking hand to his chest. With a strangled cry, he crumpled to his knees.

The governor swore. "My God, man, when you said DeSoto was ill, you didn't tell me he was dying!"

Ortiz bent, attempting to raise DeSoto from the ground. "The physician just saw him yesterday. Said he was quite fit, only the changing weather had affected his energy. The exertion of leaving the Palisade and seeing all his work undone has been a shock."

Ortiz lost his grip on DeSoto, dropping the sick man flat on his face.

Surely Cat wouldn't have... couldn't have?

Alon stepped forward, unable to leave DeSoto to breathe his last face down on the floor. Alon rolled DeSoto over onto his back. He scrutinized DeSoto's gasping breaths, how he clutched at his chest with one club-fingered hand. A distant kind of professional urgency stirred toward the old man, despite what a monster he was.

"Send for the physician," Alon ordered the younger priest. Taking his false rosary in hand, Alon bent, checking DeSoto's eyes for telltale signs of poisoning. "Father, would you like me to pray with you?"

DeSoto was too deep in the throes of heart failure to answer.

Alon laid his free hand over Father DeSoto's, reaching through the man's thin blood for the source of his ill. He wasn't sure what he would do if he found it. If Catalina had poisoned him... Alon couldn't do much without dumping DeSoto into the bay, and he'd likely end up on a pyre himself.

But nothing was wrong with Father DeSoto's blood. There was only significantly less than there should be, thanks to the good physician's leeches. It moved sluggishly, though. Alon let his awareness sink deeper, following the blood through the dying man's body, until it got caught up and pooled in the heart.

Father DeSoto's heart was only doing half the work it was supposed to.

Alon lifted his hand from Father DeSoto's clammy flesh, muttering, "Amen."

Lunurin had sabotaged half his heart. The healer in him couldn't fathom it. Had she done it with the body lightning his mother had shown her?

A terrible sinking pit opened under him. Somehow, all this was his wife's doing. He had to find her.

35

LUNURIN CALILAN DE DAKILA

Lunurin woke late. By the time she dressed and found breakfast, Alon had already gone to the Palisade.

Lunurin returned to Alon's study, determined to write back to Inez. If Inez wanted out, Inez was her own person. She deserved to feel safe. And maybe she could convince Cat... Lunurin's thoughts spun and tangled in on themselves. Why was it that every time she tried to make things right, they spiraled further out of her control? A sleepy Sina joined her with steaming cups of tea, urging her to take a break from her heaps of crumpled letters and drink.

Screams and the shattering of glass punctured the usual lull of a steaming Aynilan morning. Lunurin bolted to her feet as the study door crashed open. Two Codicían soldiers seized her and Sina and marched them out.

Lunurin was shoved to the shop floor. Shards of glass gouged her knees, threatening to slice through her skirts, which grew heavy as they sopped up spilled dye. Casama stood in frozen terror with two young shop girls behind the counter as soldiers flung bolts of fabric onto the dye-soaked floor. Each carried a bottle of salted holy water, in which floated a wooden cross. They waved them in terrified faces, eager to count any too-vigorous sloshing as signs of witchcraft. Everything was happening so fast.

The abbot stood outside, drenched in harsh sunlight, supervising the work. Isko stood motionless nearby along with some of Alon's guards, hands raised, several rifle barrels pointed in their direction. More soldiers forced the dye workers from the outer buildings, testing them for witchcraft and rooting through the warehouses.

One of the soldiers shook Sina. "You're hiding witches or gunpowder. Which is it?"

Her captor shoved his witching bottle in Lunurin's face and laid a stinging blow across the back of her neck and shoulder. Lunurin cried out, but crossed herself properly. The water in the bottle didn't move. She prayed Kawit was far, far away.

The soldier shook his head at the abbot, who waved him off to harass other targets. It was a test Lunurin had passed many times.

"What is the meaning of this trespass?" Lunurin demanded, pushing to her feet, trying not to slice open her palms. "I am the daughter of the Lakan. The woman you are manhandling is the Lakan's niece. We are ladies of the principalia."

The soldier holding Sina said, "We have orders. Aynila Indigo is suspected of harboring saboteurs. Last night the bridge was blown up."

"And what has this to do with us? We have not interfered. If you'd shown me your orders, I would gladly have opened my home to your search. You've no right to treat us like common miscreants," Lunurin repeated, struggling to keep her voice even. She was so tired of making herself small to endure the barbs of narrow-minded men.

She did not dare get angry when one wrong move would leave Isko bleeding out in the street.

The abbot had all the power here, and he knew it.

"Lady Dakila is correct. She and her cousin are blood-relations to the Lakan and, passing the witching test, are outside of our jurisdiction. We shall see if the same can be said of her charges."

The soldiers tore through storerooms and outbuildings. Every woman dye worker was subjected to a witching test.

They passed even the abbot's muster, until one of the girls behind the counter made the sign of the cross. Only it wasn't. Shoulder, forehead, shoulder. Mountain or wave; defiance, or an honest mistake? Lunurin couldn't tell.

The venomous green of the abbot's eyes gleamed in the sun.

He pointed at the girl with a long, thin bamboo cane. "Seize her."

The weal across the back of Lunurin's neck itched at the sight. In the abbot's hands a witching cane could part flesh like a razor.

Casama shoved the younger girl behind her. "No, they are good devout girls. They've passed your tests."

Soldiers dragged Casama forward instead. Passersby in the street gawked as the old woman was thrown at the abbot's feet.

"My people have no more hindered your task than I have!" Lunurin snapped, angry beyond caution, beyond sense.

"None of these women have attended Mass in months. Your charges defame holy sacraments," the abbot supplied. "I think ten lashes of the cane should help her remember that yearly confessions and regular attendance at Mass bring even the most wayward soul to God's light."

The tip of the cane made a terrible whistling sound in the air. "Stop!"

The abbot's cane hesitated above Casama's bowed back.

"You don't care about her. You found nothing in your search. What do you want?" Lunurin willed her fury not to escape her body. If the weather turned now, the abbot wouldn't need a bottle test to burn her as a witch.

"You never did pay proper penance for the spectacle you caused."

"My time in the cage wasn't sufficient penance?"

The crowd outside was growing in number. All but the abbot seemed to be aware of their discontent, like the distant rumble of thunder. Gat Alon's home was the very heart of the community, Casama a treasured elder.

The Codicians have no respect—Lunurin froze. Those weren't her thoughts, but those of Anitun Tabu, buoyed on the crowd's rage. The salt amulet at her chest burned. Through the prism of salt, Lunurin stared into the mirrored rage of the divine. Why had she spent so long resisting it? Then the salt drew tight around her soul, and Lunurin remembered. She had to protect her people. She pulled away, though it was becoming harder and harder.

The abbot scoffed. "No soul is saved unless they show true contrition. Surely if this woman means so much to you, you will humbly beg God's mercy."

But of course the abbot meant his mercy, and he had none at all.

Still, she had to try. If this devolved into a riot…

She curtseyed low to the abbot. "Abbot Rodrigo—"

Casama flinched as the abbot's cane tapped tauntingly over her shoulders, as he indicated with his chin that Lunurin must do better than that.

Lunurin eyed the glittering shards of glass strewn between herself and the abbot. Ah... he wanted her to petition him, on her knees.

Distantly she heard Sina hiss a warning. Isko appeared to be trying to bargain with the captain of the Codicían guard. Lunurin's head was awash in a haze of crackling fury and terror, as her body reminded her what came of appeasing men like the abbot and the Lakan.

Lunurin tried to will herself down onto her knees.

How many times had she lowered herself, and what had it ever gained her? Had it made her safer? Had it let her keep her family together? No!

Lunurin couldn't do it, not again.

She took the first step before she realized what she meant to do. If the glass cut her bare feet to ribbons, she didn't feel it, only the hot pulsing rage in her belly, a pure, selfish, human rage, her rage. She embraced her fury, let it carry her. Her anger was hers. Her power was hers. The sun beat down on her head as she left the shaded interior of the shop. She did not need the storm.

The abbot was still sneering at her, waiting for her to throw herself at his feet, and beg.

Lunurin seized his bamboo cane and snapped it in half. She flung the pieces to the ground. "Get out of my home."

The abbot went bright red. "How dare you. Guards!"

"No." Lunurin took another step toward the abbot, forcing him to backpedal from Casama. "No, you will call them off."

"Are you threatening me?"

"Certainly not. But think how uncomfortable your situation will become should all your servants quit. I promise, if you continue to threaten my household, you'll be scrubbing out your own chamber pot by the end of the week. I can offer your servants double what they make now."

The abbot sputtered, "You wouldn't dare!"

"Ask the governor how he likes relying on conscripted labor in his kitchens." She smiled at the abbot. "He had to hire a new taster last month. Another poisoning attempt."

The abbot paled. "You'll regret this," he spat.

Lunurin didn't flinch. "Leave. Now."

The anger of the gathered crowd bolstered her threat. Mountains and waves. Solidarity, and defiance, but even if his fixation on devilry blinded the abbot, his soldiers knew better than to start a bloodbath. They were too few. They'd be torn apart. She didn't take her eyes off the abbot as he called off the soldiers. They retreated like a pack of kicked dogs.

Then they were gone, the crowd cheered. Relief made her lightheaded, as several rushed forward to help Casama from the ground.

Lunurin laid a hand on the old woman's shoulder. "Are you alright?"

"Dayang! Your feet," Casama fretted.

Lunurin yelped as two men lifted her, setting her on one of the still intact crates.

Sina touched her ankle, inspecting the damage.

Lunurin wiggled her blue-dyed toes, waiting for the verdict. She couldn't feel any pain, but that meant little when she was this angry.

"A few scratches, nothing dire," Sina pronounced with relief.

Someone produced a basin of water and Lunurin let Sina fuss over tiny splinters of glass she could hardly feel.

One of Alon's guards approached. "Dayang, shall I run for Gat Alon? He must be informed."

"I'll write a message," Isko said.

One thing ran into another. There were the shaken employees to be looked after, time off and hazard pay insisted on, cleaning up the shop front, cataloging the damage to the dye huts and warehouses. They ran together in one long blur of spilled indigo dye, until Sina finally pulled Lunurin into the quiet of Isko's office.

"You haven't drunk anything in hours," Sina chided, pushing a cup of water into Lunurin's shaking hands.

"It would appear they didn't buy our lime story. Who would have tied you two to the collapse so quickly?" Isko asked.

Lunurin's relief transmuted to dread. It weighted her limbs like she was sinking into deep mud.

Sina turned to her. "I didn't see clearly, but it was her, right? Your friend, Sister Catalina. Did she see you summon the wind?"

Realization sank barbed hooks into Lunurin's lungs. It hurt, oh it hurt.

"No, no it couldn't have been..." The words dried to dust behind her teeth. Lunurin wasn't even sure she believed what she was saying. She'd been in denial about Cat for a long time.

She pressed her face into her hands. Cat must be scared, so scared of what Lunurin was, of what she'd done. And when Cat was scared... she could do terrible things.

A frantic knock sounded on the door.

Isko opened it to reveal Rosa.

"Sister! It's the abbot. Catalina and Inez. You have to come quick!" Rosa panted.

Lunurin bolted to her feet. "I have to go."

Sina held out a hand. "Lunurin, wait. It could be a trap."

"I don't care."

36

ALON DAKILA

*The abbot and a squad of Codician soldiers raided
your home searching for proof of sabotage. No one
was seriously harmed. The Dayang handled it.*

Isko's message reached him as he was leaving the Palisade, and
Alon damned the dying DeSoto for delaying him.

He met Kawit returning from the harbor safe house.

"Not the work of your mother's people," Kawit reported.
"They left none of the usual signs."

That was a relief, but it didn't mean his mother's hidden
village was safe. "We have to warn them the abbot is on the
hunt again. The Codicians failed to flush out anyone in my
home. They may try Hilaga next. I don't know what Catalina
told them."

"I'll go. They won't be able to land ships without a
tide-touched to guide them, but we'll retreat into Hilaga's
hidden valleys till the fervor dies down. They'll never find
us."

Alon embraced Kawit. "Tell my mother I'm sorry."

"You did as a healer must." Then Kawit was gone.

His mother's safety seen to, Alon rushed home. He found Sina and Isko alone in Isko's office. What a cozy conspiracy they made.

"How did you do it?" His voice sounded so calm. Alon didn't feel calm, but everything seemed to be happening from quite a long way off. All he could smell was blood, the memory of how it had run red past his mother's lips and down her front.

Sina stood. "Alon, are you alright? You look awful."

Alon backed out of her reach. "How did you collapse the bridge? And where's Lunurin? I know she helped you."

Sina lifted her chin defiantly, saying nothing.

"Aman Sinaya have mercy. I lied to my father and the Codicians to protect you. I swore you and Lunurin would never be involved in something like this, that it was all superstitious fearmongering. But it really was you. It's always been you. You caused the lime shortages, and collapsed the Puente de Hilaga, then tried to claim it was all faulty lime! You even dragged Isko and Lunurin into your plans."

"They weren't ever supposed to be in danger. It was meant to erode over time and until it was declared too dangerous to use. We only damaged a single span. We had no idea it would collapse so quickly," Sina explained.

Somehow hearing Sina say it, as if sabotage and treason were all perfectly reasonable, made it worse. After all, they'd only miscalculated their plan!

Alon turned to his brother. "Why by all the gods did you help them? This is treason! My father will demand their heads. You know this!"

Isko was pale, but he said nothing, his jaw set.

"I trusted you with… with everything, and behind my back you—!" Alon's hands were shaking so badly, he clenched them into fists. Isko dropped his gaze.

Sina stepped between them. "This is my fault. You can't blame Isko."

"Yes, I can! I knew you weren't to be trusted. I know you'll always put your family before the safety and wellbeing of Aynila. I know that and I thought my brother was equally aware of the danger."

"Not my family, my people. The conclave is my responsibility as much as Aynila is yours. You will not shame me for it!" Sina bit out. "You are not more selfless than I. We've all seen the risks you've taken to protect Lunurin—"

"Where is she?" Alon demanded. "If the abbot took her and you didn't tell me—"

"The abbot didn't take her, but she's gone to the convent. One of the servants came, said it was about Sister Catalina and Inez," Isko broke in.

Alon cursed. "And you let her go? Alone?" He wheeled about to grab Litao and go after her.

"Alon," Sina called. "She took her bride-price. I don't think she means to come back."

Alon tensed. "She wouldn't just run."

"It's why she helped me. She wanted out. She was going to join me in the conclave. I think she planned to bring Catalina and Inez with her."

Alon closed his eyes. So, he'd endangered Aynila and betrayed his father's trust for a woman who'd only ever planned to run away. But hadn't he known from the beginning that Catalina would always be first in her heart?

So why did this hurt so much?

37

LUNURIN CALILAN DE DAKILA

Rosa clung to the seat as they rattled toward the Palisade. "The abbot's ready to start another Inquisition! They have soldiers and new ships. When he came from his raid in Aynila, he locked himself away with Sister Catalina and Inez. Juan told Cook it was bad. She sent me running for you."

The distance between Alon's home and the Palisade had never seemed so great.

By the time Lunurin had bribed their way past the Palisade gates and reached the church courtyard, she knew she was too late.

Sister Philippa, now acting-abbess as she'd always wanted, hurried to intercept her as she clambered down. "You—you shouldn't be here! And you!" She pointed at Rosa. "You abandoned your duties without leave. I'll dock a month's pay for that!"

Lunurin seized Philippa's wrist. "Where are they? Sister Catalina and Inez. Tell me now."

Philippa's scowl twisted. "Sister Catalina is gone with the abbot on his holy mission. They will root out the last witch nest, and Aynila will finally be free of their devilish influence."

Lunurin was so cold. "And Inez?"

"She's no longer my concern. She revoked her postulant's vows and was released from the convent."

Lunurin shook Philippa. "What did you do to her?"

"Nothing!"

Lunurin flung Philippa aside as Juan descended from the abbot's study carrying a small, bloodied form in his arms.

"No, no, no!" Lunurin's voice broke in her throat like glass. And within her the goddess asked, *"How much more? How much more will you let them take? How much more must Aynila endure, while you hesitate over a few gone astray?"*

There was so much blood. The sky above went dark as Lunurin's heart tore asunder.

"But say the word, but cry my name, and we can make it stop."

Somehow Juan's voice reached her through the roaring in her ears. "They had her caned. A final penance, the abbot said, because she wouldn't confess like Sister Catalina. I tried to stop the bleeding. She's in a bad way."

Lunurin's hands fluttered over Inez's pale cheeks. "Inez? Inez, can you hear me?"

She could feel her control slipping away with every breath Inez labored for. Thunder rolled overhead, and Lunurin didn't want to resist the storm, didn't know why she should. The air grew so thick with humidity it felt heavy in her lungs.

Inez's eyes darted behind half-closed lids. Despite the steaming heat of the afternoon, she shivered.

"I've called the physician, but DeSoto collapsed this morning. The physician won't spare time for her," Juan added.

This final irony was too cruel. Lunurin's eyes burned and burned, but she couldn't cry, the prism of salt seemed to draw even the marrow from her bones. Anitun Tabu waited. Her promise had never changed. She waited, as Lunurin desperately tried to remember why she'd been fighting against her vow for so long. The heavy skies overhead promised her anything she might need, if only she asked.

Inez cried out as Juan lifted her into the kalesa. At her cry, Lunurin broke free from the goddess's terrible surety. She had to get Inez out. Nothing mattered now but getting Inez out before she lost control. Before even the salt guarding her soul could no longer hold back the typhoon tethered to her bones.

Lunurin stepped down and pressed gold coins into Juan's and Rosa's hands. "Thank you both. It's not enough, but thank you." She tapped the wave-etched cowrie on Rosa's rosary. "You have contacts other than me?"

Rosa nodded. "In the governor's house."

"Good. Get out of the Palisade, both of you. I don't want you punished for this."

Then she clambered up to steady Inez.

The driver eyed the sky nervously. "Dayang, where am I to take you?"

Her bride-price was heavy in her lap. Fear tangled inside her like so many venomous snakes. With this much gold, she could get passage on a ship, a ship anywhere. She could pay one of the Tianchaowen herb-healers to accompany them and care for Inez.

She couldn't go to Alon. The mere thought made her sick with fear. Not now that Cat was leading the abbot to his mother's doorstep. He had to know it was her and Sina behind the bridge. He'd never forgive her. How could he possibly? She'd endangered the two most important things to him, peace in Aynila, and the hidden tide-touched village. He'd have no choice but to turn her over to the Lakan's justice.

"Dayang?" the driver prompted her.

The gold promised freedom. She'd run before. When the consequences of her mistakes finally caught up to her, she always ran, just like she'd fled Calilan and then the convent. Now, it was time to flee Aynila... and Alon.

Cat was lost to her, but she'd have Inez. Together, they'd start a new life far away, and maybe the goddess would go quiet for a few more years.

Inez gave a weak moan, turning her face into Lunurin's hand her skin was cool and clammy. She'd lost so much blood.

Inez couldn't travel. Not like this.

Lunurin seized the salt amulet on her chest. Would its power fade if she went too far from Alon? Could she face her goddess without his walls of salt to protect her soul? Could she face her own rage and control it, or would she send them both down to a watery grave with whomever was unlucky enough to harbor them?

There was no choice after all.

So. For Inez.

"Take me back to Gat Alon." The words scraped out, the bars of Lunurin's cage drawing tight as the salt shackles on her spirit.

She couldn't run again. There was no escaping the consequences of her actions, or willing her goddess's vengeance away. Not this time.

～

Inez was small, and so terribly light in her grip. Each step toward Alon's front door seemed to take an age. She couldn't get there fast enough for the quick, shallow puffs of Inez's breath against her neck.

Her head swam, thirst pounding at her like a hammer. The bars of the cage over the Palisade flashed before her eyes. She felt insubstantial as dust in the wind. No more running.

She pushed her way inside. "Alon! Alon, please—"

"Lunurin. You came back."

She looked up. He stood at the head of the stairs. Late afternoon light poured around him in a river of gold, casting his face in shadow. What had she been thinking, letting him convince her that she could stand by his side even for a moment? What had it brought either of them but ruin?

"It's Inez and Cat." Desperation clawed at her throat.

"Isn't it always." His voice was so hard, it pierced her through.

"I came to warn you—Cat, she betrayed your mother, all the tide-touched, to the abbot. I'm sorry. I never imagined it would come to this."

Silence. Lunurin waited a beat, for Alon to push past her, to rush to his mother's side. Cat and Inez would always come first for her; for him, it was his mother. How could she begrudge him that?

His shadow fell over her, blocking the light. She stepped aside. His hands came to help cradle Inez. "Salt take it, Lunurin, what happened?"

"The abbot had her caned." Her voice was so small against the storm in her soul.

He lifted Inez, carrying her to his treatment room. Lunurin, dizzy with thirst, struggled to keep up.

"Isko! I need saltwater."

Lunurin clung to the doorway. "Alon, your mother!"

334

"I sent Kawit to warn them as soon as I realized the abbot had called another Inquisition. I was about to go after you. Come help me get her blouse open."

Lunurin couldn't move. He was going to stay and help her with Inez when his mother was in danger?

Alon turned to her. His expression wasn't hard or angry at all. Worry and concern were all that marred his face. "Lunurin, sit. Sit and drink. I'm going to take care of Inez."

"I betrayed you!" Lunurin wailed. Alon should lash out at her. He should do just as Cat had done, punish her for failing him. He should, he had to, because... that was the way of things, wasn't it? It was what Lunurin deserved.

Alon frowned at her. "Yes. I know that too. We'll discuss it when Inez isn't in shock."

Isko carried in a bucket of water. Sina followed, lugging one of Kawit's bags of sea salt.

"Thank you. Sina, will you boil me up a decoction of tibatib and guava leaves?" Alon thrust several jars of herbs in her direction, and then bent over the treatment bed. "Someone make Lunurin drink."

The metallic scent of blood filled the room as Alon cut saturated bandages away from Inez's back.

Inez began to struggle and Lunurin shoved away the storm of self-flagellation and anguish to scramble to her bedside.

Lunurin held Inez down by her upper arms. "Easy, easy, Inez. I've got you. You're safe now."

"Lunurin?" Inez croaked.

"Yes, I'm here. I'm here." Lunurin's voice broke.

Inez sobbed as Alon reached her mid-back, uncovering layered lashes that had cut her skin to tatters. Lunurin willed herself not to be sick. Were those... bamboo splinters wedged in her back?

"Alon, can I do anything?"

"Yes. I wasn't thinking. Place your hand between her shoulder blades. Can you do what you did before with the lightning in her spine?"

"Not higher?" Lunurin asked, eyeing the ugly weeping cuts across Inez's shoulders.

"No, I'm afraid it will interfere with her breathing," Alon said, as he pulled his brace off and set it aside.

Lunurin laid a hand over Inez's spine.

Inez's body lightning came to her so easily, frighteningly so.

"It would be as easy as this," Anitun Tabu promised. *"Easy as this for us to destroy everyone who ever harmed her."*

Inez's lower body went limp.

Rather than lean into her goddess's anger, Lunurin leaned into Alon. His spirit was so calm and still, as it always was when he healed. They'd saved so many lives working together over the years. Surely they could do it one more time. She only had to hold off Anitun Tabu's fury and her own a little longer.

~

When they were finally finished, Inez lay limp and exhausted with her head propped in Lunurin's lap. Her hands suddenly without a task, Lunurin had nothing to hold between herself and the storm. Her composure wavered. The gathering twilight cast shadows like bruises over Inez's small form. Lunurin's shame and guilt circled like sharks, eager for the first sign of weakness. Though Alon had calmed and focused his spirit for healing, dangerous currents below the surface dragged at her awareness like barbed hooks.

Lunurin petted Inez's fine brown hair back from her pale cheeks. "Inez, how—" Her voice caught.

Inez's mouth trembled. "Cat told them. She said she had to

confess our sins so they'd let us stay. Even when I wanted to leave. But she… told them anyway. So *she* could stay."

Inez's tears drenched Lunurin's lap. Lunurin wished desperately she could cry. Her dry eyes burned. The clouds above offered to cry in her stead and wash everything into the sea.

"Easy, easy, don't sob. You'll tear your stitches. Rest." Alon pressed his hand over Inez's brow and breathed out.

Inez went limp. Lunurin curled her body over Inez, as if this might shelter her. Her world narrowed to the boiling point of pain on her breast and the child in her lap. She'd have torn down the sky to keep Inez from harm, to keep her little family together, but stormcallers did not save. Every use of her power had only made everything worse, just as Catalina had warned. She'd failed her family, and Catalina had betrayed them all. Lunurin tried to suppress the anguish brewing beneath her skin, smothering any sound. If she moved or breathed, the unholy rage of the goddess within and her own grief would tear the world apart. She was too dangerous. Hadn't Cat said that? Because that's what Lunurin was, deep down. She was nothing but vengeance waiting to happen.

The unknown depths of Alon's spirit seemed far away, but then he pressed a cool hand over the amulet on her chest. "You have to calm down, Lunurin."

Had her pain always fit so well in the palm of his hands?

A cry tore from her, like a wailing wind. "Why? Has Inez not suffered enough? Why must I control myself? Why must I curtail my grief and rage? *Why? When all the world should bleed with me!*"

Alon's voice was low and urgent in her ear. "Please, Lunurin, please. I know you're still in there. This isn't what you want. This isn't your rage. Think of Aynila. Think of all the people whose lives your storm will destroy. Think of Inez."

She expected his power to flood into her, to seize her burning heart and douse her spirit. She'd always feared that trusting Alon, leaning on him, would end this way. She was born to the Mistress of Storms. She was cloud-high freedom and wild winds. She wasn't meant to slumber in the depths of the salt. If he dragged her down again… she might not rise at all. But now, she welcomed it. She didn't want to live with this knowledge, with Catalina's betrayal. She was so tired of bringing nothing but pain to everyone she loved, of driving them to such terrible choices. She was too tired to run. She would not struggle.

She pressed her hand over his. "I will be Aynila's unmaking unless you stop me. I am tired of fighting fate. Let me rest. Drowning by your hand would be a peaceful end. Offer up my head to your father. Use it to buy Sina's innocence. Forgive me. This marriage was only ever going to end in tragedy. Let it only be my death. Let it be done with me."

Alon pulled away from her, horrified. "I am a healer. How could you ask that of me?"

"What else is there?" Lunurin cried. "Vengeance is all a stormcaller is."

"This rage and bloodlust isn't yours. It doesn't have to be your only birthright."

How could he still not see it? See her?

Lunurin exploded. "You're wrong! It is my rage, because it is my grief. I wasn't born to be a martyr, sanctified by suffering. I won't decree it godly and righteous, and put out my own right eye to prove my faith like Catalina. I own it. My rage is selfish. It is bloody, petty, and vengeful. I would've torn the heavens down for my family. Who else will? No one cares to protect lost mestiza girls. This rage is all I have. I will not renounce it, even if I must die for it."

She seized his hand. She had to make him understand. She'd

failed with Cat, she couldn't fail now. "Can't you feel it too? It's in the air, the soil, the water. Our people cry out for justice and there is none. There is only vengeance, or death. How can you look at what they've done to us, to our families, to our people and *not* draw the tides in until every one of them has drowned?"

Alon's eyes burned into hers, his fingers closing spasmodically around her own and Lunurin was sure he understood. Then his expression closed like the slamming of a door. He wrenched free from her grip as if prepared to tear off his own arm to escape, and left without another word.

Lunurin's fervor drained away, leaving her fragile, and alone. So, she'd found the limit of Alon's patience.

Fitting that the terrible divinity inside her should drive away everyone she'd ever loved, if she didn't kill them first. Inez's breaths, hitched and labored, drove the brutal point home. She'd been a fool to think she could excise the seeds of destruction in her own heart to make a life with Catalina. Nothing she did would change the nature of her poisoned birthright. Could she blame Cat for escaping Lunurin's blighted fate the only way she knew how?

Slowly, Lunurin reached into her hair, lifting her mutya free. She traced the design of clouds framing a moonrise that decorated the comb, admiring the artistry of her Tiya Halili's hand in the design, memorizing the jagged shape of the silvery-grey pearl topping the hair prong.

Cat was right. Everything she'd done to try to protect Aynila and keep her family together only made things worse. Cat was right to fear her. If Alon wouldn't stop her... could she stop herself? If she could do it now, before she failed Alon again and again, before he felt nothing for her but fear and hatred...

Alon's words rang in her ears. *This doesn't have to be your only birthright!*

38

ALON DAKILA

Alon's heart beat raggedly, trying to escape his chest. His blood was a storm-swept sea, yearning to bring forth the destruction Lunurin and her goddess desired. How could he deny her when she'd laid bare the bleeding heart of her pain, the very core of what she was, and he'd recognized it? Lunurin had glowed with her fervor like a dark pearl in coastal waters. Looking at her, Alon knew why men drowned diving for pearls. Did the Sea Lady not rise at her lover's call? Alon didn't know why he shouldn't follow suit.

But then, he'd remembered his mother. How her blood had run red past her lips and down her front. Her song silenced, severed. Memory had blurred and it had been Lunurin with blood bubbling from her lips, accusation in her dying breaths, blood pouring from a long red wound across her throat. He could see it, the exact expression that would be on the Lakan's face as he demanded Alon deliver his wife's and cousin's heads. And he had run, like a coward, because he couldn't afford to get caught up in the disaster singing in his wife's blood.

He found himself in his office, the farthest room in the house from where Lunurin and Inez curled around each other, broken and bloody in body and spirit. He stared at the paperwork that represented the running of Aynila, the lives and livelihoods depending on him and his father, and he saw, all around him in fresh indigo ink, her seal. The tooth-marked wedding ring she and Isko had used to falsify documents had also addressed petitions and settled disputes. While he'd been letting the governor lead him around by the nose, she'd been doing the work his people needed. Work he'd been pulled away from to court the Codicíans, ensuring they had all they needed for their bridge, their ships, their dominion.

Isko entered. Alon stared at his foster brother. The air was so much shattered trust between them. Alon had relied on Isko for everything since his mother's banishment, when Aynila Indigo had fallen entirely to him. Even now, he couldn't conceive of any rational reason for Isko to have betrayed him.

Isko bowed to him, formal and distant.

"Why did you help them? You know, you have to know what my father will ask of me if he ever discovers…" Alon's voice trailed off, silenced by the horror of it, by the phantom press of Lunurin's fingertips into the back of his hand as she'd offered her death for Sina's innocence and Aynila's safety.

"I could see no other way to prevent your loyalties from tearing you apart. There was no stopping them, only damage control."

Alon scrubbed his hands over his face. "I know that! I know, but if you'd warned me…"

"And made you choose between loyalty to your father and the woman you love? How would that be any better than the Lakan and his ultimatums? I've seen what it does to you serving him. And I've seen what you're willing to do for her if she asks."

"She is everything you ever warned me."

"So you do see it." Isko eyed him knowingly. "And you love her anyway."

"She's killing a man. DeSoto. His heart is failing. It will be torturous, and slow, and Lunurin didn't even blink. If she were one of my mother's tide-touched…"

"Are you upset that he's dying, or that she used her power in a way you wouldn't use yours? If she'd cut his throat, would you be angry?"

"My mother taught her that so she could heal!"

"Stormcallers don't heal. Can you ask her to be something other than she is?"

The silence stretched. Alon tried to wrap his mind around everything that had blown into his life with her like a wayward squall. Even here, she'd wrought changes. Had it only been a week? She called herself selfish, said that her grief and rage would bring nothing but death, but here in indigo ink she'd begun building sea walls to protect his people.

Alon released a long, shuddering breath. "No more than she can ask it of me."

A band of lightning lit the sky over Aynila. It cast strange blue-white light over Isko's startled face. The roll of thunder that followed made it feel as if the building were caving in on their heads. Alon bolted to his feet. But the storm did not rage on. Silence reigned thick and heavy, until a single scream shattered it like glass.

He found Lunurin collapsed in the kitchen, seizing. In a jar of vinegar on the sideboard her mutya fizzed and bubbled.

Alon snatched the comb and hair prong from the corrosive solution, dumping them into a pitcher of water to stop the reaction. He stared around the kitchen. She'd clearly tried to shatter them first, with a large wooden pestle for grinding rice, and one of Kawit's bone cleavers. His whole being revolted at the thought. It would be like biting off his own fingers, an unthinkable self-mutilation.

As the damage to her mutya ceased, Lunurin's body went limp. Outside, a drenching rain began to fall.

39

LUNURIN CALILAN DE DAKILA

Lunurin woke cradled in Alon's arms. Rain fell on her upturned face as he carried her toward the river. Her spirit felt raw and burned. The paired weight of her mutya in her hair seemed to throb in time with her aching spirit.

"Why did you stop me?" Her voice grated in her raw throat.

Alon's arms tightened. "Aman Sinaya have mercy. Lunurin, you were having a seizure. I thought it would kill you. What were you thinking?"

"I was giving up my poisoned birthright, like you asked, like I promised Cat I would. Only I wasn't strong enough, not in time. If I'd only been able to do it sooner, maybe she wouldn't have been so afraid. Maybe she wouldn't have—and Inez!"

"Sina is with her, she's safe." Alon's hand gripped on her shoulder. "Stop, Lunurin. Stop. How could you ever think I'd ask you to do such a thing?"

His words filtered slowly through her rising hysteria. A terrible disorientation seized her. "But you asked me... I had to make Aynila safe. I know you're angry. You're right to be! I had to make it stop before I lost you to this terrible thing inside of me. Before I did something truly unforgivable—"

"No matter how angry I was, why would you think this was the answer? I would never, ever ask you to hurt yourself. Not even to save all Aynila would I ask you to destroy your own mutya!" Alon's voice rose in distress. He was half shouting, his broad shoulders shaking. Still, he held her so gently.

As gently as the rain falling like tears on her cheeks. Anitun Tabu wept for her. The goddess's power reached to curl around Lunurin, but couldn't connect to her burned and aching spirit. Lunurin didn't have the strength to reach back.

"I'm so tired of being afraid. Alon, I'm so afraid of what I can do with my goddess burning in my heart. I never stop till everything is so much devastation and death. All my life, what has it ever brought me and mine but grief?"

Alon's brow furrowed, his lips pressed tight and trembling. Lunurin lifted a shaking hand to his cheek. "Even you. I never wanted to hurt you as I have. Didn't I tell you taking me as your wife would ruin you? Look at the mess I've made of it. I thought... I thought if I could do this one thing, you might forgive me."

"Salt take it, Lunurin, I'm not the fucking abbot. I don't want your penance and self-flagellation. I'm not Catalina. If this is your idea of love, I don't want it. I have seen what the shattering of her mutya did to my mother! Her spirit is torn and bleeding. You've burned yourself in places I'm not sure I can heal!" Alon shouldered open the door to the bathhouse and walked her into the water. Someone had bathed recently. The oil lamps were just beginning to burn low; the light, magnified off the water, created a soft blue-green glow.

Lunurin gasped as the coolness of the river closed around her. The prayer for a sea current was musical in Alon's deep voice as he pulled saltwater from the bay. She'd not been aware of *how much* her spirit hurt until Alon applied pressure where she'd been dissolving. His presence was cool as moonlight, soothing as a compress. The sudden lack of pain was shocking.

"Oh, oh. Oh." Lunurin pressed her hands to her face, smothering the cry rising behind her teeth as she realized what she'd almost done to herself, to Alon, all for an impossible atonement.

"Do you... need to cry?" Alon asked, brushing his fingertips over the crown of her head. He was so gentle it hurt. "You can cry. I'll hold your power in check. You can lean on me. You can always lean on me. I'm sorry you feared you couldn't."

"But I failed you! It's my fault Catalina betrayed the tide-touched. It's my fault Inez was hurt. I can't even blame you for hating me—"

"I saw the study," he said.

At his non sequitur, Lunurin hiccupped on her next sob, suddenly deeply sure that he was about to tell her to keep out of his business. That she had no right to use his mother's seal. That she was unworthy of it.

Alon didn't say these things. His love was not a razor edge waiting for her to cut herself open. "I need to thank you, for all of it. You stood between my household and the abbot's witch hunt." He hesitated. "This isn't your fault. And this terrible guilt that's eating you alive... I don't hate you. I hate that I don't have better answers to all that's wrong in my city. The only choices shouldn't be bloody vengeance or doing nothing. I hate that the Codicians' 'gift' of empire is generations of trauma. I love you. How can I blame you or your goddess for transmuting all our grief into fury?"

"Cat does," Lunurin whispered. "She shattered my dugong bone amulet when she found out what I did to DeSoto."

Alon's breath hissed in.

Lunurin rubbed at her eyes, trying to stem the prickly heat. "She should blame me! Inez wouldn't have fallen into DeSoto's orbit if I hadn't started her as a teaching assistant. I should've seen something was wrong sooner!"

The raw note of hysteria in her own voice frightened her, but there was no stopping the rush of secret fears as her black thoughts untangled.

Alon wrapped a gentle hand around Lunurin's wrist, startling her. She stopped rubbing the corners of her eyes raw. "You can't always be strong. It's not your fault the Church's lofty morals are as empty as their prayers. What's come of it may be your responsibility. But it is *not* your fault."

His words burrowed deep, cracking the foundations of everything Lunurin was.

Lunurin grasped for purchase on the wet silk of Alon's barong, suddenly finding the buoyant clasp of the water not enough support. "You don't blame me? You don't hate me for endangering Aynila?"

Alon gathered her into him. "I don't blame you. You've done the best you could. We are only human. I can no more blame you for seeking vengeance than my mother could blame me for bringing Inez to her for healing. We cannot change the stuff of our spirit, and I will not hate you for what you are. You aren't something terrible that should be destroyed for the good of all. You are no more unnatural than a typhoon in the wet season. All I want is for you to see that, and to stop hurting yourself trying to be something else."

"What my goddess wants, what she asks—Alon, it will be terrible, and one day soon I won't remember why I resist her. I'm afraid. I've spent my whole life so very afraid."

Alon curled his arms around her, warm and solid. "Then let it come. I'm not sure anything else will fix all that's broken in this divided city. Let your goddess's vengeance come. I trust you to guide her storm and protect our people. I refuse to believe Anitun Tabu only intends to use up your life in pointless vengeance. Whatever you choose or do not choose for Aynila, you are my wife, and we are responsible for the Aynila that will be after your storm. I will be here beside you, no matter what."

Alon pressed his lips to her temple.

Lunurin didn't know what to say in the face of his tenderness. Vengeance was what she'd been born for, but the fervor in his gaze made her want to believe she had a future beyond Anitun Tabu's calling. He made her want to believe she had a place beside him, that together they could stand for Aynila. It frightened her how much she wanted that future, a future as his wife.

Lunurin licked her lips and tasted salt. Every bit of her Alon held above the water was dusted in salt crystals. They clung to her arms like flakes of coconut. She lifted a hand to her hair and found it stiff. She must look like one of Anitun Tabu's salt-encrusted statues after the visit of her lover's tides.

"I may have pulled the salt too hard. I was frightened for you." Alon's fingertip traced her brow, loosening a fine white dust. "I'll help you rinse."

The phrase panged with familiarity. Hadn't Cat used those words the morning of the earthquake, before everything had gone so terribly wrong? Lunurin pushed away the comparison. Alon wasn't Cat. His love was not like Cat's. And wasn't that the most frightening, world-altering realization of all?

The direction of the current reversed, running fresh once more. Alon lowered Lunurin off his arm, supporting her till her feet found the bottom. He took her hands. Lunurin gasped at the sensation of sun-warmed ocean feeding humidity into a faltering storm. Strength flooded into her. Her fingertips jittered with the sparkling feeling in her veins.

"Better?" Alon asked.

"Ooh yes." Unbidden laughter bubbled to her lips.

Alon's brow furrowed. "Are you... drunk?"

Lunurin swayed, testing the sensation. "Euphoric, maybe?"

"So... not bad?" Alon sounded very concerned.

That was silly. Lunurin smoothed away the furrow between his brows. "Not bad. Good."

Alon held her upright when she would have tipped into his chest. "Rinse and you can sleep it off."

Lunurin planted her palms on his chest. "It'll settle. I think it's just the sea change from how much I was hurting."

Alon hummed, unconvinced. "I'd like to go a week without finding my wife in mortal peril."

Lunurin giggled. "Your wife would like that too." She patted his chest, which was pleasantly firm under her hands. "I used to go months without encountering any mortal peril at all. The convent was a quiet life."

Alon snorted. "I'm familiar with your famously quiet and uneventful life as a nun. I regret to inform you it involved a great deal more peril than most encounter in their entire lives."

Lunurin pulled a face.

Alon's laughter filled the space, bouncing off the water, and vibrating under her hands.

Lunurin smiled ruefully. "Maybe you're right."

Alon released her. Lunurin noticed the current tugging her skirt-tangled legs had gentled.

"I'm fine."

"Can you untangle yourself?"

The silver buttons of her wet blouse challenged her jittery grip. "Ahh... no."

Lunurin admired the blush crawling up Alon's throat as he freed the tiny silver tambourine buttons and slid the translucent garment off. It was her turn to blush at his fingertips against bare skin as he tugged the ties of her overskirt. She gasped when he unwound her from the drenched fabric. Alon turned away quickly.

Lunurin wrapped her underskirt under her arms before the red tips of Alon's ears caused his hair to combust. Hesitantly, she lifted her mutya from her hair. Had that surface roughness been there before? Anxiety tightened her throat. What would've happened if Alon hadn't found her?

She tucked them into the band of her skirt. She didn't want to think on it. Alon's turned back provided ample distraction.

"You'll damage the silk if it dries." Lunurin tugged the stiffening shoulder of his barong.

Alon loosed the buttons at his neck, pulling it over his head, rewarding her with the broad brown expanse of his back. The lamplight gilding the curves of his shoulder blades cast a valley of shadow down his spine that she desperately wanted to trace with her tongue. Was that euphoria or desire pooling in her belly? Did it matter? Lunurin dragged her fingertips down Alon's back.

The way he reacted, she might as well have bitten him.

"What are you—" Alon swallowed hard. "This is a bad idea."

"I'm helping you rinse," Lunurin said, with absolutely no guile.

Alon narrowed his eyes. "You had a seizure. You were just giggling. You never giggle."

"But I'm not bleeding." Lunurin drew her wet fingertips down Alon's bare arm. He shivered.

Lunurin hummed, as his warm grip closed around her elbow.

"Lunurin... bathing? You're white with salt."

She considered it. "Only if I can help you too."

"This deal sounds dangerous." But Alon smiled as he drew her toward him.

Alon dipped her into the river, and freed her hair. Lunurin relaxed as the patter of rain slowed and ceased. It was bliss to melt into his touch as he massaged coconut milk into her scalp, and finger-combed oil through her hair.

Lunurin twisted her hair up with her mutya.

"Tired now?" Alon sounded almost hopeful.

"Not at all."

Lunurin found a bar of coconut milk soap, and lathered her hands. He tensed when she touched his back.

By the time she'd worked around to his front, Alon offered his arms to support her, though they both knew she could stand at this depth.

Alon kept his hands fisted, rather than splayed against her skin, as if he needed the self-control now as he hadn't earlier. His eyes followed her with keen intent that filled her with heat.

"Rinse," she commanded.

Alon's arms trembled.

"Am I too heavy?"

"No," he rasped.

He dipped to his neck. Lunurin's palms skimmed over the breadth of his chest, down his ribs. They pressed chest to chest, her hands running down his spine. Alon shivered, dark eyes falling closed. Lunurin's fingertips explored the soft but firm skin and padding over the muscles of his waist. It was comforting how sturdy Alon was. She hummed when Alon's fisted hands opened to cradle her at last.

Alon gave an inarticulate groan and buried his face in her neck, his hands clutching her waist. Then, he let go.

In protest, Lunurin wound her arms around Alon's neck.

"I can't. I'm sorry, I want—"

Lunurin scraped her nails down the back of his neck, earning a shivery whimper.

"More than I should," he finished.

"So do I."

"You're sure? It's not because I was angry, and you've had a terrible night? I don't want—"

"I want to sleep with my husband at least once." The title sat oddly on her tongue, but she tried to imbue it with the tenderness with which he'd called her his wife.

She'd fought what she was for so long, her own fury and desire, cutting off pieces of herself and swallowing them down, to be palatable, to be safe, to remain hidden as she had in the convent. Constantly sick with guilt at her inability to change herself. She was tired of pretending she didn't want him. Insisting it was rogue magic and not that his spirit against hers was the closest she'd felt to coming home in years. She'd been wrong. It wasn't Cat who understood what it was to be torn between worlds. It was Alon. He understood, and he forgave her failings as Cat never had.

"Do you want it for you or just because you are my wife?"

Lunurin tilted her hips against the hardness barely contained in his waistcloth.

Alon's hand came to the small of her back. He held her like a man drowning, and yet… if she said a word, he would let go. The knowledge made her bold. She didn't want to die having never truly been his wife.

Lunurin wriggled her hips experimentally. "This, I want for me."

A stuttering groan escaped him, his hands tracing her back, while the current tugged curious fingers over her legs.

"Can I kiss you?" he asked.

"Yes," she breathed.

Alon's mouth slotted over hers, soft and warm and thorough. He didn't kiss roughly, like Cat. If Lunurin had thought she'd find the difference lacking, she was very wrong. She melted under each gentle press of his lips. All the myriad discomforts of dehydration she'd learned to live with faded. She tangled one hand in his hair, needing an anchor.

They kissed until Lunurin was breathless. She wanted nothing between them, to be wet and naked against the warmth of Alon's chest. She hitched herself closer.

He lifted his mouth from hers, lamplight dancing in his dark eyes. "I'm going to embarrass myself if you keep on like that. It's been a while."

Lunurin pressed with purpose against him. "We have time."

"But you—"

"I want to know how my husband will fall apart under my hands."

Alon stumbled back into the dock. Lunurin followed, the water cool against her heated flesh. Gently, she lifted his mutya, dropping the pearl-studded cross behind his shoulder. She ran her tongue up the taut muscles of his neck. She squeezed her thighs around him and Alon jumped, her teeth scraping his neck. Alon let out a low whine, baring his throat fully to her.

Lunurin brushed an apologetic kiss over his flesh. "Was that good?"

"Yes, yes, please, whatever you want." His hands cradled her rear, pushing her higher up his chest. "Just don't bite off anything important." He gave a breathless little laugh.

"I'll be careful," Lunurin promised. She bent to nibble the edge of his jaw, kissing her way down the column of his neck and sank her teeth gently into the straining muscle.

Alon moaned, rocking into her urgently, creating tantalizing friction between them. Lunurin kissed the red marks left by her teeth and hummed as he pressed himself where she ached, the taut wet cloth between their bodies creating unbearable friction. She dragged her teeth over Alon's bobbing Adam's apple with wicked intent. He made the nicest sounds.

With a frustrated yank, Lunurin loosed the knot holding her wrap. She moaned as Alon's hands clasped hot against her bare skin, the metal of his ringed brace a sharp contrast.

She set about freeing Alon from his waistcloth.

"Oh please," he begged as she dragged the cloth from between their hips and curled her hands around his cock. "Tighter, please."

Lunurin was momentarily distracted. This was going to require more planning and logistics than she'd estimated.

Alon whined low in his throat. Lunurin tightened her grip and bent to bite the vee of his neck.

"Fuck." Alon thrust once, twice, his cock sliding with a fascinating hot slickness against her belly.

He came with a shout, burying his face in Lunurin's neck as she licked and kissed away the redness. He panted, his breaths making her breasts tighten in anticipation. Then, he moved. Lunurin yelped as she was hefted onto the dock.

Suddenly, illogically vulnerable without the clasp of the water, Lunurin shivered as Alon's eyes drank her in.

Alon pressed a kiss to the inside of her knee. He nuzzled there, his fingertips brushing her ankle. "Is this okay? I'm trying to minimize my chances of drowning."

Lunurin laughed, hesitation melting away. "Yes, it's okay."

Alon grinned and lifted himself to steal a hungry kiss. She was half-drunk with his kisses. Then, he tugged her close. Lunurin helped, hooking her legs over Alon's shoulders, as he proceeded to drive her mad. He kissed down her thighs. He laved his tongue where her thigh met her body, nibbling the band of muscle that flexed there.

Lunurin ached and arched, trying to tug his mouth where she needed it. But instead, Alon paused, drawing her fingertips into his hot mouth, before returning to his maddening exploration. He ran his lips so lightly over hers, she might almost have imagined it. He skimmed his hands over her thighs, tracing her shivers. Then finally, finally, Alon lowered his mouth over her center, his tongue broad and firm.

Lunurin thought her heart would explode. She forced herself still, beginning the counterintuitive task of controlling her magic while relaxing enough to tip into an orgasm without tearing the roof off. Lunurin clutched her salt pendant, struggling to sink into the space she needed, while Alon lapped dizzyingly light circles over her clit.

She pressed her palm to her mouth, biting hard to keep in any sound. Her whole body wanted to draw tight in ecstasy, but that way led to lightning and a torrential downpour. Alon's finger curled into her, and Lunurin forced herself not to clamp him in place with her thighs, holding them lax and open. She needed stillness and calm and just enough separation from her body...

Just when she'd managed to relax enough to come gently, Alon *stopped*.

He heaved himself from the water, hovering, naked, and not touching her.

"Lunurin? Are you with me? Am I not doing something right?" Alon cupped her face, evidence of her arousal smearing her cheek. He drew her palm from between her teeth. "Please talk to me. If you don't want—"

Lunurin glared. "I'm trying not to flood the city. You're making that difficult."

Alon cocked his head, tension draining away. "It's not storming."

Lunurin lifted herself on her elbows. Alon sat back, trying to give her space without falling off the dock.

"It's not?" It was true. The night was quiet. All her energy was tangled up in Alon, none spilling out to turn the weather tumultuous.

She reached for him. "It's not."

Alon grinned wickedly. "Is this why your tiya married a tide-touched woman?"

He slid his hand between them. His eyes on her face were so attentive. Lunurin shivered.

She wasn't used to being the focus, her own pleasure a soft afterthought, or forgone altogether if she was afraid to risk the inevitable storm. She gasped when he returned to the center of her, his fingers sliding through her slick folds and curling in. Lunurin cried out and Alon dropped kisses over her mouth and cheeks.

"Don't go away inside yourself. I've got you. You can let go. Just tell me what you need."

She trusted him.

"More, I need—"

He obeyed.

Lunurin let her body coil tight as it wanted. She curled her arms around Alon's shoulders, unconcerned she might crush him. Her thighs clenched, trapping his hips. She half lifted herself off the dock as he used his fingers ever so skillfully and shoved her hard over the precipice. Lunurin let herself fall without control, without gauging the tempo of the rain. She came with a gasp, her body spasming tight around Alon's fingers.

With his less deft hand, Alon stroked her hair, murmuring encouragement. "I've got you. Should I stop?"

Lunurin gasped something, maybe his name, shaking her head. She hadn't had enough of the indescribable fire in her veins, of letting it drag her under, not worrying about anything but sensation.

He captured her clit and massaged it under his thumb. Lightning flashed behind her eyes, and Lunurin cried out and came again, her thighs slick and shaking.

When she'd come down from that impossible high, lightheaded and panting, helplessly, Lunurin began to laugh. Alon smiled at her with such delight, she had to kiss him again.

Just then, there was a rush of water. They both sat up in confusion as the river surged a foot in seconds, lapping at the edge of the dock.

"That's not me," Lunurin said.

"Or me," Alon echoed.

Lunurin rose, offering Alon a hand up. She snatched her sopping underskirt. Alon made a tugging gesture and yanked all the water out of both his waistcloth and her wrap. He grabbed their damp clothes and dashed out of the bathhouse. Lunurin scanned the sky, reaching her power up. Was some natural upstream storm causing a flash flood?

Alon was frozen, staring across the river, over the ruins of the bridge at the dark bulk of Hilaga against the star-splattered night.

Lunurin turned. Past the pin-prick lights of the metalworkers' conclave, a red glow rose from the far side of the volcano. "Was there an eruption? Wouldn't Sina have warned us?"

"The ground didn't shake, and there's been no smoke from the peak," Alon said in a tight voice.

"Shouldn't an incoming tsunami pull the water away from the river?"

"It would."

"Alon—what's happening? Are you okay?"

In the moonlight, Lunurin saw he was weeping. "They're dying. The other tide-touched. Aman Sinaya reaches out for her children, dying far from her embrace."

Lunurin stared at the column of smoke, lit from within by flames feeding on the pyres of a village of tide-touched. "No, no, no! How? The Codicians have no ships that could make the approach!"

Alon, pulling on his barong, thrust her clothes into her hands. "What was I thinking, sending Kawit alone?!" He strode toward the floating pier where the bangka, outrigger canoes, were tied.

Lunurin followed, struggling into her clothes. "Alon, wait!"

"I have to go. She's my mother. I have to try," he said, already untying the bangka. His face was hard and drawn with terrible grief.

"I know you do. Just like I had to go to the convent, but if it was a mistake to send only Kawit, then you can't go alone either."

Alon's breath burst raggedly through his teeth, and she seized his shoulder. "You're not alone. We need Sina at least, Biti is there. The three of us together, we'd be so much stronger if we stopped working at cross purposes."

Alon's fevered movements ground to a halt. He shuddered all over like a carabao shedding flies. "Yes, you're right."

Together they ran to the house to rouse help.

40

◆—◆

ALON DAKILA

They'd leveled the village and put the torch to every hut.

Kawit's bangka smoldered on the narrow beach. Dawn was a blighted orange glow over the water, the light strange through the smoke. The ash-covered lava was hot under Alon's sandaled feet. More ash rained down overhead. It lay thick and white, catching in his hair. Alon pressed his sleeve over his mouth and nose, struggling to breathe the hot dry air.

They'd erected the pyres on the lava field. There were five, now burning low, multiple charred bodies tied to each stake. He counted ten. Including his mother and Biti, the hidden village had safeguarded nineteen. Some must have gotten away, surely even a young firetender couldn't be burned alive.

He barely reached the border of the jungle to be sick at the familiar scent of charred lechon rising from the pyres like the remnants of a suckling pig roast. Again, Aynila's tide-touched burned, and there was nothing he could do.

Sina stumbled ahead toward the village, screaming her sister's name. Isko—who had stubbornly refused to be left

359

behind—followed at her heels. Fires flared and died where she passed.

Lunurin dragged cold rain down the flanks of Hilaga, washing ash and smoke from the air. But every breath still ached in Alon's lungs like a thousand stabbing needles. Lunurin helped him to his feet.

"How?" The question scraped out of him. "How did they get close enough to land ships? The village should've been impossible to attack by sea!"

It was supposed to be out of range of even the *Santa Clarita*'s new long-guns. As soon as a landing vessel was spotted, a pair of tide-touched could dash it to bits on the rocks. The inhabitants could melt back into the jungle, as though they had never been here at all.

Lunurin's rain-wet hand closed around his. Was it her hand shaking, or his?

"Rosa, she told me the abbot had new ships. I didn't know what it meant. I didn't *know…*"

They moved toward the village, past the ring of blackened trees. Sina tripped and let out a terrible moan. "She was supposed to be safe—"

Sina hadn't fallen over debris. Alon was afraid to look, but the bodies half-hidden beneath the dense ferns weren't small enough to be Biti. It was the two night guards, their throats slit.

Nothing lived. The only movement came from collapsing huts, sending up gouts of sparks and ash. Desperation seized him—he tried to climb the blackened steps of his mother's porch, but the heat forced him back. He coughed, eyes streaming and burning, trying to force himself past the wall of heat, into the remains of his mother's home. It had burned so long that though Sina had damped the flames, heat radiated from the blackened husk in waves. Even Lunurin's rain evaporated before it touched the hard-baked ground. He had to find his mother. He had to know.

Sina walked past him, waves of heat curving around her body and crisping the edges of her clothing black. "I will find them. If they are here, I will find them."

How many had been caught by the smoke in their beds? Alon went on, determined to find survivors, but all they found were bodies. More lay cut down by bullets at the edge of the village near the entrance to the lava tube caves. They searched the tunnels for survivors, but found no sign that anyone had made it that far.

One trail of blood went toward the sea. Alon followed, unable to stop himself from hoping.

He came to a bluff that dropped straight down to the waves. Out among the razor edges of lava, frozen in time, lay a half-sunken karakoa, its spine broken, its oars sheared off by angry surf. And Alon knew the ship. It was the flagship of his father's fleet.

A cry dragged itself past his bared teeth, the waves leaping higher at his anguish, claiming the remains of the ship for the sea. It wasn't enough, it would never be enough! How could his father—

Lunurin pulled his attention away from this greatest betrayal. She pointed. Alon flung himself down the incline without a thought for his own safety. Lunurin's cry of alarm rang in his ears. Near the surf, in the lee of volcanic outcroppings, he found Kawit.

The older man was slumped and unmoving, his clothing dark with blood.

Alon fell to his knees, searching desperately for a pulse. Kawit's eyes fluttered. Alon tore open his shirt and yanked water from an incoming wave to his hands, pressing them where bullets had burrowed deep into Kawit's abdomen.

"Oh, Gat Alon, you should not be here. We cannot let the Codicíans have you too," Kawit rasped.

"They've gone. The Codicians are long gone, Tito," he assured Kawit.

"Your mother—" Kawit coughed. Flecks of blood, black as night, splattered his lips. "I couldn't find her or Biti. There was too much smoke and confusion. I am sorry, Gat Alon."

"No, no! I shouldn't have sent you alone," Alon cried.

"I came too late. I should've stayed hidden, I know, but…" Kawit grimaced. "I couldn't let those murderers slip back out to sea. I sent a few down, at least."

"How? How did they surprise the village like this?" Alon asked. He was losing the battle over Kawit's waning blood. So much had soaked into the sand, and with it his healing magic. Around them bloody salt crystals formed, glistening on the black sand.

Please, not Kawit too.

"They didn't come from the sea. They landed… upriver… two of the Lakan's warboats. They came around the flank of Hilaga through the jungle at dusk. I came too late, the village was already burning. I thought I could help a few get away…"

Kawit's voice faded.

Alon dumped bloody water from his hands and pulled fresh seawater into his grip. He gathered the salt and impurities into a hard crystal in his palm, till the water was so fresh he could no longer control it and it dripped out of his hands into Kawit's mouth, a survival trick he'd taught Alon long ago.

Kawit drank and gave him a thin smile. "You are a good boy. Look for your mother for me. A tide-touched Dayang should be put to the sea, not have her bones left in a burned heap."

Alon scrubbed his tears away on his shoulder, not wanting to drip on Kawit. "Just hold still and rest—"

"It is enough. I was afraid I would die alone, and no one would know what had happened." Kawit gave a bubbling sigh, and went still.

"No, no please! Don't leave me alone!" The cry tore from Alon, bloody and raw.

Lunurin dropped to her knees beside him. Her palms were torn from her descent down the volcanic scree. She seized Kawit's face in her hands, the rain and lashing wind lifting her hair.

Lunurin sang a plea to the heavens. Her power surged and Alon felt a faint rush as Lunurin breathed the storm into Kawit's failing body.

Alon grit his teeth, joining her struggle to push back the grey fog of death creeping through Kawit's veins.

Maybe, just maybe they had a chance.

41

LUNURIN CALILAN DE DAKILA

There was so much blood. Too much. Lunurin knew that. It saturated her skirts. The storm of life in Kawit's body was fading, draining away faster than she and Alon could replace it. Lunurin's eyes burned as the draw of the salt amulet stole her ability to weep. She couldn't tell if her throat burned with smoke, thirst, or her inability to cry. The sky wept for her.

It had been a massacre, and she'd brought it to their doorstep in the form of Catalina. Lunurin's head bowed under the terrible knowledge.

"I'm sorry, I'm so sorry." What a foolish, useless thing, when Alon's grief whipped the sea into a frenzy, and the searing updrafts of Sina's desperate search tore holes in the clouds Lunurin had dragged down Hilaga's flanks.

She sang down the vitality of the storm overhead, willing it into Kawit's body. Alon worked desperately to force the internal ruin of too many bullets into rightness. Lunurin could see skin knitting together under the bloody saltwater in Alon's hands, but could feel that inside, there was so much more still broken.

Kawit's eyes fluttered open.

"Dayang," he rasped.

Lunurin bent her ear to catch his words above the roar of surf.

His hand closed around the salt crystal hanging about her throat.

Lunurin seized his wrist. "Kawit?"

He held her gaze. "Do not waste your power on a dying man. It's been a long time since there was a stormcaller in Aynila. Will you grant me vengeance? For the true Lakan and her kin, for all the tide-touched of Aynila, will you cry our deaths to your goddess and see us mourned as we deserve?"

Lunurin's throat constricted, her eyes burning. It was an ancient plea. Had she not been born to answer it? She'd hesitated so long, and now Aynila's tide-touched had paid the price for her cowardice a second time.

No more.

"Yes. I am a stormcaller. I do not heal and I cannot save, but if you would have vengeance..." It was a prayer, a mourning ballad, a vow.

Kawit's grip tightened on the pendant about her neck, his brow furrowed in concentration. Lunurin's heart beat fast. The vow she'd made to her goddess in the cage burned as though lightning were tracing the words on her heart. The salt prism guarding her spirit drew so tight she gasped, but it did not break.

With a shaking hand Kawit reached toward Alon who was still trying so desperately to fix what could not be unbroken. "Gat Alon, I must beg your aid, one last time. They stole my mutya, without it..."

Slowly, Alon lifted his own mutya from around his neck.

Lunurin didn't understand what he intended. She cried out when he seized the pearl-studded cross and tugged, pulling the mother-of-pearl-beaded strand free. A paroxysm of agony twisted his face. He tucked the cross into his waistband and then, steeling himself for the shock of it, he broke the strand, wrapping three mother-of-pearl sampaguita beads into Kawit's hand.

Kawit clutched the beads. "Thank you, I wouldn't want Aman Sinaya to think I cast away her blessing."

With the aid of Alon's gifted mutya, Kawit's power focused into a single point within him, bright and shining. The salt pendant around Lunurin's neck crumbled, and Kawit's hand fell, lifeless, the last of his strength, cold seawater, and salt soaking into Lunurin's blouse.

Lunurin cried out in anguish as her spirit spun free into the storm with nothing to anchor her or hold her back from her goddess. Alon sobbed. Great heaving wails wracked his body as he bent, pressing his brow to Kawit's, his grief bitter and endless as the depths of the sea.

Her throat ached. Her lungs had nothing else to offer to the wind, horror and pain a poured offering.

And her goddess rushed into her skin like air into lungs after a deep dive. *"My lover's chosen burn, their prayers rise to me in the ash. The tide-touched of Aynila cry vengeance, and they will have it."*

It was relief, and freedom, and rage as Lunurin had only known once before.

Within Lunurin there was a storm, a hundred-year typhoon held to her bones by a thousand threads as fine as silk. For years, she had bound herself and her power down with magic and vows and self-control. Lunurin gathered up those threads in her bloody hands and sundered them all, letting her power boil up out of her body unhindered, unencumbered, untethered. Northeast, on the open water of the Great South Sea, it began. With the salt of Kawit's spilled blood, Lunurin and her goddess roused the sea. Into the sky they spun a budding thunderhead, cloud vapor, cool and dense, the tantalizing bite of seed-lightning on the tongue, a cocoon of mist and starlight, a deadly glittering raiment. Heaven's judgment would come, and by the time it had swept in over several hundred miles of warm ocean, it would bring with it a storm surge that would drown every living thing in the Palisade.

Slowly, Lunurin sank back into her skin.

She laid her hand on Alon's neck, and transferred his head to her shoulder, drawing him gently away from Kawit's cooling body. Alon seized her like a man drowning. He clutched her close, burrowing against the beat of her heart and the warmth of her skin.

Lunurin closed Kawit's staring eyes with her free hand. Then she curled herself around Alon, trying foolishly to shelter him from the rain. His tears soaked hot into her blouse.

Alon tugged her mutya to loose her bun. Her hair uncoiled heavily across her back. The rain fell harder.

It frightened Lunurin how much she trusted this man—with her life, with her mutya, with all the secrets of her past, and whatever future was before them.

The song Lunurin sang was one of mourning. The sky wept with her, the sea moaned in anguish, and smoke rose from Hilaga's peak as Amihan herself stared down from her perch.

"Ask and you shall have it, lover mine," she crooned. "I do not heal and I do not save, but whatever power I have it is yours. Let the tides turn and the sea roar. Walk with me and the sea will rise on the wings of my storm."

She bent, pressing her brow to Alon's and made her own promise. "We will drown every Codicían responsible for this massacre. We will drag their Palisade into the sea and be free of their scourge. Aynila won't mourn the death of monsters."

He gazed up, his eyes reddened with smoke and tears, starbursts of black striations visible against the deep brown of his irises. Grief carved harsh lines in his face.

Alon kissed her. He tasted of ash and salt, sorrow and rage. "Yes." The word was a growl.

He kissed her again, fervent as worship. "Yes."

He kissed her a third time, gentle as silk. "Yes."

Lunurin kissed him back. She poured all the strength of the storm into his too hot blood. Within her, Anitun Tabu whispered, *"Soon, soon, soon."*

Together they stood. Alon lifted Kawit's body in his arms and they made the treacherous climb back into the village, and across the lava field to lay Kawit gently onto the sand beside the bangka.

They found Sina in the burnt-out husk of his mother's home, clutching at the sheets of her sister's cot. They were the only thing not turned to char in the whole village.

"She was here—"

"We'll find her," Isko promised. "We'll comb Hilaga for her."

Sina threw her head back with a wail. The ground under them shuddered.

"She's not on Hilaga, the mountain would know. Biti is a Prinsa. Like me, like our mother. Hilaga knows our blood."

The next shock threw Isko from his feet. The blackened husks of the village around them collapsed, sending up sprays of soot and smoke.

Sina screamed and pressed her hands down into the drifts of ash surrounding her sister's cot. "No. Not like this."

The ground heaved, and Sina rippled with it, heat exploding out from her body so fiercely the air seemed to boil. Her fingers plucked twists of heat up out of the pores of the earth. A firetender's chant flew skyward on the updraft. Lunurin dragged Isko back, fearing they'd be scalded.

The earth went still. Sina gasped for air. "My mother. We have to get my mother back to Hilaga. Too many gods-blessed have perished on her flanks. If her chosen katalonan is not returned to her soon, the next eruption will bury Aynila in lava and ash. I'm not strong enough to hold her. The conclave will do their best, but the tremors will only get worse."

Lunurin lifted Sina to her feet, pressing the strength of the gathering storm into Sina's hot skin. "You will have her. We will not let the Codicíans keep anything they have taken from us."

~

Together, they carried bodies and the blackened bones of the dead from the doused pyres to the beach. Sina had found no sign of human remains in Dalisay's home, but three others had burned in their beds.

The four of them gathered on the beach at last. Lunurin's abraded hands had acquired a fine coating of black bone ash that no amount of rain would shift. The scent of death was everywhere.

The waves on the beach crashed and broke like the gnashing of teeth. Alon didn't hesitate. He cradled Kawit's body in his arms one final time, struggling out past the violent surf, into the waist-deep water.

Lunurin's winds carried his words back to the small party on the beach. "Aman Sinaya, Gentle Lady! This is Kawit, more maker than healer, but ever yours. He taught me how to hide in plain sight. He taught me how to stride forward into an uncertain future, no matter what might come. He knew more of salt and dye than I could ever learn. He was brave and loyal to the last, and now I send your son back to your breast." Alon's voice was raw with grief, the sea and the sky cried with him.

He released Kawit into the arms of the tide, and fought his way back to the beach. Falling to his knees beside the rows and rows of bodies and bones laid out on the beach. He seized the beaded strand of his mutya, each one a perfect carved flower, and prepared to sunder it further.

"Alon, stop." Sina's words died in the face of the shadows lying across his face, bottomless and terrifying.

"The Codicians plundered the mutya from the village. I cannot send Aynila's last tide-touched to the sea without a token by which Aman Sinaya may know them for her children." Alon's solemn voice brooked no further protest.

Alon grasped the end bead and pulled, breaking the hooked gold wire connecting them. He tucked a single mother-of-pearl bead between the teeth of each blackened skull, and into the hands of each of the four bodies, and one by one, he carried them into the sea. He named the ones he could, and then the ones they couldn't recognize or find. The surf grew rough and dangerous, threatening to prevent even him from making it back to the beach. For one terrible moment, Lunurin thought he would let the sea drag him away with the dead, before he turned and struggled for the shore.

Now, Alon truly was the last tide-touched in Aynila.

Lunurin met him in the surf, dragging him the rest of the way onto the beach.

Her storm was coming, a just reward for decades of occupation and desecration, and nothing now would turn it aside.

The time for bargaining with the gods was past. Now, even patient Aman Sinaya cried out for her lost children, and scarred Hilaga, who had sheltered Aynila in her shadow for centuries, shuddered under their feet.

Sina swayed, holding tight to Isko for support until the tremor passed. "Oh, Lunurin, soon, we must move soon. Hilaga must have my mother or all of Aynila will suffer for what the Codicians have done."

Isko swore. "Are you mad? They wiped out a village of tide-touched overnight. What can the three of you hope to accomplish, other than dying tragically? If Hilaga is waking, we run, and evacuate the city if we can."

"There will be no more running from what the gods demand," Lunurin said.

"The gods didn't protect the tide-touched, they won't protect you," Isko spat. "Aynila has been dying for years! And they've done nothing!"

Lunurin rocked back, his accusation flowing over her.

"Well? Have you anything? Excuses? Apologies? Divine portents?" Isko demanded, his jaw clenched, a pale knot against his dark skin.

Lunurin shook her head. "I'm sorry. No. But it wasn't the gods who failed Aynila, it was me. This is what Anitun Tabu asked of me when I was twelve years old, when the healers of Aynila burned. But I was afraid, and my family hid me from her sight. I put off my vows for a long time, but the price of my blessing is due, and nothing now will prevent Anitun Tabu's vengeance."

Sina put her hands gently to Isko's jaw. "Without our katalonan to sing of our fate to the gods' ears, how could they know? Amihan sleeps long between waking, whole lifetimes, and when she wakes she is indiscriminate with her fury. My mother did not dare wake her. Even now, even for Biti, I don't wish it. Aman Sinaya has many strengths, but being slow to anger can be a curse as much as a blessing. She never wishes the death of one of her own, even if it would save a thousand lives. Anitun Tabu is in the rains. She comes every season. She sees all in the eye of the storm. But with no stormcaller to call down the heaven's justice... The goddesses of Aynila slumbered and forgot themselves. Now we must remind them of their true names. No matter what it costs."

"You will all die," Isko cried.

"We may," Lunurin acknowledged. "But if we do nothing, everyone will die when Hilaga wakes."

The inconsolable sea crashed. Lunurin didn't know if any of this would matter. She and Alon combined might not be able to get them off this beach alive.

42

ALON DAKILA

Alon was hollowed out. All his rage and grief and terror poured into the sea, leaving him empty and insubstantial as sand. He didn't know where Lunurin found the seemingly unlimited reservoir of strength that she poured into the rest of them. Even then it was barely enough. The roiling bay nearly dragged them down.

Finally, they ghosted up the Saliwain on a thin pair of countercurrents, through banks of cloud that dripped condensation on their skin like tears. Halfway upriver, Alon lost his grip on the currents he'd called, the salt too dilute for him to control in his exhaustion. Lunurin, Sina, and Isko laid themselves into paddling. Somehow, near dusk, they bumped alongside the floating docks.

Alon would've collapsed if Lunurin and Isko hadn't heaved him bodily back onto land. His whole body ached from the pounding surf, his arms felt only distantly attached to him. All he could smell was death.

He drank the salted fish broth Sina shoved steaming into

his face, leaning heavily on Lunurin as he was deposited into a bed.

Hers, he realized, staring at the blue lace canopy overhead, buffeted by phantom surf and deep-sea currents. The smell of burning hair and charred bone crawled up his sinuses like drops of saltwater. Sleep didn't come. Instead, he felt trapped above his own head.

Was he alive? Was he dead? Had he slipped with the other tide-touched out to sea? Were the currents tearing him apart, rolling his bones smooth along the sandy bottom?

Lunurin draped herself along his side, hot as a brand. The thread of real sensation tethered him to his body, a shocking and intense relief. He seized onto it, desperately needing something that wasn't the churn of angry surf and the crumble of charred bone under his fingers.

"Please, I can smell them burning." He reached for her, gasping when his aching fingers clumsily bumped her arm.

Lunurin cradled his hand in hers, examining the problem by touch. She reached toward the opposite bedside and returned with a vial of her sesame hair oil. The smell was thick in the air, nearly banishing the acrid scent of smoke.

She massaged it into his fingers, dropping a featherlight kiss onto his thumb when he hissed in pain.

"Don't—" He didn't want to contaminate her with all the death he'd touched today. She pressed three more kisses to his palm, then twisted the greased brace from his hand.

Alon bit back a curse, contorting it into a grunt. Then his mutya lost contact with his skin and he snapped fully back into his body. Oh… his mutya had been feeding him the sensation of all the sampaguita beads he'd put to sea with the dead. His hand throbbed, free from constriction at last, folding into a more comfortable half-fist.

Lunurin held his mutya out to him, gold and mother-of-pearl gleaming in her cupped palms.

Alon shook his head. "Keep it for me tonight. It's sending me echoes of its fellows. I can't bear it."

"Can I help?" she asked.

Alon reached for her. It was selfish, and perhaps in the morning he would regret it, but nothing seemed real except her. Alon needed something real to counter the crushing blackness and the tug of phantom currents.

"Please…" Alon didn't know what he was asking for.

But his mother and Kawit and all the tide-touched were dead. He was alone, and he could not bear the weight of it.

Lunurin went to him. "Yes."

She kissed him and did not flinch from his hands, hands that had failed him. What was the point of his healing, and his forewarning of the deaths of his kin, when he hadn't saved even one from the massacre?

She draped herself over his body, aligning their limbs as if she knew he needed to be pressed back into his skin. Alon lay half stunned under the warm steady weight of her and could have wept in relief. He tucked his face into her neck, nuzzling into the inky softness of her hair, letting her bear him down into the mattress, till his limbs reattached and his spirit did not float free into the endless salt.

When sometime later he grew hard against the soft heat of her thighs, he shifted uncomfortably, about to apologize. To ask this went beyond selfishness. But before he mustered the willpower to pull away, she reached down, her hand grasping and squeezing exactly where he needed. He should have been red with shame, but instead he groaned aloud, bucking into her grip.

"Do you want this?" she asked. "We can just lie together. We don't have to."

Damning himself, Alon begged, "Please... I want you... You anchor me in my skin. But you don't have to. Just holding you is enough."

43

LUNURIN CALILAN
DE DAKILA

Lunurin would've had to be made of stone to deny the raw need in Alon's voice. He'd turned his face away, ashamed at being caught in the act of needing, but from whom should he ask this comfort if not her? And who else was there now for either of them? After what Cat had done... Lunurin couldn't bear to think it.

She struck a light. She wanted this to be about Alon. She wanted to see him and be with him, to give him whatever comfort he could find. The press of him into her hand was so keen. She wanted him to ask it of her, to beg her to take mercy on him.

If he did not want her guilt and penance, then she'd not let him keep this shame.

"Look at me."

Alon obeyed, anguished guilt writ on his face. "I'm sorry. You don't have to. I shouldn't have asked."

"I wanted you to ask. I'm tired of pretending I don't want you. I told myself it was just that you are tide-touched and I am a stormcaller, that it was a trick of our magic, not real.

And then I told myself it was only that your nearness relieved the burden of the salt amulet. But I'm done lying to myself and I won't lie to you. I don't want to be alone tonight. I want to be with you. I want this memory, to hold with me, whatever comes tomorrow." She kissed him and put both hands to the task of freeing him from his waistcloth.

His cock jumped from its restraints. Lunurin dragged herself from the heat of his mouth to loosen her wrap. She sat bare, her rear cradled on his thighs, his cock jutting between them. The glistening head painting fluid under her navel.

She studied his half-anguished pleasure in fascination. Despite all the horror of the day, she ached for him. The hollowness of her grief wanted proof she still lived. If something as simple as release could blunt the memories of death and drop them both into deep and dreamless sleep, it would be a blessing.

Lunurin closed both hands around him. Alon cried out and Lunurin pinned him to the mattress when he bucked. He whined low in his throat, beseechingly.

Alon traced a hand up to cradle her neck, drawing her down. He kissed her throat and the soft hollow beneath her ear. His tenderness melted the ragged edges of her grief.

"Please, I need—" he begged, low and desperate against her ear.

"Easy," she assured him. "I've got you."

She located the flask of hair oil. It poured like honey, pooling in her palm. When the whole length of him was slicked to her satisfaction, Lunurin knelt.

His smooth, slick head bobbed against her folds. She ground down, till he pressed wide and blunt against her. Alon's hands petted up and down the outsides of her thighs, his hips jumped a little, and she half expected him to drag her onto him to satisfy his desperation.

"Please, Lunurin."

Her name was different on his tongue, a prayer and a plea. There was something of worship in his dark gaze. She wanted to sink into those depths, to float in the safety of him. She took mercy, the stretch of him a deep sweet ache.

It had been a long time since she'd been intimate with someone this way.

Goddess but he was so much, like wet silk wrapped around a furnace.

His eyes searched her face. "Is it too much? We don't have to—"

"No, I—" Lunurin made herself breathe, and let her weight bring them together.

Finally, she sat firmly in his lap, so full her body sang with it. As close as they could possibly be, and his hold so tight and urgent she never wanted to leave. Instinctively, she ground down and shocked herself by coming, the sweet ache of him pulling her apart at the seams. It seemed when she wasn't terrified of tearing the roof off, pleasure came easily to her. The safety she felt in his embrace was heady as strong spirits.

When she could think again, Alon's breath was hot in her hair. He panted. His left hand gripped her hip. His right arm, slung around her back, crushed her into him.

Lunurin tried to pull herself upright, intending to properly ride the unbelievably patient man, but his grip didn't give. Lunurin put a hand to his face, and tried to move her hips. His hold tightened.

"Please, stay, just like this, please," he begged.

Lunurin went obligingly still, but he tugged her more firmly against him. "Ahh, no, grind on me, please," he groaned. "I just need to stay inside you like this."

Her legs trembled. She kissed his neck. "Let me make you feel good. Let me move for you. Let me give you what you need."

His eyes were blown wide with wanting. His dark hair lay in a broken halo about his head. The fevered need behind his eyes was as wild and deep as his grief. How could he be so gentle with her, so patient, when he had so much desperation tangled up inside him?

Alon lifted a hand to stroke her face, carding his fingers into her hair. Reverently, he once more lifted her mutya free from her bun, then slid them back in, releasing her hair to cascade around them. All of what she was, known and seen and cradled in the palm of his hands, and she'd never felt so treasured.

"This is all I need, to stay inside you. Can I? Please, just tonight. Let me know when you're done. I'll stop."

She wanted to tell him it was fine to simply take his own pleasure, that she would give him everything, but her head was swimming with bliss, all her blood replaced with hot honey and seed-lightning. His hold was so urgent, as if being locked in her embrace was really all he needed.

She nodded. "Whatever you need."

He drew her over his body, rocking into her slow and deep. He kissed her like the only clean air was in her lungs. He pulled her apart with his hands and the grind of his pelvis against the soft heat of her. He drew out every spasm and quake, until sweat broke out across her skin and ran between her breasts, her muscles quivering too much to support her.

Alon licked the salt from her skin, lifting her hair away from her flushed neck with reverent hands, his own breath hard and hot against her skin, as he struggled to hold himself in check.

He kissed the tears of bliss gathered at the corners of her eyes and pressed his brow to hers. "You're alright? I'm not hurting you?"

"Yes, yes, I'm okay. I'm very, very good," she promised.

Lunurin panted, clutching Alon's shoulders, every thought hazy in a wash of pleasure, like she were caught in a vortex of sea foam.

When Lunurin was sure that every bone in her body had melted and the next time she came her heart would stop, she squeezed his hand tangled in her hair. "Next time, there's always next time. I'm not going anywhere."

Alon nodded, his expression so fierce with concentration that at any other time she would have laughed. "Yes, you're tired."

He withdrew from her, as if he really thought she'd leave him like this, to sort himself out.

She dragged him back. "No, no, it's my turn."

She made good on her word, pushing up on trembling arms. Alon bucked into her with a bitten off shout. His eyes affixed on her—wide and wild with the need he had kept on an iron leash, just to keep her in his arms a moment longer.

"Lunurin." He uttered her name half in prayer.

"I'm here. Always." She rode him hard. His head fell back as he clutched at her, desperate to ground himself, and she squeezed back.

Then, he came.

He folded into her, burying his face into her breasts, his strong thighs tight to her back. Her hands gripped his cock, trapped between their bodies, till at last, his muscles unclenched and he fell back against the pillows. With a deep sated sigh, Lunurin collapsed over his chest.

She was slick with sweat and other things, almost clammy now as she came down while he stayed so warm. Lunurin rubbed her cheek against his chest. She breathed, letting the ebbing waves of the glow lap gently over her head, listening to the thundering beat of Alon's heart under her ear.

She expected Alon to drop right to sleep, hence her strategic position on top. But as he got his breath back, the hand on her back started tracing sweeping patterns over her skin. When he found the sensitive nape of her neck, she shivered and her belly clenched. Alon turned his head to her, his expression so concerned. He pushed her curls back from her face and dropped a gentle kiss on her lips.

Lunurin responded with a murmur.

"How are you?" he queried, so solicitous Lunurin smiled and kissed his cheek.

"Sleep now, don't worry about me."

But Alon wasn't doing that. He was moving.

He found his waistcloth in the tangled bedding. "At least, let me help you clean up."

With the pitcher from the bedside, he damped his waistcloth, wiping the sticky mess between their bodies. He cleaned her hands, pressing his lips to both her palms.

When their hands were clean, he offered her the water. Dutifully, Lunurin drank. Relief flooded through her, the dry ache she'd grown accustomed to living with giving way with each swallow. Each draft was cool and clear. Lunurin drank deep. Water had never tasted so sweet. She handed it back only when she thought another sip would make her sick.

He drank, his broad frame outlined in lamplight.

Lunurin reached for him. "Sleep now."

"You can't be comfortable." He found the rumpled pile of her underskirt and gently wiped the slick wetness dripping down her thighs and spread across her folds, brushing a chaste kiss to the point of her hip at her strangled whine in response to his touch.

Lunurin briefly couldn't breathe. It did something devastating to her heart the way he cared for her. She wanted to do the same for him.

At last, Alon curled against her side, like even a breath of space between their bodies would be unendurable, but his breathing didn't drop into the cadence of sleep. Instead, he clutched her like she was the only real thing in a sea of nightmares. The lamp ran dry of oil, plunging them into darkness.

"Without the tide-touched, the storm surge will lay half of Aynila under the waves." Alon's voice was a bare rasp against the skin of her throat.

A typhoon was bearing down on Aynila, only this time there would be no turning it aside. All of Aynila's tide-touched dead had cried out for vengeance, and Lunurin would not deny them, or the fury in her own heart.

Far out to sea, over water still roiling with Aman Sinaya's grief, the budding eye of a storm peered over choppy seas. Lunurin was still so afraid, but there was no stopping what was coming. And that was not her fault, but she must take responsibility for whatever came with her storm.

Deep inside, the goddess whispered, *"We are the ship killer. We are the wall breaker. What walks with us is death."*

No. Lunurin held this in her heart. *I will kill a hundred Codician soldiers for you, a thousand. I will wash their walls and ships into the sea, but we aren't like them. We will not kill them all sleeping in their beds. We will give them a chance.*

"How do you expect to stop the inevitable? The typhoon is coming, the sea will rise, and those who do not heed my call will perish."

She reached for Alon beside her, his bottomless grief a hole rent in the fabric of her world.

Lunurin cupped his cheek. "I can't turn aside this storm, but there is time yet to evacuate Aynila, and the Palisade if they will listen to reason. These are responsibilities for tomorrow. Tonight, rest. There is time still for grief."

As Alon's strong limbs fell heavy around her and his breathing slowed, Lunurin prayed he would sleep so deeply, not even the scent of burning hair could follow him.

44

ALON DAKILA

The day after the massacre the sun shone clear and bright. A golden day in Aynila, without a cloud to mar the haze of blue where sea met sky, and Alon was sure nothing could ever be right again.

He woke alone, the bed beside him cold. Alon went in search of his wife. The ache of the coming storm throbbed in his right hand. It was strangely comforting. She must be near. He could sense the disquiet of her spirit, a tempest churning the sea to a fevered pitch. His home, like the golden dawn, was unchanged, yet irrevocably gutted. The kitchen hearth lay cold, Kawit's collection of culinary salts untouched. Alon's sense of dissonance increased as grief sank claws into his chest.

He found her with Inez. Her internal tumult and the energy of the coming typhoon spilled out of her into the very air. It took him a moment to untangle his spirit from hers enough to realize that her turmoil had nothing to do with him.

"Lunurin?"

She looked up, her eyes burning. "I didn't want to disturb you. I couldn't sleep..."

She gestured. All across the floor she'd weighted down maps of Aynila, the Saliwain river delta and flood basin.

"And Inez?"

"No fever. She woke briefly. I changed her bandages and gave her more of the pain draft you prepared." Lunurin's hand curled protectively over Inez's head.

"Are you... okay?"

Lunurin pressed her knuckles to her sternum. "It's so much, Alon. I've unleashed the largest storm I've ever known, and it's still miles offshore... It will be stronger yet before it makes landfall."

"So you don't regret—"

Lunurin's head snapped up. She crossed the room to him. Her nearness was suffocating. He couldn't imagine what she was feeling if this was only the overspill.

"Why would you think that?"

Alon brushed a hand down her arm. Sparks of lightning crackled against his fingertips.

She grimaced and took a deep breath. The sparks dancing along the dark waves of her hair died. She let the air out slowly through her mouth, and the humidity in the room broke apart before a cool breeze. "Better?"

"Do you feel better?" Alon asked.

"No, but if I've roused you..."

Sina stumbled into the room, her eyes red and puffy with tears. "What's wrong? Is it Inez?"

"I'm sorry, I was meditating on the typhoon to gauge when it would make landfall. I didn't think about how the runoff would affect you two."

"It can't be good for convalescence. I couldn't bear it if..."

386

Sina flinched, turning away from Inez's small still form on the cot and pressing a hand over her mouth. "What will I tell my mother?"

Their shared grief seemed to fill the room, a towering wave that would surely crush them. But Alon was tide-touched. He knew how to hold a wave. He laid a hand on Sina's shoulder.

"I sent Biti to the tide-touched village. Let the fault lie with me."

Sina's expression crumpled. "Stop that. We both know you were right. She was safest in the Palisade. I never should've taken her. I never—"

"It wasn't any of us. It was the Codicíans. It ends here. We will end it," Lunurin swore. "Now come and look at these maps. If we don't see to the evacuation plans, there will be even greater losses to mourn."

The weight of lives and livelihoods in the path of the storm was staggering. There were seven hundred Codicían families within the Palisade and a garrison of five hundred soldiers, with twice that many native Aynilan servants and conscripted workers. Aynila and its outlying areas were home to almost thirty thousand, with two-thirds of the population centered around the port that would take the brunt of the storm. This was the story of the maps and figures, but in his mind's eye, he saw his city, his people. Even if this devastating typhoon managed to free them from the shadow of the Palisade, whose black teeth swallowed even the warmth of the sun, would they ever recover?

"Sina can see to the metalworkers' conclave. Alon, do you have the authority to order an evacuation of Aynila?" Lunurin asked.

Alon's hold over his emotions wavered. "No, that requires the Lakan's decree."

And his father had already betrayed the tide-touched.

～

This was a terrible idea. Alon's entire being disagreed with any plan that put Lunurin in range of his father's retribution. But even if they could counterfeit an evacuation order, he didn't have the manpower to carry it out. Furthermore, if anyone could convince the Palisade to evacuate... It would be their chief collaborator.

"What does your father want more than anything else?" Lunurin had asked.

Alon's flesh prickled with unease as he and Lunurin were escorted into the Lakan's study. The door closed.

His father didn't look up from the letter before him, scrutinizing it with a furrowed brow. "Alon, will this take long? I have—"

Alon was done playing along. How long had *he* been collaborating with the Codicíans in his father's name? Bile rose at the thought. He'd been a good son too long.

"Father, the tide-touched of Aynila are dead."

The Lakan's head snapped up. "What?"

It was a very good approximation of surprise.

"There was a Codicían witch hunt. Now I am the last tide-touched in Aynila."

Was that satisfaction he saw in the face that so closely mirrored his own?

"So your mother's band of saboteurs finally faced the consequences of their success. I don't know what they thought to accomplish, targeting the bridge. They should have left long ago." The Lakan dropped his gaze back to his documents dismissively.

Alon's fractured heart broke, the pieces disintegrating and falling into his guts, sharp burning sparks of pain. His grief seized him, and he might have faltered, but Lunurin's hand closed around his. The storm coiling within her skin buoyed him up.

"It takes a dozen tide-touched working together to protect Aynila Bay from a storm surge. I cannot do it alone. Aynila's evacuation plans assume the Saliwain will not flood. They assume there *will always be* tide-touched to protect the delta. A typhoon is bearing down on Aynila, and our defenses have been shattered," Alon said.

His father's tone turned low and dangerous. "A typhoon?"

Alon held his gaze. The "saboteurs" his father so despised had protected Aynila for decades, and he had betrayed them without a thought.

The Lakan's face went red with fury. "What precisely is the purpose of your pet stormcaller if she cannot protect us from storms?"

Lunurin stepped forward. "Not even Calilan's Stormfleet at its height could turn this storm. If we don't act, our dead will be washing ashore in Tianchao."

His father bared his teeth. "I'm supposed to believe this is not your doing? I might be better off putting you aboard a ship to Tianchao and sending your typhoon to their doorstep."

"If it were a storm of my making, I would have spun it directly atop our heads so there would be no chance for anyone to escape the fury of my goddess. I am telling you now, we have three days to evacuate to high ground," Lunurin lied.

The Lakan regarded Lunurin through narrowed eyes. "This is a ploy to separate the Codicians from their guns."

"I don't care what the Palisade does. Warn them if you want, but Aynila will bear the brunt of the destruction if we do nothing. If you sign the evacuation order, I will convince the matriarchs of Aynila that you have the old gods' blessing. With Dayang Dalisay dead, the principalia must vote for a new Lakan. Your detractors have always feared your Christianization," said Lunurin.

Alon watched his father's avarice for power vanquish every other doubt. The ignominy of being seen by the principalia as nothing but a placeholder for his wife had plagued him for years. Had that alone been reason enough for him to provide the Codicíans with friendly hulled crafts to deceive tide-touched guards? Or had it been when Alon finally rebelled, and chose protecting Lunurin over appeasing the Codicíans? What had been the final straw?

45

LUNURIN CALILAN
DE DAKILA

Inez wouldn't evacuate. She should've been easy to send across to the conclave to seek shelter high in Hilaga's hidden valleys. But sometimes Inez could summon every ounce of Catalina's stubbornness.

"You aren't sending me away. If you won't come with me, I'm not going," Inez declared, her lips pinched tight against any tremble.

And didn't she look heartbreakingly like Catalina when she did? Lunurin banished the comparison and her instinct not to argue when Cat was like this. This was about Inez's safety, and with Cat… without Cat, Lunurin was all Inez had. She'd never forgive herself if Inez came to harm in her storm. Lunurin had caused Inez enough suffering.

"I'm sending everyone away, Inez. I need to keep you safe. I'm trying to keep everyone safe."

"You're not sending Lord Alon away!" Inez's chin wobbled.

"Lord Alon isn't injured. You need to be somewhere safe well before the storm arrives."

"I'm safer with you," Inez insisted. "Please, Lunurin, you can't send me away."

"Not this time. I'm sorry, Inez."

"You're abandoning me!" Inez wailed, tears pouring down her golden cheeks. "Just like my mother. Just like Catalina!"

Lunurin felt answering tears welling up in her eyes and gathered Inez into her arms as gently as she could. "I'm *not* abandoning you. I'm going to come and retrieve you myself when all this is over. I swear."

"What if you don't?" Inez wept, clutching her neck. "What if you never come back? What if I lose you like my sister?"

Lunurin pressed her lips to Inez's brow. "You won't lose me, and I swear, I'm going to bring Catalina back to you. We are not going to abandon you, Inez. But your safety has to come first."

Inez burrowed her face against Lunurin's neck. "You promise you'll come back for me?"

"Yes."

"And you'll make Cat leave that horrible place?"

"I will," Lunurin promised.

She held Inez a long time, until at last, Inez whispered, "I'll go."

The weight of her grief and anger with Cat tangled about her neck with this new promise as she left to arrange Inez's transport to Hilaga. Both Aynila and the metalworkers' conclave were hemmed in by volcanic peaks. People could retreat to high ground. There was nothing to trap Aynilans fleeing rising floodwaters. The Palisade was easily ten feet closer to sea-level, and bottlenecked by the Puente de Aynila. In a twenty-foot storm surge, their walls would be a deathtrap.

Alon's arms closed around her shoulders. His voice was soft at her ear. "Let me send you with Inez."

"That was never part of the plan."

"I can't risk you like this."

"You'll need me to negotiate for Hiraya and all the other Aynilan hostages."

"If... *when* my father betrays us, he'll tell them what you are. They'll kill you." Alon held her so tightly. "I can't lose you too."

"You won't. Alon, I swear, you won't lose me. I won't hand myself over to them, I will walk this storm into Aynila, as I promised Anitun Tabu I would all those years ago. Nothing, not even my death, will prevent it."

"Aynila doesn't need your storm. It needs you. I need you—"

Lunurin kissed him. She wished she could press her goddess's unwavering certainty as deeply into him as it was carved into her. Her promises would have to be enough.

~

Lunurin picked at the still edible parts of the breakfast Sina had burned. At dawn they'd been woken by the Palisade church bells ringing the alarm reserved for plague and closing the Palisade for quarantine. They had been betrayed.

"*So, they have chosen to drown,*" the storm in Lunurin's heart whispered.

Blackened flecks of garlic tasted bitter on her tongue. Why did it matter if the storm was natural or not? They would die all the same if they stayed. Did they really think their walls could withstand the full force of a typhoon?

"*Let them learn otherwise,*" Anitun Tabu said.

And they would. They must. So, for Biti and Kawit, for the true Lakan of Aynila and all the other lost tide-touched, Lunurin would take responsibility. She would make the Codicians learn.

Sina had gotten the better of Isko's every attempt not to burn breakfast. He hadn't left her side since waking after the massacre.

"You don't have to eat it," Sina repeated. "I don't mind the char. I should've known better than to be in the kitchen when I'm like this."

"You can be where you like. Next time, I'll make a cold meal," Isko said.

Lunurin caved, accepting the papaya Alon had peeled and cubed instead. She'd just taken the first bite when a heavy knock sounded on the door.

"That will be the demand to hand me over," Lunurin said.

Alon took her hands. "You don't have to come with me." He met Sina's gaze. "Either of you, one Prinsa must be better than none."

"We won't send you to face them alone. Whatever comes, we will face it together," Lunurin said.

"All of us," Sina agreed.

Alon's guards didn't grant the messenger admittance. Their demand was simple: deliver the wife of Alon Dakila, María Lunurin, to the Palisade, or children from the church school would be put in the starvation cages to face the storm unprotected.

Alon's reply was already written. They sent the messenger on without delay.

Lunurin stood from her meal. "Shall we go?"

Alon growled. "Eat first. Let the Codicíans wait for once."

Outside, the sky was startlingly clear and blue but for thin bands of clouds swirling across from the northeast, carried on a low, steady breeze.

Alon boosted her onto a little black mare; Isko pulled Sina up behind him on a grey. Litao and every trained guard that

Alon could convince to stay accompanied them. Though the typhoon was not yet visible to the human eye, thunder rolled over the city. Half of Aynila was in the streets, evacuating inland with loved ones and what possessions they could carry.

But loud spoke the goddess in the thunder. *"My time is come, Aynila. We will drive them from Hilaga's shelter, into the sea, into the storm. There will be no mercy for even one of those who have defiled my name."*

Despite Alon urging people to continue seeking higher ground, a crowd swelled about them. Together they made their way toward the Palisade bridge and the doleful tolling of the church bell.

The cages gleamed against the pitch-blackened walls. Lunurin wondered if they'd already put the children into them.

46

ALON DAKILA

There would be losses. Alon was prepared for that. He would never again put Lunurin into Codicían hands and hope they'd keep their word. He'd learned his lesson on the steps of the Lakan's palace. He was relieved Sina had taken his side, arguing Lunurin out of trading herself for Hiraya.

They'd had this discussion a dozen times. There had always been the terrible risk that the Codicíans might openly torture the hostages. Lunurin promised she wouldn't hand herself over. If worst came to worst, she'd dive off the bridge into the water and Alon could whisk her out to the bay. Still, it was frightening how calm she was. She burned with terrible intent, and Alon was quite sure she wasn't alone in her head anymore.

Lunurin had dressed this morning in a style he hadn't seen since she'd been fifteen on a Calilan beach. The pious nun and the demure dayang had been shed away. The skirt was not as wide and heavy as was currently popular in Aynila. It was closer to the waistcloths he wore in private, knee-length with long tasseled modesty panels in cobalt blue that contrasted with the indigo of the wide wrap. Her indigo blouse was close fit with short sleeves, baring a teasing strip of golden-brown skin at her navel.

She wore her hair in a low tail at the nape of her neck, the top half secured in a figure eight speared through with her pearl-topped hair prong, her comb pressed into the top of the bun, rising over her head like a crown. Her uncovered half-loose hair, curls dark and coiled as deep-water kelp, was almost more indecent than the curves of her strong calves hugging the sides of her mount.

All around her pressed the crowd, more mutya than he'd seen in years now worn openly, waves and mountains etched in decorative patterns on shell, bone, and cloth, their hopes and fears and prayers buoying her up. Though their entourage was only a few stray bullets or misplaced words from becoming a mob, Alon was glad of them. Surely the goddess within Lunurin wouldn't lash out with lightning and death when so many of her people were near.

Alon half expected to see his father standing beside the governor on the bridge. But the Lakan was nowhere to be seen, which heartened him. He would deal with his father later. He needed to focus on the hostages. They'd brought Hiraya, hands chained behind her back and gagged, but only half the students from the school.

Alon lifted Lunurin from her mount. Her hands on his forearms were steadier than his about her waist.

Alon kissed her, desperate to shatter her terrible calm with something. But all he could feel within her was the typhoon drawing toward Aynila like iron filings pulled by a lodestone.

"Are you still with me?" he asked.

"Always." Her promise was echoed in the thunder.

A sailor in the crowd held out a fishing spear, the barbed bone head ringed in waves. Lunurin accepted it with a gracious bow.

"Why?" Alon asked.

"The goddess of storms is supposed to wield a spear," the sailor answered. "And the Dayang is unarmed."

"This is a hostage exchange."

"They aren't unarmed."

This was true. Alon clasped Lunurin's fingers tightly in his strong hand. He would not let another life slip through his grip. She had so much of her goddess in her now, he didn't know if she still remembered her body was mortal. They walked to the foot of the bridge.

"Governor, I asked for every Aynilan student. You're a dozen short," Alon called out.

Governor López laughed his booming laugh. "You're a newlywed, so I'll forgive your overvaluation of how much your wife is worth to me."

Around the governor bristled a regimen of soldiers, their polished rifles aimed at Alon's small party and the crowd gathered on the opposite riverbank.

"I don't know what my father has told you, but if she dies, none of you will survive the coming storm."

"Is that a threat?"

"A fact."

The governor's hard smile gleamed through his black beard. "I don't like the kinds of 'facts' you Aynilans have been inventing lately."

"That will not make them less true. Send over my aunt and the children. I won't hand over my wife without assurances you are serious."

"I will send one set. If your wife comes quietly, then I'll release the rest. Tell me, what will the matriarchs of the principalia say when they hear how you toyed with their heirs' lives?"

So they did consider the children the more valuable. The flaring of Sina's hope was palpable.

Sweat ran down the back of Alon's neck. "Send over Hiraya Prinsa then, one lady of the principalia for another. It's a fair trade."

He squeezed Lunurin's wrist tightly as the children were hustled back inside the Palisade, vanishing from view.

The governor gave the order. Hiraya, hands still chained, was released and allowed to cross the bridge. Alon didn't take his eyes off the row of rifle barrels gleaming under the beating golden sun until his tiya stood beside him on the bridge. He'd half expected them to gun her down midway.

Sweat stood out on her brow, not merely from the sweltering heat. Her jaw worked desperately at the gag, her muscular smith's arms bulging against her chains. As soon as she reached them, Sina set to work on her bindings, nearly weeping with relief.

"Now, prove to me you are serious. Send over your wife," the governor called.

"And end our negotiations already?" Alon called back. "What assurances are you willing to give me for her safety?"

"She will be exactly as safe as any of us. I will put her into the abbot's cage until she calls off the storm, or dies in it."

"You brought this storm when your men massacred a village of fisherfolk and old women."

"Jungle water witches and saboteurs, the lot of them, and you know it," the governor shot back. "Enough talk. Hand over your wife."

"If she's to go up in one of your damned cages, I want the children let down and released to me."

The governor made a sharp gesture. A burning pitch torch was put into his hand. "I tire of this talk."

The row of riflemen parted. A woman, bound and hooded, was flung down on the stones of the bridge. Alon did not need to see her face to recognize his mother. A soldier upended a jar of clear viscous fluid over her head.

The whole world ground to the slow pour of oil under the hard, hot sun. His mother twisted and writhed, struggling to breathe through the hood as it saturated. The governor's torch crackled in his hand. The stones of the bridge darkened with pooling oil.

"Send over your wife, or I will burn this water witch before the eyes of God and all of Aynila."

Alon's grip on Lunurin's wrist tightened. The torch lowered, waving tauntingly through the air, sparks falling, falling. Only one needed to catch his mother's oil-soaked clothing.

"Sina, tell me you can stop a fire at this distance," Alon rasped.

"Alon, I can't. I'm sorry, it's too far!" Sina grunted in frustration and lit fire to the knots holding Hiraya's gag. The cloth crumbled into ash and Sina transferred her attention to the chains joining her mother's shackled wrists. Heat blurred her fingers, the metal slowly turning red.

"They have Biti too." Hiraya had spat out the gag at last. "Don't fold."

She wrenched at her bonds, her own fingers twisting intricate patterns, adding heat to the miniature forge between them. The metal in Sina's hands went soft at last, dropping sizzling to the ground. Hiraya was freed.

"Let me go, Alon." Lunurin's voice was calm and clear.

"I won't lose you both. You promised me you wouldn't hand yourself over to them."

"*I will lose no more of my lover's blessed to Codicían pyres.*"

Lunurin twisted her wrist and somehow she was free of his grip and striding across the bridge.

Alon's heart sundered.

She sparkled under the beating sunlight, threads of lightning dancing in the dark fall of her hair. They gleamed along the barbed head of the fishing spear in her grip.

When she was halfway across the bridge the governor called out, "Stop. Throw down your weapon."

Lunurin stopped but she made no move to comply. "Untie the woman and let her cross to me."

Alon dared to hope that Lunurin really would dive off the bridge.

"Why should I? What if you try something?"

"Then you can shoot us both down," Lunurin answered.

The torch swept lazily through the air, every pass closer and closer to his mother's head.

"Drop it," the governor ordered.

"Release her. Release her and I will hand myself over to you."

The air in his lungs was so thick he couldn't breathe. The tension stretched.

"Not until I have you back in chains where you belong," the governor answered.

Thunder clapped, loud as a mountain sundering. Before the echoes had died, a sharp crack and a gout of smoke cut the air as a rifleman panicked and discharged his weapon. In his peripheral vision Alon saw Isko fall. Sina screamed. The torch in the governor's hand flared wildly and he flinched, flinging it away.

Time slowed as it spun through the air and landed on his mother's skirts. Fire licked up her body like the closing of a burning fist. Alon cried a prayer to the sea, seizing every bit of the bay he could reach and dragging it toward him.

"Who fired?" The governor pointed toward Lunurin. "She has a spear, for God's sake. God gave you steel and guns! Seize her. I need her alive!"

Lunurin's spear arched through the air. It disappeared with a wet red spray into Governor López's thick black beard.

Then Alon's wave crested the bridge. He dragged half a dozen soldiers into the water with his mother and Lunurin. And the bay kept coming, eager and angry. It rushed up and over the Saliwain's banks, flooding into Aynila.

Alon couldn't stop it. He was on his hands and knees beside Isko, trying desperately to stem the bleeding. He couldn't lose anyone else!

47

LUNURIN CALILAN
DE DAKILA

Lunurin dove forward. Her hands closed on a hank of Dalisay's blouse as the wall of seawater caught them, dousing the spreading flames and sweeping them into the river. All around her the armored bodies of soldiers were dashed upon the stones of the bridge. The sea was angry and Alon was scared. They had to get out of the water.

The wave crashed down. Lunurin curled around Dalisay, desperate to prevent the churn from tearing them apart. Lunurin didn't know which way was up. Her lungs burned.

Finally, they broke the surface and Lunurin struggled to drag the saturated bag off Dalisay's head. Air, she needed air. The swirling current disoriented her. It was all she could do to keep them both above the water. They spun, helpless as a rudderless raft.

Suddenly hands seized them. A human chain of rescuers had waded out into the angry rushing waters. Extra hands dragged them both free from the river's grasp, and back onto the bank. Lunurin crawled to Dalisay's side, pressing an ear to her mouth, unsure if she was breathing, as one of their rescuers bent to cut her free from her bonds.

Her breath came fast and shallow, pulse weak and fluttery. Sections of Dalisay's skirts had disintegrated in the water, revealing red burns snaking up her legs.

Lunurin laid her hands over Dalisay's heart.

A breeze rushed off the water, chilling her wet skin. Like she was spinning up clouds out of the bay, Lunurin reached deep into the waves of salt that curled so protectively around Dalisay's spirit and bore her up on a strong steady breeze into the sun.

Dalisay woke, gasping. She grabbed Lunurin, dragging herself up. With a shaking hand she pointed and signed, "Get me to the water. I have to stop the bay."

Lunurin twisted and stared, disoriented. The bay was still rushing in, up over a low point in the Saliwain's bank, pouring into Aynila like a spilled pitcher. Where was Alon? She bent, lifting Dalisay's slight frame, carrying her toward the river. Their rescuers pressed close, ready to drag them back if the current should grab them.

Lunurin struggled to make sense of the situation. The bridge was empty, the soldiers had retreated. The Palisade's gates were closed. The lone figure of Governor López hung pinned to the gate by her spear, like one of his sacrilegious hunting trophies.

On the parapets, soldiers labored to turn their cannons from the bay to point out over the bridge and Aynila.

Lunurin set Dalisay on the bank, so her scalded legs were in the water. The inward rush of water slowed, then ceased, lying like a vast still pond, but the Saliwain didn't resume its seaward flow. Dalisay's countermand played tug-of-war with the bay. Lunurin stared in horror at the path of destruction one wave had wrought in its inland rush. Debris bobbed and swirled aimlessly in the water filling the streets.

"Find my son. Stop him pulling the bay, before he kills himself," Dalisay signed.

Lunurin ran for the bridge. Alon's wave had carried them a way upriver.

She was conveyed through the crowd quickly; at times her feet barely touched the ground. She found Alon and Sina bent over Isko, who was drenched in blood. Lunurin's heart crawled into her throat. Not again. Please, not again!

Hiraya stood over them, her eyes trained on the Palisade battlements.

"Alon!" Lunurin cried. "Stop, you're flooding the city!"

He didn't react to her voice.

"Get down!" Hiraya shouted.

Lunurin flung herself flat as the two main guns protecting the Palisade gates were lit.

There was a roar, and the great guns shuddered and split down their barrels. Shrapnel exploded in all directions. Men were blasted down from the parapet and black splinters rained down over the bridge.

"Hiraya? Are cannons supposed to do that?" Lunurin screamed.

Hiraya made a complicated gesture, and the splintered teeth of the Palisade all around the broken wrecks of her cannons flared, flames spreading quickly. "Mine are. Now we need to move back quickly. They'll figure out soon enough which barrels I sabotaged. We mustn't give them time to get Biti. They put her up in one of those cages."

Lunurin pressed herself through the last few bodies between her and Alon, falling to her knees at his side. "Alon, release your hold on the bay. Let it go. I pulled your mother from the water. She's safe."

Alon blinked glassily at her, his spirit stretched thin

between the vast spread of the bay and how much he'd sunk into his brother.

"Focus on Isko. Let's get you out of the line of fire," Lunurin repeated.

Alon let go, and strength flooded back into him from the bay. Isko stirred at last, cursing loudly as Lunurin and Sina grasped him under the arms and dragged him bodily away from the bridge.

"Good, strong lungs, not filling with blood," Sina panted as they hauled Isko into a side street behind the first row of buildings back from the bridge.

The sound of cannon fire recommenced, as more distant gun mounts were primed. Smoke rose thick and black over Aynila's port. Several of the larger ships still anchored in Aynila's bay foundered and sank under the onslaught.

Lunurin stared at the spreading devastation; the northeast wind of her typhoon would push the fires from the port into Aynila so quickly. "They'll level half of Aynila before my typhoon makes landfall."

"More than that if they get the *Santa Clarita* on the water," Hiraya observed.

Isko swatted at Alon. "Leave it. I won't bleed out. It's enough."

"If you die on me..." Alon's hands trembled, he'd poured so much energy into the healing. Lunurin bent, feeding strength into Alon's blood like a wind over still seas.

Dalisay found them. Two of Alon's guards carried her on folded arms; her burned feet wouldn't bear her weight. Casama, Alon's dye mistress, followed at her right hand.

"Drag down the storm now," Dalisay signed. "We'll sort friend from foe out of the wreckage."

There was power in Dalisay's order. The goddess within

Lunurin paid heed to the will of a true Lakan, chosen by Aynila and blessed by the gods.

"If her storm doesn't sweep in over the sea, there will be no surge," Alon pointed out.

"You'll have to pull one for her," Sina said. "If the water rises, they'll have to evacuate."

"You saw what I did! I'll flood the whole city. There aren't enough tide-touched left to protect Aynila," Alon protested.

"We will do it." Casama, Alon's lead dye mistress, spoke up. Old and bent with age, her eyes were only for Dalisay. "If we have one katalonan to pray for us, we can hold off the floodwaters the old way. We have enough women who still have their mutya," Casama continued.

Alon's brow furrowed in confusion. "How?"

Dalisay signed, "By wading into the river, to remind Aman Sinaya not to drown her people. We can hold the Saliwain in her banks. I cannot sing the prayers, but the Saliwain will hear me all the same. Pull only the bay. You saw, Aman Sinaya is angry, she will rise if you bid it."

Alon turned to Lunurin. "Can you do it?"

Lunurin held his gaze. She tested the fervor of the tempest within her. Could she spawn a second storm?

"I must." Lunurin stepped from the cover they'd found. Alon and Sina followed, leaving Isko, Hiraya, and the others with Dalisay.

She needed to see the sky.

The black smoke boiling up from the port had blown inland, filling the sky with a greasy grey film. Cannons spat fire between the teeth of the Palisade, and death rained down on Aynila.

They needed a storm. Lunurin's lungs trembled as cannon fire thundered in the air.

The sun beat down through the smoke with a strange red-orange light, casting a pall over the city. Lunurin reached for her mutya to release her hair with trembling hands. The thrum of power in them stilled her.

She couldn't do this. It was too much. Aynila might have been able to weather one of her storms, but two? The second hammer blow would fall tomorrow, when they were already storm weary and weakened. Biti and the other children might still be swinging high in cages over the Palisade. And there had been no evacuation—there were servants, conscripted workers, even stubborn, fearful Catalina. Would Lunurin be the death of them all?

"*Has Aynila not suffered enough?*" the goddess within her howled. "*Let us rage! Let us feed our pain and our anger into the sky! Let the streets of the Palisade run red with blood! Let them suffer as we have!*"

Lunurin's protest drowned in the awesome fury of a goddess captured and unmade while her people were exploited, taught to forget the names of their gods as their katalonan burned. When would it end?

"*You would deny me now in this final hour? Are we not of one heart?*"

But Lunurin was afraid. She always had been. "I can't! Not again! I can't face all the death that will follow."

In her mind's eye all she could see were storm-wracked bodies bloating in the sun. The dead of the Palisade and Aynila would dwarf her worst nightmares.

"*Do you think this fury is mine alone? It is a prayer whispered by a thousand tongues, secreted in a thousand minds as they ill-make the sign of the cross and hide their mutya and forget my true name. On their will, I will be an unstoppable storm, and you would deny them all, for fear? Over a few lost ships and one gone astray? One who has turned her face away time and time again? You made me a promise. There is a covenant between us. Daughter, cry my name and set my fury upon the world, or run, and be a daughter of mine no longer."*

Lunurin stared across the river at the Palisade and willed herself to act.

On the bay, a great black bulk moved ponderously around the Palisade. At first Lunurin didn't understand what she was seeing. Then, the behemoth swung broadside and thunder boomed with no lightning to herald it.

The *Santa Clarita* was on the water. She ate chunks out of the other vessels in the port like a frenzied mako shark. The maneuverable long-guns on her deck picked high-value targets in Aynila.

Modern galleons were built for destruction on the water. The *Santa Clarita*'s tall masts were outfitted with metal rods, her timbers soaked in fire-retardant boric acid, and her belly of gunpowder netted in grounded chain to prevent "accidents" of the type Lunurin had orchestrated as a child. An impervious floating fortress, the *Santa Clarita* would level Aynila, leave it smoking rubble just as her conquistadors had left the village of the tide-touched.

Lunurin was cold with fear. Alon's hand closed on her arm.

"Lunurin! We need your storm!" He shouted to be heard above the cannon fire.

"I can't!" she cried. "If I do, Aynila will be destroyed just as surely as it would be by Codicían cannons!"

Sina seized her other hand, feeding heat and warmth into the bottomless freezing pit of fear in Lunurin's belly. "You must. Even if it means the death of everyone within the Palisade, you must. Our loved ones are just as surely dead if we let Aynila burn."

"Aynila has survived such storms before. We will not leave you to weather the aftermath alone." Alon stared into her eyes. "You are the only one who can give Aynila a tomorrow to recover in. The time has come, even gentle Aman Sinaya cries at last for vengeance. Amihan herself would wake Hilaga. We have put off Anitun Tabu's reckoning long enough."

The goddess within Lunurin laughed, and it was a terrible sound. The fear that had driven Lunurin for over a decade filled her up to the brim, but she wasn't alone. Lunurin squeezed Sina's hand, drawing on the steady banked heat of her presence. Alon was like a vast deep sea, curled around her.

She took a deep breath, easing the quiver in her lungs. "Let down my hair."

Alon reached for her hair prong. Her hair cascaded down past her hips. She remembered the slap of saltwater and schooling clouds. The tumult and terror roiling under her skin spilled free with an inhuman howl. It tore out of her, along with all Anitun Tabu's endless rage.

Clouds spawned above rising smoke, piling up and up, an eye peering down over the center of the bay.

She spun it up out of Sina's fiery determination to free her sister or die trying, out of the endless well of Alon's grief for the tide-touched and his people. Lightning flashed and thunder crashed over Aynila, louder than cannon fire.

Lunurin reached toward the sky. She threw her spirit into the clouds, into the arms of Anitun Tabu, crying her name. The goddess caught her in an upswell of power. Riotous joy flooded into her veins, and Lunurin welcomed it in.

"But ask it, my daughter, and it is yours," Anitun Tabu promised. *"Only come to me and free me from my shackles."*

"Yes. Anitun Tabu, Goddess mine. Give me the storm."

The towering thunderheads deluged their bounty of rain in a wall of grey. It swept across the water, caught them up and slammed down. Lunurin threw her head back and laughed.

The *Santa Clarita*'s gun hatches darkened as the full broadside rolled forward.

Lunurin threw the storm at the galleon. The wind roared in her ears, but they'd laid anchors securely in the sheltered bay, there was no turning her. Lightning danced over the water, illuminating the *Santa Clarita*, crackling harmlessly over her soaring masts and dissipating into the bay. It wasn't enough. She wasn't enough.

She turned to Alon, half-blinded with rain. "I can't. I can't sink her. I can't turn her—"

The cannons boomed. Lunurin watched them tear swaths through the streets of Aynila. On the hillside, the near wing of the Lakan's palace was in flames. She'd failed before she'd even begun.

"Together, we'll sink her together," Alon said. "I just need to touch the bay."

She leaned into him, letting his steadiness fill her with strength and calm. Alon did not waver. Lunurin reached for Sina's hand too. She wasn't alone. Not like the first time. No one could pull her from Anitun Tabu's arms now.

Lunurin smiled a terrible smile. "You know, my name means 'to drown.' My mother meant it like 'she drowns in blessings.' But I think this is what Anitun Tabu always intended."

48

ALON DAKILA

The port was chaos. Sailors swarmed the docks trying to put out the fires spreading over ships heavy with cargo. A junk from Tianchao and several of the largest vessels had already been sunk.

Alon guided their small party. They'd left Isko with his mother and his guards to hold the bridge. Finally, they came to a narrow pier. It was lined with vessels not yet on fire, whose crews scrambled to turn their small lantaka cannons up toward the Palisade walls. Hiraya rode double with Sina; as the firetenders passed, fires smoldering in the rain died. One of Aynila Indigo's captains urged them into the shelter provided by his karakoa.

Hiraya directed Lunurin's attention upward to where cannons squatted along the top of the Palisade like fattened black hogs. "You need to disable the main gun in the corner of the Palisade. They can swivel it, and we'll be in range."

Sina, her expression a mask of concentration as she crushed out every spark in range, said, "Try not to blow it up too spectacularly. We're in range of shrapnel now."

Lunurin made a face. "Do you know how hard it is to be precise with lightning?"

Alon squeezed her hand. "You can do it."

Lightning illuminated the port like cracks in the heavens, through which the noon sun still leaked. Armored conquistadors clustered around the cannon like furious ants. A searing arm of lightning stretched from the clouds, touching a single fingertip to a barrel of gunpowder. The cannon platform splintered into kindling. Men tumbled down, their screams carried on Lunurin's winds. Some cooked alive. The smell was greasy and rank, a metallic, burnt-hair scent that clogged Alon's sinuses.

Alon swallowed hard and reached for the bay, prayers he'd never used before heavy on his tongue. But though his waves crested onto the galleon's decks, they could no more turn the *Santa Clarita* than Lunurin's wind. Still, his waves rushed toward the Palisade, crashing higher and higher along the walls, water rushing through drainage grates with a willingness that frightened him. The sea was so angry.

Alon had grown up around those blessed by the gods, but healers worked inside the limits of a human body. He'd never seen anyone wield power like Lunurin, not even his mother. It appeared to cost her nothing, as if the only thing tethering her feet to the ground, keeping her from being lifted and enrobed in the storm she'd called, was her decision to stay beside him.

But she alone couldn't sink a galleon in the sheltered bay. She needed the sea itself to turn on the *Santa Clarita*, and he had to give it to her. She seized his hands. It was like drinking lightning, exhilarating and terrible. But all the energy in the world didn't change the fact he was one man, and the bay was vast. It was like sinking a single hook into the mouth of a whale. He could pull with the strength of ten men and the line would only rip free. He needed a dozen harpoons, and others to pull with him.

Head swimming, he pulled away. "If I pull the bay any more, I'll lose control and overwhelm the Saliwain again."

Alon's chest tightened at the thought of those brave women, waist-deep in the river, praying it would not rise, with nothing to shield them but their mutya and the whisper of salt in every Aynilan's blood. He could feel them, two dozen bright spots along the margin of the Saliwain, their mutya infused with his mother's power, holding the line for all Aynila.

The *Santa Clarita*'s cannons fired. The dock beside them splintered.

Lunurin flung out an arm, warding off the worst of the shrapnel with an upward gust of wind. "Then I drag down the storm, and we see who comes out the worse for it."

"No one's evacuated!" Alon protested.

"They had their chance." Death was in Lunurin's eyes, her grief howling in the wind. Despite Hiraya's and Sina's best efforts, Aynila was burning. "You gave them every opportunity, every warning!"

"Let me try, once more." Alon lowered himself into the water on the outrigger of the karakoa. If he touched the salt, maybe he could summon the rogue wave Lunurin needed, or at least dislodge the *Santa Clarita*'s anchors enough to turn her. If the Palisade lost their floating fortress, they'd have to evacuate.

Letting his awareness sink into the depths, he cried out to his goddess, "Please, Aman Sinaya, I haven't the strength alone. Even you must want vengeance for all your lost children. These are the ones who came in the night. These are the ones who burned them."

But the vast spread of the bay did not speak back. Aman Sinaya had grieved many lost children, and Alon wasn't like Lunurin, with a goddess burning in her eyes. He was only one tide-touched. So he reached for the sampaguita beads of his far-flung mutya rolling along the bottom of the bay with the bones of all his dead.

Alon pulled till his own blood thinned with the endless weight of salt, till his voice seemed to shred in his throat. And from his mutya came a whisper like waves lapping on a sandy beach.

"Gat Alon! Stop!"

"Young lord, you will stop your own heart."

"Can he hear us?"

"Can anyone hear us?"

"We burn, and no one hears our anguish."

"I can. Who speaks?" Alon asked the waves.

"We do!"

All across the choppy water of the bay, between the *Santa Clarita* and Aynila, stood ghostly figures, rocking up and down with the waves. Alon beheld the lost tide-touched of Aynila who he'd consigned to the sea. In the heart of each ghost hung a single sampaguita mother-of-pearl bead. Together, the beads made a garland spread across the waves, one ubiquitous in every Aynilan's life from birth to death, filling the air with their brief extravagant sweetness. These were kaluluwa, the souls of the dead, Aynila's ghosts, and he'd gone too far. Healers this close to the realm of the dead rarely returned.

He tried to pull back, but his mutya held him as surely as if it were still bound about his neck. Then he saw Kawit. He stood, feet planted ankle-deep in the water beside the prow of the karakoa. The rain slashed through his ghostly form. In his hand, Kawit held three mother-of-pearl sampaguita beads. He strode toward Alon, showing no sign of his grievous wounds.

"One cannot pull the whole of the sea alone. Aman Sinaya, our gentle lady, has been bound down since creation so that she will not drown our people. It takes the work of many to raise her up. Give me your hand. We will pull together."

Kawit's gnarled hand closed strong and sure around Alon's, cold as deep water. Kawit pulled him up till he stood on the outrigger.

"You shouldn't be here," Alon said. "You all should have gone on. Why hasn't Aman Sinaya taken you back?"

"She waits until we are ready to travel. We will embark once the bones of our murderers lie at the bottom of the sea, when the shadow of the Palisade does not block the sun."

When Alon reached for the sea this time, fifteen tide-touched spirits were with him, their magic forming an invisible glittering net within the saltwater of the bay. He offered up the prayer and they pulled together. The sea came spilling into the arms of the port like a whale being dragged from the depths. Out in the bay rose an indigo beast, awakened at last. It curled over the *Santa Clarita* higher and higher, like the laho of long ago. But there was no one to call off this sea monster. There was no one left to pray for mercy.

Even as the *Santa Clarita* deployed their secondary oars, desperate to turn into the wave, Lunurin and Sina twisted together cyclones of hot wind, harrying the *Santa Clarita* till she was broadside to Alon's wave. Somehow, they'd sundered the central mast. Men fell from the deck into the sea and were dragged down by hungry currents.

"Now, Alon! Release the wave now," Lunurin said.

As if he had any control. It was Aynila's vengeful ghosts that held the wave, and they would not be satisfied with merely foundering the *Santa Clarita*. Oh no.

The wave crashed, a hammer driving the *Santa Clarita* down.

Had it been a normal wave, she might have risen. But with fifteen tide-touched to pull the water where they willed... the bilge pumps had no chance. Lightning flashed. Alon did not dare flinch from the light.

Where the *Santa Clarita* had gone down, the surface of the bay boiled, but only air streamed to the surface, as if the sea floor had swallowed her whole.

Alon's creation raged on, a great amorphous wall of water. It hit the Palisade with a thunderous crash, salt spray mixing with the rain.

The water within the Palisade surged, two feet, three, then four.

Warm, living hands seized him and dragged him aboard the karakoa.

"Alon, if you pull much more, no one will be able to wade out," Lunurin pointed out.

"They'll never open the gates," Alon finally admitted. "They'd rather drown."

His ghosts now ringed the Palisade. He doubted they'd let anyone living pass.

Sina pointed to a section of the Palisade not yet burning. "Lunurin has a plan, we can open the wall."

"We will hold, so the innocent may yet slip free of the trap," Kawit promised. *"But not for long."*

The karakoa lurched forward into the choppy water. Captain Capuno on the rudder had pulled out his mother-of-pearl mutya and was rubbing it as he prayed, eyeing the bruised, swirling clouds overhead.

Sina swept her hands out toward the huge tree trunks that made up the wall. Bright sparks leaped from her fingers, hitting the wall just above the waves. The sparks burrowed in and down. Soon the smoke of Sina's below-ground blaze billowed over the sides of the karakoa. Lunurin twisted her hair up to lighten the rain and not damp Sina's fires. Together with the rowers they huddled low and waited, listening to the crackle of burning pine.

~

"Ohh, get us out of here!" Sina shouted, and every sailor on the oars gave a great heave as the Palisade wall began to waver. Hiraya caught Sina before she was pitched off her feet.

Lunurin, at the prow, let her hair down. Wind rushed along both sides of the boat before racing to the top of the Palisade.

The top of the wall began to sway. Simultaneously, Alon reached for the water he and the other tide-touched had shoved into the Palisade, yanking it toward the bay. The weight of the water bowed the wall outward.

The Palisade creaked, but held. More smoke billowed from the water line. The wind moaned through the shattered teeth at the top of the wall. A corona of lightning danced just over Lunurin's head in a strange mimic of a saint's halo, casting a blue-white glow. She spoke a word he couldn't hear over the howling of the wind and raked clawed fingers through the air in a twisting pattern as the rowers pulled them away from the Palisade.

A great groan rent the air, and the Palisade splintered. Eighty-five feet of wood swung down. It hit the water and the bridge with a tremendous splash, destroying the left side wall and collapsing a pylon. They would have capsized, but Alon pressed alongside Lunurin, and together—with her wind and his hold on the sea—they split the wave, salt spray raining down.

The buildup of water within the Palisade began to gush outward.

Alon curled his hand and commanded it, "Halt."

Kawit's ghost waded up the falling water, pulling the sea after him like an indigo tapestry slipping off his arm.

The soldiers guarding the main gate swarmed to the breach.

Guns pointed down from the ruined parapet at them. Lunurin twirled a finger through a strand of her hair and sent a howling swirl of air up. It plucked men like straw dolls, tossing them spinning into the air, and hurtling down to shatter on the water.

More men boiled from the opening. A row of guns pointed out at the karakoa. There was a flash of smoke.

Sina shook her hands out, flinging sparks into the water. "Alon! Do something. I've flashed their powder, but they'll reload."

But Alon couldn't do anything but hold, as every ghost cried out in one voice, *"Drown them! Drown them all!"*

Ghostly hands rose. Men screamed and went down, drowning in water that hardly came to their knees.

This was different than sinking the *Santa Clarita*, its lives distant specks swallowed by the bay. He could see the terrified white faces of the soldiers, gasping desperately for air, then gone. Some broke and ran, but there was no escaping the vengeance of the dead. Long had the ghosts of Aynila craved vengeance, and at last they would have it.

Alon pulled all the salt he could reach. A wave of water from inside the Palisade washed the soldiers into the bay. They sank quickly in their heavy metal armor. It was a quicker end than a ghostly shallow-water drowning.

Soon there was no movement from the gap they had opened into the Palisade.

Alon pulled the sea to him and lifted the karakoa up, sailing it through the gap in the wall, following Kawit's ghost.

The devastation inside the walls was… Alon had no words. The rising water was covered in a thick layer of ash and debris. Splintered bits of buildings and window shutters floated by along with bodies of men who'd been on the parapet when Lunurin had brought the wind and lightning, and those his ghosts had drowned. The karakoa rowed through streets that were now canals, passing wet clumps of feathers and fur, poultry and vermin mixed together with debris.

As they rowed toward the church, Alon had the rowers rap on second-story windows, telling people the Palisade gates were open and they needed to get out to higher ground in Aynila.

A soldier waded toward them, his gun held above his head over the floodwaters. Alon looked away as Lunurin's lightning crown crawled down from her hair, curling around her arm. But there was no crackle or smell of burning flesh.

"Wait! Wait, for the love of God! Don't shoot or fry me, please."

Lunurin leaned around the prow of the boat like some terrifying figurehead. "Why shouldn't I?"

"I convinced the guards to lower the cages, and the Lakan would probably be upset if he lost one of his best spies."

Then, the man's unremarkable face clicked in Alon's memory. He'd last seen that face screaming in terror as Lunurin threw him out of her window.

"He won't need Codicían spies by the time I'm done," Lunurin said. "Where are the children?"

The man winced. "Still caged, the abbot has the keys."

Sparks of lightning danced around Lunurin's fingers like fireflies. Alon didn't dare touch her.

"What's your name?" Lunurin asked.

"Pedro de Isla."

"What became of the shipyard workers in the barracks?"

The man clutched nervously at his gun, his right hand crudely bandaged where Lunurin had relieved him of two fingers, as the boat came alongside him. No one reached into the water to help him aboard, not with the eerie way Lunurin's lightning crackled.

"There was talk of another strike, or worse. The governor ordered his men to lock them into the barracks before noon."

More lightning crawled down the inky length of Lunurin's hair.

"If I get them out somehow…" Pedro's voice trailed off hopefully.

"If you get the barracks unlocked, let the workers know they can escape the rising water by heading across the bridge into Aynila. When the guards on the other side capture you, try telling Litao that you did Gat Alon's wife a favor and she promised to consider letting you live."

Pedro heaved a great sigh. "I suppose that's the best offer I'm going to get? Lord Alon, your wife is not a generous woman. You'd expect a nun to be more merciful, God's grace and all."

Lunurin smiled very sweetly. "Your god can't help you now."

Pedro stared into the turbulent sky above. "Yeah, I figured that."

He began trudging through the waist-deep water back the way he'd come, toward the shipyards.

"They still have my daughter, not to mention two dozen other Aynilan children," said Hiraya.

"They won't keep them," Lunurin promised, gathering and hurling her shawl of lightning upward into the roiling clouds.

49

LUNURIN CALILAN DE DAKILA

They rowed up the main boulevard, the church belltower scraping the turbulent sky before them. As they grew closer, Lunurin wasn't sure if she could bear to walk into the sanctuary.

Lunurin shivered, and jumped when Alon pulled her into the warmth of his chest.

"Go sit with Sina and her mother. I don't think it's possible to be cold near a firetender," he said gently.

"This is alright," Lunurin whispered, tucking chilled fingers under Alon's forearm.

"Are you ready?" he asked.

Lunurin nodded. "Will you help me bring out Anitun Tabu's statue from the sanctuary? It's not right to tear the church down on the goddess's head."

"Of course."

Rain swept from the sky, making skirling patterns across the rising floodwaters that spread like a wide lake in the plaza before the church.

"Could you forgive me if I tried to save her?" Lunurin asked.

Alon's grip tightened. "If it will bring you peace. I can forgive you Catalina."

"I know she betrayed them. But I cannot be the reason she dies."

"You may save her from the storm, but she will still face my mother. Someone must answer for all the dead tide-touched of Aynila." Alon's voice was firm, but not cruel.

Lunurin leaned into his strength greedily, desperate for his solidity and substance. Here they stood, at the center of the destruction she had wrought. There was so much blood on her hands. It didn't matter if her goddess had demanded it of her. She'd opened her heart to Anitun Tabu's fury, and now rage was all she would ever know.

"I promised Inez I'd get Cat out. I can't let her die like this."

"I understand."

Lunurin turned, pressing her lips to the corner of Alon's mouth. "You are too good for me, and too kind. Too like your Aman Sinaya, plucking storm-wracked ships from the sea when they don't deserve it. But if a man as good and just as you can love someone like me, then perhaps there is still something within me that is not destruction and rage. Something worth loving."

Alon kissed her brow. "Even if it feels like that now, I know that isn't all you are. It's worth weathering even this storm to stand by your side."

Lunurin squeezed his arm, grateful beyond words for his steadiness. When she was on the verge of spinning off into the madness of the storm, he was there, dependable as the tides, ever-present as the sea, a vast depth by which she could tether herself to humanity.

The bottom of the karakoa scraped cobblestones, and the rowers looked to their captain for direction. Capuno approached Alon. "Gat Alon, you will have to raise the waters or go the rest of the way on foot."

Sina pointed. "There she is!"

The cages hung just above the floodwaters. Lunurin couldn't pick out Biti from among the others. They'd crammed the children in too tightly, three or four to a cage.

"Will you be able to open the cages or do you need the key?" Alon asked.

"We will bend the bars with our bare hands," Hiraya declared.

"The others will be in the sanctuary," Lunurin said.

Alon lifted Lunurin, setting her into the water. He supported her till her feet found the bottom.

Lunurin waded toward the church, pulling up her hair as she went. She didn't want to have to carry children out through a downpour and hail. When she stumbled over unseen debris, Alon caught her about the waist.

Finally, they mounted the steps of the church, where the water was only ankle-deep. Lunurin considered the huge, intricately graven wood door. She gave it a tug.

"They've locked themselves in?" Alon asked, staring in disbelief at the locked door and the rising water. "Could Sina burn through it?"

Lunurin frowned. "Maybe, but we'd choke everyone inside on the smoke. The water's rising. They can't stay low to the ground. Besides, it would take too long."

Alon winced. "Yes, of course."

Lunurin threw her shoulder into the door, testing the jiggle and trying to remember if it was possible to bar it from the inside. "It's bolted, and the doors open out, so it can't be barred from inside." Lunurin tapped the gold ring on her finger, eyeing the large keyhole. "Alon, can you force saltwater through the keyhole and into the interior mechanisms?"

Alon gestured, pushing the water away from them in a wide circle. He worked his gold brace off his hand and scooped up a jelly-like globule of saltwater, pressing it into the keyhole. Lunurin slid her hands under his and pressed the gold of her wedding ring against the metal of the keyhole.

The damaged fingers of Alon's right hand, looped in burn scars from her last attempt at precision lightning, lay smooth along the backs of her hands.

"I'll be careful," she promised.

Alon's chest pressed to her back, steady, always steady. No matter what, he would hold. "Do what you have to."

Lunurin called lightning. It came, tangling ropes of it. There were no seeds to be had in a storm like this. They spooled out of the sky like skeins of silk thread winding around Lunurin's arms. She pulled the lightning in tight, holding it away from Alon's skin, feeding it into her hands, through her ring and into the door.

Seawater boiled around the metal. Alon drew more water from their feet, and Lunurin kept pouring lightning through the mechanism of the lock, knocking chunks of rust plating off the surface of her ring. Bit by bit, the internals of the door crumbled.

Lunurin stopped, but she didn't release the lightning, liking how it coiled around her arms like the shawl she'd abandoned in the chaos. Alon dropped the saltwater, flexing his hands as if he disbelieved their wholeness.

"I didn't hurt you, did I?" Lunurin asked.

He shook his head. "It just tingles."

They seized the huge metal ring and pulled. The door bolts gave way like sand. Water gushed in to fill the space, and people screamed. Lunurin pushed her way forward, lightning her lashing shield, fully prepared to murder the first person who pointed a gun at them. But clustered on the steps around the altar were only the priests and sisters of the abbey, and a great many servants. They weren't even all servants from the convent. Many were from public buildings and the governor's mansion who had sought shelter at the highest ground available within the Palisade. The school children were standing on the benches, already in water to their ankles.

"You can't stay here," Lunurin said to the people huddled around the altar. "The water will keep rising. Not even climbing onto the roof of the church will save you. You have to cross over into Aynila. Come, we've brought a boat. The children can be carried safely out. The rest can wade. You cannot remain here."

Abbot Rodrigo appeared from the side chapel behind the altar. "Witch! Deceiver! Do not listen to her. She brings the storm. Any who go with her will surely be cast into the rising seas. The only salvation is to remain and pray to Our Lady María of the Drowned for intercession."

A ripple of confusion passed through the servants who stood knee-deep in the rising water.

But then Juan moved. The tall freeman had two of their youngest students, one in a sling on his back, the other in his arms. "You have a boat for the children?"

"Yes, in the plaza," Alon assured him.

Juan took Rosa's hand. "Come, Rosa. You can hold on to me when the water gets too deep."

They went out past Lunurin and Alon in the doorway, and there was a surge of movement as the other servants followed. They collected children from the school, lifting them up onto their backs and shoulders.

"Cowards! Sinners! Faithless sheep!" Abbot Rodrigo shrieked. "God will never forgive you for abandoning his house to follow a witch!"

Quickly, the church emptied of its congregation, a crowd forming on the church steps as they navigated the descent into the floodwater. Only the truly faithful clustered around the steps of the altar, its altar panels inlayed with stolen mother-of-pearl, and the statue of Anitun Tabu.

And halfway between stood Catalina, frozen in the aisle.

Lunurin held out her hand. Lightning crawled along her veins, bright as moon-poured silver. "Please, Cat. Come with me."

Cat bit her lips, her arms wrapped tight around herself, half turned to the altar.

"Let me take you to Inez. Your sister will never forgive me if I leave you to drown," Lunurin begged.

Cat's expression contorted on a sob.

"Sister Catalina doesn't have a sister," the abbot interjected. "She died weeks ago in a water witch's bloody bath."

Lunurin focused all her attention on Cat. "Please, Cat, I know you don't believe that. Inez misses you so much. She's been safely evacuated from the storm—"

"You brought the storm!" Cat wailed, but took a faltering step toward Lunurin.

"Not for you." Lunurin held her arms out.

Cat wept bitterly, stumbling down the aisle and falling into Lunurin's arms. Lunurin cradled Cat close, lightheaded with relief.

Cat threw her arms around her neck. Her words tumbled over each other, her tears hot on Lunurin's skin. "My sister, tell my sister I'm sorry—I'm sorry, I'm so sorry. God have mercy, Lunurin! Lunurin, I love you and I'm so sorry."

"Hush." Lunurin held her tight. "You'll tell her yourself. I've got you now. I'm taking you home."

Cat looked up. Tears filled her large brown eyes. "I'm not like you," she whispered. "I am not Aynilan enough to marry and raise little brown heathen children. I've no place in Aynila!"

"I can make you a place."

Cat shook her head and dragged Lunurin down for one hard, hot kiss. Her apologies smothered against Lunurin's lips.

"I'm sorry—I have to—"

The heat and desperation of Cat's kiss was so familiar, for one stunned moment, Lunurin melted into it, not noticing when Cat's arm around her neck turned choking tight.

"Lunurin!" Alon cried, lunging toward them.

"Kill the witch, save the nun." Cat gasped the words into her mouth, her arm swinging down, a dagger clenched in her delicate hand.

Lunurin twisted, pushing Cat away, and losing her footing. Cat's wild swing skimmed down her forearm and Lunurin watched in slow horror as it sank deep into Alon's belly.

A soft, almost confused, grunt passed his lips, his hands clutched tightly around the hilt of Cat's dagger. Then his grip slackened, and he crumpled. His temple struck the edge of the pews. He lay unmoving as the floodwaters ran red with his blood.

Cat dropped the knife. "They're witches, witches sent to lead you astray from God." Without a glance at Lunurin she turned, stumbling back toward the altar and the abbot.

He smiled benevolently from his perch at the highest point of the altar steps.

Alon did not stir.

Lunurin screamed. Lightning uncoiled from her body in all directions. In a blink it crossed the sanctuary.

It struck the abbot in the chest, throwing him against the huge altar panel. The vast panel wavered, rocking on its narrow base.

Those gathered on the altar steps panicked, scrambling to escape the fall zone and Lunurin's lightning, jamming themselves up the choir stair to escape onto the roof.

With a sound like a sigh, the huge altar panel swung down, crushing the abbot's stunned form. More blood spilled down the altar steps to dye the floodwaters red.

Lunurin fell to her knees, grappling with the dead weight of Alon's body to lift his face clear of the water. Her hands slipped in water that was blood, so much blood.

"Alon! Alon?" Lunurin's voice rose in hysteria at how heavy and still he lay in her arms.

Thunder rolled and the stained-glass windows shattered, Lunurin's storm pouring inside the church.

She couldn't feel his breath on her neck. It was all she could do to press her shaking hands to Alon's wound, trying desperately to stem the hot pulse of blood.

"Please, please," she begged, rain and hail rattling off the pews and her bowed shoulders. "I can't lose you. Not like this!"

How had he gotten in the way? Why had he? He was tide-touched. He could've torn Cat off her with a wave of floodwater!

Lunurin curled around Alon's head and sobbed. Lightning crashed. Twisting cyclone winds tore tapestries and paintings from the walls. They rent the air with her grief, and she urged them on. She lost herself in the storm, her last human tie taken from her. Let it be done. Let it all end here, with her, with him, together.

She cried out. Her anguish and her tempest moaned through the halls of the church, making the very walls vibrate.

The doors of the church flew open, one tearing off its hinges as the wind howled outward, carrying the door skyward.

Sina pushed her way into the church, through cutting winds and the staccato beat of rain and hail.

She seized Lunurin's shoulders. "Lunurin! We won't get the children out if you tear the church down on top of our heads."

Lunurin turned away, pressing her brow to Alon's.

Sina tried to drag Alon out of her arms.

Lunurin growled, throwing out bands of lightning to ward Sina off.

Sina yelped as lightning raised rippling burns on her arms. "Get up! Lunurin. Get up and help me lift him onto the pews. If we can stop the bleeding, we can get him to his mother!"

Lunurin stared at her cousin, uncomprehending.

"He's not dead yet! He's bleeding too well," Sina cried.

Lunurin forced herself to cooperate with Sina's manhandling Alon's limp body up onto a pew, without releasing the pressure on his wound.

Sina bent over his head, pressing her ear to his mouth. "He's alive. He just hit his head. Please, Lunurin, the hail!"

Lunurin took deep slow breaths, trying to will away her desperation and panic, and the wracking sobs shaking her body. Her lungs ached. Slowly the wind calmed; the rain and hail that was falling inside the church dissipated.

Sina squeezed her shoulders. "We're all going to get out of here. Do you have enough control to cauterize with lightning, or do you want me to try?"

Lunurin closed her eyes tightly and analyzed the lashing rage of the storm overhead compared to the stillness of Alon under her hands. "I can do it."

"Good."

"Step back. I don't want to hurt you."

Lunurin called and the lightning came, a tad messily, through the shattered window frames, coiling around her wrists like eels. Hot lead dripped down and sizzled.

Lunurin focused her attention and pressed the bands of lightning coiling between her fists down. Alon's body jerked with the force of it, but she was careful to keep her lightning from interacting with the storm of his brain or heart. Slowly she lifted her hands. Charred pieces of Alon's barong flaked away, revealing the wound a few inches below Alon's navel had been sealed.

Sina hissed in sympathy. "It'll do. C'mon, the sooner we get him to his mother, the better."

It seemed oddly fitting that after Alon had carried her semi-conscious body down the church steps after their wedding, she should do the same for him now. Sina brought the statue of Anitun Tabu out of the church beside her.

Lunurin did not look back. She didn't want to know if Cat had made it to the roof or if Lunurin's winds had plucked her free. Ten years she'd loved Catalina. They'd been through everything the Church and the abbot could inflict on them, and yet, for it to end like this... She'd never imagined Cat's poisoned faith would bring them here.

They waded across the plaza to the boat, overflowing with women and children. Capuno had perched the rowers out on the outriggers to make more room for evacuees. Ropes had been thrown out to give those wading something to hold on to to keep their footing. Room was made for Alon. Lunurin wedged the statue of Anitun Tabu beside him, demanding that her goddess watch over her husband. She walked alongside, keeping one hand clasped tightly around Alon's, willing him to wake. As they went, they gathered up a deluge of evacuees.

When they reached the Puente de Aynila, they ran into a crowd of shipyard workers and other Aynilan servants who'd fled when it became clear the water wasn't rising over Aynila. Once they'd made it to the gap, Sina helped Lunurin carry Alon across to the bridge. Hiraya followed, Biti on one hip, Anitun Tabu's statue balanced on the other.

Dalisay met them on the bridge, where she was sorting the wounded for triage. She cried out when she saw Alon still and bloody in their arms.

Lunurin swayed when she stepped out of the floodwaters onto the surface of the bridge. The matrons of Aynila and Dalisay had indeed held back the rise of the bay, keeping the Saliwain in her banks. Dalisay helped her and Sina lower Alon gently.

"He was stabbed and hit his head. I had to use lightning to stop the bleeding. Please tell me I haven't killed him," Lunurin babbled.

Thankfully, Dalisay ignored her to focus on healing her son. She lay her hands on his head, hissing under her breath till Alon jolted awake with a shout.

Relief broke over Lunurin like a wave. She held him down by the shoulders until he stopped thrashing so his mother could tend to his gut wound.

"Lunurin?" Alon asked.

"I thought I'd killed you!" Lunurin wailed.

"Not killed, just a little knocked about... are we on the bridge?"

"You've been unconscious for ages. I didn't know what was wrong!"

"Well, I did get stabbed if I recall," Alon supplied, his breath hissing out of him as his mother did something and the lightning burn spreading across his middle faded from angry red and weeping to a few shades paler than the rest of him.

Helplessly, Lunurin began to cry, the rain falling harder, hail pounding down across the bridge.

She saw Alon signing to his mother as they were scolded for his condition, but she was sobbing too hard to make sense of it. Slowly Alon sat up. He kissed her cheek and pulled her tight against his side. "Help me up. Let's finish this."

"Get everyone off the bridge," Sina told Dalisay.

Sina knelt down on Alon's other side, worry weighing heavy across her broad shoulders. Alon, braced between them, came wincing to his feet. Lunurin urged the wild power of her storm into his blood till sparks of lightning danced over all three of them, and he was able to stand, swaying, under his own power.

Lunurin turned Anitun Tabu's statue to face the Palisade. The governor's pale staring eyes watched them with accusation where he hung pinned to the gate.

The Palisade looked much less imposing. Most of the eighty-five-foot wall was reduced by half, as if a huge dugong had come up out of the sea and grazed along the top of it, tearing out huge chunks of three-needle pine trunks as easily as seagrass with its blunt crushing teeth.

Lunurin let down her hair, clutching her mutya in her hands. She had wrought this, all this. And at last, her goddess rode the wind in joyful euphoria, her name returned to her. Anitun Tabu, freed from her enslavement, freed from false prayers reducing her to Santa María of the Drowned, Our Lady of Sorrows. She walked the skies again, Lady of Storms and Vengeance once more, arbiter of heaven's judgment.

Lunurin twisted her fingers through her hair, spinning together wind like loose abaca fibers into rope.

"What will we be, stormcaller?" asked the twisting winds as they pulled their fellows into their dance.

"You will be wall breakers, shredding wood and powdering stone. Grow tall, bridge sea and cloud. You will be cyclones," she commanded.

Her cyclones drank in the bay with the roaring fury of sea dragons.

Alon pulled, and the bay surged up into the Palisade as if it were a goblet overflowing with wine. Out over the water, a dozen wraith-like lights shone like fallen stars. An arm of water crawled up onto the bridge, dragging the governor's body down off Lunurin's spear and into the depths. Aynila's ghosts would have their due.

As Alon's water doused her fires, Sina reached deep into the ground. All these islands were volcanic at their core.

The land under the Palisade shivered, a carabao shedding flies from its great black hide. Lunurin guided her winds up into the Palisade, where they ripped apart buildings of stone and wood like kindling. Bit by bit, the Palisade fell.

At last, only the belltower rose above the choppy waters. Lunurin turned her eyes away from the dozens of clergy clinging to its roof.

She gazed into the eye of the storm as if she might look upon the goddess's face, and she cursed the church and all in it, calling down Anitun Tabu's wrath. "Lintik ka! Tamaan ka sana ng kidlat!"

A band of lightning, so thick it lit the sky like the noonday sun, struck the tower as a huge rogue wave broke over the roof, sweeping bodies into the sea.

The lightning hung in the sky, a blue-white bridge between the clouds and the rising sea, and in it stood the Goddess Anitun Tabu. Several hundred feet high, she was garbed in light. Her dark head crowned in lightning. Tears ran down one side of her face, the other smiled. In her hand, she held a great spear. She spread her arms. *"Thank you, Daughter. You have restored me to myself. You returned to me my name when I had all but forgotten it. You have freed me and our people from the scourge of the Codicíans' endless hunger. A hundred years from now, they will be singing songs of the feats of Lunurin Stormbringer. No more will we be saints of storm and sorrow."*

Anitun Tabu pressed her hands together and bowed. Then, she was gone, and the roll of thunder that followed was so intense it drove Lunurin to her knees. The belltower fell, crushing what was left of the church roof, before sinking slowly into the sea.

For the first time in weeks, Lunurin felt no rage at all. She was empty of everything but herself. She was like a cracked clay pot, the divine drained away, leaving nothing but a husk.

She had done it, what a hundred tide-touched over the last twenty years had died attempting. The Palisade was no more. The governor and the abbot were dead by her hand. Had she not envisioned their deaths a thousand times?

And yet, it had cost her Catalina. Lunurin had killed her, drowned her with all the other Codicían martyrs. Her arm ached dully where Catalina had cut her. She stared at her hands. Hadn't this whole terrible nightmare started to protect Cat and Inez?

"It is done," her voice rasped, raw and hollow. "I have done just as the goddess always wanted. We have had vengeance for all our dead. I killed her! It was selfish and terrible, but I loved her, and I killed her."

Then Alon's hands closed around her shoulders. "You've saved us. You've saved all of us."

She turned into him and wept out all her bitterness and grief on his shoulder. Tomorrow, tomorrow she would face the typhoon she somehow had to guide around Aynila, but today she would mourn all she'd lost.

Alon gathered her hair. He twisted it and, slipping her mutya from her unresisting fingers, secured her bun at the base of her neck. The weight of her mutya bowed her head, but it stopped hailing. They were both too tired for more than that. This storm must run its course.

50

◆━◆

ALON DAKILA

Alon released the sea and sent it streaming back into the bay, carrying with it all the wreckage of the Palisade. He was so tired it felt like pulling hooks out of his own flesh. One by one, the ghosts of Aynila's tide-touched sank into the waves, until only Kawit still stood in the swirling devastation of the Palisade. He turned to Alon and bowed, his mutya gleaming like moonlight on night-blooming sampaguita in Kawit's hand, and then he was gone. Alon's ability to sense his far-flung mutya winked out, as those he had gifted them to traveled beyond his ability to sense, into Maca, the underworld. The ghostly sweetness of sampaguita perfuming the air faded at last.

Lunurin had folded in on herself. She'd been emptied, scraped from the inside, all her great strength poured out into the storm. Alon clutched her close, irrationally afraid that if he let her go, she'd slip away and join all his other ghosts. Sina shored his other side, and slowly they began the long walk back to solid ground.

The Saliwain had never seemed so wide. His head throbbed, and his lower left side was one huge ache. His blood felt very thin, though it still sang with the energy of Lunurin's storm.

They were a sorry group that met Litao and his mother on the Aynilan side of the bridge.

Alon and Lunurin sat heavily beside the other wounded, less as a choice and more because Sina had caught sight of Isko and stumbled to his side.

Alon instructed a dozen of his men to find out how many of the evacuees who'd been living and working in the Palisade had no family in Aynila that could shelter them tonight. Among them were a handful of Black men, two women, and a young boy who'd been illegally enslaved by Codicían families. Juan, with his command of Aynilan and Codicían, was their spokesperson.

Alon had no idea where he was going to put so many people, but it needed to be the first order of business. He sent guards to see how many of the portside boarding houses had escaped the barrage with minimal damage, so they could get the very young and the old undercover quickly.

Through it all, Alon intentionally kept his back to what was left of the Palisade. The great waves he'd pulled in had been quick to pour back out to the bay, but the last six feet of water was slow to drain through the debris caught in the jagged teeth of what was left of the wall.

He was numbly going through the motions of disaster relief when someone caught his arm, dragging him back to the present. Lunurin was still ghostlike, but her anguish was buried deep. She was good at that, perhaps too good.

"Open up your warehouses."

"They're half-empty, just dirt and a roof. We shipped almost everything out before the wet season."

"But farther from the port, less likely to be damaged," Lunurin said. "Dry dirt and a roof are all we need for tonight. I'll talk to some of the local food vendors and get a warm meal served to everyone, and woven palm sleeping mats." She squeezed his hand. "Don't wear yourself out."

Alon ordered Litao to go with her and see that all she asked was done. The sooner they got people out of the rain, the better.

Then he did sit down, before he could fall down. But here was Isko with two lists, one of all the Aynilan children recovered from the church, and one of every Codicían prisoner Litao and his men had snatched from the mob. Alon handed the first list over to Sina. She would know who everyone's closest relatives in Aynila were and where they could be found.

Finally, Alon cast a critical eye over the Codicíans that his men had plucked from the stream of bodies evacuating the Palisade.

Two of the cosseted Codicían wives sat drenched and dazed beside Aynilan servants who had dragged them out more or less against their will.

There were a handful of soldiers who had given themselves up, including the Lakan's spy. There were two dozen woebegone officials of various ranks, from accountants to one of the governor's tax collectors. All the way up to the second mate of the *Santa Clarita* who, along with a dozen sailors, had defected rather than face the storm.

Alon had them all herded into another one of the warehouses farther from the waterfront. He set a rotation of guards, excluding the spy, Pedro de Isla. While the guards were busy ensuring their captured Codicíans would go nowhere for the night, Alon had Pedro set free.

"So, my lord, has your lady wife forgiven me? Or is mine to be the first head on her pike?" Pedro asked, rubbing his wrists and tightening the crude bandage on his right hand.

Alon stared hard at him. "Yours would be the second head. She already has the governor's. And I still don't know. But there has been too much death today, so I'll not leave you to her mercy."

Once Alon had handled the situation with the spy, they had word from the palace.

Lakan Tigas was dead. Suicide.

He couldn't bear the expression on his mother's face, satisfaction warring with fury.

Alon thought he'd wrung out all the turmoil and grief he could feel after seeing his father's karakoa sunken at the massacre of the tide-touched village. He was wrong.

Really, there was only one thing to be done. Alon returned to the bay and pulled from it every still beating heart he could find, until he couldn't tell warm blood from saltwater any longer, and the pain in his side forced him to his knees. His guards at last carried him away at his mother's orders, seawater streaming between his hands as he tried to drag one last body from the clutches of the bay. Alon was too exhausted to protest.

51

LUNURIN CALILAN
DE DAKILA

At dawn the next day Lunurin found herself nestled into the prow of a mid-sized sailed bangka. She had one strand of hair free and carded her fingers through it, luring in a breeze to fill the tripod sail, sending the craft skimming toward the purple-grey behemoth on the horizon. She hadn't wanted to leave Alon's side. But with his father's abrupt... abdication, his many duties to his mother and his people could no more be delayed than Lunurin could ignore the typhoon she'd spun.

He'd charged Litao to accompany her. Litao sat across, looking like he would prefer to be anywhere else. A crew of six hardy sailors seemed to agree with him.

"Don't worry. We will not sail into the typhoon, only skim along its edges and run before it, leading it safely around Lusong," Lunurin promised.

It was a relief to use her magic the way Anitun Tabu's blessing was supposed to be used, to safeguard her people. The sea breeze filled the raw emptiness inside her, washing the poison from her wounded heart as if with gentle rain. On Calilan, the stormcallers went out no fewer than three to a vessel with the Stormfleet, with a tide-touched to gentle the waves. Lunurin had never needed anything more than herself. With the shoreline of Lusong receding into the distance, and the great typhoon bearing down on them, Lunurin becalmed her summoned wind. They foundered, directionless, in the sea. Then the captain turned them, charting a course that would fling them around the southern edge of the island.

"Are you ready?" Lunurin asked, as every rope and tack was battened down, and the captain secured his tie on the rudder.

"I only hope we can outrun such a typhoon, Lady Stormbringer."

Lunurin let her hair down. The wind direction changed as the eye of the typhoon reacted to her presence and shifted track. "We will."

The wind caught in the sail with a crack. They were flung forward, balancing on the outer bands of the typhoon's wind like a spinner dolphin in the crest of a wave. The sky was the bruised violet of a typhoon sunrise.

Lunurin braced herself in the prow, her hair whipping in the wind, smelling the salt and ozone of the typhoon as they rode the great ocean swells some thirty feet high. It was exhilarating. She'd missed this. When she sang out a prayer in thanks to Anitun Tabu, the sailors and Litao sang with her, the glory of it infectious. Lunurin might have been nestled between her tiyas Halili and Kalaba out with the Stormfleet that guarded the barrier islands.

She wished desperately that she could've shared the joyful side of her magic with Catalina. Perhaps, if her love had seen Lunurin as she was meant to be, Cat would not have had so much fear for the abbot to twist and poison, turning her against her own people.

But that was an empty and pointless wish, and Lunurin released it to the typhoon winds, letting it tear from her hands along with so many other what-ifs and hopes she'd held inside her heart, for a future for her and Catalina, free of the Church's oppressive presence.

These foolish but painful hopes welled up and she found herself weeping, the outer rain bands catching them up and drenching them, washing her tears from her skin. Lunurin grieved and the typhoon rent its mirrored sorrow upon the open ocean.

52

⬦◆⬦

ALON DAKILA

They'd found his father's body in the chapel, kneeling before his golden crucifix. His tambourine reliquary laid on top of a suicide note addressed to Alon.

Its contents were like leaded weights digging holes into his heart.

The old gods must truly favor your mother, if the Codicians could not relieve me of the burden of either her or the wife that turned you against me. I suppose you expect me to hand the city over to you, as if washing one fortress into the sea will mean anything when the Codicians return to level Aynila next year with a war flotilla. I have decided I'd rather oblige than remain until you realize your mother is nothing but a jungle mangkukulam who deals in sneaking curses and sabotage. She is not fit to be Lakan. Your betrayal has doomed Aynila.

Lakan Tigas Dakila of Aynila

Hate, grief, and a feeling of abandonment he very much did not want to examine gnawed alternatively at Alon's battered insides.

~

Two days after the Palisade washed into the sea, as the last trailing rain bands of Lunurin's typhoon vanished to the south, and his wife with it, a face Alon recognized entered Aynila Indigo. It was the spy, Pedro de Isla, looking no worse for wear and amazingly unremarkable for a Codicían soldier with only eight fingers.

He'd abandoned his armor, styling himself an Aynilan sailor. With his dark hair and tanned skin, it took another look to tell he was not mestizo.

"Gat Alon, I've held up my side of the bargain."

Was it relief or disappointment squirming in his chest?

"I need more proof of it than your word."

Pedro bowed. "If you will but slip your loyal guards, I will lead you right to the she-cat's cage. I do wish you would associate with women less prone to biting. At this rate, I'll have no fingers left to run through my pouch of gold."

On the excuse of taking Inez for a checkup with his mother, Alon escaped his guards and followed Pedro to the outskirts of Aynila, into the hills near where the volcanic adobe rock for the new bahay na bato style buildings was quarried. Unsure what to expect, he had Inez wait with the horses. He was led into a cellar beneath a small nipa hut. And there, behind a padlocked door of woven bamboo, was Catalina, significantly worse for wear but alive. Alon hadn't been entirely sure she would survive when he'd pulled her muddy and hardly breathing from the water and charged his father's spy to keep her hidden.

Pedro rapped on the doorframe. "Good morning, hell-cat. You can stop calling me a lying Codicían dog now. You see, here is Lord Alon, who bid me keep you hidden for a few days. If you hadn't made the first two escape attempts, the padlock wouldn't have been necessary."

Catalina snapped a water-warped prayer book shut and gave him such a black look, Alon took a step back.

"Alive, mad as a wet cat, but all in one piece," Pedro crowed, quite pleased with himself. "I'd say you can go in and speak to her, but I don't know what she'd do to you. Since I haven't been paid, I still have a vested interest in your wellbeing."

"Catalina. Before my mother is appointed as Lakan, I'm having you sent away from Aynila. It won't be safe if anyone knows you survived," Alon said, and retreated up the stairs, his task discharged.

Catalina jumped up. "Wait! Alon, where's my sister? What have you done to her? ALON, you son of a murderous sea witch!"

Alon turned to glare at Catalina. "I saved her life! Just like my murderous sea witch of a mother, which is more than you can say. If you hadn't betrayed Lunurin and all of Aynila, you could be with her now."

Catalina's expression crumpled. "Please, let me see her. You can't send me away without letting me see her."

Alon wanted to tell her no. The fewer people who knew Catalina was alive, the better his chances of getting her out of the city without his mother discovering her. But he relented at her tears. Catalina was the sort of woman who even cried beautifully. Though ragged and imprisoned, she was stunning. Despite the memory of her knife sliding into him, he could understand why Lunurin had fallen for her. And he wasn't so hardhearted as to deny Inez the assurance her sister was alive.

"Don't make me regret this," he warned.

Then Alon left her, all but flinging himself out of the cellar into the humid mid-morning air with relief, letting Inez know that she could go down.

Pedro followed. "Lord Alon?"

Alon paid the man half a gold piece.

"The rest of your pay to come to four gold pieces upon her safe removal from the city," Alon said as he dropped the gold into the man's palm.

They settled in to wait.

Sometime later Inez came rushing out of the hut, her round face wet with tears. She took one look at Alon standing on the covered veranda and dashed around the corner of the house. Her sobs grew more muffled. Despite himself, Alon discovered he was sharing a panicked look with—of all people—Pedro de Isla.

Pedro took another puff on his cigarillo, blowing two long streams of smoke through his nose. "You aren't paying me to keep track of that one."

Alon frowned. He didn't like the new habit, popular among sailors and even his own guards. He'd seen Litao showing Sina how to roll one the other day.

"You stay away from her," Alon ordered as he crossed the porch and headed after Inez.

Inez was easy to pick out in her bright white-and-indigo-striped skirts amidst the tropical underbrush encroaching on the abandoned hut. She'd gotten deep in among the trailing lianas. Her mobility was increasing. His mother had removed the stitches a day ago.

Alon, side aching with each step over the uneven ground, made plenty of noise as he approached. Inez didn't like to be startled. She'd crouched under a spreading clump of banana trees.

Alon let his hand hover uncertainly over her head. "Inez?"

"I'm sorry," she muttered, face hidden in her skirts. "I don't mean to keep making a spectacle."

Alon wished he could bend down beside her, but standing and lying flat were his best options right now. "No spectacle. No one here but the frogs and the birds. I can go if you'd like some time to compose yourself."

Inez sniffled into her lap, her shoulders shaking with sobs. Alon fought the instinct to rub her back. It was still particularly tender.

"I'm sorry she upset you."

"I'm such a burden, and it's all my own fault. Are you... really going to send me away with her?"

Alon blinked. "No, you don't have to go anywhere with your sister if you don't want to."

"But I'm the reason you took Catalina to the hidden village. I'm the reason your mother almost died. She said... She said your mother is going to have all the mestizos sent away, our mixed blood makes us traitors."

A dangerous slow boil of rage simmered through Alon. He tore his gaze from Inez, searching out the spots of blue sky shining through the canopy of green.

"Neither my mother nor I hold you responsible for what happened. You needed help. We are healers. It is our duty to provide that help, even if it puts us at risk. Lunurin is also mestiza, my mother wouldn't—"

"Lunurin is different. She is your wife, and they call her Stormbringer... She has power," Inez interrupted.

"Lunurin loves you. She would never let you be sent away if you don't wish it. Come, I'll take you home." Alon offered Inez his hand.

Rising gingerly, Inez asked, "Am I a terrible sister if I let her go alone? I wanted... I had hoped to have her forgiveness, but she's so angry. I don't want to speak to her again. She said if I don't go with her, I'm consigning my immortal soul to hell."

"You are not terrible, and I'm sorry Catalina can't see past her anger to realize you're doing what's best for you."

"Isn't that terribly selfish? How do I know what's best for me?"

Alon shrugged. "I think, of any of us, you deserve some time to be a little bit selfish. If you ever decide you want something different than what you want now, I will help you get there."

Alon hoped Lunurin would return soon. He felt inept to offer aid beyond Inez's immediate physical ills. But Lunurin had promised she would try to weaken the typhoon, out over the open water between them and mainland Tianchao, so as not to set their city killer on other people. Even if she'd done the impossible and they'd cleared the far side of Lusong, she would be tired, and they would sail back under the power of mortal winds.

As they walked back toward the hut, Inez's words kept circling around his head. He suppressed a groan. Alon hadn't intended to speak to Catalina again. If at all possible, he never wanted to look at the woman. If he did, he might think about how she was the reason the tide-touched of Aynila were dead. He might remember how very close she'd come to plunging a dagger into Lunurin's back. And then, he might do something truly unforgivable.

Alon still had fine black bone ash under his nails. No amount of scrubbing would remove it.

But Lunurin would return soon, and Alon wouldn't let Catalina wound his wife like she had Inez. If he'd had any idea, he never would've brought Inez at all.

He squeezed Inez's hand. "Would you wait by the horses? I need to speak to your sister."

Inez nodded and went to pat the little black mare on the nose.

Begging his goddess for mercy, Alon descended once more.

Catalina was angry, pacing the tiny room in agitation. "You've poisoned my sister against me!"

"You did that well enough on your own," Alon said.

"She is mine!" Catalina spat. "She is all I have in the world, and you've... you've..." Catalina pressed to the door, her eyes wet and pleading. The change was jarring. "Please, bring her back! I need to speak to her. I need her to understand!"

"Inez doesn't want to speak to you."

Catalina's expression changed like a coin flip. "Liar! You're keeping her from me!"

Alon stared at her. If he cared at all about what Catalina thought of him, she would've been devastating. He wondered distantly if she had always been like this, blowing hot and cold, without warning, keeping those who loved her constantly fighting to get back into her good graces...

Catalina dragged her hands through her disheveled brown hair. She wailed, "You did this! You made my baby sister a murderer! You and your witch mother!"

Alon wanted to reach in and shake her till her teeth rattled in her skull. But he made himself stay put. He didn't want to know if Cat had any more surprises up her sleeve.

When he was sure he wouldn't shout, he said, "Inez didn't kill anyone. She's far less a killer than you."

Catalina's voice shook. "How dare you?"

"Even if you don't count all the tide-touched dead because of your betrayal, you tried to kill Lunurin. You nearly killed me."

Cat pressed her hands to her face. "He said I had to cast her off, with all my sins. They said the storm would stop, that I could have my sister back—"

450

"How can you claim what you did was for Inez when you let them strip the skin off her back before you'd see her sent somewhere safe?" Alon said, out of patience with Catalina's twisted words.

Catalina's face flushed, her breath coming hard through her teeth. "Don't lecture me! I had to make sure her soul would be saved."

"Listen to me. If Lunurin hadn't gotten her out, Inez would have died. What kind of salvation or forgiveness is that? What kind of god wants the blood of children, of people who never did anything but help you?"

"Then why by all the Saints did you bother pulling me from the sea? You should've let me drown with the other true believers. Then at least I could have been a martyr!"

"Because I'm not as cruel as you are. I won't let Lunurin believe she's responsible for your death, not even if you deserve it."

Catalina bared her teeth at him. "She won't ever love you! No matter what you do, she won't ever love you the way she loves me."

He wasn't as immune to her barbs as he'd hoped. This one caught and tore a great gaping wound in his chest. Instead of holding it inside, hiding it under stoicism and layers and layers of calm, for once in his life Alon yelled back. "Good!" he shouted. "By all the salt in the sea, and all the mercy in Aman Sinaya's heart, I hope Lunurin never loves me like she loves you. I hope she never again tears herself apart and shatters pieces of herself for me. I hope my love never betrays her or makes her hate herself or her goddess. I hope if I ever hurt her like you have that she stops my heart rather than love me through every wound. If that means she will never love me as she loves you, then I will die a happy man."

"She's a murderer!"

Alon turned to go, upset she'd riled him. "So am I."

"No—wait, please, wait!" Catalina was all desperation again. "Will you let me see her before I'm shipped off who knows where?"

Alon wanted to deny her. He wanted with all his heart to protect Lunurin from the daggers of self-doubt, from the lies and anger and all of Catalina's twisted faith. But if there was ever a chance that Lunurin wouldn't hate herself, her magic, and her goddess for her role in the Palisade's destruction, she had to see Catalina and know beyond a shadow of a doubt that Catalina's death was not on her hands. Even if Catalina's love was a slow poison and agony, even if Alon knew somehow, Catalina would use this to cause more pain. She was so like his father that way.

He had to try. He couldn't let his wife suffer the terrible, bitter grief he suffered now. He wanted Lunurin to have the closure his father had stolen from him.

"Yes, when she returns, I will let her know where you are. But, Catalina… whatever you did or said to Inez, know this: if you try to hurt my wife, if she returns to me with even a scratch on her, I will turn you over to my mother's justice."

~

Lunurin returned in time for the funeral. Though calling it a funeral was an overstatement. His mother had agreed to a private interment of the body. They buried him in the Christian manner rather than immuring him in one of the living mortuary trees that had held his family's remains for centuries. He was not tide-touched and Aman Sinaya would not keep a gentle watch over his bones.

Standing over the yawning black pit, Alon was grateful for Lunurin pressed close against his side. They'd wrapped his father in a simple white shroud. The outline of his body against the black dirt wavered before his gaze.

Lunurin squeezed his hand. "Just because he died for them, doesn't make his words true."

Slowly Alon lifted his father's beloved tambourine reliquary over his head. The cold gold beads had none of the comfort of his broken mutya, only the terrible weight of his father's final words. Extending his hand over the open grave, Alon let the familiar beautiful gold beads fall through his fingers and disappear into the earth.

There would be no Christian prayers and no consecrated ground. Even if there'd been a priest to say them, the Church did not abide suicides. Had his father concerned himself with such details of his chosen faith? Alon didn't know. Still, he hoped his spirit would find some peace with the talisman he'd chosen.

Then he turned away, leaving the gravediggers to their work.

53

LUNURIN CALILAN DE DAKILA

Alon didn't want to return home after the funeral, insisting on going to the port to check on the few Palisade evacuees who hadn't yet found family to take them in, nor work and lodging elsewhere. Lunurin went with him. She understood his not wishing to be alone with his thoughts, but worried he was overestimating his recovery.

When Alon yanked them both out of view of his guards, Lunurin half expected him to sit down to have a good long cry in private. Instead, Alon took them to the docks where a familiar karakoa had been repaired, ready to sail.

"Alon, why?" Lunurin began, and then she saw her. Catalina, alive and well, looking so irritated she couldn't possibly be a drowned ghost.

Locked in some kind of contest of wills with Captain Capuno, Catalina was hardly recognizable without her habit and veil.

Lunurin couldn't move.

Alon squeezed her hand. "She's been disarmed. Go, talk to her."

Moving as if she were underwater, Lunurin stepped aboard and brushed past the captain. She curled her hands around Catalina's shoulders, holding her at arm's length, desperately needing to prove to herself this was real.

Lunurin breathed deep, memorizing Cat's smell, the feather dust and sesame oil scent of her hair, the paper and indigo ink of prayer books still clinging to her.

Catalina froze. Then, she let out a choked sob, reaching toward Lunurin as if she would embrace her, but Lunurin did not pull her close. Lunurin was speechless. Her heart was lodged in her throat like a stone. Alon tipped his head toward the prow of the boat. Lunurin sat opposite Catalina on crates of dye while Alon and the captain stepped onto the dock to give them privacy.

With difficulty, Lunurin cleared her throat. "Where are you going?"

"Your husband is sending me to the Codicían settlement in Simsiman. He says if I wish to continue living as a Codicían nun, I should arrange for my travel from there to Canazco in New Codicía as soon as possible." There was accusation in Catalina's tone.

"Will that make you happy?" Lunurin asked.

"Happy? Your husband intends to push all the Codicíans on these islands into the sea, and you want to know if I'm happy?!" Catalina snapped.

The words cut at Lunurin through her exhaustion and shock. "Alon will guard Aynila first, but yes... once the datus, lakans, rajs, and sultans of the other islands know we can hold Aynila against them, it won't be long before there are no more Codicían shipyards east of Canazco."

As she said the words, Lunurin knew them to be truth. The divine within her swelled, and Lunurin didn't fight. Whether Anitun Tabu had put her hand over Catalina and preserved her from the lightning, or Aman Sinaya had carried her up from the depths, or if it had only been Alon, being far, far too forgiving. Whatever had happened, Lunurin had not murdered her lover. If her husband and her gods needed her to guard this city... she wouldn't neglect her duty. She would embrace it with her whole heart.

Because Alon's father was right about one thing. The Codicíans would not accept the loss of their pearl of the East. They would return. Lunurin wouldn't let Alon and Sina face the war she'd started alone.

"How can you accept such a terrible thing? It would mean women like us would have never been born!" Catalina cried.

Lunurin reached across the space between them and took Cat's hands in hers. She squeezed tight. "Our fathers came in violence. As soldiers to take what riches they could find in spices, silk, pearls, and women. As holy men to take from us our histories, our gods, and all the wild power of our islands. For twenty years, we endured their endless hunger, but no more. Our gods will not be forgotten. They will not be remade into saints and martyrs. Our gods walk once more and so long as we remember their names and true faces, we won't stand alone."

"Your gods are not mine." Catalina's face twisted with anguish.

"I know that and I'm sorry. I wish it were different."

"I—I don't know how else to live."

Lunurin nodded. "Tell Abbess Magdalena that I hope she will find a place for you in the convents of Canazco, as if you were as much her own flesh and blood as I am."

"You won't come with me?" Catalina asked.

Lunurin shook her head, a bitter smile on her lips. "No, Cat, you know I can't do that."

Catalina began to weep. "Inez is abandoning me as well!"

Lunurin tore her gaze away from Cat's small shoulders shaking with sobs. She stared out over the turquoise waters of the bay. Cat would never understand that she was the one who'd pushed all of them away, that it was her faith that made loving her impossible.

"I will look after her as if she were my own sister," Lunurin promised.

Still holding Cat's treacherous, beloved hands in her grip, Lunurin leaned forward. She gathered Catalina into herself with one arm, pressing Cat's soft frame into the strength of her own, knowing it would be the last time. "I loved you, but I cannot go with you."

"Then this is goodbye," Catalina whispered.

Lunurin remembered a small silver weight tied into her sash and untied the corner. Her Aunt Magdalena's silver crucifix gleamed brightly against the deep blue silk. Alon had returned it to her before the burial.

"Take this with you. Maybe it will remind my aunt what you are to me." She draped the rosary over Cat's head.

Lunurin rose from the crate and stepped back.

"I'm sorry!" Catalina blurted. "I'm sorry I destroyed what we had, and that I hurt so many people. Please, won't you let me try to make it right?"

It was everything Lunurin had longed to hear since Cat had shattered her dugong bone amulet, but it was far, far too late.

Still, a part of Lunurin wanted to fall back into Catalina's arms. It was on her tongue to apologize in return like she always had, to say that it was her fault, that she should have protected Catalina better or trusted her more. She somehow should have prevented it all from spinning out like this, and of course, of course they could always try again. But this was a different kind of ending.

"I'm sorry. There will be no fixing this or us."

"Do you... forgive me?"

Lunurin breathed in, so deeply her chest ached with it. All she could see was Alon's blood staining the floodwaters red. "No, and I'm sorry for that too. But I loved you, and I will always remember you as the one good thing that the Church ever gave me."

She turned, leaving Catalina in the prow. She stepped onto the dock to stand beside Alon. Cognizant of his injury, she wrapped her arms around his shoulders and pressed her face into his neck.

"Did you hear and say all you needed to?" Alon asked, his voice low against her ear.

"I did. Thank you. Thank you so much."

Alon pressed his lips to her temple. "I know what a heavy burden your goddess's vengeance is. If I can ever lighten your load, I will, I always will."

Alon's hold was so gentle. The weight of the future lifted from her shoulders.

She wasn't remaining as penance, she realized, or even for duty. Lunurin was staying for hope, for him.

~

From the steps of the Lakan's palace, she could see all Aynila spread before her. There were open wounds torn across her face, where Codicían cannon fire and typhoon winds had caved in homes and turned streets to rubble. But like the dugong matriarch, Aynila had survived her hunters. Her wounds would heal over and scar, badges of victory against the odds. Alon had been right. Aynila was resilient enough to weather any storm. In the distance, on the center delta of the Saliwain, the ruins of the Palisade gleamed like shattered bone, a great beast slain at last, its body returning to enrich the soil. Beyond that, mighty Hilaga slept, no smoke at her peak, her rumbles of discontent quieted.

Alon leaned into her shoulder. The tidal pull of his joy was infectious, drawing her attention back to the square. Not even overcast skies could dampen the festival atmosphere of the packed plaza. All of Aynila had turned out to see the anointing of the Lakan.

"Ready?"

"No," Sina said, twitchy and nervous beside Lunurin. She'd fought accepting a speaking role in today's proceedings, but Hiraya had insisted that this was what Amihan wanted. Her family were seated with Isko and Inez among the gathered principalia on the steps.

Alon grinned. "It's too late to run now. We're starting."

"If I light your mother's hair on fire, it's your fault," Sina hissed.

Lunurin gave Sina's arm a commiserating squeeze. "That's why you're last, once her hair's been decently saturated."

Alon snorted, struggling to control his expression as a heartbeat throb began on a set of drums. A hush fell over the jubilant crowd.

The palace doors opened and Dalisay descended the steps. She was garbed all in indigo and gold. Casama's best dye artisans had worked for days on the petal-shaped panels of translucent piña fiber adorned with crashing waves. Her shattered mutya on her breast gleamed like a reflection of moonlight broken on deep water.

Dalisay was like Aynila: scarred, but not defeated.

At the sight of the true Lakan, Lunurin felt Anitun Tabu swell within her. For the first time in her life the goddess in her heart did not rage. She did not weep nor rail with grief. Anitun Tabu was with her, and Lunurin wasn't afraid.

Lunurin lifted her mutya from the complicated bun Sina had helped her arrange. Her hair uncoiled, spilling white sampaguita flowers into the playful breeze she sent dancing over the crowd. Lunurin took a deep breath and sang. Her voice did not tremble. Her lungs didn't quiver. Her voice rang clear and strong, rising over Aynila to the very ear of her goddess. The steady beat of the drums kept pace with her heart. Lunurin sang down the ambon, raising cupped hands to the skies.

Over the steps, the clouds parted. Anitun Tabu peered down, and sunlight crowned Dalisay in glory. Rain fell like a sigh. Each drop was momentarily transformed into a pearl, a dozen miniature rainbows glinting through the air. Lunurin sang, her heart swelling with joy that was not tainted by bloodlust, and hope not tempered by fear. Let the whole world hear her and know her for what she was. No more hiding. She would never again make herself small.

At last, Dalisay descended. With grave dignity, she knelt at Lunurin's feet.

"Katalonan, will you grant me Anitun Tabu's blessing?" Dalisay signed.

"Dalisay Inanialon, will you stand for Aynila though storms should come?" Anitun Tabu spoke through Lunurin, her voice rolling across the plaza in the thunder.

"I will."

Lunurin lowered her cupped hands and anointed the Lakan in rainwater. Lightning embroidered the clouds and thunder clapped.

Lunurin stepped back. Alon took her place. In his hands he bore a gleaming gold-lip oyster shell filled to the brim with seawater. Lunurin had taken him to dive at the old beds. They had walked the wreckage of the Palisade and discussed the future of the central delta, as a school not only of healing, but for all who wished to reclaim the old gods' blessings.

"Katalonan, will you grant me Aman Sinaya's blessing?" Dalisay signed.

"Dalisay Inanialon, will you make Aynila a safe harbor, where all can seek Aman Sinaya's mercy?" Alon asked.

"I will."

Alon anointed the Lakan in seawater.

Sina took his place, bearing a small obsidian dish filled with finely ground charcoal.

"Katalonan, will you grant me Amihan's blessing?" Dalisay signed.

"Dalisay Inanialon, will you see that Amihan's fires are tended? As my hearths are guarded so I will guard yours," said Sina.

"I will."

Sina dipped her fingertips in the charcoal and drew two lines down Dalisay's cheeks from under eye to jaw.

Lunurin joined hands with Sina and Alon, and together they cried, "Aynila, too long have we spent in mourning, today we celebrate. Rise, Dalisay Inanialon, Lakan of Aynila, chosen, anointed, blessed!"

Dalisay rose and the crowd roared its approval until the stone steps beneath Lunurin's feet trembled. A swirling blue and turquoise flock of spark-striker birds rose from the peak of Hilaga, Amihan's messengers carrying word to her ear. The clouds broke apart, the last drops of rain gracing Lunurin's cheeks as the sun shone bright on calm cerulean waters as far as the eye could see.

They descended into the plaza. There was feasting and dancing, and under the open sky, the memory of her wedding banquet seemed another lifetime. Without Palisade walls looming, the life and community she'd always yearned for was here. Aynila had seen her do her worst, and rather than shun and fear her, she was addressed as Lady Stormbringer. Her heart had never been so full.

When she was panting and giddy from the dancing, she and Alon wound their way to the edge of the crowd. Alon found some space at the foot of the steps. Lunurin could've sat beside him; instead, she settled into his lap, laughing at his expression.

He stared up at her, his hands closing hesitantly about her waist. "Do you want to stay? If you're tired…"

Lunurin smiled, fanning herself with a buri palm fan. "A while longer, at least. Look how much fun Inez is having."

Lunurin pointed to where Inez and a dozen other Aynilan children were engaged in a game of tumbang preso, tossing empty oyster shells from the feast tables to knock an opponent's coconut half off the step.

Lunurin curled her arms around Alon's neck, resting her hot cheek on his shoulder. "Just let me get my breath back."

Alon leaned back on the steps, bracing his elbows, making himself into a more comfortable place for her to sprawl.

"Your side?" Lunurin checked.

"I'm fine," Alon assured her.

Lunurin reclined, gazing up. Overhead, stars pierced through the indigo tapestry of twilight. Lingering tufts of cloud caught the last of the sunset like drifts of yellow ylang-ylang flowers. Together they watched every streak of sunset fade, listening to the children play and the strains of music and laughter drifting through the night.

"Do you want to stay?" Alon asked again, his voice hushed and low.

Lunurin peered down at him, trying to read his tone, and the way his hands had slipped away from her waist.

"With me, I mean. Married. It all happened so quickly, life and death, and no real choices. I don't want grief and a few moments' weakness to be the reason you stay. I wouldn't expect—"

Lunurin leaned down and kissed him, stemming his unspooling doubts. "I didn't stay for grief. I stayed for you, and for hope. Storms will come, and it may be that Anitun Tabu hasn't yet tasted her fill of vengeance, but I had not known shelter till I found it in your arms."

Alon curled a strand of her hair coming loose from its bun around his fingertips, and kissed her brow. "I can be that for you, for as long as you need safe harbor."

~

AUTHOR'S NOTE

The oldest extant black Madonna statue in the Philippines is over 450 years old. She is beautiful, dark featured, her near-prayerful hands delicate and expressive. She is first described in Spanish accounts from 1571, when they found natives near Manila worshiping the wooden anito statue on the beach in a "pagan manner". Many miracles and answered petitions were attributed to her power. The Spanish quickly declared the statue to be the Virgin Mary, and moved her into the Manila Cathedral, where she remained until 1606. Our Lady of Guidance is now enshrined at the Ermita Church in Manila. Most interesting and heartbreaking of all is that the name and origin of the goddess has been lost to time, although some theories suggest she is an Animist–Tantrist Anito or perhaps an East Asian goddess, due to her monolid eyes.

I wondered what her name was, and most of all, I wondered if she was angry her name had been forgotten. This proved the spark from which *Saints of Storm and Sorrow* sprung. As I delved into the history of the early colonial Philippines and read how babaylan (Visayan pre-colonial shamans/priestesses, analogous to the Tagalog katalonan) led rebellions against colonial rule, I began to wonder: what if all the legends and stories were true? Accounts of the Bohol rebellion of 1621 recorded that babaylan Tamblot would intercede with the diwata to shake the mountains to throw off Spanish musket fire, and say that they could summon flame. This inspired the firetenders and Sina, my favorite pyromaniac.

Later dios-dios messianic movements of the 1880s inspired the healing and water control of the tide-touched. Their affinity for salt is a nod to bohol salt and the many unique salts produced in the Philippines.

Finally, Estrella Bangotbanwa from Iloilo, who is perhaps one of the most famous Babaylan, was renowned for calling down rain just by letting down her hair, for summoning storms and ending droughts. She inspired the stormcallers and their function in the Stormfleet.

The Spanish brutally suppressed these movements as rebellions against colonial authority, but also as religious blasphemy.* After the Bancao rebellion of 1622, the Spanish burned the temple to the diwata, executing many "rebel priests" and burning one "in order that, by the light of that fire, the blindness in which the divata had kept them deluded might be removed."† This and other incidents of Spanish brutality inspired the burning of the tide-touched healing school and the massacre of the tide-touched village.

I chose to represent a goddess-dominated pantheon to honor the tradition that katalonan and babaylan were women (cis and trans alike), and took direction from the Tagalog creation story my grandma told me, which names Amihan,

---

* *Incomplete Conquests: The Limits of Spanish Empire in the Seventeenth-Century Philippines,* Stephanie Joy Mawson (2023).

† *The Philippine Islands, 1493–1803,* Emma Helen Blair et al (2009).

the kite, as deity of the northeasterly winds. Aman Sinaya is the primordial Tagalog goddess of the sea and protector of fishermen. Finally, I chose Anitun Tabu, the Tagalog goddess of wind and rain, to replace the traditional Bathala, Supreme God of creation and the sky. I was always too angry at heart to resonate with my grandma's frequent, resigned exclamations of "bahala na", a somewhat fatalistic phrase and philosophy towards life which can be translated as "whatever happens, happens".

So if nothing else, I hope that you will hold your anger to your chest and never forget from where it springs. I hope you will use it to make the world a better place.

ACKNOWLEDGEMENTS

First thanks must go to my grandma, who told us her stories without ever flinching. Who lived hard and loved hard and sacrificed so much, but still found the time to write poetry just for herself. She never got to read the poem that inspired this novel, the retelling of the Tagalog creation story. Still, I think she would have loved it.

And to my father, who passed away suddenly in 2023 of pancreatic cancer. I never expected to be working through my first round edits while keeping your bedside, and discussing how best to ruin mortar and collapse bridges around med schedules and doctor appointments. I wish you could have read the book you helped me write. But I know I'll find you by the river.

Thank you to my agent, Ramona Pina, who was prepared to kick open doors for this story, when it felt like hundreds had already been slammed in my face. To Katie Dent, my amazing editor at Titan Books. Thank you for always wanting to see more dragons. Also many thanks to Michael Beale, who brought fresh perspectives when we had gone quite cross eyed, and to Louise Pearce and Kevin Eddy, who provided their expertise. Also to the rest of the Titan team who answered my many questions and supported this story: Bahar Kutluk, Katharine Carroll, Kabriya Coghlan, and Claire Schultz. And to Nat MacKenzie, whose amazing cover design still makes me giddy with joy every time I see it.

Thank you as well to Bienvenido Lumbera, *Philippine Studies: Historical & Ethnographic Viewpoints*, and Ateneo de Manila University for granting us permission to use Lumbera's translation of early Tagalog Tanaga poetry, which made for the most romantic proposal I could think of.

My endless thanks to my husband, Robert Johnson, who gave me the support and tough love to actually start pursuing publication instead of hoarding all my stories to myself. I never would've sent that first query without you. To my mother, who helped me connect with so many writing mentors over the years. To my sister, who never reads, but listens to every revision at the gym. Soon you won't have to suffer your screen reader butchering Tagalog. Thank you to Tita Rosie for all the Tagalog checks and research help. And to Meighan Arce, who introduced me to fanfiction and got me started writing in the first place. Here's to over a decade of story swaps.

Finally, to the huge community of writers who've been friends, mentors, critique partners, beta and alpha readers, *Saints* would not be the story it is without you. Thank you to Mic Domenici, my amazing PitchWars mentor who went above and beyond and really helped me to shape *Saints* into the story it is today. To Kerry Schafer, you have been so generous with your time and patient with all my endless publishing questions, thank you. To Mia Tsai, who I consider my Asian writing auntie, thank you for talking me off the ledges and out of corners and for being so ready to celebrate all the highs and lows of publishing along the way.

To my betas and critique partners—Ben, you've read this book more times than anyone except me, and I couldn't have gotten this far without your insight. Many thanks also to Faye Delacour, Ysabelle Suarez, Eleanor Strata, and Mary Zambales; this story has been through so many iterations, getting better all the time because of your help.

To the whole Pitch Wars class of 2021, I could not have persevered without you all, and especially to Alexandra Kiley, Lillian Barry, Lisa Allen, Chrissy Hopewell, Abigail Barenblitt, Megan Davidhizar, Konstantinos Kalofonos, Jenny Kiefer, and Aimee Davis, whose generous sanity reads kept me going both during Pitch Wars and in the long aftermath.

To the whole Gsquad, especially Keir Alekseii, Logan, Erin Fulmer, Kyla Zhao, Mel, Adria Bailton, and Meredith Mooring. Thank you for always listening to my at times glacial progress on this story, and for cheering me on.

Thank you also to The Filipinix Writers Collective, FilTheShelves, The Inclusive Romance Project, and the Ramoniacs. The community and support you provided was invaluable.

ABOUT THE AUTHOR

Gabriella Buba is a mixed Filipina–Czech writer and chemical engineer based in Texas who likes to keep explosive pyrophoric materials safely contained in pressure vessels or between the covers of her books. She writes adult romantic fantasy for bold, bi, brown women who deserve to see their stories centered. *Saints of Storm and Sorrow* is her first book. Find her online @gabriellabuba and at gabriellabuba.com.

THE AFTERLIFE OF MAL CALDERA
BY NADI REED PEREZ

Mal's life is over. Her afterlife is only just beginning...

Mal Caldera—former rockstar, retired wild-child and excommunicated black sheep of her Catholic family—is dead. Not that she cares. She only feels bad that her younger sister, Cris, has been left to pick up the pieces Mal left behind.

She enlists the help of reluctant local medium, Ren, and together, they concoct a plan to pass on a message to Cris. But the more time they spend together, the more they begin to wonder what might have been if they'd met before Mal died.

Mal knows it's wrong to hold on so tightly to her old life. But she has always been selfish, and letting go might just be the hardest thing she's ever had to do.

"*The Afterlife of Mal Caldera* is a profound unravelling of a life... that leads to a bright and vivid afterlife packed with characters to die for!" Rosie Talbot, bestselling author of *Sixteen Souls*

TITANBOOKS.COM

SONG OF THE SIX REALMS
BY JUDY I. LIN

Uncover the dark past of the celestials in this melodic tale inspired by Chinese mythology and Daphne du Maurier's *Rebecca*.

Xue, a talented young musician, has no past and probably no future. When her kindly uncle is killed in a bandit attack, she is devastated to lose her last connection to a life outside of her indenture contract.

Xue faces a lifetime of servitude—until one night she is unexpectedly called to put on a private performance for the enigmatic Duke Meng. The young man is strangely kind, and surprises Xue with an irresistible offer: serve as a musician in residence at his manor for one year, and he'll set her free of her indenture.

When the duke whisks her away to his estate, she discovers he's not just some country noble: he's the Duke of Dreams, one of the divine rulers of the Celestial Realm. The Six Realms are on the brink of disaster, and the duke needs to unlock memories from Xue's past which could help stop the impending war. But first, Xue must survive being the target of every monster and deity in the Six Realms.

For more fantastic fiction, author events,
exclusive excerpts, competitions, limited editions and more

VISIT OUR WEBSITE
titanbooks.com

LIKE US ON FACEBOOK
facebook.com/titanbooks

FOLLOW US ON TWITTER AND INSTAGRAM
@TitanBooks

EMAIL US
readerfeedback@titanemail.com